3, —

ONLY THE DEAD KNOW BURBANK

ONLY THE
DEAD
KNOW
BURBANK

A NOVEL

BRADFORD TATUM

HARPER ● PERENNIAL

NEW YORK ● LONDON ● TORONTO ● SYDNEY ● NEW DELHI ● AUCKLAND

HARPER PERENNIAL

This novel is a work of fiction. Any references to real people, events, establishments, organizations, or locales are intended only to give the fiction a sense of reality and authenticity, and are used fictitiously. All other names, characters and places, and all dialogue and incidents portrayed in this book are the product of the author's imagination.

FIRST EDITION

Designed by Jamie Lynn Kerner

Library of Congress Cataloging-in-Publication Data has been applied for.

ISBN 978-0-06-242875-2 (pbk.)

16 17 18 19 20   OV/RRD   10 9 8 7 6 5 4 3 2 1

FOR SOPHIA LACRAMOSA,
the Vampire Girl of Central Park

ONLY THE DEAD KNOW BURBANK

PROLOGUE

I see them (if you can call it seeing) feint toward the open street, their resolve failing like bad teeth. They are not cops. Their badges of office are printed paper in plastic sleeves dangling from polyester lariats as if they're junior managers at a hotel convention. He checks the address that rides in blue ink on the creases of his palm. She coughs into her fist. And I would spare them some sympathy if I wasn't their object.

They are two.

A he and a her.

They almost break my heart. They haven't done their homework. They haven't made the doing *specific*. He ambles up my walk irresolute, listing like a lothario who has been asked to pick up Tampax before the third date. Cued to the duty, uncommitted to the task. And she's no better. Her hips have petrified, calves pumping like pistons unused to the slap of a hem. And once they get here, once they knuckle-tap twice and announce Child

Protective Services and hear no reply then try the knob and feel the door give (I always leave it open), what do they find?

Nothing. Expanse. The chocolate shag still furrowed from the vacuum blade fully forty-six years ago. Stale air. The kitchen hinges virginal under a second coat of paint. Dust in the sinks. No furniture. No crumbs. They'll lump around for ten minutes or so, checking the bedroom. All the closets. Save one. The one that shelters the greening plumbing and the mice and the dark. The one where no living child would dare linger. Not breathing. Not blinking.

A rumor.

It is a game we play, my landlady and I. I get more quiet than usual and she conjures up a winter passion for my welfare—*Oh, that poor little darling in 602, she's up there all alone. I can't imagine where her parents have gone*—knowing I've sat in these rooms alone for four decades, chaperoned only by tangles of spider floss and yellow afternoons. I wonder sometimes what they would think of me if they ever actually caught me. A girl just shy of the exit of her adolescence. Long black hair, pale gray eyes. Long-limbed and thin. Cheekbones and breasts full of promise but shunted in their strides. They might see my skin as flawless if not for its sallow hue. They might think my full lips pretty if they weren't so freighted with an old woman's regrets.

I suppose I could leave here, tuck myself beneath a nice quiet garbage heap in the shade of that ominous *H* that still beckons and chides from the spine of Mount Lee. But I can't leave my view of the studios. Everything happened there.

Perhaps it was enough to have held the drowsy wrist of dear Mr. Pratt when he took those first star-making steps backward. To have whispered in the doubtful ear that allowed Bela's black lips to spread and dare the world a taste. To have had one finger on the knife switch that woke a world to a thrill of lightning that could do more than just spark our televisions and power our vibrators. When nightmares first learned to speak English and the flickers were hot as scissor arcs. I won't take credit for the genre, no matter how many times my name may surface in deep blogs dedicated to such ephemera. *The Phantom Girl of Stage 28*. *The Vampire Girl of Universal City*. It is difficult to know which legends to trust. Which are born of the idle breath of gossip. And which shadows still have the heft to haunt.

Confusion breeds nostalgia. And these are confusing times.

CHAPTER 1

I wasn't always in love with the dark. I remember a Bavarian sun, ambering through my eyelids, the veiled light sitting hot on the tender corneas. When I dared open my eyes, the sunlight would sear a white circle onto the retinas. Closing them again, I would delight in the black suns that wavered in the hollows of my skull.

That was my first camera.

We lived in woods so ancient some trees still bore the wounds of gladius and pilum, deep longitudes from the days when centurions tried to recruit from the chalked Celts and found themselves quartered in bronze pots, a feast for the Aesir. Our village lay on the outskirts of Laupheim, the town where Carl Laemmle would be born, near the Rottum river in southern Germany. And although it may have appeared a paradise in the daylight, these were closed climes no soldier of Christ could fully purchase. The priests were misled when they pronounced our burg converted. Those were not crosses over the markers of the dead but Thor's hammer lending fist for the dead's last fights. This Jesus of the east was only tolerated for he had gained his wisdom, like mighty Odin, hanging from a tree wounded by a spear.

An open field could not be planted. It was common knowledge such empty expanses served as the incestuous beds of the old gods. Elder groves were left standing for fear the trees might be witches in arboreal suspension. It was well known cribs made of elder delivered up quiet babies in lingering stupors, their spongy bodies blotched with mysterious bruises and cuts. An elder log tossed on a solstice fire could summon the devil. The sewn fields of our village flowed around the bases of such trunks like great snakes sleeping at silent and terrible ankles. Alderwood was a favorite of the nixies and other water sprites and therefore could be used only for well roofs and sluice gates. Willows were known to uproot themselves at night and follow foreigners to their deaths. With such innate motive properties, willow wood was a favorite for witches' brooms. Ash trees had healing powers, while the buds of a whitehanded birch could cause madness. We children were cautioned never to pick the last apple of the season or our teeth would turn to angry wasps that would nest in our greedy stomachs and brains.

Life in our village required an advanced understanding of diplomacy. The woods teemed with all manner of fairy folk, each with its own etiquette, customs, and particular channels of offense. A trip to the outhouse could be delayed upward of ten minutes in obeisance to all the attendant rituals needed to avoid maladies as divergent as tapeworms to chronic flatulence. And if for one minute we doubted the necessity of all these calisthenics, there was proof enough in the myriad deficiencies and deformities that surrounded us. Cows born with six heads whose milk stunk like vinegar belonged unerringly to those who dared cross the thresholds of their homes with their ax blades facing heaven. Wens that wouldn't heal, diseases that fed on nose tips and ear-lobes, all were justified responses to any rudeness leveled at the little people.

My own grandmother, once a hive of energy, suffered until her death from a listlessness so pervasive it could take a full minute simply to lift a teacup. And how had she been cursed? As a newly married woman, she had indulged in a dalliance with a Jewish petticoat salesman. When dawn came, after her tryst, a smile would not leave her sleeping lips. Her throat was covered with livid love bites. A gentle blow to the head, a bracing douse of icy water, nothing would rouse her. It was clear she was a victim of a vampire. Suspicion immediately turned to the undergarment salesman, as everyone knew Jews had no life force of their own.

He was caught at sunrise rocking gracefully with his morning prayers under the shade of an alder tree. My grandfather hammered the ash stakes into the four cardinal points of the Jew's body and quartered him cleanly with his best ax. He was buried in four separate graves, each site divided by a north-running creek to prevent his reeking soul from crossing and thereby coaxing his flesh back into service.

It seemed my grandmother's transgression had left her more than lushly exhausted. She was full with child. My mother was born loathed. But my grandfather was too conscientious a man (as his concern for the soul of the petticoat salesman had shown) to slake his vengeance on the innocent. Besides, my mother was extremely fair, even if she was a cub of Beelzebub. He thought her red hair would keep the boys away, at least until he had extracted several seasons of work out of her. He was wrong.

I don't know why she carried me to term. She was feared by the people of our village. It's not that they were afraid of witches.

Witches were as common as clover in my village. It was her. The wantonness of her that mystified them. Widows crossed to the other side of the path when she approached, spitting three times as she passed. It was rumored she knew the language of slugs and cats, that she could turn the teeth of a violent man to glass, so I'm sure she knew the herbs that could have stilled my quickening. But she let me grow, her pale freckled flesh becoming harder and rounder. By the winter solstice my time had come. She made a fire of green willow branches she tore with her left hand and stood naked in the smoke until the blush of the first winter sun. Then she walked to an open field, her skin and hair still reeking from the willow smoke and, squatting in the chamomile, pulled me from her body without a single sound. A young cowherd, up early from delivering a breech calf, said he saw her raise the afterbirth to the sun before swallowing it whole.

I remember her touch. A song she would sing.

My mother disappeared one evening when I was still in swaddling. She stuck me in a sack and tacked me to a tree beside the summer scythes, an empty dipper at my dangling feet. I was found by my grandfather, who was furious. He was convinced I was destined to be as wicked and unruly as she. I spent years listening to him brine himself in his own invective whenever her name was mentioned. And I learned to hate parts of my body.

I don't know how old I was when she finally came back. I had all my molars and had suffered shamefully through two cycles of my monthly bleeding. She was wearing a striped dress of yellow and black, high collared and badly worn at the hem. Her slim waist was bound up in a secondhand corset, the whalebone shrill through the cheap batting. My grandfather opened his mouth to protest. But one look from my mother and the sound was stilled in his throat. I remember black flies crawling at the corners of his drying lips. She offered no explanation, no greeting. She merely held out her arms and I came running, like a planet drawn to its death by an immovable sun. She had brought a mule with her. In place of a saddle, a man's pinstriped coat was draped over the animal's backbone. She sat me on the bundled coat and we walked the twelve miles to Ulm.

The mule's spine cut deep into my cursed places. My rattled thoughts were not on my mother's sudden return, her purpose in repossessing me. The animal's belligerent shifting caused a welcome if fearful friction that addled my mind and kept it seared to where my grandfather had taught me it should not linger. I was courting devils with goaty faces and long dexterous limbs who would stuff me with spider sacs and stitch me shut. I tensed my insides and focused ahead, on the back of the woman walking before me. Even under layers of rank flounce and cheap twill, her backside lolled like a possessed pudding, a moveable confection for the damned.

The tree finches and frogs lost their voices. We were leaving the forest. The path became more packed. The wind reeked of sour congregations, open pits buzzing with the smell of fingered copper and ammonia. I was afraid. It was the farthest I had ever been from home. We were nearing people. Nearing strangers. We stopped at a clearing of fresh stumps, the raw circles still skin-bright and smelling of raped pine. She turned to me and, lifting the edge of her skirt, applied it to her wet tongue. She sponged me with the rough fabric.

"You can't face townsfolk looking like a whore fit only for a two-penny upright," she said. Her touch was practical and love-less, three rough strokes that raised the blood on my cheeks and chin. She tore a strip of cloth from her soiled petticoat, pinched it between her teeth, and ripped it cleanly in two. She raked her hard fingers through my hair, gathering it into two greasy hanks. She tied these into limp horns on either side of my head.

The beginning of power is when fear turns to wonder.

So it was the devil I was finally to meet.

CHAPTER 2

The path must have given offense, for what was once living earth lay scabbed with smooth black stone cut at sharp angles, set tightly as snake scales. I had never seen cobblestone before. Two feeble creeks, wrestled straight, ran foul on either side of the path. Rising just above the running filth were ledges of smooth stone that ran the whole length of the main street. The barns and hovels were not made of dung and sticks. They were built like enormous coffins, set on end, shiny as beetle wings. The porch rungs grinned like skulls. Each building bore a curse in a bold symbol above the door or over expanses of bewitched air where the symbols seemed to float in perfect stillness. Behind these expanses, headless and armless torsos were trussed in straight-stitched cloth with cruel-looking shoes and cagelike hats. Other windows were filled with bloodless meat, hanging from hooks, obviously meant as offerings, never for civilized consumption.

All the buildings seemed to be patched together with the same hard angles, the same unwavering lines fit only for boxing the dead. This was no quaint city square. This was the ripe hell spoken of by the skalds. A half place where she-demons wore human faces and stuffed their deformed bodies in bell-like dresses and hid their cloven feet in spade-shaped boots. The males wore collars of thinly pounded bone, cunningly constructed to look like cloth, that pushed the blood purple into their naked chins. Bulbous felt and feathered hats covered what surely must be their horns. I reached up and touched the loose hanks that sprang from my own head. I feared I couldn't fool any of these creatures.

The mule caught a scent and lifted its head. Its short legs began to churn. I was jostled forward. Small sparks shot from beneath its tiny shoes as it loped over the stones. Then it stopped before a post and waited. My mother lifted me off the animal and tucked the coat I had sat on under her arm. It was warm and damp from the combined heat of our bodies and I moved to stroke the mule's velvet, but my mother slapped my hand away and pushed me toward a doorway blocked by two swaying shutters. There was a smell of sawdust and spilled beer. A tinny music trailed above raised rough voices.

The men looked up. All I could see at first were men.

Fair heads. Raw blood in their cheeks. All wore mustaches, grotesques things damp with beer froth that camouflaged their wet leers. They wore rolled sleeves with black in the bends of their arms and a similar black in traces of crude tattoos that rippled over sinews and veins. I had seen tattoos before, in sigils and runic spells that arched over the hearts of certain men in my village, protecting them from blights, busted bones, and other evils. But these men in the tavern were stained with what looked to be a child's musings. Dull dripping knives and silly skulls and overfed women ready for their bimonthly baths. These men must have been repositories for devils and these marks on their skin kept the demons caged.

All eyes hung heavy on my mother's passing but she seemed not to notice. She walked straight toward a table in the back, pushing me before her. The table was strewn with the lounging bodies of several women, all overripe and spilling from their tight bodices. All I could see at first were their lush backs and the dull black of the hair piled above their small ears. They could be sisters, so common was this black hair among them. I was later to learn this color was a badge of their profession, a requisite rinse of coal tar thinned with vinegar and pine spirits that distinguished those in the life.

All but one.

My mother's rebellious red locks cleaved the throng of night-headed whores. They parted reluctantly like corrupt petals spreading for a ravenous bee. And what was at the heart of this ruined flower?

A man, of course.

Volker Kemp.

But such a man. He was veiled in smoke of his own making, a soft red ember glowing from a dark stub in his teeth. He had full lips as lustful as any woman's. His black mustache curled on waxed tips to the smooth boundaries of his face. He wasn't dressed like the other men, radiated none of their roughness or weakening desire. He glistened with a relaxed sheen. But he wore no silk thread. The glow was an effect of his eyes. Just his black liquid eyes. Flanked with a spray of thick lashes, those eyes pierced one like fingertips beneath bodice buttons. I knew of such eyes, knew they belonged to wicked gypsies who could steal years from your life by counting your teeth. But still I stared back and must have smiled, for I felt my gums grow dry as my smile was returned and my cursed places began to tremble. He seemed pleased by my discomfort and his eyes surged. But I did not look away.

"You should have warned me she would be so becoming," he purred, his eyes never leaving mine. When he leaned forward I could smell traces of bergamot laced with his tobacco. "You know, love, if you put on a little weight, washed that face and neck of yours, you'd be quite a pretty little pet."

I had never heard myself referred to as beautiful, not even as a possibility, and I could not stop the blood from rising in my face.

"Enough perhaps to rival mamma," he added, enjoying my blush.

The other girls clucked at this last comment, but my mother's eyes spat hot grease and they recoiled.

"I've changed my mind, Volker," my mother said. "She ain't for the life."

"Only if I say so," Volker said, relighting his failed cigar.

So he wanted to make a whore of me. Had I known then that I would never know the company of a man, would I have complied?

His lips curled but not into a smile. The subject was closed.

My mother grabbed me roughly. I struggled out of her grasp, afraid.

"You mind if I show her something?" he said. "Or do you want to keep frightening her?"

He didn't wait for a response but laid an arm over me and led me toward the back. We passed an enormous cabinet fixed to the wall with great brass brackets. It was flanked by two life-size women carved from pillars of boxwood. They were draped in mourning shrouds that revealed the red of their thimble-hard nipples. In the main cavity of the cabinet was a model of a medieval city. There were crenelated castles and twisted alders. Small rough roads with minutely carved bramble that led into dark holes laced throughout the diorama.

To the side of the cabinet, sitting on a milking stool, sat a plump woman sucking a sausage through a slit in her upper lip. The slit was deep enough to separate her lip at the philtrum and with the ballast of her fleshy cheeks, the sides of her lip hung down like the flews of some great hound. She rose at Volker's glance and bent to a brass crank at the base of the cabinet. There was a wheezing as if a bellows had taken a deep draw of air and then a rattling sound that finally released into a flood of tin and snare. A martial dirge came through dirty gauze.

I watched transfixed as a small figure of death, complete with shroud and scythe, snaked out of one of the holes. From another set of holes a parade of wooden people—serfs, knights, maids, and tradesmen—wound their way upward, their stiff bodies bending with clockwork age as they approached the black figure. The specter raised his tiny scythe with four neat clicks, then descended upon the people, one by one, as they passed. Death clipped them neatly into halves that fell open at tiny hinges. They reassembled before passing once more into the dark.

Volker watched my face, feeding on the horror and delight there, then pressed my arm and whispered close, the citrus of his bergamot tangled warmly with the sour wind of his words.

"That's not all I wanted to show you, love. That much about life you must already know. This is new."

He pulled me past a beaded curtain into a dark room. He sat me upon a beer barrel, wetted to keep it cool, and turned away with a grin. When he faced me again he held a small oak box with a brass flange at the top. He held the box to my face and nodded for me to press my eyes into the flange. Surely I would go blind or mad or worse. But the strange box pulled me toward it. I was powerless.

Inside was a small fat woman. Naked, she was amply cushioned by the pillows of her breasts as she lay on a small couch. She wore a bemused smile, completely unconcerned that I, a giant by her reckoning, was staring down at her. Volker asked if I was ready. I did not know for what. He turned a small crank and the little woman jerked to life. In shudders. In blinks. In atoms of movement her limbs began to unspool beneath me. I watched as she reached behind her, producing a shiny brass trumpet, her smile spreading as she arched her plump bottom and placed the mouth of the instrument into the pleat of her ass. I swore I could hear it sound. Then, suddenly, the trumpet was gone and she was back to her original position, her knowing smile in mid blossom when the box went dark.

"I bet you never saw the likes of that, my love."

I could only shake my head.

"That is the future of delight, my child. The future of *dreaming*."

CHAPTER 3

That night, in Volker's apartment, I listened to their voices from my place on the ground. Volker had a flat above the bar, one room with a plank floor partitioned by a blanket behind which the bed was kept. This was the primary place of business and all efforts of civility had been funneled there. On my side was a sheet metal stove, a basin, a small work bench with smooth lengths of dovetailed oak still in the jaws of a vice. A coping saw and planes were mixed with a beaten kettle and a few chipped cups. I understood that he made the boxes where that cunning little woman with the trumpet lived. In the far corner was strung a dimpled canvas upon which someone had painted his best impression of an enchanted grove. Single-stroke trees with impossible flowers. In front of this was the couch I had seen in the box.

"You've spent every dime I've earned building that shitty little box of yours," my mother said.

"And I'll earn every penny of it back once we have the proper scenario, my love."

"She's no actress. The plan won't work. She doesn't have the stuff." (Had my arrival been some kind of audition? And had I already *failed* it?)

"Then let me press the rosebud. She'll have stuff enough."

"You *touch* that child I'll kill you myself."

These weren't threats, they were well-trod paths, and I soon lost interest. My attention strayed to a strange black box in the corner. It stood on three stalks, as thin as cricket legs with a wrinkled accordion snout and a drooping fisheye at the end. I got up from the floor and walked to it. I reached out, sure it would shudder at my touch, but the eye didn't blink. It had a drape of cloth at the back. When I looked beneath it, I saw a weak pin of light in the darkness. There was the couch, the backdrop. But not as my eyes saw them. Through the skull of this thing, the image had been tipped upside down, reversed and somehow flattened. The image was hard, brittle to the tap of my nails. This was not enchantment. This was human cunning. Something far more terrifying than a devil's fork.

Near my feet was a slotted box full of glistening edges. I pulled one out of its pocket. It was cold and clear and heavy. A perfectly parceled square of air. I thought of the floating symbols I had seen in town and realized they had merely been larger expanses of the same substance. Conceivable. Manufactured. Something other than fear was elbowing into my brain, and I lifted the glass for closer inspection.

A ghost grinned back at me.

My fingers fumbled and the glass negative crashed to the floor. The voices stopped. I heard feet. Volker pulled me roughly from the shards. He wore a thin undershirt and I could see the angry russet of his breasts. He raised his hand to strike me. This I understood. Expected, even. But my mother's grip was fast and stopped him. He spun around and the fist meant for me landed flat to the side of her face. Her head snapped, then righted. Her eyes were hard and clear.

"You stay away!" my mother shouted as Volker calmly turned toward me.

"Well," Volker whispered, raising a silencing hand to my mother but keeping his hot gaze on me. "What have we here, girl? Damages," he said, flicking his eyes to the broken glass negative on the floor. "Property lost."

"Volker, please," my mother said. But it was not a plea for me. It was a warning to him.

"I just want to be reasonable," he purred. "Something of mine has broken. Now something of hers must break. Like value for like." His smile was wet, his lips as red as washed cherries. He extended a hand toward me and I shied away, my terror rounded by a faint but sharp delight.

"I can make it up to you, Volker," my mother said evenly. "Leave her alone."

"We are discussing *value*, my dear. Not a stale redundancy. No, the responsibility is with the perpetrator. Unless you have some hidden spell on that dexterous tongue of yours that can make glass knit like flesh?" I watched my mother recoil as Volker turned back to me. He brought the tips of his forefinger and thumb to his face and let them gently trace the black sheen of his mustache. He approached. I could smell him then. The damp spice of his skin dulled with sleep, the tart fermented sugar of his breath.

"*Mother?*" (Was that the first time I had called her that?) I saw movement, a blur of her as she darted toward something I could not see. He had his hands on me then, his hot slender fingers that seemed impossibly strong and somehow soothing. I tried to push him away but his pressure increased.

"Struggle, child. Do. It only makes the rose sweeter."

"Volker!" My mother's voice sounded like a muffled shot. He turned, amused by the ridiculous threat. Then his black eyes went wide as my mother leaned into him and then stepped back. In her hand she gripped a long shard of broken glass. I could see a ghostly half face, a length of neck and truncated shoulder at its triangular tip. It had color on it now. His hands went to her shoulders, settling hard there, an exhausted partner at an all-night waltz, and she plunged again, holding his sagging body with renewed vigor. She entered him again and again. She stepped back from the spurts of blood, a cat avoiding a spray of hot milk from a cow's teat, then let his body crumble to the hard wood. She dropped the shard and looked at me.

"We can't stay here."

I boiled the water that washed her cuticles clean. I watched her strip from her spotted slip, toss it over the lifeless thing, dress in fresh linen, lace her low boots with small grunts. When she was ready, she lifted a cloth from a stump of black bread and cut two thick slices with the coping saw. One she handed to me.

"Eat it now. I don't know when we'll eat again."

She cleaned the crumbs from the sawteeth and hung it back at its place on the wall. I was still chewing when she blew out the lamp.

We stole unseen through the sleeping streets, passing the night in the forest, sleeping under piled hazel leaves in the root crotch of a red oak. The stars were hot above us and night birds called in fading halftones from night-steeped perches. I could hear my mother's breathing grow deep and even. But I could not sleep. I wasn't thinking of his raised fist. Or the peeled wonder of his eyes when the shard of glass first struck him. Or the man, once living, who my mother had bled. I was thinking of the magic box.

MY MOTHER PROVIDED. WE SLEPT IN BARNS AND SPARE BEDS, HAYRICKS when no people were to be found. She would snare the eye of the men hacking wheat in the fields or working behind the counter in stores, disappear for an hour or less, and come back with all we needed. There were sausages and mutton joints, pails of fresh milk and beer. Once even a tiny cake of soap that smelled of ashes and jasmine. A few nights I woke up seeing Volker's lifeless eyes, a red bubble of spit forming at his pretty mouth. My mother would only look at me harshly when I woke her.

The old gods lost their grip. The fairies faded. For how could my mother have slept so many untroubled nights if their reach were real? She would laugh when I asked her, saying the truth was in our bodies, in the trials that didn't kill us. Rules had reign only if we played by them. And her life was proof enough. It didn't matter how hard the floor, how late the hour, or how poor the food and drink. Nothing could weaken the beauty that men saw in her. Her allure was structural. A thing as real and transporting as an iron bridge.

We were in a café near the Austrian border when the war began. Overnight, men changed to marching songs above their steins of beer and grew pronged mustaches like the kaiser. There was a frenzy among them. The company of women held new value. We had not eaten for three days when a strange-looking man approached us. He was dark, tall, spider thin, with feverish brown eyes. We were sipping hot water from our cups, desperate to keep our table, for it was raining outside, when he stuttered something. My mother regarded him with her usual cool until he reached into his vest pocket and pulled out a krone. She rose, assuming the offer, resigned to work. But he motioned for her to sit.

"No, no," he stammered. "I don't want any of that. Draw you," he said. "I want to draw you."

"*Draw* us?" she said. "That will *still* cost you."

He asked when last we ate. My mother did not answer. She simply summoned the waiter and ordered the entire left half of the menu.

He wanted us both as models. Our lives took on the quality of new homeowners in an old house, discovering papered-over doors and following cloth-wrapped wires to cold ends or sudden fires. For us to begin work, it was necessary to accompany him to his studio in the *Hauptstrasse* in the remote Viennese district of Hietzing. He was adamant about this, saying he was soon to be married and needed to provide his would-be wife with certain assurances as to his marital fitness. He would refer to her as his wife, she to him as her husband, and it was how I would eventually know her. Apparently their living in sin begged for the ballast of certain bourgeois conventions.

Following him meant crossing the Austrian border. As we had no papers this seemed an impossibility, but he seemed unconcerned. His father had worked as a railroad official in Tulln and he knew every man on the line. We briefly conversed with the conductor and told our place of birth, our general health. He seemed more impressed by our command of German than any answers we gave and showed us to a second-class cabin. The artist ordered hot tea and cream cakes. He made sure the blinds would remain drawn. Then he refused to ride with us. My mother saw this as an advantage, the easiest coin ever to grace her purse.

But I was disappointed. He possessed a quality that enthralled me, a kind of detached concentration, a naive misanthropy too self-obsessed to be of any real harm but forbidding enough to be compelling. It was a quality I would encounter with other greats, other condemned. I ate the cakes and watched my mother doze against the gentle rhythms of the moving train. When I was convinced she slept, I rose, took a sip of cold tea, and left the compartment.

The aisles were narrow and smelled of wet wool and furious tobacco. Young men loitered stiffly in their new uniforms. I burrowed through the milling bodies, over brass buttons and the butts of rifles, and slipped past the sleeping porter at premier class. Here the air was cool, almost refined. Compartments hummed like men's clubs full of boyish officers buying boots and prop monocles. They toasted and saluted one another with wine flutes full of thick German beer. They wouldn't drink champagne. They thought it was their duty to already hate the French.

I found the artist alone in his compartment playing with his hands. His knees were tucked to his chest. His eyes were transfixed by his own fingers that splayed then grouped into steeples and cross-bridge supports and a hundred other dexterous variations. He whispered something under his breath, a charm against the dark, a snatch of nursery song, and I realized just how young he was. How happy he was in his solitude. I knew I could not disturb him.

The train aisle burst with voices. Three drunk boys, their field grays stained with spilled beer and ashes, pushed past me, honking a whoring song. My eyes were nearly level with the crude eagles cast on their belt buckles. I saw *Gott Mit Uns* inscribed there above their untried sex, their Brandenburg cuffs falling loose off their pale boyish wrists. There was a gut-flutter in the air, a feeling of sudden Christmas in that narrow corridor. Boys ran as if with exposed knees. Ran toward hidden tree forts and secret creeks. Ran green broke away from their mothers' calls. I was confused by the rush of hot bodies. More confused when I realized they were all flowing back into my own compartment.

The show had begun. My mother was naked below the waist, the thatch of her exposed sex burning auburn above her translucent thighs. She held a pickelhaube over each breast. The shallows of the helmets were barely deep enough to contain her, and I thought how little imagination she must have. The compartment was stuffed to capacity. They were soaring now, these newly minted soldiers, borne up into the pink galleries of common lust and shame. I thought surely some railway official would break upon the scene. But there he was, the conductor, down on one knee in his blue uniform and gold fob, clapping as loud as the rest. But lust was not their only focus. Humiliation of the meek is the real pleasure of the mob.

From among themselves, they had found their idiot, a muscular youth of incredible height with enormous hands and red knuckles, a plowboy, perhaps, from the wilds of Württemberg. His blush fell like carrion among these buzzards. He had black hair with heavy wet bangs that shielded his ice-blue eyes. They pushed him to his feet, then pulled roughly at his belt and peeled his trousers to his knees. He stood there, buffeted by the jeers while my mother dropped the helmets and threaded her fingers into the loose fly of his worn drawers and pulled him free. There were cheers and sharp whistles. I watched a dense hatred clog the corners of his lips, but he said nothing, just swayed like a nearly felled tree while she pumped him with her hand. She frowned theatrically when he failed to respond. Ten other men were at the ready, their trousers puddled at the ankles. They rushed toward her, but she bristled, her eyes flashing like flints. But still they came toward her. And then she began to sing. It was an old song. The plowboy knew it or was quick to the tune, for he took it up. His voice was strong and clear and he held the song at a great height as it spread out over all the men, over all the boys and the countryside. Their lust cooled. This was her intention. Untried crowds could turn ugly and she was only looking for pocket money. The plowboy, still singing, lifted his trousers to his waist and refastened his belt. The windows spun into cream ribbons of gold and green. The fear and confusion left them, and the trenches toward which all were headed became mink-lined. The conductor dipped his gaze to his watch and was pulled back into crispness, into timetables and the language of lanterns, and he righted his cap, flipped my mother a coin and left the compartment soundlessly.

The show was over. My mother pulled her camisole over her bare back as if she dressed by candlelight, alone. The men milled out beneath their corrected buckles and buttons, flipping coins and paper to the worn carpet as they left. She looked at me, knowing I had seen it all, but simple nakedness could never expose her. She patted the seat beside her. I sat. She pushed my head to her lap, still humming.

"Sleep," she said bending to pick up her earnings. "Austria soon."

CHAPTER 4

It had just stopped raining when the train slowed into the station. I woke up in the adamant gray, hungry, still sluggish from the pastry sugar I had eaten the day before. My mother pulled me to my feet. Steam hissed past the window. Voices. Raised lights. The artist stood in the door of our compartment, staring at us with his mantis eyes, regretting his purchase perhaps, unreadable. There were shouts from the platform, long coats beneath double-headed eagles shouting names and numbers as the train emptied of its main occupants and the men mustered like marbles stacked in a child's game. The artist turned. We were meant to follow.

Weather threatened again, so we walked quickly up the Hietzinger *Hauptstrasse*. The houses rose up like monstrous bakers' models, floors stacked one upon the other, burnt sugar soffits and lintels of bitter marzipan never meant to be eaten. Women passed us, their hair pulled so tightly into buns they looked like rabbits held by the ears ready for the axe. All with high collars and hard eyes that would skip like stones from the artist to my mother to me. This was Hietzing, in the thirteenth district of Vienna, fingerbowl of the Hapsburg court, where all the dirty linen was rinsed. A place where the shrubs were as well tended as bankers' children, where quiet syphilis and pennyroyal abortions were portioned out by doctors who scoffed at Freud from Biedermeier night tables before the lights were snuffed out.

He stopped in front of a house, a particularly malevolent neoclassical confection capped with a virulent growth of ivy that reached to the top casements. He knocked distractedly. He had no key. In fact, he carried no metal in his pockets, a residual from his several months in prison on a pornography charge. But we knew none of this then. The door was opened by a plain girl in a vertically striped dress. Her eyes were the faded blue of empty medicine bottles and they looked at us, fell, then were picked up again as she lifted to her toes to kiss her husband. She lowered her head as we passed. We stood in the clean foyer, arms tucked to our sides to take up less space, feeling profoundly, I think, like the luggage we were.

False husband.

Fake wife.

And us a perfect addition to the blissful mockery.

The hall we stood in was drunk with respectable smells, sharp furniture polish and smoky wood soap and another smell like pine spirits but muddier. The outgassing of oil paint as it cures. The counterpoint of their marriage was evident in all their effects. On the walls were his paintings. I knew it even then. Frank vaginas below blank stares. Then an heirloom candlestick discreetly gleaming. A portrait of his last affair, with a dead and yellowed infant at her breast. An exquisitely chased vase of tube-rose. This simple pattern of extremes echoed through the entire

house. Theirs was a relationship of unresolved fifths and synco-
pated thirds and I suppose modern for all that. I could understand what he saw in her, what a distant and treacherous shore
called to him every night and the respectable anchor of teacups
and spoons she provided. But what did she get? Houseguests he
insisted on flaying to their quaking fundamentals? Perhaps he
was a husband in more common ways. I had heard peasants cou-
pling, heard the cries that were not from pain. But he seemed too
frail for such exertions. Surely it was only his gaze that entered
you.

We were shown to the servants' mess, to a big bowl of broth
with spaetzle and black bread. When we finished, we were taken
wordlessly up the back stairs to a small room with an iron bed
and nothing else. We were to keep factory hours—that much
was made clear by his wife. We would be required to be at her
husband's disposal for twelve hours a day during the week and
eight on the weekends. Compensation would be meals, a bed in
the studio, and a few kroners, which was far more than Klimt or
his cronies paid, she told us. We were tired. Still hungry. And we
agreed. We were meant to share the bed, sleep if we could, and
be ready for work in the morning. But I didn't sleep that night.
I thought of the artist. His hands. His eyes. His morning-bird
jerkiness that even then had become precious to me.

We followed the light, chasing the thin rays across the worn
wooden floor from dawn until the last leaning beam, standing,
crouching, kneeling, leaning, unfurled on the bed or floor, willing our muscles past their spasms, evening our breath to endure
yet another hour of scrutiny. All the while his eyes never left us.
He worked in a fashion apparently discovered by Rodin, a way to
blow the channel between the optic chasm and the hand, where
the eyes never left the model, and the hand laid down a firm

indelible line from mere trust. Rodin's motive may have been as simple as lust, his eyes never wanting to miss a single play of light on such soft and ample female flesh, but there was nothing so warm at work here. Our artist's gaze was that of the surgeon, the vivisectionist. We were not people but rather objects that defined space, a delineated mass radiating a single contiguous line that he quickly translated with blind gesture. He sat on a low milking stool, a stack of blank sheets balanced on his knees, a quiver of pencils at his thin ankles. He worked incredibly fast. Finished drawings drifted to the floor in some furious autumn, littering the planks beneath his shoes in a silent but volatile soil.

Breakfast was weak tea and a biscuit, perhaps a piece of cold sausage, left on a tray on the floor near where we slept. We would awaken and hear him chewing in the corner, already crouched on his stool, eating the same cold food as us. That first morning I was innocent to his expectations. I swallowed quickly when I noticed him and then stood in my rumpled clothes, my arms swinging slowly in their sockets, trying to inspire. He simply stared. It was then that my mother stood, smirked, and pulled her camisole over her head. She was clear of her bloomers and bending to unroll her stockings when he shot an arresting hand into the air.

"That," he said.

My mother froze, pulled her stocking to the swell of her thigh, and looked up. His pencil began to move and she froze again. In mere seconds it was over. I moved to pull my own shirt off but he waved me down, his gaze taut on my mother. I sat on the bed, still dressed, angry and bested. I had been slow, had failed to please, and now he would be farther away from me than ever.

With the waning of the winter light our hours grew shorter. Some days we didn't work at all, just huddled in blankets, idling, while he sat on the floor with trampled tubes of gouache and jars of colored water, irrigating stacks of drawings with washes of unlikely hues. I loved to watch him work, loved to see his brush fill to dripping with some violent orange and see it seep to the pencil-thin boundary of me.

But my mother grew restless. The few times he did want her services she was stiff and quick or she hardly moved at all. Then one morning he brought a young man into the studio. He was thin and dark and unshaven, a street-worn twin of the artist himself. He stood by the windows, deeply shadowed by the weak winter light, staring into the street he had just left, perhaps amazed by his new perspective, while the artist molded the stale linen on the bed. He motioned for my mother and whispered something to her. Her expression was blank, only her fingers moved, the meat of her thumb rubbing the opposing pad of her index finger. What he wanted would cost him. The artist jerked his head and she flopped on the bed. The young man followed and they made love in shattered stills until the light was lost. All I could do was watch.

We were constantly naked by this time, never knowing when we would be needed. The young man had arrived early and began to remove his coat when the artist's wife appeared at the door and motioned to me. She had a robe with her. She draped it over me and led me from the room and shut the door. I didn't want to leave. I was angry the stranger had replaced me. But there was something else adding to my reticence. Something about him that lingered sharply. Something in the skin surrounding his eyes, a blue tightness that veiled his stare and made me think of Volker Kemp.

"You may call me Frau Schiele," she said. She did not ask my name. I was led downstairs and introduced to several men in bankers' collars and dark coats. They were passing sheets of the artist's work among themselves. Their voices would rise as they turned the sheets in their fingers, exclaiming about the tyranny of tea spouts and how the design of bed linens was fertile ground for a revolution.

"No, no, Herr Moll! There must be shades of the *eternal* in the tines of that fish fork!"

Many words were spent debating the proper balance of negative space in wallpaper patterns. It was explained to me they were part of a movement called the Succession. I wanted to hear more, to understand how stylized daisies could free a man's soul. But the artist's wife pulled me into a deep curtsy and showed me to the back parlor. She set me in a comfortable chair and gave me a large bright book with pictures. After months of the raw veracity of the artist's images, the pictures seemed childish and false. I didn't need to be excluded from what was going on at the top of those stairs. I could have found some way to fit into the frame. So what if they touched me and opened me? The artist would see me and I would be safe. Under his gaze I would be as safe as if smothered in goose down.

I was never to sleep in that upstairs room again.

My mother had won. Her bigger body, her fuller breasts, the accommodation of all her hollows had defeated me. I slept on a bed made for me near the stove. I took my breakfast now where we had begun, at the servants' table, usually with one of the picture books Frau Schiele was so fond of giving me. I would stare at the round heads of the animals standing upright like humans, their snouts smeared into unnatural smiles, and try to imagine them without their ridiculous clothes, truncated legs splayed, tongues lolling, vying for the artist's attention and immortality.

One morning, I slammed the book in frustration. I raised

the book to throw it when my hand was stilled. The artist's wife took the book from me gently and placed it closed on the table.

"That's not how we treat books," she said. "If you don't like the pictures perhaps I can get you another."

Her stifled affection must have needed an outlet, for these were the first really civil words she had said to me. I told her I didn't like the books, any books. They were too full of gibberish. She smiled. "You can't read," she said. "Of course they seem like gibberish." I must have blushed, for she told me not to be embarrassed. Reading was simple once one knew how. She left and came back with a thin book with large pages filled with bright pictures of common things. There was scribbling next to each image.

"My mother taught me with this," she said, flipping the pages with the tips of her pale fingers. "It's very simple."

Cup. Table. Floor. Spoon.

This is how the days passed. Like an explorer with his telescope slowly twisting a foreign vista into focus. Soon the scribbles had meaning. Then held more interest than the pictures. She taught me rhymes and we would chant these over tea, sometimes completely forgetting to drink from our cups before they grew cold.

The artist was finally married. We were not invited to the ceremony and heard no details of it upon their return to the house. Real life was beginning to inform their lives and we were still only on the fringes of the real.

We saw less and less of the artist and my mother.

As a tonic against his absence, Frau Schiele would take me out on fair days. She had a pink-and-cream crepe dress made for me for these occasions that was too stiff to bend in. I would trail behind her on the *Hauptstrasse*, gazing happily at the other trussed-up mothers and children who passed us. She showed me the summer palace and the big park with the little white hut that looked like it was made of spun sugar.

"That's where the waltzes come from," she said.

We ate flavored ices and fed pastry crumbs to the ducks on the banks of the Danube. One day she took me into a shop where pens and writing paper were sold and told me to pick something. I assumed she was going to teach me to draw.

"No," she said. "Proper young ladies must learn to write with proper ink. Pick what is comfortable and we'll get started."

The house smelled heavily of wet oil paint when we returned, and the wife must have taken this for a good sign for she hummed gaily to herself as we headed for the kitchen. She made me change into my ordinary clothes, now faded and sweet-smelling after so many washings. She untied the parcel and fitted the nib to the pen. Then she unscrewed a pot of ink and smoothed a fresh sheet of practice paper to the top of the table.

"Let's begin with your name," she said, tipping the pen toward me.

I refused to take it. In my village it was common practice not to name bastards. It kept us neatly in the realm of things, of that which could be handled or altered according to use. Names gave things a soul.

"I don't have a name," I said, looking at the blank page.

The wife seemed confused. "Surely you've been called something."

I remembered Volker, in heat, had spit a common noun at me once that in my language was *Mädchen*, which meant simply "girl." I told the wife this. Her face darkened. This was the kettle calling itself kettle, the fork answering to fork. I stared back, my heart pumping in my ears, thinking I had somehow offended her. She cleared her throat and, spritely once again, said, "Maddy's a pretty name." I might have gotten a soul that day.

I HAD HEARD THREE CHRISTMASES FROM THE DARK EGRESS OF THE stairwell, the distant mirth and ringing china of three sets of birthdays when I woke up one morning with a slight cough. Frau Schiele used my new name when she told me to stay in bed while she went to the chemist's. As soon as she left, my mother strolled into the kitchen. She was wearing a thin silk kimono, a gift from the artist, and it clung to her greedily. She plopped herself on my bed and grabbed me.

"Who gave you that name?" she asked coldly.

"It's mine now," I answered, trying to break free from her.

"She's given you quite a few nice things."

"A few." I could feel the pain begin to rise in my wrist from the pressure of her touch.

"And now you feel special. A regular lady."

"She'll be back soon," I said.

"You were better off before. Names only trap you."

"Let me go." I wiggled hard and managed to break free.

"I won't keep you, *Maddy*." The name sounded false and dirty in her mouth. "She can have you for what little she has left."

"What do you mean?"

"Haven't you noticed? She hasn't much time. Neither of them do." She smiled and squeezed my arms. "It will be just us soon enough."

I watched the artist's wife closely in those following weeks. When she lifted a teacup to her lips, did she leave a final sip for the ferryman? Did crows refuse to scatter at her approach? She still liked to take me to the outdoor concerts and we went frequently. News from the front was bad. The lawns around the band shell were peppered with young soldiers propped up in wheelchairs, rushed into old age. The ones who could stand applauded at all the wrong places. The others screamed at every cymbal crash. They were wheeled away like broken toys by plain nurses whose charges could no longer appreciate a pretty face. But I still loved to hear the music, to wear my stiff little dress and pretend there was only this shallow beauty in my life.

We were seated close to the orchestra one Sunday. The musicians had just begun to play "Roses from the South." I was probing a back molar with a tongue still cold from a flavored ice when the tooth suddenly gave away. I tasted blood and looked up to the artist's wife. She stood and coughed to clear our path. When we were at a discreet distance, her gaze fell to my gloved hand, the tips stained now with the browning blood, a small pearly kernel in my palm. She gently pushed the ice to my lips and told me to take as much into my mouth as I could. The raw socket ached, the ice too cold to offer comfort. I was afraid to drop my tooth, thinking it could be used in a charm against me, so I gripped it as best I could in my covered hands. It seemed a shame to leave, but my gloves were now soiled and no longer fit for public.

When we came through the front door, my mother was sitting on the landing steps, her kimono loose at the breast. I wasn't happy to see her. But still there was a pull, a feeling that I owed her something. I held my tooth out to her. "Look," I said. She snatched it from my open hand. Seeing the ball of ice straining in my cheek, she ordered me to spit. I looked to the artist's wife, who still stood next to me. She seemed distant, curious as to what I might do. I spit the pink ice in my mother's hand before I could think. My mother got to her knees and rummaged around beneath the stairs. Frau Schiele slipped her hand into mine. When my mother faced us again, she had a lacy ball of spiderweb in her fingers. She tipped my jaw open and, looking defiantly at the other woman, stuffed the filthy ball into the raw socket in my jaw. She packed it deeply with the tip of her little finger. The pain ebbed immediately. I was afraid to probe the dusty clot that roiled my gut but soothed so quickly. What was I to do? The artist's wife had seen this shameful, primitive doctoring, and back came the dirt floor of my grandfather's hut. I shivered in the frilly dress not fit for me, not fit for anyone like me, and felt the tears brim in my eyes.

"Take that filthy thing out of your mouth," the wife said gently. She held her white hand below my lip like a silver bowl. I loved her then, the artist's wife. And hated myself for feeling so. I dropped the red tangle into her palm and watched her fingers close around it, making it disappear. My mother merely smiled, saying nothing.

WE WERE PLAYING TWO-HANDED *SCHAFKOPF* IN THE MORNING COOL OF the kitchen. The chill of fall was in the air and the stove coals were banked red but offered only a weak heat. I was trying to remember the card values, aces-eleven, over-three, under-two, the tens unchanged. Trumps were too few in the thirty-two-card deck. There had been arguing earlier from the floor above. The artist and my mother had not reconciled. I played an ace. The artist's wife coughed. When she laid her trump on the table, her card was dappled with tiny flecks of red. She looked at me wide-eyed. For that moment, we were equal. Two children staring at one another in white horror. Then she was doubled by waves of coughing so wet and violent she sprayed the bib of my dress. A throatful of blood splashed to the table, soaking the deck, obliterating the suits. She shuddered and pulled for breath, but none would catch in her filling lungs. I screamed for the artist. He rushed into the kitchen, half-dressed. My mother was not far behind him. She watched from the threshold as he bent to lift his wife, his thin back buckling like a whittled truss straining to contain a collapsing roof. The wife wheezed hard, her eyes flaring white. His long fingers played deftly over the tight laces of her corset and then leaped to catch the paring knife my mother tossed him. He sawed at the laces. They popped like the support cables of a failing bridge and he caught her as she spilled to the ground. He screamed for a doctor, snared now in her panic and unable to leave her.

My mother did nothing. She just stared down at the frail bellows pumping frantically on the floor. I was on the street before I could think, screaming for a doctor, my dress smeared with red, my lips chalked with terror. A young man dropped the hand of his companion as he ran to me. He searched my body for wounds but I yelled, "Inside, inside," and tugged at his starched cuff. He stumbled behind me as I led him up the landing and to the kitchen.

Her breath was a shambling machine now, a pump organ kicked in anger, sounding only foul notes, pathetic flats, not human anymore. The doctor was quick about his work. His finger swept the cavity of her mouth, progressing deep into her throat. It lingered there, then was thrust out as she gagged and vomited a stinking slosh of cake and blood. He sat her up. She heaved her first real breath.

"Help her to her room," he said. I moved first but was repulsed as the artist laced his arms beneath her knees and hoisted her, with the doctor, out of the kitchen.

"Maddy, dear," she said weakly as she floated from the kitchen. "Your poor *dress*."

The artist never left her side. He beat back her fever with

rags wrung in alcohol. He cradled her wilting wrists. He brought broth and flowers and thimbles of cool water, which seemed to be all she could get down. I could hear my mother moving about in some remote corner of the house, away from us, away from the artist's newly rekindled attention.

After nine days the sheets barely moved with her breathing. Doctors could do nothing now. The artist asked me to fetch his drawing board and pencils. When I returned with them, he was on the bed with her, his knees curled beneath him, naked, weeping. I backed from the room, then stopped when he began to kiss her. This was not the greedy appetite I had seen so many times before. This was something new. The kisses were tender at first, slight scuffs over her scalding throat. Then his tears caught fire and his movements became impassioned. She moaned beneath him, unnamable. His lips and fingers began to knead her skin and sheet-white breasts. I watched his long brown fingers trace the soft crests of her ribs, the skin stretched taught like something left in the sun. She arched in a daze, her eyes veiled. He reached a bundled fist below the sheets then unfolded himself above her, lengthening like a shadow, and thrust. She moaned. Her brow clouded, then slowly crashed. His tears fell on her shoulders that were too weak to receive him. It was life slowly extracting death, holding up a single silencing finger to that which is made of silence.

When they were finished, he slipped out of the bed. She slept. Still naked, his eyes never leaving her, he picked up his pad, the shaft of his pencil. She opened her eyes one last time, just long enough for him to trace the gesture. The artist died three days later, on All Hallows' Eve. He died from the same Spanish flu that would take a hundred million others.

I tried to mourn them but my mother only scoffed. She told

me we had existed, finally, only at the side of their lives. We had been looked at, distractedly loved, holding trays and chairs, never really one of them. But I did not believe this. The house was aggressively empty without them and I could find no comfortable spot, not even among those I had thought brought joy. I refused to scrub properly at the stain on my dress. I needed at least that to know I had been touched. My mother, in many ways a kind of virus herself, was far more practical. She stripped the pillows from their cases and boiled them, then stuffed them full of provisions from the larder, hard circles of cheese and stone-shaped loaves of bread, canned beets, and candied fruit peels. In another pillowcase she stuffed all the wife's jewelry, a few silver candlesticks, and a few sheets from the artist's sketchbooks. She knew the families would descend soon and take inventory. With the war as good as lost, they would need every asset they could muster. On our last night in the house, she lit a fire. I watched her as she burned the bedsheets, her profile shadowed hard by the mindless leaping light. I asked where we would go.

"Berlin," she said.

CHAPTER 5

I knew I would never see Berlin. Already I could feel the pathogen ignite in me, could feel the icy tendrils of the disease lift me up out of my skin. I tried to keep my head clear, fighting hard against the gathering haze. I remember leaving the house. My mother did not bother to lock it. I was trying to follow her down the empty street, but my feet did not touch the pavement. I was carried along on the cold, slippery backs of phantom fish. I stumbled. I could barely split my feet fast enough to stop my vomit of blood from staining my shoes. My mother was angry. A hard jerk under an arm. The world torn loose and spinning as she pulled me harshly back into the artist's house. On the floor, near a fire. My mother was in a corner, mumbling something. Chanting. She was coughing herself now, spitting distractedly, never breaking rhythm. I saw her lift a small nacreous object to the light. My tooth. She took my tooth and placed it in a small metal bowl. She had a mortar of sorts, a hard little mallet with which she pounded the tooth, crushing it into fine powder. I heard her

spit and watched her finger swirl the powder into a hard pearl of
pink paste. Her eyes were open but sightless as if the very horizon fled from her stare.

In my fever, we were in a cave. A frozen cave brittle with blue
and pale green ice. I begged for blankets. But she blew on me, a
sharp breath that cut like honed flints. Her chanting increased
and I saw the flash of a small knife. She held my middle finger in
her hand and flicked the tip of my fingernail with the blade. She
took the nail chip in her fingers and kneaded it into the paste.
Then she plucked a hair from my head and wrapped it around
the ball of paste. I watched, delirious, as she pushed the pearl
of my hair, fingernail, and ground tooth into what looked like a
leathery thistle.

"Hair, nail, and tooth," I heard her whisper. *"The sisters that
never die."*

She raised the thistle to her mouth and spat blood on it.
She then took the thistle and placed it in my mouth, settling it
gently upon my tongue, whispering, her thumb circling my dry
lips three times before the flesh knit and sealed the thistle inside
me. Had there been a needle and thread? Had I felt tiny stabs
through my feverish lips?

There was a high, incessant whistling in my ears. I wanted
to sit up, move closer to the fire that I knew burned in the room,
but my body would not respond to thought. It lay there, in the
snow, on the floor of the cave, in the cold that became increasingly chill, increasingly real. I pushed my lungs but my scream
died behind sealed lips.

My mother ignored me. Between her fingers she twisted a
length of thread, fine and clear as if wrought from glass. This
she wove between my paralyzed toes, binding them together in
a series of intricate loops and knots. She did the same to my fin-

gers, trussing them together so tightly I could not move one hand free of the other. The thread began to circle my legs, winding up my calves and thighs, pressing my arms to my sides, willing them to mesh, the flesh turning to clay, swallowing the creases between limbs, my body losing all delineation, reverting back to some limbless amoeboid state. I writhed like a worm, sent panicked signals through my spine and nerves, but communication was cut. I was buried in my own flesh, sewn into my own skin like a death shroud. Was this the pinnacle of the illness, the last hideous crest before death? This hateful oneness, all individuality worn away until I was nothing more than a soft bolus awaiting the gullet of a god?

The last thing I remember seeing was a creature in the corner, a human form, firm on all fours like a wolf, its back arched hard in a feverish curve as torrents of blood flowed from it lips to the blackness of the floor.

CHAPTER 6

I awoke in darkness. If you could call it that. I was conscious. But not living. Half-finished. Uncured. You enter a concert hall where a powerful symphony has just played. You see the stage, the seats where the audience and orchestra once sat. You feel a resonance of great sound, but there is no music present. You are this great hall.

Empty houses that had once known joy must feel this way. Battlefields where the grass now grows.

I had no heartbeat. No lift and retreat to my chest. It is a vibration you miss only by its absence; blood coursing through its channels, organs churning out their chemicals and bile, bones on their hinges and intestines squeaking. Blinking. Breathing. All this background noise of living that we mistake for silence. The void was deafening, yet still I *was*.

I don't know how long I lay there drenched in this nothingness. A day. A week. Finally I had a dream of breathing and willed my chest to heave, but the breath was not needed. I could remember. Words. Feelings. Faces. The artist's wife. Something dimmer in the shape of my mother. The house. The last night. The cave. The thistle. And as soon as my mind fell to this thought, there it was, its rough case pressed against my palate, dry upon my drier tongue. The feeling came gradually, prodded and willed into flowing, but it came. And so I thought of fingers, palm, wrist, and something stirred there with me in the dark. How long did it take to raise my hand to my lips? A month? More? But slowly it came, like lead flowing into the mold of a tin soldier, the memory and the movement coming on at once, flowing into empty recesses and filling with mass, filling with me.

There were laces there. My mouth had been sewn shut. I pulled hard at the stitches. Did they tear? Or was it the flesh of my lips? I felt no pain. Only the pressure that was relieved in tiny echoing plinks. When the thistle left the purse of my lips, I was filled with a dim but frightening implication. If the thistle was real, then the ritual was real. That meant my death had been real. Or had it? Perhaps this was the dream of death.

To know, to know for sure, I needed to move, to pierce the darkness and what lay beyond. I remembered wood, the roughness of wood, on floors and crude cabinets, pithy and hollow but oddly strong, and this hardness above me, this stoppage, this was wood. A lid. A box. I willed my heels. They sounded on wood. I was in the box. A coffin. Was that the word? Casket. Buried. In the box, buried deep, in the box with the lid, shut blackly above me.

There was panic, the memory of panic, but panic without purchase, just the ghost, the flicker of it across my mind, for the box and I were the same. I simply wanted to know what was above the box. The box wouldn't mind. The box would comply. I willed my wrists to bend, my palms flush to the surface above me, and then I willed *Push, push hard,* and the stoppage gave, a muffled grating of loose gravel and soil that sifted into the box as I continued to push.

The dirt filled my eyes but didn't sting. It only settled there as would a burst of different air, benign, expected. The lid hadn't been nailed, set upon me as it was in great haste. The grave was not deep, dug as it was in complete exhaustion. Was this my mother's last effort before she died, when she assumed her charm had failed? And as the lid finally tumbled off my body, my eyes slowly focused on the pitted landscape around me. No head-stones. Just quick crude crosses either nailed or lashed at the apex, stuck into the ground, namelessly. Whole crops of crosses over acres of shallow mounds. A harvest of death. I willed myself out of my box and stood. Then I walked. Small pyres of smoldering effects were everywhere. A final effort to slow the disease, they smoked in the wine-colored evening. Horn combs heat-twisted into sea-creature shapes, charred crib slats and blackened sau-cers, bone-handled buttonhooks still glowing like pokers. Pho-tographs, letters, charred and left to fade from what the flames could not finish.

If there was a sense of sadness it was a remote feeling. I looked on all this with more fascination than horror. Horror requires a kind of consent from the victim, and I was past all that now.

I knew I was still in Vienna, for I could smell the brackish signature of the Danube. I could see barges moored along the canal. I knew I was no longer in the thirteenth district. I was later to learn I had been stumbling around in the wilds of the Kaisermühlen in the twenty-second district of the Donaustadt. This would account for all the available burial space. But at the time I could have been wandering the surface of the moon.

A greasy light spilled onto the wet cobbles of the quay. The air was rank with a tarry heather that flaked off pitch torches lit against the airborne pathogens. The light came from a riverside beer hall, once robust in its patronage but now filled with the old and infirm who had escaped induction or disease. Fat old men with imperial side-whiskers and beer-blistered eyes focused only on the shallow dregs of their steins. They were seamen, barge captains, and stevedores, idle now that all the empire's supplies were spent at the front. I looked like what I was, a child newly puked from the grave. My entrance, as they say, raised the roof.

"Crippled Christ, look what the cat dragged in."

"Step into the light, darling. Let's have a look at you."

"God in heaven what a stink."

"Steady there, Hans, that brat is dripping with plague."

At the mention of plague, I could feel a cold recoil from all those present. Then one of them stood.

"Can't have that," said the one that must have been Hans. "Not while *we* can still lift a stein to our lips."

My life, if one could call it that, would have been so much different if they'd simply asked me to leave.

I didn't feel the first blow, nor the second or third that ramped into a steady hail of angry fists. I was aware only of a kind of adamant concussion, a velocity of outrage, as if I were safe in the confines of some metal cage let loose over a rocky incline, tumbling, rocking, jolting, but vaguely aware of the intent of the impact, not the impact itself.

I felt myself leave the ground, my body arching in space as I cleared the far edge of the bar and landed on the slimy plank floor. I held no breath that could leave my body.

There was more rough jostling as boot heels slammed into the orbits of my eyes and the bridges of my cheekbones, but where bones should have cracked and splintered, mine gave, pliant as marsh reeds. The mob redoubled their efforts, terrified at the sickness they thought I harbored, frustrated at my resiliency, but I was above them now, swerving in the unconcerned trajectory of a common housefly as it avoids the dull swat of human hands.

Their fury finally reached its climax and I felt myself lifted up again. They ran me through the door, each holding a limb in a grip that could shatter kindling, slamming the crown of my head into the jamb, but again I felt only a ripple of concussion through the jellied chambers of my spine, a wind that thrilled in passing. I was falling through space again, in the soothing openness of water-cooled air, tumbling in a languid free fall that almost delighted.

There was a soft implosion, the cymbal hiss of a parting surface that enveloped me in some slower substance. I saw the surface of the Danube seal over me, the white froth of bubbles from my impact squirmed past my open eyes in furious schools. The darkness swallowed me slowly.

I don't know how long I brined in that silent green water. I recall the sleeping darkness, the almost audible whisper of the currents that gently buffeted my body like a lover rousing me to love. The sacks of my lungs had filled with water and weighted me to the bottom. There was no flesh to decay, no methane that could siphon into my tissues and buoy me to the surface. I drifted. Freshwater snails curled into the conch of my ears and little fish frolicked in the hollow of my open mouth. If we knew how serene death really is, how merciful the dark gesture that helps us shed the sea chests of ourselves, would we still fear it?

I was roused by the sound of dripping water. I could feel pressure in the pit of each arm, an unsecured weightlessness. Voices conferred, whispering as if afraid to wake me. I felt two fingers press my jugular, a rustle of cropped hair as the convexity of a head was held to my chest. I was being lowered when sight bled into my open eyes and I saw I was in the hands of a giant.

He had a sallow face the color of candlewax and sunken at the cheeks. The lids of his eyes seemed swollen and unbearably heavy but could not hide the bright blue irises that stared dully back at me. He had black hair, shorn nearly to the skull, running in wide patches on either side of his head. But the top of his head was flat, hairless, a calcified rusty color with patches of florid green patina. The lip of this plate, for I realized it was a metal plate, was flanged at the crest of his head and dipped past his hairline, beaten somehow to mimic the curve of his forehead. A crown of four mismatched bolts had been drilled through the lip, into the living bone, securing it there. Even in my present seemingly impervious state, I marveled at the radiant pain he must have endured, the huge, blind fumbling will to live that could leave him content to be so diminished and yet still breathing and blinking and feeling. I didn't know who was the greater wonder, he or me. There was something familiar about him, despite his modified appearance. I felt a little peal of pleasure as one might feel in the remembered floor plan of a childhood home despite it being demolished. He was the plowboy. The one forced into my mother's lap in the troop car. The one who demurred. The one who could resist her. I must have smiled, for his colorless lips spread into a thin grin that revealed the broken pickets of his teeth. But there was warmth there, a dull thud of recognition. Many candles had been extinguished behind his eyes but this one still burned.

"Put her down, Mutter," a voice whispered. "She'll be all right now."

Crouching near the giant was another man, short and plump with wide-set brown eyes and cropped red hair. He wore a long walrus-like mustache that dangled past the ledge of his chin in two rough points.

"I assure you he's quite harmless, despite his frightful appearance," the walrus said. "I had great plans for him, but his limited faculties, alas, offered even more limited theatrical possibilities. But no matter. He has his uses. That plate he wears is really quite a blessing. French shell in the pits of Verdun peeled his skull like a boiled egg. I'll never forget that whistle. He was quite fortunate we still had our field surgeon with us."

I was on the ground now, but the giant refused to slacken his grip.

"It's okay, Mutter. You can let her go."

Mutter blew like a horse, blinking hard, then mumbled a wet growl and retracted his large hands.

"I should dispense with introductions," the walrus began. "I am Heinrich Meir-Aichen, but that is beating a banality. Please, call me the Trout. I assure you the name is more indicative of my tenacity than any aquatic prowess. And this conspicuous fellow is Mutter. I never learned his real name. The boys always called him Mutter, for he acted so like a mother, always making sure we were dry and fed. Always doing for others. And what shall we call you, my little water baby?"

I moved to speak but felt a great surge of water flood my throat. I pitched forward and vomited a few liters of the Danube. I tried to say something, but all that came out were tarnished leaves.

"No matter," the Trout said. "Perhaps we could—"

"Maddy," I said finally, rasping it out with the sound of a long idle grindstone.

"Maddy, yes. Short for Madeline I assume."

"*Mädchen*," I croaked.

"*Mädchen*. Quaint. A tad literal, perhaps."

He stood, his greatcoat almost reaching the ground. Around

his waist he wore his ammunition belt. But where cartridges and grenades had once hung were tubes of dry sausage and triangles of cheese.

Mutter raised himself to his full height and began walking.

"Our camp is not far," the Trout said. "Perhaps you would care to join us in a modest feast?"

I said nothing. I could feel the pull of deep, open spaces, quiet depths, and silent floors where a nullifying sap could be allowed to saturate me. It was my first time experiencing this sensation. I did not know the earth is always calling for the dead. But something kicked, some involuntary muscle that still quivered for the light, for the human.

"Or we could picnic here," the Trout continued, deaf to the monumental struggle inside me. "By the water could be quite pleasant."

He produced a knife and cut a disk of sausage and held it out to me. I took it and remembered where it fit, stuffing it dryly into my mouth. My jaws rose and fell, but the mass tasted of ashes. I kept chewing, but no saliva flowed to reduce it. Flecks of fat and dried meat dribbled from my lips as my jaws continued to work.

"Or perhaps you're not hungry. Perhaps you don't eat at all."

His tone grew quiet as I felt him eye me. His hand slapped my face and I felt the breeze of it as my head snapped to the side. I heard Mutter whimper.

"You can't feel that, can you child?" the Trout said. "In fact you can't feel *anything*. Isn't that right?"

I said nothing.

"You were quite dead when we fished you out, my dear. So perhaps, as the Americans say, let's stop beating around the bush."

He took my face in his hand, studying it, waiting for a welt that never appeared. A memory of fear, a feeling of awful exposure surged through me.

"Please," I said. "Don't throw me back into the river."

The Trout smiled, parting the tails of his great mustache like a curtain.

"Throw you *back*, girl?" He chuckled wetly. "I have far more use for you than the fishes. I'm too jaded for miracles and I can no longer believe in God, so I shan't waste a moment in awe. Suffice it to say there are gift horses and they should not be regarded where they chew. Now I had quite a reputation before the war, was known as quite an impresario, a showman who had the good fortune of performing for several distinguished personages not unknown to the Hapsburgs. Therefore I feel I can offer you, with utter certainty, a thrilling theatrical opportunity, one for which you would have to wait centuries to entertain its equal. In short, my dear, I can make you a *star*."

CHAPTER 7

"Pathos, pathos," the Trout was explaining over a scrap fire of textbooks and single shoes. Mutter was softening a cheese rind over the low flames with a pair of spectacles bent into a single-pronged fork.

"The empire is lost," the Trout said. "The kaiser is as crazy as his father if he thinks otherwise. The war will cease by summer, and what do you think the masses will crave as they sift through the ashes? That ridiculous flickering train of Lumière's? Pathos! Hope! Three matinees a day of a two-act *resurrection*!"

Mutter was chewing on the blackened rind, having resumed his sewing. It was a dress meant for me, frilly with great capped sleeves painfully redolent of the pink-and-cream dress I had but dyed a dutiful black with diluted motor oil. The scenario had been all worked out and we were late into rehearsals, but still the Trout felt we needed inspiration.

"I don't eschew the possible revolutionary aspects of the flickers," he said, blowing on his fingers. "But movies are dynamite in the hands of infants, fondled with their fuses wet. For now only the *theater* can offer real edification, spiritual, emotional, or otherwise. Mutter, hurry up with that hem. We need to go over that last business with the box."

I suppose there was genius in our presentation. If not in the execution, at least in the audacity of the attempt. It wasn't a play, really. Not in the purist sense. There were elements of theatricality but just as much sideshow flimflam. There was a moment right after my "death from the Spanish Menace," as the Trout referred to it, when he would place a small cone constructed from a modified ear horn over my chest and invite an audience member to listen for any signs of life. Satisfied that I was truly departed, I was respectfully deposited into a black pine box and slowly nailed shut. The Trout would dramatically hold each nail over his head, pinched between his taut fingers before driving it with great purpose into the dark pulp. Mutter, now dressed in a frayed chasuble, would ring a small bell between each strike of the Trout's hammer. I was then lowered into a pit, while Mutter shoveled dirt on top of me and then left the scene for his costume change. The Trout would launch into a desperate prayer for my redemption, ascension, and hopeful resurrection. This speech would end with his tearful collapse onto the fresh grave, where he would raise his head one last time, streaming eyes facing the sky, and say, "But death shall be vanquished on the wings of a father's final love" or some such claptrap, and poor Mutter, visibly panting by this time, would reenter, now in crepe beard and wire crown, a monolithic Jesus, and lift the box out of the grave with a two-handed squat. With the box on terra firma once more, the Trout would select an audience member, usually a woman, to whom he would graciously offer the hammer and aid in removing the seated nails from their supposed final resting places. This took some time, during which the Trout would indulge in some vaguely humorous patter that I always felt undercut the moment. With a heft and an impassioned grunt, the lid would fly off and I'd pop up, wide-eyed and giddy, the grateful beneficiary of an end-curtain miracle. The Trout and I would embrace, father and daughter reunited past death, while Mutter would strike some cribbed ecclesiastical pose. We would hold this dreary tryptic until the trickle of applause began and the Trout sprang back to life to pass the hat.

As the saying goes, we killed 'em in the sticks. To me, the allure was trivial. I was growing increasingly sensitive to the dualities of life. All those wet eyes that greeted our trite finale, the soldiers with their tin jaws brandishing their iron crosses, screaming the names of their fallen friends. The souring widows and sonless mothers. All that roiling hope, all those fervent wishes, wasted, spinning like rogue stars into an empty pocket the gods never tended. So perhaps I was to blame for what happened next. If we were going to hawk discount redemption, when the real agency of our act would have had us burned as witches, didn't we owe it to the rubes to give them a better show? If the whole prestige of the thing was my miraculous recovery, wouldn't it be better to chuck that corny bit with the ear horn and let them *feel* my dead self for themselves? The Trout liked this idea but thought stopping the show to have the audience line up to prod me might disturb the organic flow.

"Well then, don't bother lining everyone up," I said. "Just pass me around."

"Like a *collection* plate! My God, you have the instincts of *Bernhardt!*"

The next day we tried it. It was the pathos the Trout had dreamed about that took me in its many arms, an army of exhausted and woe-brimmed eyes, hearts stuffed so full of loss they split. I was thrilled at this new direction and wanted to sit up and shout, but I stayed limp in the anonymous hands. I could feel the knots of calluses through the thin fabric of my dress, the rooty fingers that made the satin rasp as I spilled in to frailer holds. I could smell stale mucus and cheap kraut, the pure notes of sour mash and the thrum of tobacco, boiled onions and pork fat and stale prayers. All the phantoms of private grieving. Fingers skimmed my throat and cheeks, lingering like bald mice, feeling for life, lifting me to the wiry ears of the old. Voices squeezed out names of the dead. Greta and Recca, Gerhart and Maude. Soon there were no transitions, no faltering stoppages, just one ragged flow of woe upon which I was borne like some blasted raft.

In the distance I heard Mutter growl. Or perhaps I felt it, for it was that low, wet, throaty rumble of his he let loose whenever someone snatched the last sausage without asking or the Trout raised his voice to me. I was willing my limbs off the alert when I was crushed into a chest of stiff priestly black. I felt the sinews of thin but stubborn arms that locked me into a smell of wool and frankincense. I felt the chest swell with air, a whistle down the pinched pipes.

"Death to the unclean!" it screamed. "Vanquish this hell-spawn of Satan, this incubus of decay."

I dared not struggle and fuel his argument, so I lay there limp, crushed in his fervent grip, my limbs flailing behind me. "Destroy the undead! Kill this *nosferatu*!"

I could hear the approach of Mutter. Then I heard the voice of the Trout.

"Father, please. You're disturbing the performance."

"This is no performance," the voice above me hissed. "No

human child could still its vital pumps to this degree and still be called living. There is but one explanation. Vampire! *Undead!*"

And here he made a sudden gesture that brought cries from the crowd. Peeking through a tangle of my eyelashes, I could see he held a wooden stake high above his head, crudely whittled to a sharp point. I could feel Mutter's frantic heat, hear his strained breathing as he stood near me.

"A mere *illusion*, Father," the Trout tried to soothe. "Humble stagecraft, I assure you."

"There is craft I'll grant you," the voice wheezed. "But of a far darker cast." And he shook the stake above his head, his fist draining white.

Mutter feinted forward.

"Try it, you profane filth, and I'll run her through," the priest said.

I felt Mutter recede.

"Now, now." I could hear the Trout wending his way through the crowd toward me. "You must repose yourself, Father. These illusions are designed to be effective, and perhaps I should be flattered at the depth of their deceit. But really, put the child down and let us finish the show."

"Child? Did you say *child*?" the priest said. "Could any natural mother's *child* withstand this?"

He set the stake between his teeth and gripped me with both hands before shaking me so violently my teeth rang like hooves clacking on cobbles. Mutter whimpered and lashed out, but the priest was quick. He dashed between the dregs of the crowd, away from Mutter's grasp, letting me fall to the ground, one ankle only in his wiry grip as he ran with me bumping and flailing behind him. The crowd surged toward the running man, clogging Mutter's path. He pushed and clawed and shoved through the swamp of thick bodies, screaming in his awful denuded tones that held no language, only pain.

"Up there!" a voice in the crowd rang out.

I felt myself ascend, my head slapping rhythmically upon the hard edges of steps. Up and ever up until we burst through a door and stopped.

"On the roof! The *church* roof!"

Mutter threw himself at the rough stone of the church wall, finding purchase in the irregular surfaces, grinding his fingers into the rotting mortar, leaving bloody flecks like ashes from stamped cigars as he worked his body to the belfry.

"Stop! Stop!" my captor screamed. "Or by God I'll do it!"

I could feel the point of the stake at my heart and I could feel the bubbling up of voices from below, shouting, screaming, crying out in anguish and dare.

"Kill the Serbian whore!" (How did I become Serbian?) "Kill the daughter of the Dracul!" "Aw, come on! Let 'em finish the show!"

Mutter had reached the copper rainspout that crested the slate roof and he swiped at the priest's ankles, but again the old man proved quick and he lifted his feet in time and sent them crashing upon Mutter's already bleeding fingers. Mutter let out a bellow, but still he held on. The priest lifted his foot for a second blow but Mutter caught it, his enormous fist easily enveloping the old man's narrow arch. The old man screamed as the stake fumbled out of his grip. His hands churned in the air, trying to catch it, and I felt myself freed from his grip. A communal intake of breath from below seemed to buoy me up for an instant. Then a huge concussion of dread from the rapt throats beneath me signaled my slip and steady descent. I heard Mutter howl as my body breezed past his huge shoulders. I fell in a blinding veil of whipping hair. Then I hit the ground and lay there in a tangle of bad geometry. A circle of spectators surrounded me. I heard the Trout push through the crowd and plant his feet by my silent form.

"Stop!" the Trout shouted before the horror of what had just happened could congeal.

Mutter cleared the roof and subdued the old man with a single slap.

"Never before," the Trout continued in his booming bravura, "has the theater been subject to a spectacle of this magnitude. Not from the soul-shattering pits of Oedipus's orbital gore nor from Faust's foul demonic temptation has the human coil been so profoundly and effectively unraveled. You came to see life triumph over death. You came to see a father's love vanquish the hoary darkness of disease and demise. Where would you have seen this? Why, the stages from London to New York could never have served up so thrilling a diversion as you have been privy to this day. Only here could you be witness to this apogee of theatrical entertainment. Only here will your eyes and hearts swell with the miracle of our craft. Yes, I say 'miracle,' for what is great art if not the impossible made possible? Ladies and gentlemen, you have been chosen. You have been marked for ages to come. For only here could you witness what will linger in your brains forever! Only *from* here could you depart and be just in saying, 'Yes, by God, *yes*, I was there that day. I saw it with my own eyes. I saw the disease-ravaged shell of a frail little tot plummet ten stories to the unflinching soil to lay broken in a heap, crushed, nay it shall be said, *dead*.'"

"And yet you will also see a sight that will thumb its nose at what you deem possible," the Trout continued in full glory. "I implore you, ladies and gentlemen, hold fast to the knowledge that all you will observe is stagecraft, the mere whimsy of the theatrically inclined. But enough! For now we have come to the pinnacle of our humble play. You will see me turn to this lifeless form you see before you and with the power of the redeemer coursing through my shaken and shattered soul, with the beating thrum of ten thousand angels surrounding this dire scene, I shall shout, 'Rise! My child, rise! In the name of the Lord, *rise!*'"

I assumed that was my cue. I milked it for all it was worth. I fluttered an eyelid. The crowd gasped. With a frail moan, my lips parted. Then my head tilted to the side. My eyes fell open. I blinked hard and a smile bled across my face.

The Trout rushed to his knees and wrapped me in his arms.

"You see, ladies and gentlemen, with love all things are possible."

The applause drenched us like spring rain. The ground was pocked with falling coins, hard kroners, and fluttering *Papiermarks*. Mutter was back on the ground, scooping up our winnings as fast as they fell.

"Not bad," the Trout whispered as he lifted me to my feet. "We should get that crazy reverend on retainer."

CHAPTER 8

It was in a small outdoor café near Kagraner Platz that I first learned of Dracula. The Versailles treaty had yet to descend with its full crushing bulk so a simple meal of pork schnitzel and weak beer could still be had for a few pieces of silver. I was diligently chewing my meal, lifting my napkin to my lips while I pretended to swallow, giving what I considered to be an excellent impression of any living girl out for a simple dinner with her two doting uncles. Fresh from our recent triumph, it was a relief to have the talk veer toward something other than bits of stage business and blocking, but my mind was caught on an earlier comment, the one made by the crowd as I felt them sour, the one about me being a Serbian whore, the daughter of Dracul.

"*Dracula*, actually," the Trout corrected. "Son of the dragon, in literal translation, and son of King Dracul of Romania. But the allusion really refers to Mr. Stoker's old penny dreadful."

"Romania? But why call me *Serbian*?"

"*Blame*, my dear. Serbia, to some, is responsible for our recent troubles. But we can hardly fault so ignorant a mass for its poor geography. You are guilty by proximity. Another of the German virtues."

"But why do you say that?" I asked. "Aren't you German?"

"Born in Germany, yes. But not German. Not by any strenuous German standard. No, for a sterling example of an iron son of the fatherland you would have to look no further than to our own Mutter here."

The Trout clanged a fork still holding a slice of schnitzel on Mutter's metal crown, and Mutter swatted him away, growling.

"Good Hamburg stock, aye, friend? Why, a great uncle of his was a cannoneer for Frederick the Great. His proud blood flows all the way back to the berserkers of the Visigoths who first hacked their way into the Rhine Valley almost a thousand years ago. Good German stock, this one. And good German steel."

Here he tapped the plate again, but Mutter was too engrossed with his chewing to notice.

"No, my father was a rag picker from Kraków. You can thank him for my finding you. He always taught me the value of other people's garbage."

He saw my eyes glaze at this last comment and was quick to smile.

"I mean you no disrespect, my dear, but the subject rankles. My Germany was the Germany of Beethoven and Goethe and Spengler. Not little metal men with their little metal minds. War is a mercurial thing, horrific for its complexities but beautiful in its simplicity. It gives one the experience of being alive with the tyranny of a drug. That is why it attracts us. The recent unpleasantness was a cancer in the German body. It needed to be cut out, and perhaps the patient might complain from a bit of tissue loss, but it was an operation that could be performed only under the chloroform of defeat. Today's disturbance teaches us that we must never take our critics too seriously, even if they hold little sharpened sticks to our chests. Which reminds me, have you wondered what would have happened had he actually done it? I was positively breathless after your little fall. What are the limits of your particular gift?"

"But what *are* you then," I said, ignoring his question, "if not really German?"

"Me? A Jew, my dear. I thought that was clear."

A Jew, I thought. Filthy, bat-winged legends fluttered in my mind. "But where is your tail if you are a Jew?"

The Trout laughed, to his credit, and patted me softly on the head.

"My tail? I keep that tucked up my ass. It reminds me to chew my food better."

We were getting up to leave the table when we were approached by a little man with lavender spats and striped trousers. He held his hat to his chest like a résumé, gesturing with it slightly that we might notice it and appreciate its latent value. He clicked his heels and ducked his head in imperial fashion, but his cheeks crimsoned when he saw the Trout's mocking blank stare in return.

"My compliments, gentlemen, lady," he said, clipping the tails of his words as if they were cut from some sour rind. "If I may?"

The Trout knew from the quality of his costume what fortune this person augured. But he also knew that power respects nothing more than that which mocks or ignores it. So it was in the guise of an afterthought, with studied nonchalance, that the Trout motioned to an empty seat at our table and slouched with rehearsed slovenliness into his own.

"My name is Erich Zann," the little man said, spitting out his tart consonants, "of Decla-Bioscop studios."

He offered his card. The Trout refused it.

"Never heard of it."

"The Studio Babelsberg? In Potsdam? I assure you it's the largest in the—"

"Are you by chance a *theatrical* producer?"

"Motion pictures."

"Motion *pictures*," the Trout repeated as if the words had been scraped from the sidewalk. "And here I was getting all aflutter. Well, state your business and be done with it."

The little man was visibly ruffled but could find no graceful retreat. "As I was saying, we have a production deal with Universum Film AG—"

"*UFA?*" the Trout almost shouted. "What are you proposing, sir, that we should make a *hygiene* film? Perhaps the proper way to recognize a contagious French tart or how to clean one's ass with a bayonet?"

Something in me sparked. A pale recognition. Was that bergamot in the air?

"I can assure you, since the end of the war," the little man continued, "UFA is barely under the direction of the military. We enjoy the full confidence of Deutsche Bank and are working toward privatization. And I can assure you we have staunchly avoided all hygienic content."

"Surely not *all*." The Trout laughed.

"That's not what I meant. Our productions are quite proper, at least as far as the health and safety of our employees is concerned. What I mean is—"

"Take a breath, little man. We have all night."

The Trout was having a grand time.

"What I mean is, we are currently scouting for talent and I was fortunate enough to catch your performance this afternoon. The child and the giant were superb, but that last . . . *feat* . . . I'm not quite sure how you managed it." The Trout smiled smugly. "That was something I'm sure we would be honored to commit to film. The scenario was a bit weak, if you don't mind my saying, but I'm sure you could come up with something more coherent."

The Trout bristled and the air chilled around his eyes.

"More *coherent* than the antediluvian dichotomy between *life* and *death*?"

"Perhaps coherent was an unfortunate choice . . ."

"Say what you mean, then," the Trout snapped.

The little man looked sick.

"I'm sure we all can appreciate the great themes, sir," he began, chewing on the words as if to soften them, "but one can never underestimate the . . . *palliative* effect of entertainment on—"

"*Palliative?* Is that what you're selling? Perhaps we should all emulate the Americans then and disburse with storytelling altogether."

"Please, again, I don't have your gift for—"

"Perhaps we should construct our scenarios around the noble themes of *train robberies* and *pie throwing*. Is that what you mean?"

The little man balled up his face, then let loose for all he was worth.

"*I simply meant that film is a relatively new medium and I think it would better serve your genius should you devise a plot suited to the limitations of the moving picture.*"

This escaped in one breath.

"I can assure you I can offer you a contract, all of you contracts. It would mean relocating to Berlin, but I'm sure you would find plenty of diversion there."

But the Trout had stopped listening after the magic word. He had been called a genius, something all artists suspect of themselves at one time but never bother denying until they hear it from a separate source.

"I'm sure we can come to some arrangement, if the terms are amenable."

The little man brightened and extended his hand. "Wonderful," he said. "I shall be in touch."

The Trout stared at the pale, extended appendage.

"Leave us," he said. "Before I change my mind."

THERE WAS A LIGHT RAIN FALLING AS THE TRAIN HEAVED OUT OF THE station. Mutter took the seat opposite me, his hands placed neatly on his lap, his side acres of hair combed wetly over his ears. He smelled of lye soap and breakfast grease. I watched his chin, as still as a porcelain vase on a high shelf, and thought of our last train ride together. Were there pictures behind his eyes, moments sweetened or soured by memory? Did he remember the child who'd spied him with his pants tangled around his ankles? Like the last time, the artist sat apart from my companion and me. This time the Trout was in the second-class car, his lap full of pages with berry-blue fingers from the frantic quill, chasing down the scenario he was contracted to deliver upon our arrival.

I was flirting with a different anxiety. Berlin meant public: public of a very different and discerning kind. We would no longer be living in a vacant lot and playing to rubes and believers. I needed to fit in. Pass as living on a daily basis. And so this would be my role, the part I would play. I would no longer be a stage illusion. I would be as baffling and intimate as a card trick. I would pretend to live, to raise and lower my chest, and smile and blink and chew and walk and turn and frown. I would close my eyes and pretend to sleep and open them and pretend to wake. And if someone touched me and felt the dry chill of my skin or sat too near and sensed the stone-stillness of my body, they would only think, *That poor child, she needs a better coat.* My best and only defense was the belief that people like me did not exist.

CHAPTER 9

The *Berliner Luft*, or *Berlin Air*, was famous for the dread it inspired. Like the stink of night sweat that bleeds through soap, the smell was not at first apparent as we pulled into the Lehrter Bahnhof. It was only as the brake steam cleared and the porters lowered the compartment windows that I felt the first tingle of regret. There was an alkaline ether in the air that could have been the essence of brick if bricks could breathe. It was an avaricious smell, something heated up in angst, then cooled too quickly, not content to be merely breathed. It had to leach out a part of you and replace it with something similar, like those malignant fairies who took human children and left crude effigies in their birthing blankets.

I watched Mutter move more slowly than usual as he pressed himself to his full height, a warning grumble in his throat even as he lifted his arms to lower a woman's bag. He held the bag for a moment, inching it toward his great chest as if he had forgotten why he had done it. The woman, blond with watery brown eyes, expected no shining future but did seem to want her bag, and so she held her arms in front of her, her head slightly bowed, coaxing with syllables but not words. The aisle began to fill and the woman was jostled and her desire for it seemed to wane.

"He can keep it if he wants," she said finally. "I have nothing in it, really. Just my son's, what *was* my son's cap."

"No," I said, putting a hand on Mutter. "It's hers," I said. "Hand it over."

"Where was he wounded?" the woman asked.

"Verdun."

"I lost my boy in France too. Please," she said, her words becoming thick and peaked, "he can have it."

We watched her thread her way into the crowd. The upsweep of her colorless hair, the tendrils pulled loose and soft from the journey, exposed the pale nape of her neck that glowed solely for us, for the only ones who were watching. We had no other baggage, only the bodies we had brought with us, and I decided we would wait for the Trout on the platform, let him make an entrance.

Mutter opened the woman's bag. She was right. There was only a worn flat cap. Mutter placed it on his head, and the effects of the war seemed to evaporate from him.

The platform was lined by a colonnade of Romanesque arches capped by enormous half circles of modern paned glass that finally gave way to more pragmatic bows of cross-braced steel trusses as if the station had simply run out of history. Assembled under these arches, in rows as orderly as their twisted and truncated physiology could offer, were heroes of the Second Reich, the trench fodder who had found their way home or at least to the city where they hoped to eke out a living from pity and the reclaimed garbage they sold. There were stalls of pencil stubs and

those of cigarette stubs, watch chains and pocket pens, spectacles
of all strengths, and stalls that sold just the cases. Handkerchiefs,
parasols, and pocketknives. In fact, anything that could be lost
or discarded resurfaced here in this goblin market of the forgotten. The sellers all wore or displayed their iron crosses, second
and first class, and some even had neatly penned placards that
named their regiments and the action they saw, all in the bloodless prose of the dispatch. They either squatted or sat or leaned,
their amputated stumps wrinkled and pink as unbaked loaves
or stuffed into laced leather sheaths that ended in hooks or pegs
or crisply pinned-back fabric. They were quiet behind their orderly stalls, smelling faintly of pomade and their proximity to the
ground, patient as winter wheat.

One seller, a prim man with cheeks shaved so closely they
kicked even the gray light of the station, wore the sleeves of his
pressed serge suit folded and pinned behind him like the wings
of a grounded duck. If he missed his arms, the rigor of his parade
ground stare gave no indication. Nor did he seem in the least
bothered by the nature of his merchandise. In rows as neat as
military graves he displayed postcards of women in the most
shocking and rude aspects of compromise imaginable. There
were torture scenes with bodies trussed in rope or chains, torsos
twisted in balanced curves like pinup saints with painterly slashes
of blood, women wearing just their peasant braids engaging the
attentions of reluctant livestock. Women with other women,
a whole section with just gardening implements, another with
brass band instruments. I was curious to purchase one, if only
to see how he would conduct the transaction and still maintain
his steely demeanor, when my eye stopped on the leer of what
seemed to be a Moroccan slave girl. She was tied to a tent post,
her breasts thrust forward, arms laced behind her. Her eyes were

blindfolded by an elaborate sash dripping small coins, but the sweep of her nose, the defiant plump of her mouth, left no doubt. It was my mother.

The voice of the Trout rang out, "There you are, my minions, loitering by the French postcards?"

He picked up the card and gave it a quick once-over.

"Never would have suspected you for the oriental, my dear." He tossed the card to the ground.

Mutter was quick to retrieve it and place it neatly in its slot before the seller could even take a breath to shout. I looked behind me, back at the postcard stall, and what flooded me then? Was I happy to see her, relieved she too had somehow survived? Gratified she was employed if still in the skin trade? No. It was dread. Or perhaps it was the Berlin air.

CHAPTER 10

I'm afraid you misunderstand me, sir." Erich Zann continued from his chair. "It's the recontextualization of *horror* we are after."

"Fairy tales," the Trout slurred.

"Perhaps if you read the scenario of our project currently in preproduction, the requisites might become clear." He tossed a typed stack of pages bound with three brass studs toward the Trout. *The Cabinet of Dr. Caligari* was the title.

The Trout was at a loss. He rubbed his word-worn eyes and tried to force a complicit smile, but failed at this and looked manageably panicked.

We had arrived at the studio only an hour previous. The space was massive but stifling, the enormous arc lights throwing entire afternoons at the still-drying timbers of the false fronts, releasing the fresh solvent of pine tar in the superheated air. It was a world as fake and presumptuous as me. I felt strangely at home. The Trout flipped the pages as if movement might jar the sentences to life, like a mutoscope divulging its secrets.

"Why horror?" he finally asked as the pages stopped rustling.

"Let's just say horror has universal appeal."

"But horror is a discount emotion," the Trout said. "A mere reflex to shock. I'm trying to give the audience something equally universal. Hope, faith in the continuum."

"They don't want *hope*," Zann said, leaning back in his chair. Sweat pooled at his collar. "They want their nightmares made *safe*."

"And you think these silly little funhouse flats you're building, you think that informs horror?"

"I think incorporating expressionist principals into a new medium like moving pictures is extremely innovative and communicates perfectly the unbalanced interior of our protagonist."

"You mean that skinny line-boy in the body suit I've seen prowling around out there? He couldn't scare up a hand job on the Alexanderplatz."

"Herr Veidt has impeccable theatrical training," Zann quietly enthused. "I think if you actually watched him work you'd find his portrayal quite chilling."

The Trout stood with a sudden snap of his knees. He held his pages in front of him, a week's worth of effort, and ripped them in two with one straining pull. He kept his eyes pinned to the little man in the chair before him.

"Give me twenty-four hours," he said, turning on his heel.

Zann stood and clicked his heels to the Trout's furious back.

"They want monsters?" the Trout whispered to me through gritted teeth. "I will give them night terrors that'll have 'em shitting blocks of ice."

THE STUDIO HAD PROVIDED US WITH LIVING QUARTERS, A FRESHLY framed box with two cots and a desk above the shooting floor. From this, Mutter and I were banned while the Trout worked rewriting his scenario. We sat on a wooden platform, on crates stuffed with still-fragrant hay that held the huge bulbs of the arc lights. These lights had a terrible habit of sputtering and then exploding in the middle of a scene, so bulbs were in constant demand. We were silent during the shooting, but this was a habit of the theater. The barnlike structure echoed with hammer blows and ringing telephones and the steady loping cadence of the spinning film that white-coated cameramen beat through the guts of the slender cameras. The cameras held instant fascination for me. It was the sound of tiny galloping horses, tethered to a moment, pulling it into eternity. It was the heartbeat I should have had.

These magnificent machines seemed wasted on the scenarios they were forced to film. The gestures were too broad, too remedial, like a language made of only the past tense. I was confused by the pale lavender base over the actors' faces, the gray-green grease paint that shadowed the eyes, the red eyebrows and blue lips. I learned later this was due to the sluggish exposure speed of the orthochromatic film. Even the camera operators and directors had to wear smoked goggles that would "slow" the lights and give them the translated naturalism that would ultimately be printed and projected. The whole process seemed unnatural and worried, what with everyone standing around in their white lab coats calling one another *Herr Doktor* like half-assed pharmacists before even the simplest request. I had expected the otherness of my artist's studio back in Hietzing, not this tight Prussian efficiency. This was a factory. They would be as at home making rifle butts or rug beaters as moving pictures. What these people were filming was not life, not as I had witnessed it. And what made me qualified to pass such judgment? I was a student of living, of every gesture and nuance and smirk. Life was what I aped to go unnoticed. Watch a face hit with joy or fear and do you see? This clumsy running leap over the fence of the feeling? It is subtle and awkward and reticent. People do not *want* to feel. They resist. Only when the moment is overwhelming do they give in. But then it is a natural thing, like a fall from a high place. We are seized by it as by gravity. We don't kick our legs in descent to hit the ground faster.

The Trout's twenty-four hours came and passed and no pages were produced. Just shrieks and frustrated shouts from behind the plywood door of our little garret. Herr Zann just smiled, somehow imbued by the Trout's pangs of labor. Perhaps he saw them as the only true emotion in the place. He was one of those men whose proximity to greatness made him immune to its sting and he was willing to wait for whatever creature burst forth from that sealed little room. Mutter grew restless and once, when a light was called for, he lifted the enormous apparatus and placed it as casually as a dinner plate. After that little exhibition his services were much in demand and he tried to recruit me in his labors.

But my only interest were the cameras. I would spend hours just looking at them. So pure, so simple, so economical in their design and function. Yet inside them seethed endless horizons that could never fill the temptations of ten thousand Pandoras. The operator was a large man whose bones had been reduced to rumor from the slurry of flesh that rounded his angles. He was immensely fond of fried potatoes and I made it my singular mission to keep him supplied with hot salted platefuls just to be near him. In his tight-fitting coat he looked more like a butcher than a technical professional, but it was clear after a single day watching him work that if a picture was to have any stylistic pulse, it would be entirely due to his efforts. After a week of grinning at my mooning face he finally took pity on me and let me follow him to the stock room. It was as quiet as a witch's circle in there, the air sour-smelling with chemicals. And in the bloodred dark, like a fat druid with his sacrificial scythe, I watched him carefully open the camera.

"The stock is male when it goes in," he said. "Fickle and shallow, nothing on his mind. Then it is threaded through the gate here and light touches it for the first time. The image is burned and in that moment a marvelous thing happens. The film becomes *female*, enthralled, stained with secrets that she will only whisper in the dark. It is a marital occasion, this transformation. So we must dress."

Here he stuffed his stubby fingers into white gloves and chuckled at my wide eyes and said, "We must handle her like a lady in love now, gently."

I watched his thick wrists slowly extract the reel and tape the tail down, writing a few numbers or key words on the tape, then tucking it away among the other exposed reels before reaching for a fresh roll. "The threading of the film is the most important part," he said. "You screw this up, my little cabbage, a whole day can be lost. You must know the path of the film through these sprockets like you know the way home." Then he doused the red light and we were just two creatures in the dark, one breathing, the other as silent as the countryside, the snaking crackle of the celluloid the only other sound with us.

THE DAYS PASSED WITH STILL NO BUTTER CHURNED IN THE TROUT'S milky brain. Mutter moved on to location, but I wanted to learn more and so was left to fumble my bridal ceremonies in the dark.

I was given dead leader, lengths of film with no emulsion, with which to practice. I wrestled with endless strands of the stuff for days, mangling most of it in the process. My small fingers were pinched in the cogs, torn in the teeth of the sharp gears. But I had no blood that could foul the sensitive mechanism. From my cuts drifted only an odd pink dust I could clear with a breath before I started again. When the studio slept, I kept at it. I pictured the sprockets as turnings in a coiled river, my hands blind captains that never longed for land. Over and over. Until the snags were smoothed, the path cleared. I was finally allowed to remove and catalog the exposed film. I would watch the footage meter turn over slowly, my anticipation growing as if arriving at some wonderful destination. The numbers finally settled to their maximum count and I would snatch the camera from its stand and plunge into the dark. I became good at this, better than the cameramen themselves. I could have the film out, looped and labeled, and a fresh roll taut in the cogs and back out on the floor before the director could even miss me. Then one day, instead of leading me to the dark, I was shown to a ceramic bowl filled with a dozen broken eggs.

"What's this?" I asked.

"Rhythm," the cameraman said, handing me a wire egg-beater. "The eggs are for resistance. Start whipping and feel the count, three to the second. One whisk for each second."

He looked down at a small stopwatch. I heard it click. "Begin."

I dipped the beater into the eggs and began my rotations, counting under my breath. The whites began to froth, splattering onto the wooden platform.

"Stop," the cameraman said. "Again. *Three*, child. No more. No less." I heard the click of the watch. "Begin."

"But what for? Why am I doing this?" I asked.

"You are wasting time," he said looking at his watch.

"But why," I asked, wondering if my loading had been somehow unsatisfactory.

"Because your big uncle Karl is going to be directing pictures soon and you are the only one I trust to run the camera." He winked at me, curling my fingers around the whisk in my small hand. "I used to run the camera for Lang. Now look at him. He's all set to go to Hollywood." Was that the first time I had ever heard that word? "But first you need to build up your wrist, lock the rhythm in the bones there."

That was all I needed to know. I spent my nights with a running stopwatch pressed to my ear until I thought my brain was powered by a mainspring. I don't know how many eggs were sacrificed in the service of my proficiency. I whipped through what seemed like a hundred dozen of them each day, and when the basin was finally full of wintery meringue, shooting stopped and the cook made everyone omelets the size and consistency of cumulus clouds. Only after weeks of this, when Zann finally complained about the excess of our dairy bill, did the cameraman ask if I would like to try the real thing. He reached for my hand and held it there in his.

"Your hands are cold. You feeling well?" he asked.

I nodded, and he turned my hand over in his, looking for swelling, a sign of stress. Finding none, he smiled as if down at a lucky penny, and said, "You got filmmaking wrists, my dear." He took my stool and dragged it over to the camera. "You don't worry about a thing but the count, okay? Three turns in one second exposes sixteen frames. Sixteen frames are one second of film. We build the image by the second, so keep the count steady like you did before. But be easy with the rotations, let the spool do the work, the counterweight will take care of the upstroke. Just keep the count nice and steady. Try it."

The brass handle was warm where he had been holding it and I felt the warmth drift into the curl of my fingers, the coolness on my own finally eclipsing it. I turned the crank slowly and the machine shivered awake. This was a whole new world. Nothing dull and domestic in these turnings like with the eggs. This creature of brass and wood came to life under my volition. It whirred and crackled, and it wasn't hard for me to surrender cause to the machine, to let the life that churned in that narrow box bleed into me. This was the real osmosis of the enterprise. It lived. It turned *me*.

The director spoke *Begin* and the actors jerked to life and I felt that leap in my nerves, what cables must feel in the duty of carrying current. I was that fine, finished cog in the god of clocks, weighing all moments equally, parceling out to each a single second, even turns regardless of the truth conveyed or the artifice indulged before me. I was judgeless and served only the steady round sweep of the big hand. I pressed my cheek to the lacquered wood and swore I felt heat there, perhaps friction but something more, a metabolic blush from such steady feeding of this repetitive diet of frozen stills, the lie of motion. How like me, I thought. By the mere accumulation of dead things it provided the perception of something living. How could one say we were not kindred?

I turned that little crank over a hundred features, sometimes blazing through one whole scenario in a single day. I watched the cameraman work, his lips and fingers greasy from his buckets of fried potatoes, spitting out positions and righting light beams, tinkering out there in his own cosmos that was hung with only three stars. One key light and two fills. All he needed to illuminate entire little three-walled worlds. There was no formal instruction; we worked too quickly for that. All was taught by example. "Light always throws at a slant," he might say to a gaffer. Or "Curb that spill over there, keep half that face in shadow." It was the lighting of the old masters he was after. A crisp transformational singularity cutting through the dark and illuminating the martyred saints, the tortured faces of Ribera and Caravaggio. Those who toss the look of these films to the abstract expressionists miss their history. I pored over too many fine art monographs to gleefully hand over our textured shadows to the block printers of Die Brücke. It is only the light, after all, that has survived.

CHAPTER 11

I took everything in. I watched shoulders and fingers and mouths and eyes, saw how light was a chisel against the fumed oak of shadows. And how shadows could be shaped into jagged corrals that could hide what the studio couldn't afford to light. Mutter became especially adept at this. With his great strength, he had the luxury of anticipating contours. With the massive burning arcs perched like parasols on his shoulders, he could place the lights as easily as brush to canvas.

Then one morning came forth the Trout, calf-fragile and quaking, the tails of his great mustache limp as raw strudel. In his fist, like Medea's slaughtered brats, he clutched the bruised pages of his scenario. He was the pulp of Jacob after the corrections of the angel.

"Get me Zann; he must hear this!"

A dramatic pause. And when Zann arrived, his breakfast napkin still tucked into the collar of his starched shirt, the Trout did not even wait for him to sit before he began.

"We begin in a graveyard."

My God, how many times would those words be spoken by second-rate screenwriters in need of beer money in the decades to come? But in those days, on that day, it was something new. Zann's attention was polite. The Trout had commandeered a battered phonograph used to infuse emotions in the actors when the scripts called for actual feeling. And upon the lopsided turntable he placed a disk of the "Lacrimosa" from Mozart's *Requiem*.

"A bell tolls over a humble pit," he began, "*in pace requiescat* mumbled by a lean priest . . ."

I'll spare you the rest of the overheated pablum that warbled out of his gullet that day. It was little more than a dusky wash over our previous and already dim scenario with a few worn highlights cobbled from the Brothers Grimm. A mother dies, leaving her toymaker husband and daughter to fend for themselves.

Instead of moving to the city and getting on with their lives, the father becomes paranoid, obsessed with his daughter's mortality to the point of constructing a huge mechanical man whose one purpose is to defend the daughter from death. The father's will is strong but his craft isn't quite up to the task. Desperate, he snares the dark charms of an old crone, promising her anything if she'll just get his oversize toy off the worktable. She agrees. For a time the daughter and the big mechanical lug seem the best of friends. Then the crone's vengeful intentions become clear. In some corny rose-tinted flashback we see the crone as a young woman, jilted by the toymaker as he frolics in the chamomile with the girl who will one day become his dead wife. Crone blows (literally) some pretty persuasive smoke into the windup man's face and gets him to try to kill the daughter. The toymaker, conveniently lingering by a window, rushes in in time to somehow push the crone into the creature's path. Crone gets throttled and father and daughter hug in a slow iris into blackout. Now, all the time the Trout was gesticulating to the back row, my head was exploding. I saw monochrome eyes electric in hatred. Needles purling through hanks of dead flesh. Murder and madness all in corpse white and funereal black. The clockwork creature held some especially horrific possibilities. And in the stunned if polite silence that followed the Trout's frothy performance, something welled up in me, something tarry and intoxicating, an overwhelming desire to hurt, to make the frail and modestly clothed bodies in that room squirm.

"That's just a basic template," I blurted. The Trout looked stricken. "The real horror is in the execution."

Zann cleared his throat, shooting a slightly apologetic look to the Trout before looking back at me. "Go on," he said. The Trout huffed distractedly.

"The creature, for instance," I said duskily. "What does he look like?"

"I was thinking something oddly grand," the Trout interjected quickly. "Something like the mid-Renaissance automatons of Braccelli's 1624 folio etchings from *Bizzarie*."

"Bullshit," I spat. The word was like a knife in the air. But I could not stop myself. "*Flesh*. The crone should claim the creature by covering it in a dead man's flesh. We could see it grow over the gears before our eyes. "

"That's disgusting." The Trout chuckled.

"It'll save a fortune not having to build a goddamned working *doll*," I said, staring at Zann. "Mutter here could play it."

Zann said nothing, merely raised a single eyebrow.

"And the crone," I went on. "The crone manipulates the creature but not with some stagy smoke pot."

"How then?" Zann asked, his interest building.

"When I was still learning to load film, I left a reel in the box and we accidentally shot over it. I realized you can expose film more than once. That you can create ghosts on demand, if you establish the proper parameters. I was thinking something like that for the crone. Her murderous eyes over the creature's innocent ones. Her jealous hands bleeding through hands that hold the daughter's throat."

"It will be all but unwatchable!" the Trout spat.

"Interesting," Zann said, nodding. "How would you get the flesh to grow? Over the . . . *doll*, I mean."

"Single-frame exposure," I said, not quite understanding the concept myself. "We build the illusion of movement one frame at a time, Herr Zann. It is quite possible." I had no idea how this insight had come to me. It simply bubbled out with a passion I did not recognize as my own.

Zann nodded again. I felt something retreat in me then, a gentle slithering away into darkness that left me feeling weaker but still somehow triumphant.

"You're not seriously entertaining implementing these de-generate parlor tricks," the Trout scoffed. Zann would not even look at him. "What about the great themes?"

"Great themes don't sell tickets. Not without encourage-ment. The medium must move forward," Zann said, rising. "And *collaboration*, when carefully measured, is the most motive cre-ative force I know. Don't you agree, *Herr* Trout?"

CHAPTER 12

We began production on our nameless project in a warm month of 1919. The Trout was reticent behind the scene. The camera to him was a cheap interloper, an agent of reduction that must be appeased like some alehouse tart. But he was under contract to write *and* direct, and so he listlessly rose to the task. He had been soured by the theater, and framed every shot long and wide, floating in the embrace of the proscenium. When I suggested different focal lengths or actually moving the camera, he would shriek like an anti-vivisectionist.

"Cut off legs? Cut off heads? Who could stomach the sight of such aberrations?"

I knew the camera could be more than a passive observer, but I needed more informed instruction.

I did not have to wait long.

My body in its new state did not need sleep. My consciousness was always available to me, like a pistol on a night table. And while the others slept, I made a habit of roaming the empty stages even when I had no tasks to rehearse. Death is round, like a mother's arms, with a breast that can nourish with a flow of dust. And at that breast one night was Volker. I know now he had been with me in whispers from almost the first mention of a contract at UFA. But then, that night, his presence became as real and terrible as any waking encounter. He stood in a pool of light from some far source, impeccable, the seams of his trousers straight and hard, and in his eye sockets were mouths. Straight white teeth where the lashes once grew. He bowed. I felt the anticipation of an embrace. He was not here to hurt. But he was no longer content to merely insinuate. He opened his mouths, the practical and the others. Earth poured from them, in thick fecal dowels, forcing his lips and lids into strained O's. The soil coiled about his shoes, speckled with worm casings and leaf rot. The effluvium of the grave.

See this earth, I heard him say in my mind. *It is what is left of men. It is clay. And all stories are made of such clay. What is your story about?*

"I want to know how I should shoot it."

How can you shoot what you don't understand? What is your story about?

"A mother dies."

Mothers die every day. What is your story about?

"Fear?" I said.

And?

"Loss?"

And?

"Anger?"

Yes. Anger. Revenge.

"Hopelessness."

Precisely.

"Monstrosities."

Yes, but not the monster. The monster is innocent. The anger is not. You must show this.

"How?"

See first. Then show.

"But how?"

Like this.

And the artist's wife, decayed, fouled in death, stood before me. Dirt in the pits of her teeth, eyes eaten in a brickwork of maggots. I flinched. Volker smiled.

Yes. Make them feel it. Make it unsafe. Push the camera to the rim of the grave, then see the staring eyes inside the box. Go back to the rim of the grave and see the grief playing out there. They will see the tears of the living but still think of the mother in the box. The audience is swine, my girl. Push their snouts into the shit. Make them feel it.

"But Zann wants nightmares made safe."

Nightmares can never be made safe. They can only multiply. The teeth in his face shut, in strict tandem. But his last syllable lingered on the dark like a sigh.

And he was gone.

That morning I saw the entire movie in my head. The proscenium smashed, pushed past comfort, maybe even coherence, but vital, new, and because I was only the camera operator, completely useless.

What saved me and the project was not the spontaneous triumph of artistic righteousness or the Trout's epiphanic bow to my night-born acumen. It was budget. With the signing at Versailles, the first spasms of Germany's fiscal collapse were keenly felt. It was printed in every daily that the empire would be fined nearly 132 billion marks in reparations. Although the Great Inflation had yet to fully descend, the Prussian capacity to enable fear gave way to almost all productions losing nearly two-thirds of their budgets. We had originally been assigned a small crew of six to help with lighting, set moving, and camera operation. But after the treaty, we were pared down to just us three. It didn't seem to matter to Zann, who was desperate to keep the chloroform from his own production deal, that our scenario called for *four* principal actors.

"You are actually in an enviable position," Zann said when we were summoned into his office.

"How so?" asked the Trout wearily.

"As luck would have it you already have two of this studio's most competent technicians in your cast." He was referring of course to Mutter and myself. But the Trout was just winding up to toss out the money changers.

"You still think *technicians* can tell stories?" he said disgustedly. "I suppose you believe the pigment grinders are responsible for the Sistine Chapel? Or the dolt who thought up the chisel should take credit for the *David*?"

I could hear our project's unborn cries, and I refused to see it cleaved from the womb.

"We can do it, Mr. Zann," I blurted out. "Between Mutter and myself, we can move the lights and run the camera. I can teach Mutter the camera rhythm, and we'll shoot practical so we can minimize lighting."

"And who the hell is to play the pathetic little girl if you're busy fiddling about with the furniture?" the Trout bellowed.

"I can do both. The part's not that demanding."

"Isn't it?"

"What choice do we have? Isn't that right, Mr. Zann?"

The Trout puffed.

"Just so," Zann said finally, with reserved admiration.

"Judas," hissed the Trout. "I suppose next you'll be saying you can *direct* the damn thing as well."

I didn't have to say it. Without the buffer of extra crew, the Trout defaulted to his natural state of narcissism. He was always before the portable mirrors Mutter hauled to the location. And I would set up the camera, adjust for light and angle, leaving the Trout his great pliant face for the molding of his emotion. It went unspoken that I would make the actual film.

It was our third day. We had packed Mutter like a prospector's mule, prepared for any contingency. He was hung with spades and picks and a shallow stack of wooden grave markers aged with dry-brushed oil paint. Cold pork sandwiches and kraut were stuffed into his pockets while what costumes we could muster were rolled like bedding at the nape of his neck. And on the cornice of his shoulder perched the camera, an idiot magpie primed to repeat the lies we would feed it.

There were still open spaces within the city then. Among these was a vacant field where the dregs of disbanded regiments still congregated. They would muster in the cool, still hearing the rude cries of bugles, and float the ghost of decorum among their crippled ranks. The privates huddled around one meager fire, the officers around another. Wild blackberries steamed on the briars they burned, exploding with tart floral scent. It was from among this crowd that I hoped to recruit our extras. We could offer them nothing but a few scraps of cold lunch and our attention, but they practically jumped at the chance. We found the man in charge, a lieutenant colonel who had somehow managed to keep the defeat off the sides of his still-shiny boots. We conveyed our needs, the mock grave we needed dug, the grave markers we needed placed. And then someone to play the priest. He sobered at this last request. A priest must be a man of peace, pliant and understanding, with all his limbs. And preferably free of scars. But here the men seemed to suffer from some congenital defect. Every one of them had the thin pink stigma of a saber duel on the meat of one cheek. And what scars that could have been obscured by whiskers or side-burns had been proudly razed for display.

There was but one field officer who might do. He was an artillery sergeant whose battle prize was a cranial cut that barely crested his hairline. To properly display this he had shaved his head, but we had a wig in tow. The problem was his lack of legs, blown off before the final offensive. I was thinking of the best way to skirt this when the Trout strode toward me, his lavender face and vermillion eyebrows blazing with impatience.

"Why the hell aren't we shooting?"

"The priest has no legs," I said.

"Good Christ, then prop him up!" he bellowed. "This inspi-ration I'm nursing won't last all goddamn day, you know."

I changed into my wardrobe while a petty officer blew cadence to synchronize the gravediggers. My getup was ridicu-lous, a frilly empire-waisted thing seventy years out of date with wads of petticoats and bloomers. The Trout had wanted a bonnet as well. But this I refused under the pretext of lighting difficul-ties. He did succeed in getting me to rouge just the pout of my lips, however. I looked like a demented china doll. Which may have been what he was after.

The grave was dug. German engineering, precisely six feet deep with no vertical incongruity, the dirt neatly piled and graded beside it. I had fires set at the peripheries so the smoke would imitate fog. The legless sergeant waddled forward on his stubs when I called for places. I looked at his attentive face, the bits of reheated bean clinging to his chin. He was transparently relieved to be of use once more. He was the height of a child.

"Get two of his buddies under him," I shouted. "And tell them to be still. Put him in the frock coat. We'll never see below his waist from the angle I'm using. But we need the height for the background. Do you have the bounce, Mutter?"

Mutter unfurled a heavy white sheet with a hole through the middle.

"Get the camera in the pit and stake the bounce six inches below the dirt line, lens through the hole. We need to see the rim of the grave."

Mutter grunted.

"The sun will be where we need it in about a minute. Give a nice backlight. The bounce will let us see your lovely faces," I explained to the men.

"What the hell are you doing?" the Trout whispered harshly.

"Shooting from inside the grave."

"What about the frame? What about the proscenium? How will we see the action?"

"The grave *is* the proscenium. Where the hell is the requiem bell?"

"This is ridiculous. You can't shoot up our noses."

"What is this scene about, Herr Trout?" I asked.

"Not about our goddamn septums, I can tell you."

"It's about *fear*," I said, facing him.

"What?"

"Fear of death. Fear of the grave. We put the audience in it from the beginning, they'll think your tears are for *them*. Now, please, the sun is almost perfect."

It felt strange hearing Volker's words rasp past my lips. But in truth, I was doing far more than quoting him.

The Trout was silent. Then he turned on an intake of breath and patted the bottom of his chin.

"Just keep the shadows nice and thick under here," he said, walking away. "I tend to get jowly from that angle."

I moved a few stray embers from the fire near the mouth of the grave and had one of the men feed it wet brush. Another wafted the smoke over the stuttering aperture, waiting for it to pool. I then instructed him to gently fan it, creating a spectral effect and eliminating the need for a standard iris out. Mutter crouched in the bathtub-size hole, and the Trout shouted, "Begin," and I, as his daughter, collapsed onto his quivering shoulder with my ridiculous porcelain-looking head. The artillery sergeant looked panicked. I called, "Cut." The Trout raised an eyebrow but seemed curious as to what I might say.

"I'm sorry, fräulein," the artillery sergeant stammered. "We are Lutherans. I don't know the Catholic requiem."

"It won't matter," I said. "Just say what you know."

"Now hold on," the Trout said, pulling away from me. "He can't just blabber on. He's a bloody priest. He must show some bloody decorum."

"The film is silent, my dear Trout. People will only see his lips moving. Just think like a priest, sergeant."

I called, "Begin," and the sergeant began quoting ordnance calibers and load procedures, his fingers cutting the air in the sign of the cross. The Trout began his speech, projecting needlessly, biting the back of his wrist in mute anguish. I shouted, "Cut!"

"What the hell are you doing?" he shouted. "We have half the scene left."

"I'm moving closer," I said, lifting my head from his shoulder, "for a tighter frame."

"But what about my performance?"

"We don't need it for that angle."

I looked to Mutter. He checked the footage meter and gave me a thumbs-up.

"This is an impossible way to work!" the Trout said, ripping at the tails of his waxed mustache.

"I'm only shooting what we can use."

He snorted, a frustrated bull at odds with the shade of red flashing before him, and stormed off primly. I shot two more angles and then did a series of extreme close-ups. Brimming eyes and worried brows. Hands gripping or too tired to grasp. I wasn't sure how I would incorporate this footage into the assembly. But there was Volker at the edge of my periphery, his grinning dirt-filled eyes prodding me forward.

When I had all the coverage I needed, I instructed the Trout to take a break. He anxiously agreed. I led Mutter into the pit with me. I explained that I needed two pieces of wood to simulate the interior walls of a casket, which I was going to use in an insert of the dead mother as seen from inside her coffin. He grunted and went searching the vacant lot for materials while I wiped off my lipstick and matted my hair. I had decided I would wear a veil over my face to mask my obvious similarity to the daughter but also to evoke a spectral quality to the corpse.

Not enough, I heard Volker whisper in my mind. *They have to believe you're dead, my girl. Have to know it. You must show them.*

"But I can lie perfectly still."

Not enough. The dead are hosts to living things.

And here his pale manicured hands burst out of the earth near my face. I jumped back, surprised I could still be startled. The webs of his fingers teemed with tiny spiders.

The dead are playgrounds, he said, grabbing the back of my head and thrusting the fistful of scrambling creatures into my mouth.

I lurched with revulsion. I could feel them fluttering in there like frenzied chocolates, the tentative tips of their dry-bristle feet teasing the insides of my cheeks.

There is no reason for your fear, my girl, Volker purred. *Remember what you are and it will fade.*

The revulsion slowed. The fear began to ebb. I felt a creeping coolness, an almost drowsy chill. I lay back into the earth, composed, as if in a tepid bath. In that state, Mutter must have found me. I suppose he set up the pieces of wood he had found. For when I came closer to my senses, I could feel them there behind my head. I gave a turning motion with my hand and half heard, from the distance of the grave, the whirring of the camera as Mutter turned the crank. My eyes glazed in a death stare. My lips fell open and the spiders spilled out in one frenzied black stream. I whispered, "Cut," and sat up. Mutter stared hard at me. A thin whiff of rot issued from the gulch where his flesh met his metal plate. He placed a hand hard on my chest and furrowed his brow.

"Dead again?" he said.

I realized then, the giant only spoke when he had something to say. His ice-blue eyes were wet.

"Only sometimes, Mutter," I said, gripping his callused finger. "Only when I need to be."

I ended the scene, still in the grave, shooting through the windshield of an ancient Aachener, while two privates shoveled earth over me to total obscurity.

That should make them soil their linen. Volker snickered in the dark.

CHAPTER 13

For the creation sequence, I adhered to Volker's directive. Push their faces into the shit. Make them feel it. I shot through gauze, through gobs of axel grease to simulate a breach of tears. I began with a slow overhead pan of the assembled clockworks. It was a fairly pitiful effort, given the slimness of our budget. We made do with what looked like the wreckage of a windup railroad arranged in vaguely human form, but this was only the establishing shot. The actual transformation was something new. Our crew of enlisted men were deft thieves and managed to procure two complete pig carcasses. From these I had intended to "build" the muscle of the creature through the accumulation of stop frames, but we were at a loss as to what muscle to put where. I had found a knife and sharpening stone in one of the prop closets. But where to cut? If we had wanted to kill the pig, I had several suggestions from the enlisted men. But we needed shoulders. Thighs. A chest. The pigs seemed like indifferent clay.

The Trout stepped forward. Puffing, he took the knife and whetstone from Mutter and, in a flurry of scrapes and flashes, honed the blade like a true professional. "Once the son of a butcher . . ." He sighed.

"But I thought your father was a rag picker from Kraków," I said.

"Who said anything about my father?"

He tested the edge with the meat of his thumb.

"Perhaps one day the door will finally be closed on poor Darwin," he said with concise rasps upon the stone. "One day the world will realize we are all just sons of pork."

And with two silent swipes of his knife he had the chest of the creature spread wide.

"Same pectoral configuration."

A deft flurry of cuts.

"The shoulder and biceps insertions, indistinguishable from our own."

Then he slammed the knife into the beast's neck, severing the head with a surprisingly vicious stroke. He lifted the head and, pulling hard on the jaw, dislocated it with a crack.

"Even the teeth and those triangular jaws. How many men have I met with jaws like that? And with similar appetites?"

Then he went to work. He had the major muscle groups in pink gelatinous mounds in no time.

It took the entire day. We would place a mound of muscle, roll sixteen frames. Cut. Then place more. Repeat. Until what greatly resembled a flayed human lay warming on the table under the arc lights. For skin we used the pig's own, cutting it into strips and shaving the bristles from the spine with a straight razor. I stitched the cold waxy sheets into squares that could be molded around the recognizable appendages. The head was a cabbage or some other orb-shaped roughage, covered with a tea towel upon which I would project Mutter's face in what is now known as a poor man's process. We had no idea this hideous doll stuffed with decomposing meat, puckered by tracks of black suture, would become so imitated, so iconic. (Caveat: Much has been made, among those who bother with such things, of the similarities between our creation sequence and the one in Edison's 1910 single-reeler of *Frankenstein*. All I can say in response to such suppositions, apart from being understandably insulted, is that I never saw it. Nor any other imported film at that time. The war, by imperial decree, had necessitated a ban on all enemy products. And this included not just Virginia tobacco and peppermint chewing gum but all foreign melodramas as well. To a defeated people, horror was serious business.)

The climax was supposed to be the strangling of the child. We shot the sequence but ultimately decided it to be too tame. We had been contracted, after all, to reproduce the fall that capped our live show. And so I set up the camera in a long-wide on a cobblestone street across from a half-timbered wurst restaurant that would look sufficiently Bavarian to the international eye. We had established a game between the girl and creature, a flying game where the creature would toss the child higher and ever higher. It was easily a fifty-foot drop to the stones below. And in the one editless longshot I had planned, the fall would be impossible to fake. I had never taken a fall this unforgiving, but a rehearsal was out of the question. We were already running the risk of uncomfortable inquiry shooting on a public thoroughfare. We had one chance. On the roof of the restaurant, Mutter held me tight in the high wind. He was nervous.

"You need to toss me," I said to him. "Up and down, like we did down there."

A thin whimper bucked from his throat.

"Mutter, like we did down there," I repeated, trying to soothe him.

"Too far," he said. "Breakable." And he gently flexed the cervical joints of my neck.

"But I'm *not* breakable. I'll be fine."

His face set hard against my request.

"We have to roll, Mutter, please. Just toss me. Toss me up and catch me."

He made a tentative throw and caught me clumsily.

"Higher."

He growled.

"Higher, Mutter."

He tossed. The wind caught me for a second in a crosscurrent before he snatched me back into his arms.

"He needs to do it higher," the Trout shouted from below.

"Come on, Mutter. Real high. Like heaven. You remember the heaven game?"

I counted to three and felt his arms cock like giant springs. His smile was dull as he let me fly. He scrambled to catch me but I planted a foot on his chest and kicked out of the orbit of his grasp. But something was wrong. I was falling headfirst and the comet could not be corrected. I remembered fear. I fell for what felt like an eternity.

Then I landed.

There was a sickening thunder in my ears as the wedge of my jaw stove my clavicle girdle. A sharp crackling explosion as my eardrums exploded. Then white. A deep, pervasive, granular dun color, the true absence of light. There was the rasp of footsteps. I blinked. I was not on the ground. I was suspended in the white. I saw high-button boots. Crisp pant cuffs. A whisper of bergamot.

Ah, you silly girl, Volker said. *You've wrecked your new toy. Now what fun will you have?*

"But it's not possible."

Isn't it? Even gods have limits.

"But I didn't know."

Consider yourself duly informed, my girl.

I unspooled. Crystalline thread played out across the numb universe.

"But I need to finish. How can I get back?" A billion open doors tried to suck me into their voids.

Finish? You have finished, my dear.

"My film, my story."

You remember that? he asked with a curious crack in his voice.

"I must finish it."

Then there is a way.

"What way? Please, I must know."

Are you sure? You will give up ever really dying. You will never rest.

"Tell me."

Will, he said.

"What?"

Will. Will yourself home.

And then wet ashes at the base of my tongue. The promise of pain. Of whole houses of pain. But it never came. Yellow tears fell into my eyes and clouded my vision. Mutter was crying. He held me tightly in his arms. My head lolled at an unspeakable angle, a dull pinkish dust congealed in a wound that circumnavigated my neck.

"We thought we might have lost you," said the Trout from his full height.

"Did you get the shot?"

"Of course. A masterpiece. Can you move?"

My eyes rolled rudderless in their sockets. "Where are the others?" I asked.

"Fled," the Trout said. "What horrors they might have witnessed in the trenches I suppose were nothing compared to your little tumble."

"Will they tell?"

"And who would be fool enough to believe them?"

"Lay me on the ground, Mutter," I said.

He spread me gently on the cracked cobbles. I looked up at the sky and sent a tiny explorer down the channel of my spine. There was wholeness, break, wholeness. A corporeal Morse code. Just a message. Just information. And how to mend it? *Will*, the ghost had said. How? *Will*. Simply think there are no bones to knit. There is no flesh to heal. That was the wisdom. That was the will. The will of being *past* any break.

There are no bones to knit.

There is no flesh to heal.

My body was mine again, and I sat up.

CHAPTER 14

I'd had no first day of school, no cold Christmas mornings bleary with anticipatory heat. No birthdays. I had no reference for the sickening flutter in my guts as I waited in the screening room. It was only when Zann finally arrived for a showing of my first assembly that I realized the sensation was not malignant.

The Trout arrived just as the lights dimmed, an affected scarf around his throat. We ran the film without titles. I warned the Trout this would be the case, telling him the title writer was backlogged and how ridiculous it would be to postpone the screening when words were really a formality after all. This was Volker's logic, and I fear I had trouble sounding convincing, but he wanted complete silence for this first outing. Our nightmares have no soundtracks, he explained. Silence is the natural state of dreaming.

But there *was* sound in that little screening room. The leafy clatter of gears, the beetle-wing rustle of celluloid sprockets cupped then released. The dull hiss of the carbon arch that burned hot as the sun as it tossed each image a battlefield distance to the screen. Zann was rapt, his eyes wet but unblinking. Even Mutter seemed transfixed. I watched little of the film myself. I was too busy watching them. And in so doing I became acquainted with the ambivalence that would soon define my attitude toward my own finished work. The Trout sat behind us. But his deep silence testified to his total immersion. When the film ended we sat in the dark for a full seven minutes until I bothered to raise the lights.

"My God," Zann managed to whisper. "What have you done?"

The Trout was on his feet at the first hint of criticism, knives out. How badly he wanted to please.

"I was thinking of Wagner's *Parsifal*," he almost wailed. "At least through some of the more pathetic moments—perhaps a bit of *Die Fledermaus*, to lighten things up."

The Trout was talking music, talking treason.

"A little fluffing, a little parsing. We can change it."

And my eyes hardened ineffectively in the dark. But Zann didn't need my remonstrative looks. He already *saw*.

"I don't think so," Zann said slowly. "I wouldn't touch it."

"Well, when the titles are in it will flow a little better . . ." The Trout trailed off.

"No. No titles either."

"No *titles*? How will the audience follow the . . . ?"

"Just as it is," Zann pronounced calmly. "A *true* silent. The first of its kind."

I billed myself as Maddy Ulm, I suppose in deference to the city where I first encountered Volker, first encountered what would become moving pictures. But the name meant nothing to me. To myself I was still nameless, too young and green to understand the associative power of labels. The Trout was credited as director, but Zann assured me I need not formally claim my contribution to the picture. He had been privy to the Trout's bouts with ego and doubt, had seen me work, grave-deep with Mutter, had seen the red glow beneath the editing room door deep into the night. And he wasn't entirely dismissive of the Trout's efforts. He offered him a three-year acting contract with a two percent bump per year. But me he sat on his lap and stroked my cold knees and purred the words I so badly wanted to hear.

"You may be German cinema's first true genius, my little dear," he said. "How would that mantle sit on these frail shoulders?"

Quite nicely, I assured him.

THE PROJECT WAS DUBBED *THE TOYMAKER* AFTER MUCH HEATED DELIBeration. It was a wink toward the irony we were sure our audiences would appreciate.

One morning, a month later, I walked onto the shooting floor and all the cameras stopped. The air became peppered with the discreet applause reserved only for the nearly great. I was led to the front of the stage and awarded my own tiny white director's coat. It was cut to my child's frame and presented by none other than *Caligari's* creator, Robert Wiene. And what was the Trout's reaction to this new appreciation? Was he grateful my efforts had made him a contract player? He quoted Nietzsche.

"'You will never get the crowd to cry hosanna until you ride into town on an ass,'" he said, dressed in the foppish heels and pantaloons of a seventeenth-century cavalier. He was working as a third lead in one of Zann's costume epics and seemed tired and miserable, but I was too excited to be moved by his philosophical bitchiness. I had my white coat. I was a *Doktor* of cinema. I had my future. But such laurels have a price.

I usually avoid mirrors. They reflect a defect only, an oft-recited lie that invariably distracts from the thorny truth that festers in the dark inside me. But that night, the night I received my coat, was different. I wanted to see myself. Just myself. To revel for a moment, an evening perhaps, in the badge of my achievement. That coat had much to answer for. It had to soothe every terror, balance every abandonment. It had to provide a new skin, a new reflection not bathed in ignorance and littleness. It had to cloak me in love.

The makeup room was the perfect place for this. It was banked with a row of mirrors. Sixteen reflections and one object. Me and my magnificent white coat. Yes, I had originally thought the coat an affectation, an unnecessary formality. I'd thought it was an impractical garment that belied the filth of real film-making. I did not realize it was an intoxication that commanded respect. I was standing in my own light, my own warmth, the white coat snug at the waist, comfortable in the shoulders, looking, I hoped, directorial, regal. A force of presence and vision. When Volker appeared.

Lovely, my girl, he whispered. *A vision of purity.*

I was startled. I could never get used to his manifestations, not when they came this suddenly. He had appeared in the mirrors, but not beside or behind my reflections. Now, he *was* my reflection. When I moved, he ghosted my gesture, tethered to me as if stitched through our hearts.

You take direction well, he said. *I was afraid you would be dull. But you've proven more responsive than your mother.*

I didn't know what to say. Should I have been grateful? My mounting dread made that feeling impossible.

"Thank you," I said.

For what? I haven't given you anything you won't be paying for. Did you think me charitable, my dear?

I thought the use of body, my limbs, my voice, my movements, had been my part of the exchange. How could he have accomplished his vision otherwise?

I was only partly right. He swept into me like a sudden fever. My legs buckled and I was thrown to the floor. I felt him trickle through my hips, cold as mercury, and flow into the joints of my knees. Then pressure. I choked back my revulsion as I felt my knees violently pulled apart.

A singular vision is a lonely vision, my girl. An artist will starve on so sparse a diet as his own genius.

"Please," I rasped. "Don't do this."

Struggling is a poor defense. It only makes the rose sweeter.

I leaped to my feet, but he tripped me to the ground. My head sounded hollowly on the floor.

Be still now.

"Stop."

Have you thought you might enjoy it?

"Stop!"

I had a girl working for me once, not much older than you.

I felt the cold of him infuse my arm. It shot straight into the air, sprouting thoughts of its own. It then landed on a makeup table that was just within my reach from the ground and scrambled over the surface.

Pale as night flower, sweet has honey from the hive.

My fingers scrambled over slick pools of spilled powder, a greasy clot of face paint. Hairpins. Worn rouge brushes.

She swore she anticipated my attentions more than a whole bucketful of sweet custard. More than a whole head of candy floss.

I felt my fingers settle on a long smooth object. It was round at one end. Hard and tapered at the other. A hand mirror. My arm came down violently on the edge of the table. The oval of the glass shattered into tiny ponds that kicked with reflections of the corners of the room, the tables, my own terrified face.

That's right. It doesn't need to be huge, my girl. Anyone with experience will tell you that. Just durable.

In my hand was just the tapered handle. I felt it navigate toward me, off the edge of the table, into the line of my sight, past my face, past my chest and waist, until it disappeared beneath my skirt.

It's stamina that counts in this game, I heard him whisper in my skull. *Long languid strokes. For an eternity.*

CHAPTER 15

er *Kietz* has no translation. *Kietz* is a stubborn word, much like jazz, irreducible from its national argot. It is a word that will readily melt in a spoon or gin glass but not on foreign tongues. And like jazz, it speaks of whole worlds fed by dusky appetites as black and viscous as opium tar. But the *Kietz* is not of music. It is of flesh. Ten thousand thighs in ten thousand flavors spread in rented rooms or on the chill of civic brick. Entire meticulous matchstick trusses of hope erected, crossed, and ultimately crushed by rouged women and girls who survived by reclining and receiving for the fatherland. In typical Prussian logic, prostitution was technically legal. But verbal solicitation by sex workers was not. The solution was simple. Whores had to *look* like whores. There were *Chontes* and *Demi-castors*, *Fohses* and *Minettes*. Ratty "pharmacies" of surly twelve-year-olds with nicotine-stained teeth and proficient fingers who were "prescribed" and thus known as "medicine" to their clients who discreetly referred to hair tint as the "color of the pill." Pregnant

Munzis, whose allure lasted only until their labor pains, worked the strictly delineated Münzstrasse that abutted the territory of Amazonian boot whores who advertised their specialized perversions by the color of their knee-high laces.

Not all were so brash. Standing quietly near the boarded kiosks of the main drag, in what could have easily been mistaken for a criminal lineup, worked several Kontroll-Girls all with their weekly venereal health reports hanging around their necks. Shivering silently under the bulk of their practical coats, they were the cautious vice of middle-class husbands and optimistic clerks who didn't mind sacrificing a little lascivious illusion for the privilege of peeing the next week without screaming.

The north Berlin night belonged to women. And under the sodium lights that lined the Alexanderplatz, lights that threw jaundice, not gold, great flocks of them wheeled and preened. Caged in shedding furs and souring paint, waiting, breathing slowly, they fought for crumbs from the pockets of old men and crippled boys. It was late fall. I had been working second unit during the day and researching my next project at night. Volker was very clear as to the subject of our next endeavor and had taken it upon himself to educate me. There were many girls on the *Platz* that night, hair shorn hard to the jaw, reedy shoulders slendered from hunger. They clutched half-empty purses, their black gums flashing between brief bursts of laughter. Most worked in pairs, similarly dressed, tossing price/duration ratios veiled in the droll repartee they were known for, the *Berliner Schnauze,* as it was called.

But these did not interest Volker. He wanted a country girl, shabby now with use but still cradling green pastures somewhere behind her eyes. A girl the audience would believe had been forced into the life through the burden of dreams. Away from the lights the girls were quieter. Volker entered them like ill-fitting suits, his features and masculine limbs ghosting through their troubled features as the chill of him made their flesh ripple. And then he would slip from them silently and shake his head and flit to the next. I was propositioned a couple of times myself, and each time, Volker would send a fierce chill into the prospective john, halting would-be negotiations. We were calling the night a loss when my shoe caught the lip of a cobblestone and sent me flailing to the ground.

"Easy now, little dear," a voice said above me. The voice was not Volker's. "Where is such a little darling rushing off to in such a hurry?"

I looked up from the ground as a firm hand settled on my shoulder. He was a tall man with white brows and close-cropped blond hair that bristled defiantly in the cold. His sleeves were rolled and there I saw two crude tattoos, both of women kneeling, one with a halo, the other in garters thumbing a stack of cash. The saint and the harlot. His forearms bellied like great tunas as he lifted me to my feet, and when he smiled I saw two neat rows of gold teeth, each set with a tiny centered diamond.

"Thank you," I said, feeling Volker expand like methane within me. I moved to leave, but the tattooed man stopped me with his lucre grin.

"Wait, now," he said. "We've only just met. Let me at least be neighborly and buy you a little something."

"I'm fine."

"Don't you like sweets?"

"Not especially."

He reached into his pocket and removed a small pale green cylinder of cellophane-wrapped candy.

"Not even a nice piece of taffy and a little chat?"

"No, thank you."

"But you soiled your pretty little dress when you fell," he said, popping the candy into his mouth. He chewed slowly as he held the soiled edge of my skirt in thickly callused fingers. "Let me at least buy you a new one. With some shoes and a new pair of stockings? I could make life quite pleasant for a pretty little girl like you."

Volker had had enough. He rose like swamp gas from my guts. I could feel his misty jaws spread to my lips, his tongue filling mine with the dusty taste of the grave. It was a horrible sensation, like suffocating on one's own breath. And I was made to speak.

"Look, friend," I began in a voice studded with a ghostly bass. "Keep your cheap trinkets for the half-silks that don't know no better. I ain't *sellin'*, follow? I'm *buyin'*."

The blond pimp stroked the sides of his mouth as a chuckle shook his chest.

"*Buyin'*? For you?"

"That's right." I could feel Volker spread my feet in a defiant stance. The blond pimp shot a hard crack of laughter into the night that billowed in the cold.

"Cut the shit, kid."

"You got a stable, or do I take my money elsewhere?" Volker asked.

"Easy, now, easy," the pimp said. "I got what you need. Let's just hope you got what *I* need."

I reached into the pocket of my dress and pulled out a roll of marks. The pimp reached for the money, but Volker flashed his death head through my features in a new unsettling trick, spiraling me into a sudden and sickening blindness. And the pimp pulled back suddenly, his eyes growing young with instant fear.

"I require something of discernment," Volker purred. "Not this shopworn cunny you wrap in paper and hawk by the pound. Something fresh and real and *alive*."

The pimp regarded me thoughtfully with his colorless eyes and then said, perhaps a bit too theatrically, "You need Tanzi. She is a very great artist." And here something like respect softened the predatory edge in his eyes. "You, my dear, need Tanzi Fluke." But he couldn't show her to us tonight. The club where she worked refused minors. I would have to come back as someone else.

Heading home that night we passed a poster hanger's cart. A few stiff brushes hung from the push handle like captive mustaches, but the cart itself had been abandoned. I saw the poster hanger, a few paces down the block, bent over the wet back of a poster as wide as his reach. He lathered it with economic strokes, then flung it. It stuck in starchy suction upon the modulated surface of the brick. He had hung several posters already. All the same. *Der Spielzeugmacher*, the posters read in a blocky expressionist print. Under these words, with heavy blacks and halftone, was the figure of Death, the twin scythes of his iliac crest cutting potently if sexlessly into the image of a beautiful young woman in his arms. The woman wore a gossamer shroud. Death wore only his shoes. And ghosted behind this, taking up the entire field of the image, a cadaverous face with lifeless eyes. Eyes that could be watching this grim couple but watched us instead. And there above the brow, a metallic plate, flat at the crown, riveted to the flesh. Mutter. It was Mutter's face.

Der Spielzeugmacher. The Toymaker. It was my movie, there in multiple refraction. The image of our film setting in the morning damp waiting for the sun to seal it. And then for people, real average people, to go and see it. *The Toymaker* at the Marmorhaus. Not even being dead could dull the thrill of that moment on that empty morning street.

Volker slipped from the tenement of my chest and congealed to near solidity. I could see the pale tubes of his fingers yearning for the substance to touch the wet surface of the freshly hung poster, his eyes lit up as if by a million birthday candles, smiling hard.

"We've done it," he whispered aloud, not bothering with the private acoustics of my skull. "My God, child, we have *done* it."

Film is born in emulsion, cured in brine much like amniotic fluid. But it can claim passage through myriad canals. It is an orphan born of a thousand mothers and no father.

THE REVIEWS WERE GOOD. THAT MUCH I REMEMBER. A CRISP JOURNAL hitting a desk like the report of a cap gun and Zann smiling fresh from his coffee and tooth powder, pointing only to a headline that read, "*The Toymaker*: A Perfect Parable of Our Times."

Lichtbild-Bühne called it a "paean to the national angst, sure to find purchase among those haters of Death with an appetite for grim fantasy."

Der Film was a bit more tepid in its praise, calling it "a film confident in its ability to inoculate the lurid seeking public against lesser horrors."

Film criticism was in its infancy then. Writing duties trickled down to third editorial assistants whose usual bailiwick was correcting syntax in theatrical reviews. Much ink was spilled in service to the struggle meant to define a criteria for film, and so it was not uncommon for these reviews to devolve into personal tirades and petty airings. It was an historical moment for us. For the first time, words were not subject to imperial censorship. So it is not difficult to understand why these pens were often as easily aroused as adolescent erections. The new freedom made horny little boys of our somber journalists, little boys slipping for the first time between the slippery sheets of a new republic.

"They're calling it an antiwar film," I said, looking up from the paper. "They say it's the 'viewing duty of every freedom-loving German to witness again the caustic fruits of unchecked hubris and fanaticism.' What are they talking about? It's about a sad little man trying to protect his daughter."

"Who cares what they say?" Zann chuckled. "They *like* it. People will see it. If the anti-Wilhelmian slant bothers you, there are several others who think you made a pro-military, anti-disarmament film." He tossed a crumpled handbill to the desk.

"*Der Stürmer*? Isn't this an SA publication?" I asked.

"Yes"—Zann grinned—"and those adenoidal little brown shirts are screaming your praises on every street corner. They say the creature's a 'clarion call for the immediate mechanization of the military.' The murder of the crone a 'prescriptive tribute to the manipulative tentacles of the Jewish banking cabals.'"

"That's awful."

"You can't *buy* press like that, my child."

"But the SA," I said.

"Listen to me, my little treasure. The only time you have to start worrying is when they *stop* screaming."

CHAPTER 16

Tanzi Fluke trolled the Jägerstrasse at midday in a wedding frock flecked with raspberry jam intended to simulate congealed blood. She walked alone, although the street is full of her. A pig is snug to her full breast, spit foaming on its triangular jaws. She calls the pig "republic" and the breast "the people." That evening greasepaint will hollow her eyes to re-create the effect of high sun. The pig will play itself.

It had been an open invitation offered by the blond pimp, an invitation to see this Fräulein Fluke when the "mood so moved us." He had told us where she performed and what she could be had for, introduced us to the schlepper who would guide us through the reeking maze of the Friedrichstadt slum where her *Nachtlokal*, or nightspot, could be found.

It was easy to forget I was unchaperoned, so present was Volker's presence. Easy to forget I was sealed up in this child's body. Years had passed, but I remained changeless. I was forced to gaze into mirrors and see my budding breasts shunted by the blight of my death. My high forehead slightly hypercephalic. Blocky teeth. And a voice that would never descend from its peak. A whole menagerie of transitional forms that mocked eternity. And so Volker had explained with a mocking lilt, *Where do you think this Tanzi Fluke plies her trade, child? You think she collects tickets at a kiddy park? Or hawks peppermint sticks on the* Hauptallee? *She shakes her ass for cash in the pits where the parents go. You must be clever and show a second self if you ever want to inspire anything more than pats on the head and warning stares.*

We were seated in the makeup room at well past midnight. I had memories of my last occasion with him in that room and was nervous. Nervous enough to sit curled on a makeup table, my knees dusted with stray powder. Not that my posture could protect me. But since the success of our last film, I'd hoped his view of me had changed. I hoped he saw me as something more than merely recreational.

"What do you mean?" I said, my eyes scanning the tables for hard cylindrical objects just in case he had a relapse.

What do I mean? he scoffed. *You live among papier-mâché palaces and day-rate princes. Can't you figure it out all on your own?* He left my body then and sat in the chair opposite me. His image did not waver. It was as solid as he could manage, a viscosity much like dark blue ink. He wanted to impress his point, not haunt.

"You mean I should dress up?"

"So you *do* have a mind up there," he said, poking a spectral finger through my temple. "But you must abandon your sex. Little girls never look smaller than from the height of mommy's heels."

"I should dress as a boy?" My legs relaxed. There was no threat. It felt like we were peers. If not peers, then at least co-conspirators.

"We'll give the suggestion of a gentleman. A top hat and coat. Perhaps a monocle. A mustache, of course, to veil those ridiculous teeth."

"I can't possibly wear a mustache."

"Oh, you must. It's the key to the ruse."

"It will tickle."

"Less than a bouncer's fist, I assure you."

"But I'll look ridiculous."

"And that's why you'll look like you belong."

It was a midget's suit, a costume for a bit player, evening attire for a layer of business that gives depth to the frame but no real dimension. I had seen the suit lurking in the carnival shots of *Caligari* and tried to imagine the man who had worn it. I could sense the personality entirely, the sweat of excitement when he first put it on, which cooled to exertion as the day progressed. Then boredom. Turkish tobacco and the tear-shaped burn on the cuff where he might have fumbled for a match. The waxy stains at the cuffs where his fingers had worried, waiting to be noticed, waiting to fill the suit with more than just a cold ring of pomade at the collar. We found a beaver skin opera hat that Volker cocked over one of my eyes. Over the other he slid a monocle. My face he made up as a woman's, hanging my lashes with heavy black fringe, rouging my lips and cheeks. "You'll be no more noticed on the night streets of Berlin than a postman shuffling through his daily rounds," he assured me. And he was right.

The streets were gorged with creatures like me. Hot girls in sorority huddles. Line-boys made up like sailors. And willowy half-sexes with throats like long pours of cream in fabric that must have cost six months of salaries. All moved quietly to their chosen debaucheries as orderly as petty clerks in quests for daily bread. And I moved with the same measured intent, returning no glances, no proposals. Just another masquerading member of the predator class. The schlepper spotted me first, tipped my elbow as gently as a pot of afternoon tea. And I turned to him and shrank at the darkness of his smile, black from chewing opium tar, and doffed my hat. I felt my mustache slip, and I pressed two fingers there as if it were a habit of mine in times of anticipation. And he turned for me to follow. He led me down intestinal streets, back alleys, and open sewers where I had to mirror the careful algorithms of his steps to keep my shoes dry. Trade commenced in those dark crevices, one head seeking pleasure, the other only sustenance. And here was the religion of Berlin, sacrifice only in service to the appetite. A thousand crucifixions on the moon.

We stopped on a quiet street. The only light seeped through the pane windows of what was once a funeral parlor. Crosses in flecked gold were on the glass, and arched in letters that once held the proprietor's name was the word *Totentanz*. Death dance. Black wreaths flanked the double doors. They were made of painted thousand-mark notes, worthless now from the Great Inflation. And over the door, written with great skill, were the words *Der Tod Trägt Seine Schuhe*. Only Death Wears His Shoes.

I thought for a moment of *The Toymaker*'s poster, of our own cobbled Death (fate or mere symmetry?), when the schlepper reached toward the door and tapped a quick code that made the paper wreaths rustle. The doors digested this for a beat and then creaked open, spilling wicked light at my feet. I dipped a finger and thumb into my vest pocket to fish out a tip. The schlepper's grubby hands were already sticky upon mine and wrestled the notes from me with a proprietary sneer as he ran into the night.

There was a girl in the doorway now, in immaculate mourning attire. She was a few years my senior, with white chalked cheeks and blacked eyes. She bowed to me and I thought to

curtsy but bowed as well. I stepped past her, toward a crop of
black candles that guttered in three dense rows on gold stands.
Below these stands were rows of shoes on stone shelves. Each
pair neatly partnered. The girl waited for me to remove my shoes,
then motioned for me to cross my arms over my chest. As I did,
she gently pushed me backward into the waiting hands of four
more girls. They were dressed in shiny mourning black. Pretty
pallbearers. They held me prostrate while one girl gently removed
my monocle and another placed two pennies on my eyes and I
felt myself pulled through the cool sweep of a heavy velvet drape.
I could sense a brighter light that leaked past the poor seal of the
coins on my eyes. I was tipped to my feet and the coins fell before
I could catch them. But I did not bother. The establishment had
correctly predicted delight and not scrambling greed.

The room must have been the parlor's chapel at one time, for
the shadows spat up a few ecclesiastical elements. High-backed
chairs that could have held deacons were arranged around tables
shaped like coffins. Upon each table was a silver dish that held
an icy liquid. Pearls of condensation obscured the deeply chased
crosses etched on them. And in the dishes were stiff petals, white
roses, like chips of ice. Pinspots were the only light, directed
harshly onto these bowls of white petals. So in the deep dusk
only the fingers of the patrons could be seen as they reached into
these bowls and bit with the crisp report of breaking glass. It
was quiet in there, but not silent. For there was a feeling so pervasive it seemed capable of sound, a low, soothing hum of never
mind, of being swept away on some numbing current. I jarred my
senses after I was seated and placed a petal in my mouth. I willed
it to heat. And there was such a startling redundancy I gave a
small cry. These petals, brined in a solution of chloral hydrate

ether, re-created perfectly the cold slipping down of death. The icy caress that soothed to a near stop of the heart and lungs. The soft velvet black that crested and threatened to shunt the lights of the eyes. Whomever was responsible had access to secrets denied the living. Volker left me through my wide and impressed eyes and wafted to an empty chair at my table, smirking as he vaguely congealed.

"Questions, yes," he whispered. "But first the show." Had he been here before?

The pin lights dimmed to a thrumming of harp strings, a circular twining of treacle chords too mawkish to be an authentic overture to any serious heaven. And we all sat there in the dark as the strings grouped into silly concentric harmonies building to a gold spot that bathed a small stage. Four Negro musicians as somber as snakes lifted brass instruments to their mouths. A cymbal was struck, and a slow, limping New Orleans–style dirge squeezed out of their gold flanges.

Up the aisle came a cortege of all-naked girls, pale as birch, the nappy rugs of their pubic patches trimmed into the symbols of international currency. On their shoulders was a casket covered in black patent leather and this they carried to the dance floor in the center of the room and placed on two gunmetal sawhorses. They turned toward the audience and began a solemn shimmy, and I could see they wore only sheer knee-high stockings beneath their ululating nipples. A drum roll silenced the brass and the girls fell to a single knee. At the crash of a cymbal, the lid of the coffin blew open and a flurry of deutschemarks fluttered over the crowd like locusts blackening a field of barley. And out of the maw of the box rose up the most spectacular woman I had ever seen. She wore a black leather mask that hid her features, but her body was of such perfect fluid proportion it was impossible to imagine her clothed.

She stood before us, composed, while the patron's eyes explored her. Then she commenced to wring her body into the most piteous contortions. There were not the usual hinges in her limbs and spine. Her bones were quicksilver and she poured herself into backbends and splits and handstands and flips with a dizzying fluidity. All the while the Negro band slogged on, flogging her with the sedulous, even shuffle of their tune.

She finally worked her way to the top of her closed casket and stood bleached in a blue-white spot. There was a blast from a trumpet and the lights suddenly went black. A second blast and she stood in the spot covered in spiders, a writhing arachnid mass in female form. Another blast, and darkness. Then light, and snakes filled her shapely silhouette. Darkness again, and when the lights came up a second later she was dressed in a tight-fitting sheath sliced up to her hip. The orchestra launched into a hot jazz number, and as she began to jitter to the quicker beat, the lids of all the coffins that had served as tables blew open, the frigid rose petals shattering as they hit the floor. Out popped naked girls, their bodies blackened. White glistening bones painted upon them, they formed a primitive circle around the masked woman.

The dance that ensued might have celebrated the first pagan feast of Samhain. The brass was ditched for drums, loud deep resonant drums, a chorus of gorged heartbeats that bleated and prodded the dancers into rhythmic squats and hunched backs. This was not a dance of white women, and the guttural shouts from the band were not the street sounds of Berlin. This was some Pliocene bacchanal where the survival of the species was becoming assured. Fingers flashed and the first flecks of blood fluttered to the warming skin. The band's shouts stretched to shrieks. The old gods were among us. Blood flowed, smeared in brownish vermilion on jaws and chests and thighs. The lights began to flash, strobing to the frenzied beat, and the dance devolved to a feast. Glimpses of mouths and fists and teeth flickered past pupils the size of quarters. And in the flashes, Volker took on a solid aspect, his very real attention riveted to the re-created carnage before him. The skeletal girls swarmed the masked woman, heaping themselves upon her, bared teeth and talons hailing down in fury.

Then the girls were still. Onstage was a tangle of cannibal props, painted femurs and rib cages, cooling to the steady tattoo of a single drum. The lights faded. Then the lights blared brightly and the jumble of bones was gone. The masked woman stood alone on the stage, naked. The applause was immediate.

"My God," I whispered. "How did she do it?"

"Haven't you guessed?" Volker grinned as I turned to catch his surly eye.

The tables were righted and the dance floor cleared. The band launched into a rough Strauss that brought a few couples to the floor. A topless girl in sequined shorts and heels threaded her way through the recovering crowd pouring *Sekt* into short glasses she pulled from a leather belt she wore over one shoulder like a bandolier. Volker sipped from a glass she handed him and drank from the syrupy swill.

"The Germans have no business with champagne." Volker grinned again and asked if I was ready to meet her.

"Tanzi Fluke?" I asked.

"Who else, child? Wasn't she magnificent?"

"Doubtless. But that woman we saw dance tonight is nothing

like how you described the lead. She's no country girl still rimmed with sunlight."

"How can you be sure?"

"I have eyes, don't I?"

"Then perhaps you should widen your understanding of the effects of sunlight."

He nodded and I looked up at her approach. She was dressed in a simple red dressing gown, her mask still in place. She sat with an English cigarette in her lips and looked directly at Volker. But then she leaned forward, her eyes still upon him, the cold tip of her cigarette hovering in expectation. A flame appeared from the tip of his finger and I saw it curve with the intake of her breath. I must have looked foolish, gaping at this simple ceremony, for they both shared a conspiratorial glance and laughed.

"Welcome back, darling," she said, removing her mask.

It was my mother's face that smirked back at me, unchanged from her image on the postcard or even my last living memory of her. She dragged deep on her cigarette and her eyes squinted against the smoke.

"I see you've flourished since my absence," she said.

I was immediately furious. I wanted to weep. I wanted to scream at her until her eyes bled. I wanted to fall into her arms. But I did nothing. I stood to leave, but she held me down with a pressure on my wrist. She peeled a loose tobacco leaf from her tongue and said, "Don't be that way, darling. Look at the success you've become."

"What are you talking about?" I whispered harshly. The memory of tears flooded back, but only dust would gather in the corners of my eyes. "You left me *alone*. You left me *terrified*, you heartless bitch. Why didn't you wait for me? Why did you leave me?"

"Crawling out of coffins can be quite profitable." She smirked.

"I didn't know where I was. *What* I was."

She only seemed amused by my anger and hurt.

"Well, you obviously found your way."

"Was that your plan?"

"What are you braying about? After all, I left you in capable hands."

"*What* hands?"

"Why, your *father's* hands, you silly little tart."

And I looked to Volker, who held up a single hand in a helpless gesture, and I knew it was true.

"You don't think I'd leave you with just *any* well-shod monster."

"It's true. I've always had a weakness for fine shoes," Volker purred, and I wondered how long they had planned this little reveal. Hadn't she murdered the son of a bitch to protect my dignity? Or was that bullshit too? Of course it was. A witch of her cunning could have stilled his heart with a single glance. How many midnights had he left the echo of my skull to scheme with her? So this was her plan, let me learn from the miserable ground up. Let me struggle and thrash my way to cinematic competence, then renown. And all so she could highjack the train for her own aggrandizement.

"If you think for one second I'll put that blackhearted whore in my movie you're—"

"You'll do as you're *told,* child," Volker growled. "You just remember who pulls the strings."

And he stole into me with that icy blade of his invasive

presence and made me stand. I could hear his laughter in the hollow of my skull as he insinuated into the joints of my knees and I began a jerky step toward the dance floor.

"Stop it," I shouted. "I'll do it. Just not like that."

"*As you wish*," he whispered, and I felt the door of me shut behind him.

"Just remember, my girl, Poppa is only ever a wish away."

CHAPTER 17

I suppose in many ways the story of *Zipper* was ahead of its time. It predated the body horror of Bava and Franju by several decades and its frank dealing with the conditions of a postwar populace was considered by some to be more sensitive than De Sica. But there is little savor in accomplishments that are not completely one's own. The scenario was a grim one, made worse, if that were possible, by the relish with which I was forced to tell it. And so the frigid tide of Volker's prompting rose once again, the cold, dull knives of each syllable shattering upon Zann's open ears.

It was the story of a whore, a nameless streetwalker known only by her profession, an anonymous pigeon jerking in a park (establishing shot). We see her beheld in the low beams of desire. The sour salt of some thumb pries apart her lips to assay her teeth. The ripeness of one breast is tested like winter fruit. We see her chosen, used, discarded. But in her eyes, over the rhythmic admiration of some dandy, a spark, a fearful hope. And for what does she hope? To dance. To sparkle, perhaps. To be more than the gentle ruin she is. And so she defies her station, her class. She elevates herself to a stage, a mere two feet above the fingers that once possessed her. And she dances, if it could be called that, flecked with cheap glitter and bangles, grinding her cartilage to the shearing beat of a *Tingeltangel* bar. She dances for brutes, for degenerates still wet from fitful sleeps, for old, old men who remember when waltzes were revolutionary. Her life hardly improves. The abuse she endured on the street merely follows her backstage. But her dream is still somehow served and she is nothing if not indentured.

Then one night a poor student sees her perform and is helplessly smitten with her. He sends flowers, flirts, keeps his hands in his pockets, and the possibility of a prosaic life casts its weird light on her. She goes with him. But she has transgressed against an intractable law of economics. When she is finally missed from the stable of her cruel and very blond pimp, his retribution is swift. One evening during her number, he pulls her from the chorus line and in a very public demonstration of wrath and in what was to be our only moving crane shot, guts her, slicing her from belly to clavicle. He miraculously flees the scene unhindered, leaving her bleeding upon the stage that once offered much solace. But death does not claim her. She wakes to the adoring face of the student, weak and bandaged, grateful as he nurses her back to some semblance of health.

We iris out from her staring eyes, pulling back to see her standing before a full-length mirror. She regards her torso wrapped in a curious tangle of interlocking gauze, wrapped tightly like a gift we doubt she will appreciate. Curious, she peels. She beholds her scar, a double highway of puckered skin.

And between the puckers a stretch of something foreign, something metallic. A zipper. She has been fitted with a zipper. Like a human purse. A woman-shaped frock. And now the student enters, his arms full of their meager evening. He sees that she sees, but he is not shocked. He is not repelled. He is happy to see her up and about. He inspects the wound officiously and is pleased it is healing so well. And here the horror begins to seep. For it is shortly revealed that the student himself, the bumbling, lovesick schmuck, is indeed the party responsible for her freakishness. ("A medical student who dabbles in the occult," that is as much detail as I am allowed to impart to Zann, and his wide, stunned stare tells me that is enough.)

A slow pan down the length of her zipper, her new mark of servitude. Her old life is now lost to her. She is fit for nothing more than to be his hausfrau, his toy, his creature. And slowly the weight of this answered prayer descends on her. When she balks, he threatens her with the zipper. Smiling calmly, his fingers edge toward the pull that if opened will reveal what? Her still-beating heart? A dusty cupboard of shriveled organ and bone? The place that once harbored her dream? Close-up of her single unblinking eye as a tear of dreadful despair glistens down her cheek. It is a nightmare beyond reckoning.

Then one day while slogging home the nightly kraut she spies a flyer for a traveling carnival. Rides, clowns, and curiosities (close-up on her face, a rising dread and determination).

She gets the student drunk. He sleeps. She sneaks out to the tent show. And there is her old familiar world somehow made more horrible and more dear in its desire to grovel and entertain.

She is spied by a hideous old mountebank. Taken with her beauty, he concocts a use for her. He shows her to the tent of

exotic wonders, where common girls dress as Persian slaves. It is
rank and cheap and horrible, but there is music and dancing and
the old dreams have their sway and she is compelled to join them.

We see her onstage, dressed in the silks of a concubine.
Taken in ecstasy, she is magnificent. The audience is captive until
she reveals her wound. Horror resounds. But the mountebank
won't be gypped. He begins a chant, clapping and pounding and
prodding. *Zip-per! Zip-per! Zip-per!* And she makes the turn, I
suppose, chooses the love of the audience over what dry horror
might lie beneath that sphinxy enclosure. She toys with the silver
pull as we slowly pan behind her. Her dance slows to her final
dance. Her hand begins its descent, and the zipper loses its bite.
Backlit. A nova. A precursor of how the world might finally
end. She lowers the zipper's pull to its base, opening herself for
the last time to the rabid approbation of strangers. Her face is a
placid pool of release. Blow to white. *Fin.*

"It's marvelous," says Zann. "Terrible. Of course we'll need
more dance numbers for Miss Fluke."

Volker took no chances with even an overture toward collaboration. He perfumed his influence, pumping it full of heady
pheromones, thinning, insinuating, polluting every dry estuary
of my being. And if I tried to shunt his presence, deafen myself
to his rampaging will, I was met not with some racking punishment but with withdrawal. Like any good pusher, he knew what
I needed, what I craved. His drug was an unshakable feeling of
confidence. So if I tried to purge myself, retreat into my own
devices, I couldn't. I wouldn't. Even the imagined emptiness of
him was more than I could bear. He ruled through the tyranny
of addiction until my need became completely indistinguishable
from his desire.

Mutter was the only one to notice the change. He would stare at me from beneath the hot metal drum of his arc light, the sweat running into his eyes the only thing making him blink, and say, "Maddy? Maddy?" and I would stare back from some great depth of exhilaration and ride the rest of the scene.

The picture had been cast even before the pitch. The part of the blond pimp went to the one actor who auditioned for it, the tattooed pimp who had introduced me to my mother. Our chance meeting on the street that night had been another of Volker's clever setups. His was a convincing performance, I must admit. I was later to learn he'd done a brief stint with Reinhardt's company before trying his luck with the flickers. For the mountebank I might have mentioned the Trout, who by this time had kept steady pace with Jannings, at least as far as his corpulence was concerned, and was so bloated and blurred by drink and continued disappointment as to be all but unrecognizable. I seem to remember him stopping me in the commissary one day before we began shooting. His mustache was wet from watery beer and the moisture ran into the deep folds of his chin. He was miles from feigned indifference, desperate, blubbering about old times. But Volker made me sneer and sealed my mouth and made me turn away without a sound.

The zipper effect held some fascination, as tactile things do for the junkie. I remember watching my hand hold a honed knife over my mother's abdomen while Nick LaRocca's orchestra bleated through "Bluin' the Blues" on the phonograph. This wasn't going to be some cheap effect. As she shared my condition, we were going to do it "practical." The tip of the knife sliced her torso as if through tallow, bloodlessly. My mother looked more bored than amused. I placed the long upholstery zipper into the cut that wafted pink dust and threaded the thick needle. I was looking from some promontory of myself, a small observer crowded by Volker's cruelty and desire. I remember the stiff satisfying sutures that held it there, the dip and tug and pull, over and over, in neat puckered rows. And then a rise in heat as Volker and I gazed down on her white pubis. I felt the chill of power men must feel, the ever-forward that compels any engagement, be it war or business or fucking. And my hand was between her legs, tucked into that cold hollow like some vegetable yet to emerge from its husk. And I was upon her with my cold lips on her cold neck and breasts. The sound of Volker's murmurs and cries was as crows cry before carrion as he fired my fingers and hips. He made a habit of this, between shots, during shots, whenever the mood struck. And I was the guiltiest of all. For it was during these ravenous interludes that the narcotic of him was the sweetest.

A movie must have been shot, some sort of assembly made. For in those rare moments when Volker would ebb and I was left to myself alone, depleted and nervous, I could see Zann's eyes. That penetrating glance of his, delivered askew, the glance reserved for the endowed, the truly imbued. But I was beyond praise.

There is no survival instinct among the dead. Only the clean, organic directive to merge. Volker may have been an exception, but I was not. I had entered the house of the host and was resigned to my plight as a tool for eternity. I was such a tool for what could have been years. Time means nothing to the dead. Once my mother and Volker realized I could effectually function as a corporeal bridge to their lust, I was exhaustively exploited to this purpose. Years of Berlin nights were but a single night to me. Hot jazz bleated from the same sweating horns with only a slight variation in the tunes. I recognized a change in venue only from slight differences in lighting. Sheets were either satin, silk, or Egyptian cotton, but their surfaces were all witness to the same predictable rhythms. Only one night do I remember. I was roused from my self-inflicted stupor by a stutter of orange flames that leapt up black velvet curtains. The room was full of smoke and through the vapor, stacked at the foot of the brass bed, like prop ice blocks, were hundreds of empty gin bottles. Next to me was a sour redhead, flat on her narrow back, breasts lolling into her downy armpits, deep in a drunken sleep. It was the firemen themselves who had to tell me my bedmate had been none other than the notorious Anita Berber.

The nights were the tithe I paid to the glory of my days. For it was during the days that I worked on my craft. I spent years perfecting the edit on *Zipper* while doubling as camera operator and editor on several other pictures. I had no portrait like dear Dorian Gray to map the trajectory of my debaucheries. My face and body remained a blank canvass so Zann never showed concern. But Mutter was far more discerning. He watched me for nearly six years without saying a word. Then one day that all changed.

I was dragging myself from editing one afternoon, having just put the finishing touches on *Zipper*, the vapors of the images I had just seen dispersing between blinks, when Mutter stood before me, blocking my path. I veered to avoid him, but his arm came down like a gentle wrath and he held me by the shoulder and looked deeply.

"Darkness," he said. "Darkness too long inside Maddy."

"Mutter, get out of my way. I'm needed on Stage Five."

"Movie finished?" he asked, referring to *Zipper*.

"Yes. Just now."

"Happy? Picture happy?"

"Yes, I'm quite happy with it, I suppose," I said testily. "Don't ask me that. You'll get me *thinking* about it again. Let me pass. I'm late."

"No," he said calmly, not moving. "Must fix it. Fix darkness now movie finished."

I waved my hand to swat him away, but Volker's strength could not be greater than my own. And Mutter caught my tiny fist in his hot yawning grip.

He growled, looking down at me. "Must fix it."

CHAPTER 18

The church steeples of Berlin were little more than negative space defining a changing sky.

Mutter entered the first church he recognized as one, carried me in his arms like dry sticks ready for the fire. It was the fall of what must have been 1924. And he brought the cold with him on his clothes, brought the smell of exhaust and dirty concrete and the small shouting voices of the street, before the heavy wooden doors swallowed us both. Mutter stood there in the silence, stood there whimpering among the empty pews and souring frankincense. An old priest appeared through the gloom of the sacristy brushing crumbs from the shoulders of his worn vestment. As soon as I sensed him I went limp, my eyes glazed, arms slack though my senses stayed sharp. I had been taught to be wary of priests.

"What is it, my son?" the priest asked. His accent was foreign. "I am Father Verhoeven. How can I ease your suffering?"

Verhoeven. A Belgian name. I had to stop a rousing Volker

from curling my pink lips into a grin. *Here was how Christ leeched the metal from a man.* Volker chuckled distantly. *Made him choke down the confessions of murders.* I imagined him with two fingers held stiffly to the cardinal points of the cross, dispelling the guilt of a German sergeant who might have plundered the priest's own home. *For the rape of his sister, ten Hail Marys. For the burning of his father's crops and bayonetting of his mother, seven more. Another sheep sheared by the hand of the Lord.* This was Christ's plan. Forgiveness more steady and overwhelming than any blitzkrieg. And this must have been his weary summation of the lumbering monster full of limp child that came stalking toward the altar: some poor blasted soul who had murdered an innocent, another mortal sin to be expunged by a mere wave of the hand. Father Verhoeven sucked in the air that would neutralize the guilt and also deliver the last rites. But the monster shook his horrible metal head.

"But this child is dead, my son," said the priest.

"Not dead," Mutter rasped. "Sick. Sick inside."

The priest laid a single finger to my throat.

"But she's as cold as the grave," he said.

"Demon inside," said Mutter under his filling eyes. "*Fix* her."

The priest bent his head to my chest. He smelled of cheese and sweat. His ear was prickly on my skin.

"She has no pulse, my son. Please. Come unburden yourself."

And all might have been well with Volker if he could have contained his rising excitement. A priest, after all, might be fun. He made me cough and blink and sit up and grin at the priest's falling jaw.

"Holy Father, protect us," he whispered.

"I'm afraid you caught me napping, Father," I said as innocently as Volker's stink would allow. "You must forgive my friend. He's frightfully prone to hysterics. The war, you know," and I motioned to Mutter's metal plate as if no other explanation were needed.

"But you had no heartbeat." The priest fingered the cross that dangled from his neck.

"Now how could I be conversing with you," I said, "if that were true? Unless it's a miracle. Do you believe in miracles, Father?"

"No," he said slowly. "God help me, I don't. But I know men's hearts. And I know the sound of lies."

And here Volker could not resist a bit of small-time theatricality. My eyes turned a fierce black and my lips twisted into a vicious sneer. The priest's eyes were unmoved as he stared back at me, shadowed in the candlelight.

"Bolt the door, my friend," he shot to Mutter. "Then come and hold her feet."

"Don't tell me you're going to *believe* this metal-headed idiot!"

Mutter put me down on the hard carpet of the aisle. There was a rodent panic somewhere at the base of my skull, a frantic cleaving as Volker tried to will me larger, stronger, more violent. I heard the door bolt slam. I leaped to my feet and, shrieking, ran toward the exit. But Volker's fear soured the drug of him, and I came to what senses I had left.

"Mutter," I whimpered. Volker collapsed my body hard to the floor.

"Hold her, my son!" bellowed the priest. "Hold that writhing serpent hosted in this innocent house!"

And Mutter descended upon me like twenty tons of breathing brick. He knew my tensile strength, knew my deathly resilience. And all pretense of tenderness was crushed with his weight. Volker hissed and thrashed my limbs in flailing jerks. My eyes lolled in their sockets. I screamed and spat and moaned.

"Please! Please, dear *God*! I'm just a little girl," I howled. *"I'm just a little girl!"*

But the priest was unmoved. He mumbled sacrament as he returned to me with his pyx and glistening aspergillum. He removed a wafer from the pyx and, crumbling it, sowed the powder over my eyes. He flicked his wet branch.

"Water and crackers?" I gulped with laughter. "Water and *crackers*?" What good were his toys of office? I spat a black glob directly in his face. He wiped the bridge of his nose with his plowman's hand. His eyes set hard and he dropped his pyx to the floor and threw his branch behind him. He slowly lowered himself to his knees. His hand shot to my throat and pulled my ear to his fevered lips.

"Now you listen to me," the priest whispered harshly. "Quit this child now. Flee this fragile vessel. Leave not a shred of your cantankerous offal. Or I swear by my most holy troth I will hound you. Whether you flee down to the ninth circle of hell or seek solace in the ass-crack of Moloch himself, I will find you and grind your rank and blasphemous pulp to grist." The priest held me close, the tension of his grip so like the rictus of ecstasy, the hot spittle of his invective sizzling deliciously where it fell on my cheeks. "And I will shit you out again on Satan's hoof," he shouted. "Are we clear? And if you think for one second I can't do it, you feculent son of a bitch, look deep into my eyes and call me *liar*." His eyes were wide, flooded with a hatred so like passion, his pale irises ringing with a condemnation so like desire. But there in the pits of his pupils, girded by what he thought was the privilege of his office, of his crosses and candy glass, fluttered tiny angels of fear.

And Volker surged.

The priest tried to pull away, but my small and icy hands

clapped firmly to the wet stubble on his cheeks. I pulled his face to mine and crushed my lips to his. He bucked frantically as my tongue pushed past the gate of his teeth and I could taste the sour nausea boil up inside him. Then a sweetness, flowing and tart and ferric filled my mouth and I felt my teeth on the tender flap of his lip, digging, tearing, forcing the blood to flow. I was nearly numb with fever. Then a sharp blow hit the back of my head and I felt his lip give with a sound I could have only imagined.

"Stop, Maddy!" I heard Mutter howl. "Stop!" Mutter's hands were on me, his roughness welcome as a lover's caress and I was floating, gliding, it seemed, toward the bolted wood of the door. I felt my small body shatter upon it with echoing peals of delight. And I was on my feet, screaming, laughing, my eyes burning with wild fury. Mutter lurched toward me and my hands fumbled upon the bolt, my nails tearing. Then he froze, stopped by the voice of the priest.

"No, my son!" the priest shouted. Then, softer, "Let her go."

I threw myself into the gray light of the day. I paced as if caged on the steps of the church. The streets seemed filled with sighs of parted lips and whispers of half-closed eyes, a whole world in recline, ripe for my vicious attentions. Then just as suddenly I hated it. Hated it all. And the hooks of my thumbs were raw upon the waist of my knickers and I was crouching, the cold public air hard upon my exposed ass. Nothing came, of course. But in my mind I left an offering on that topmost step, giddy at how the world would now have to sidestep my crude imagined eloquence. The door opened. Mutter was there. His face was composed now, all the fear and violence cooled to ash and brushed away. He said nothing, just bent down gently and pulled up my knickers and smoothed the tumble of my dress and lifted me high into his arms. Volker receded like gas from a choked tap, crowded out, perhaps, by such a surfeit of ordinary love. I felt the old unworthiness flow back into my small body, cold like the sheets of an abandoned bed. I wrapped my arms around the neck of the giant as he began the walk home. And I cried. Dry hacking sobs. Cried like the left-behind little girl I was, the daughter longing for the return of the happy hell of her poppa.

Mutter put me back in my room above the shooting floor, propped me in the corner like golf clubs still wet from the green, my body ringing from its abandonment. Mutter expected no conversation, no thanks as he set me on my feet, righting my straps and buttons. With the meat of his thumb he kneaded the stiffness of my cheeks, shaping a face he might recognize. Then he pressed the hollow of his massive palm to the top of my head. I felt no heat there, just the pressure of his gesture.

Mutter knew in his simple way that I belonged more to the world of things and that "sleep" and "rest" would be like the admonishments of a child to a doll, would have no meaning for me. My spring had broken; my gears had clogged. And now I was repaired. Temporarily, at least. Or so he must have reasoned. For why was he smiling? What lies had the priest told him that made his face curl at the corners like that? Could he sense, somehow, the priest's prescription, whatever it held, was soon to be filled?

CHAPTER 19

Two weeks later it came, brought up by Zann like room service. He didn't know the trauma I had endured. He had news. And he was anxious to tell it.

"I trust you're rested," he said by way of introduction, even though there was nothing to indicate this. I had been languishing behind vacant eyes since Volker's departure for what felt like weeks. Refusing to dress, to even leave my bed. Where was he? Then sitting down on my still-made bed and pressing his small fingers together between his knees, Zann stared into the air before him. He had the distant look of the enlightened, a look I had seen on the faces of the witches of my village when their throats would brim with incantations honed to end a blight. The stupid softness of the faces of the young men I'd seen leaving the company of my mother. Something good had happened. Better than good. Transformational. I waited for his moment to crest, recede enough for the egress of speech. And then clearing his throat with a small plosive, he began.

"*Hollywood*," he whispered, letting the name linger and expand with the cold authority of the Jewish God. A name, if he could, he would have spoken without vowels. And turning to me with wet eyes he said, "Hollywood just called. Universal Pictures wants to release *The Toymaker* in America." His voice sounded unused, fresh from its wrapper. "In Chicago, Philadelphia, and, goodness, what was it?" I watched him fumble with a slip of folded paper. (What was this hot stirring in my lap? Was that bergamot I smelled or Zann's bay rum fouled by sweat?) "Cincinnati!" he shouted triumphantly. "Some lovely spot in the undulating wheatfields of Ohio, if I'm saying that correctly. Have you heard me, child?"

My whole body was suddenly shot through with a shivering tumescence, with a narrow urgency like a boy racing home with the plain-papered promise of a skin magazine under his arm. Poppa was home.

"When?" I almost shouted. Volker tugged at the muscles of my small legs and snapped me to my feet.

"Soon," Zann said, startled. "A few months I suppose. They requested several prints."

Mutter growled. But the vistas behind my eyes exploded with visions of platinum-blond angels with rouged knees and glittery tap pants, neon welcome signs flashing over the trampled expressways of their cervixes. The room felt small, cheap and suddenly shabby. Zann waited like a child holding the edges of a still-wet finger painting. And one floor below I could hear the lope of counterweights in their lacquered boxes. The whip of raw stock through sprockets. And raised voices crying "again," and "once more please," the din of practical filmmaking. The sound made me sick.

"I'm going," I said. And I waited for Volker to ignite my veins and burst through my surface to lead this new glorious charge with his sharp words and reposts. But something had suddenly quieted the ghost. I looked at Zann's face, at the confusion lingering at the corners of his eyes. I felt a stab of shame. My mind reeled as I frantically searched for Volker's cold and confident passion. He was silent. But I was not alone. Something new was there. Mutter stepped toward me. "I'm *going!*" I hissed. And Mutter's brow furrowed.

" W-What are you talking about, child?" Zann stammered. "You can't just *g-go* to Hollywood. You have no contract. You have no *introduction.*"

"My *picture* is my introduction." I was terrified, teetering on some new and adamant precipice of myself.

"But that's folly. The picture may never play California. Besides, you have a future here."

"A future?" I spat. "With *my* work fouled by the name of that preening pig?"

"Then we'll make pictures with *your* name on them. Please, my dear. Don't be hasty."

And just like that my sudden resolve faltered. I looked at the floor. It seemed as soft and swallowing as the sea.

"At least until we get the reviews on *Zipper,*" Zann said. "Please, child. These things must come at their proper time."

Proper time.

"Who cares about their *fucking* reviews!" I shouted, my eyes wild above my gaping smile. "Germany is *shit*! What she thinks is *shit*! There is only *one* place to be if you are serious. And it's *not* here, bowing and mewing behind some ridiculous white coat!" Volker surged. He raged through me with a shrill sweetness as

Zann looked on in horror. And Mutter reached to grab me. This is what Volker had been waiting for. His pupil was finally standing on her own hind legs.

"Let me go!" I shouted. But Mutter did not even look at me.

"Where . . . ?" he said to Zann in his dull bass. "*Where* is this Hollywood?" It was the most cognitive sentence I had heard him utter.

"What?" Zann asked, recovering slightly.

"Show me where," Mutter said.

I don't remember them leaving me. I drifted into a twilight shot through which the crisp glare of opening-night searchlights and champagne soured mouths. When I was jolted back into consciousness I was being lifted in the dark. I felt myself dropped into some muffled dusk. It smelled strongly of Mutter, his size and sweetness. I tried to scream. But a lid slammed over me. I heard the resolute chink of a lock. I beat on the walls as I felt the floor beneath me tilt. I was jostled about with Mutter's enormous collars and pants. I felt something sharp hit my head. A book. An English primer. And another book. The small atlas Zann must have given him. Where was he taking me? I thrashed among the soft and jagged effects, screaming, raining my tiny fists against my blind cage. The only response to my tantrum was the sickening heave of my tiny closed world, a rhythmic thump as we descended what must have been stairs. The sharp smell of pine on the shooting floor; the magnificent vacancy of the quiet studio. When I could smell the exhaust of the night air, I was rattled to the ground. The lid of the trunk was opened, and Mutter's enormous face filled the horizon.

"Shh," the giant said, a finger to his lips. "I take to Hollywood," he whispered. I tried to push past him. He blocked me with his immovable head. "I take."

"Why?"

"Maddy knows," he said with a growl. "For *Maddy*." The lid fell just before the lock. Volker was not convinced. He made me thrash until my body was raw and limp. Exhausted, sullen, I remember looking through a tear in the canvas of the trunk. I saw a sinuous curl of smoke lithographed onto a poster. The smoke congealed into the countenance of my mother, in lidded bliss. And over the magenta nipples of her exposed breasts someone had drawn two scarlet swastikas. *ZIPPER* HELD OVER! was plastered at a drunken angle over the image.

I lurched forward for what seemed like hours, days perhaps, but Volker's nervous vigilance never calmed until I smelled the brine of the sea. I could hear voices, bells, money shuffling over palms, then feet on slats, now on solid plank and a feeling of descent. Down and then down again. The stink of rats. Bilge. And from far away, ghostly and cold, the disembodied cries of deep and distant whales.

CHAPTER 20

The priest's cure had not been holy. Merely geographical. Pagan. *To cleanse your friend,* he had told Mutter, *simply get her over a large body of water. Then the evil cannot follow.* And Volker, cajoled by the tyranny of his own hunger, was made complicit in his own undoing. What was it like to lose him? It was a gentle blindness. An almost imperceptible deafness. To lay in the grave and lose, shovelful by slow shovelful, what made the world worth knowing. I was only let out of my trunk when we boarded the train headed west. In the cramped luggage car Mutter slowly opened the lid. The weak light burned. I did not try to run. I did not raise my head. Mutter had to lift me out like a scolded dog.

"Maddy?" the giant asked cautiously.

"Yes, Mutter. Maddy. Just Maddy." And with my weakened hand I slapped him hard across the face. He only blinked. Then smiled. "Why did you do it?" I screamed. He put me gently to my feet. "Why?" I hollered at his lumbering back. He didn't turn around.

Mutter loved Maddy. Mutter make Maddy well. But Maddy was not well. She was sick. Sick from the absence of Volker. Sick from the need of him. Sick to the core of her cold and stilled heart that without him the realization of all her dreams, all her grand cinematic desires would be dulled and desultory, worthless as water upon rock. Mutter's regret was in his silence, in my staring hollowness that could not offer him even a weak smile in gratitude. It took days on that westbound train for the ambition that had sparked back in Germany to quicken into something I could finally, cautiously, recognize as my own. All my own. And when it did, when it finally dawned it was a shallow thing. A shallow and hungry thing.

There was nothing to do but stare out the window. I lay tucked in my seat, lulled into some false reverie by the bland blur that raced past me. I was defeated by the emptiness of the country. I saw nothing but fields and telephone lines. A small shack in the distance. And mile after mile of vapid blue sky. Where was this nation of people? Chicago radiated its septic signature for twenty miles before we slowed at the station, but then it was just a uric choke of frightened cattle. Where were the gangsters? The molls and bootleggers? Did they spring from a carpet of cow shit like the miles of cornfields that surrounded the city? Where were the great cities and hamlets? Was America just an inflated rumor?

Changing trains in Chicago to the Santa Fe California Limited, I noticed a change in character among the passengers. The locals left and a new creature took their places. They were girls, mostly, all in line-dried cotton with cheap tint on their cheeks, clutching cardboard suitcases and creased copies of *Screenland* in their corn-shucker knuckles. They were the new breadwinners, whose fathers mourned combine-severed limbs or manure-hosted infections, sent out in droves to keep home fires from failing. And they were willing, willing to spill their youth and a little farm-tanned tit for a shot in the flickers. They were drawn to Hollywood like bacilli to putrefaction. And as the train drew farther west, they replicated just as virulently. Some fell into clutches of loose gossip, but for the most part they remained silent, eyeing one another like competing chemists guarding the formula to their unpatented charm. And I was one of them. Less than one of them for I possessed none of their leggy and matured arsenal. They all avoided me, as they would avoid anything small and dark and contagious. Mutter slept. His capacity for sleep was matched only by his capacity for food and without one he indulged in the other. But I did not sleep. I did not even close my eyes and pretend. The quiet shouting was too loud.

My fledgling ambition might find roost past the gates of Universal Pictures, for that was where I had decided to take my chances, but nature herself only wanted me buried. And toward that end she filled what functioned as my mind with the intoxicating honey of open spaces. During our crossing I had been safe, secure in my trust of the dark in the cramped but amniotic angles of Mutter's trunk. But once propped in my seat, gutted by the unspooling of the miles, ten thousand leagues of planted and abandoned dirt shouted love songs of the grave at me. There were great downy arms in those songs, a sharp ginger breath that siphoned out between the pebbles and the shale and whispered of hollows only my shape could fill, of a longing only my pale and tiny mass could quell. I do not know how the living desire. But these cold siren soughs from dirt that stuttered past my eyes were what could soothe most frightened midnights, were what filled me with a longing greater than any lover's absence, more tender than any mother's memory. And what of my mother? Had she heard of my leaving? Was she furious? Jealous? Proud? I would never know. I knew then the only thing that would keep me aboveground was the narrowness of my desire.

My only defense was living.

And for several jostled days, the skipping of steel wheels over the gaps in the rails a surrogate heartbeat, I was gently convinced that something vital stirred in me. The illusion only ended when the train was still. And with the stillness came a second death. Mutter slept fitfully as the train huffed at the platform. The air was heavy with orange blossoms, but what was that smeared over the distant shrubs and low hills? What was this nauseating operating-theater brightness scattered so absently in the atmosphere? Sunshine. I was used to it in seasoned decorum, veiled in the marine mist of the Danube, discreet behind branches, laced behind brick. But this display. This was obscene. I couldn't imagine any population of leaves, flowers or fronds, any ocean of steeping algae that could possibly require the blaring attention of so much rude and unforgiving light. Mutter opened his eyes.

"*Wo sind wir?*" he asked.

"In English," I said, tossing him the primer I had been studying. I peeked through the dirty window next to our seats and saw the hopefuls yawning on the platform in a spill of hard sunshine. They stretched and righted the seams behind their knees, shook their heads like new-broke colts in the fragrant air. I slumped back into the vague curve of my seat and squinted. I would have given both my aborted tits for even a thimbleful of respectable fog.

"Are we here?" Mutter asked in his heavily accented English.

"We couldn't be anywhere else, my dear," I whispered back.

Taxis were waiting and the girls piled into these, no longer strangers to one another. Or slid into the beds of beaten pickups owned by aunts and uncles as shabby as the folks they had left half a country behind. There was a flurry of greeting and hefting and leaving. But of course there was no one waiting to meet us.

CHAPTER 21

Universal Pictures was a smallish spread of white stucco buildings, vaguely crenellated, a lower set of gigantic dentures left in a pasture. If I had known anything about fake Spanish architecture, I would have recognized it as such. Later I would compare it in my mind to the taco stand/carwash soon to be erected on a corner of La Brea and Sunset. But then I merely gawked at the folly of leaving such massive dentition among the cow shit and creosote.

I don't remember a sign of any kind. The only way I was sure it was the studio was by the fleet of Duesenbergs and Durant Stars parked on the circular gravel driveway. We crunched up to the front entrance. And holding open the screen door, Mutter let me inside.

It was dark. On benches of tiger oak sat roughly thirty girls, all wearing an equal number of conflicting scents that fought for atmospheric supremacy like caged cocks in some miasmal ring. There was talc and tuberose and honeysuckle, starched linen, lye and lavender. Not to mention the soft marine stink of lip rouge from sixty heavily lacquered lips. There was little conversation. A polite compliment upon a particularly unspectacular pair of pumps or a question about how one had achieved such shine over her finger waves. But for the most part they were silent, shifting only in careful jerks like wagons loaded with nitro.

Girls went in. Girls came out.

There was no place for us to sit, so Mutter stood and I crouched in the corner. After a few moments a sour-looking secretary slunk out of some inner office, a clipboard pressed to her chest, and asked our names. I mentioned we were there to see the boss.

"Mr. Laemmle?" she asked. But I would have been just as effective in my answer if had I suddenly launched into "Deutschland über Alles." She jotted something down on her clipboard and motioned us back to our places on the floor.

I don't remember losing consciousness, that room-heated slipping down that passed for sleep in me during extreme moments of boredom. Mutter was slumped to his side, breathing in great even waves. Slack in his thick fingers was a half-eaten chocolate bar, the remains of a cartoon rabbit staring up from the mangled wrapper. I had no idea where he had gotten it. The afternoon had grown long. The girls were gone. There was only one other change in our surroundings. On the main office door was a sign: *Will resume at 9:00 tomorrow. Good luck!* We had missed it. Slept through our one chance to be seen, possibly heard. I stood up and crossed to the sign. I fingered through my primer, to the translating dictionary. Perhaps the word *resume* did not have as final a connotation as I had thought. I noticed the door was open. At the receptionist's desk, a nail file lay by the cradled telephone, the seat empty but still warm with the suggestion of rose water. I peeked through the main door and noticed another door marked *Private*. That's where he was. Whomever he was. The granter of wishes. The dasher of hopes. The door was closed but through it I could hear noise, a shifting of linen, the soft complaints of bodies in sleep. The halls were just beginning to fill with the smell of late-afternoon coffee. I put my hand to the private knob. And looked back at Mutter. He nodded his head. What the hell . . . we'd come this far. Let's see if my ambition had grown legs. And perhaps something between them. My eyes cooled to grim as I pushed the door open.

A man and a girl.

On her knees she was my height, and as her face turned toward me I could see crumb-colored ingots of sleep still in the ducts of her eyes. The man leaped back as if stung from the girl's now-shut mouth and screamed something, his face flushing. But all I could see was the look on the girl's face. She was my age, at least in actual years, and in that brief moment of recognition I wanted to hold her, welcome her as a kind of cousin by telling her that I too had paid for my tutoring with a similar coin. But all she saw was a bleak child. A ghost of a left sister or distant niece whose standing and seeing could mean only the worst about her. She had settled for the lies of the last chances and never again could her act be a gift to some far-off husband, never could it shoulder surprise or inspire love. She had given it away for noth-ing. And probably without lunch. She must either now totally succeed and file this act as dues or be dashed into an oblivion of drink or drugs or homecoming.

Lifetimes from now, such an act would be inconsequential. By the end of business she would have a deal and be well on her way to her own fragrance line. But we still believed we were decent in those years after the first Great War. We still needed to believe our atrocities were self-defense, not self-serving, and so her act was monstrous.

Her arms rounded in the air, a shoulder arcing to accommodate her dress strap. The flat pink of her breast was packed into her best calico. She stood then and head down, so far down, she scurried from the room.

"Just what the fuck do you two think you're doing bargin' in here?" the man bellowed. I noticed then Mutter had sneaked up behind me. Mutter tensed.

"Pull up your pants," I said evenly, placing a calming hand on the giant. Where I got the balls to say that to a man in his position, I'll never know. I must have heard my mother say it.

The man looked down and I realized then how young he was. Younger even than Mutter. His fingers dribbled over the buttons of his pants and he raked his fingers through his hair and fluffed the lapel of his suit coat.

"I'm givin' ya two minutes to make your play," he said, trying to pump the authority back into his voice. "Just to show you the kind of guy I am."

"You will give me all the time I require, Mr. Laemmle," I said quietly. I didn't wait for him to ask me to sit. Confidence gripped me like a sudden seizure. Mother would have been proud. "My name is Maddy Ulm. And this is my associate, Mutter." *Associate?* I was spit balling like crazy. But somehow I knew the only way to keep the man's attention was to act like I belonged there. "We have recently come from Germany, UFA, where our picture, known to you, I believe, under the name of *The Toymaker*, was recently acquired by your company for foreign distribution."

"The what?" he asked, reaching for a cigar.

"*The Toymaker*," I repeated, my confidence beginning to show its seams.

"Wait," he said, lighting his Upmann. "You don't mean *Der Spielzeugmacher*?" His accent was impeccable. Why wouldn't it be? His father, who owned the company, was from the same part of the country as we were.

"Precisely."

"Well, *guten Tag, Schatzi*!" he said, puffing through his smile. "Hell yes. Terrific picture. You were the little girl, right? Jesus. We've got it out in limited release, but with any luck we'll be hitting the majors. Why didn't you write you were coming?"

"I didn't realize it was necessary." Was this really happening? Was Volker right after all?

"Terrific. I'll tell the kids over in juvenile to start a buildup. Maddy Ulm, is it?"

"Yes, sir," I said, smiling at Mutter. "But, please, what precisely is this *buildup*?"

"Just for publicity. Get you on the roster."

"*Roster*, please?"

"Christ, you're green as grass, aren't you? That's no dig. It's refreshing. Half these mice come in here and try to tell me my own business."

"This is an *acting* roster, then? For to act?"

"What else?"

If I'd had a beating heart it would have been racing. Sinking.

"I fear a mistake has happened," I said.

"What?" His eyes cooled reptilian. "What'd you mean? That wasn't you?"

"It was, but my interest is not in acting. I wish to *direkten Filme*."

"*Direct* pictures? Jesus Christ. *Already*? What is *with* you kids? You think we hand out megaphones with the free coffee?"

"But I *have* directed, Mr. Laemmle. Two pictures in Germany."

"Two? *What* two?" he snapped, puffing.

"The one you have seen and—"

"Hold on. I don't remember seeing *your* name above the title, sister."

"True, but I was the one who—"

"Okay. Show's over, all right?" He put his cigar in its tray and sat down at his desk, moving papers around his desk with empty authority. "I don't know how they do things in ol' Deutschland but here in the good ol' USA we don't toss the helm of five-figure pictures to scabby-kneed little girls." Knees must have been much on his mind. He stopped moving his papers and looked up. "Look. I'm sorry. That wasn't . . ." I couldn't help but shiver in front of him. We had seen the rawness and the worst of him. The impression he had made upon us had escaped his control and he could have none of that. He bent over his desk and scratched something on a sheet of company paper and handed it to me.

"You can use this in the commissary," he said. "Get a hot meal. Put some roses back in those cheeks, huh? No hard feelings? Think about what I said, about acting. Nobody wants to *direct*. Who wants to work that hard?"

My God, how Hollywood fears burning a bridge, even where one does not yet exist.

"Try the roast beef," he shouted to our backs. "It's fresh every day."

So I had failed. Perhaps he was right. Perhaps my best course of action was to lather myself in cheap paint and ratchet my way through a series of discount emotions, just like my mother. The thought sickened me. But at least Mutter could eat. And what were my raging dreams compared to his empty stomach?

The studio streets were filled with sheiks and cowboys and the weird stagnant heat of the California sun. The sidewalks we

walked on were not real. The trees that lined them seemed preoc-
cupied. They held our attention but not our trust. Men in stained
coveralls with old-world mustaches pushed pieces of the sky on
silent rubber casters. Professional pratfallers with their barroom
noses and crippled gaits, ingenues under white powder and parasols. All moved with purpose, quick to ten thousand different
schedules, factory workers slipping from the cracks of time, un-
conscious of their tiny tributes to the impossible and the dead.
Here, despite appearances, everything had been birthed within
the decade, some things within that very day. And appearances
were all that mattered. I knew I might survive here.

CHAPTER 22

The commissary was not hard to find. Mutter smelled it before he saw it, loped like a barn-soured colt through the beef- and cabbage- and coffee-smelling doors. It reminded me of one Sunday's biergarten, when the Trout had been feeling prosperous, but the scale was off. There was simply too much of it. It yammered on, table after table, cup after cup, steaming carcass after steaming carcass like a fugue composed by an idiot. It had a large wooden bar that served beer and even hard liquor for the asking, and its rounded edge was banked two-deep by lipsticked men and women with faces that reminded me of sheets too often laundered. Fleets of waiters in ankle-length aprons served food on thick buffalo china with pale blue company globes crested on the rims. Roman centurions elbowed over the rainbows shimmering off the slabs of their roast beef, *Property of Universal costume* winking from the seams of their leather baldrics. It was a madhouse subsidized by the inmates. A stale and drunken house party that had severely outlived its weekend.

We were served coffee without asking. Then, moments later, two plates heaped with steaming food. Mutter didn't bother with the formality of asking for mine. I sipped from my cup only for comfort, feeling the warmth borrowed then dissipate as the liquid slowly trickled from the corners of my mouth. We were being watched.

He was average. Average of face, of build. He wore the clothes of any studio workman, a plaid shirt, cuffed to the elbows, a flat cap, laced boots. In his lap was a large white pad, and in his fingers he held a slender tube of charcoal, gingerly, as if it might burn. His strokes were fluid and precise, made without looking, much like my artist had done all those years ago. It was only when his hand stopped moving that he looked to his work. I assumed he worked in some designing capacity—sets, costumes—but he lacked the pronounced effete quality typical of those practitioners. He might have been a grip, simply easing half an hour before returning to the heat of the stage. But his gaze was not casual. It burrowed. Even when he stuffed a cigarette between his lips, his eyes never left us. When he caught my eye, his face was sullen, unapologetic. To sketch us was his right. He removed his cap, then placed it back on his slicked head. I nodded, thinking this was his crude greeting, but his eyes flashed impatience. He removed his hat again, holding it above his head impatiently. Then I understood. He was not drawing me. He was drawing Mutter, and he wanted Mutter to remove his cap. I shook my head slowly, careful not to further spark his intensity. He threw his pad and charcoal to his seat and arrived at our table in a few angry strides.

"Wasn't I clear?" he began. His voice was deeply etched from cartons of cigarettes and strong coffee. "The light is perfect and I'm due back in editing in ten minutes."

Mutter chewed in animal bliss, unaware of our interchange.

"My friend is very sensitive about his condition," I said quietly. "He never removes his cap to strangers."

"Isn't he afraid of appearing rude?"

"We can barely pay for this food, let alone worry about manners," I said. "Anyway, how do you know there is even anything of interest under there?" I pointed to Mutter's cap, which twitched with the motion of his jaws.

"Instinct," he said.

His face hardened under his silence and I noticed two deep cuts, wrinkles perhaps, that shot down the length of both cheeks, humorless creek beds that pulled at the corners of his mouth. It was a face made from heavy blows, a testament to rough weather.

"The war?" he finally said, his eyes narrowing at the promise under Mutter's cap. "I must see it."

"Never to strangers," I said with a slight nod of my head.

"Lon," he said, thrusting out a rough hand. "Now we're friends, right?"

"Lon?" I said looking at Mutter chewing. "Is that short for something? Should I know it?"

"Leonidas."

"I prefer that."

"Well, the brass prefers Lon, and I prefer working. Friends?"

I said nothing. Just mouthed another swallow of tepid tea and offered the cup's stolen warmth for him to shake.

"Listen," he said, flashing a rare but brilliant smile. "I don't expect him to parade around in here. Let me see if we can use Mary's dressing room."

I didn't know what this man with a laborer's face really wanted. I just knew he offered a change of scenery, a dark corner perhaps, away from all this loud flesh, and there was something clean and honed and earnest in his manner. I was beyond harm. Mutter could take care of himself.

I began with "*Liebling*," whispering to Mutter in German, explaining why we needed to follow this gentleman.

"English," Mutter said, wiping the grease off his second plate with a heel of bread.

"This man wants to draw you. Without the cap, Mutter. Do you understand?"

Mutter understood. He stuck out his tongue and made a farting sound with his warm mouth.

"Listen, buddy," Lon began. "You like chocolate?"

How he knew this to be Mutter's weakness was pure animal instinct.

Mutter nodded, and Lon said, "I have bricks of the stuff back at my place."

Mutter's eyes glazed.

"I just want to draw you. No one will see. You'll be safe with me. Okay?"

Mutter stood up without a single look back.

We stopped in front of what seemed to be a charming cottage made of pale blue clapboard with yellow flower boxes that rose up between two buildings of tan stucco. Posies unfurled in cherry red stasis in the fake loam of the boxes, the petals stiff as cow hooves. They were molded from sheets of colored Bakelite, scentless, impervious to weather, a thin layer of grime dulling their natural shine. He knocked on the Dutch door and entered without being prompted.

The inside was in marked formal contrast to the folksy exterior. It was the size of a bowling alley, complete with an attached powder room, bedroom, and a spacious sitting room whose walls were lined in quilted salmon-pink shantung. Regency sconces glowed mutely under weak filaments and curvaceous cabriole legs and Aubusson needlepoint writhed and sprawled on every surface. There was the smell of freshly washed children from a silver bowl of flowers on the mantel, and in the corner sat an old woman in Quaker black, her gray head tilted to a small jigsaw puzzle on her lap, a smote of coal in a smooth pink throat.

"You got that near done, Mother Philbin?" Lon asked the old woman, looking down at her half-finished puzzle. She smiled and pushed another fault line in place, nodding slowly in the private rhythm of her consent.

"This is Mary's mother," he said, still smiling at the old woman. "I didn't get your names."

"Maddy Ulm," I said. "And this is Mutter."

"That's simple enough. This is Maddy and Mutter, Mother."

The old woman lifted her head and bowed slightly at the neck. I curtsied back, Mutter blinked, and Lon smiled, pleased at the simple ceremony.

"What's wrong with her?" the old woman asked. "What's wrong with you, child?"

"Don't mind us, Mother," Lon demurred. I didn't know then Lon's own taste for the dusk, how surefooted he was among the rust and bone of the charnel house. I was just another shade of familiar gray locked in the grease sticks of his miraculous paint box. "I'm just going to be doing a little sketching and we'll get out of your hair."

There was a faint sound, a dry gasp as another piece of her puzzle slipped into place.

"I owe you some chocolate, don't I, buddy?" Lon strode to a pearwood taboret stacked with heart-shaped boxes. "What's your pleasure? Soft centers? Cherries? Nougat?"

He slid a box from the bottom of the pile. A note was attached to the red satin ribbon: *Dear Mary, Forever, Burt* in spidery script.

He guided Mutter to the seat of a wide fauteuil near the fake fireplace and placed the box in Mutter's anxious fingers. There was a tenderness, a reverence in Lon's gaze, as he watched the muscles jump in Mutter's temples as he chewed. It was a lover's touch that lifted the brim of Mutter's cap, a movement so fluid, so full of purpose, it barely stirred the silence.

"Jesus, Mary, and Joseph," he said in a gravelly whisper. "You glorious son of a bitch."

He was a connoisseur of the wrecked.

"Mortar shell?"

"Verdun," I said.

Lon's fingers tripped the condyles of Mutter's bolts with a soothing brush.

"He's a masterpiece. You have to get this on film."

"I have," I said.

He paused, his sketchpad almost quivering on his lap.

"You what?"

"That's why we are here."

"You made a picture?"

"*The Toymaker.* We make in Germany. They are distributing it, Universal."

"*Distributing*? You didn't come here to *act*?"

"I directed the picture, but I have the misfortune of not having my name on it."

"I know the feeling." He grinned, his face rippling into what seemed like thousands of dry furrows.

"I am serious," I said.

"*You* directed? How old are you?"

"How old?" I shrugged my shoulders. "Does this matter?"

"No. But if it's true, I'd bet you'd be a first."

"Then finally I am first at something." And I tried to smile. Which seemed to charm him. He put his hand on my knee.

"You're very unusual, kid. Keep that."

He gave us assurances. Told us our "situation" would be handled with the swift and ruthless rectification only fame could motivate. And all during these fatherly growls, he sketched and Mutter laid waste to two more boxes.

Upon saying good-bye, Lon handed us two cards, business-size, a publicity photo of himself rendered in line with the words *Don't Step on That Spider! It Might Be Lon Chaney!* in emergency red beneath it.

These were our studio passports, our all-access passes to every inch and offering at the studio's disposal, good for a cup of coffee, a three-course meal, or a rubdown at the administration building's exclusive Emperor's Club. So armed, we were set loose onto the backlot until that evening, when Chaney promised to meet us for dinner. I have since seen such little slices of ephemera sell at auction for a yearly wage. But then, on that dry and overbright day, their value was more immediate, as they were the only pieces of paper in our possession that the studio might consistently honor.

CHAPTER 23

The backlot was a haiku of half sentences, a communication of remembered time and borrowed place for supreme insiders who need not bother with completing a thought. Scene painters sneaked nips of gin in the shade of a massive drawbridge that floated unmoored in the dust. A whole street of plaster and timber facades ran like a madman's rhyme to nowhere, twisting into hapless alleys and dead thoroughfares, great vaguely European husks of dream villages empty as walnut shells. And next to this a wattle and daub reconstruction of my own village, complete with plywood pillory and whipping post. A castle in one-eighth scale compressed the distance as it sat on the valley end of the Santa Monica Mountains. And below this, in actual size but severed like a shark-attack victim at the waist, were the massive arches of Notre Dame's cathedral. The detail was impeccable, the saints' faces only just beginning to flake in the dry wind. It was up these steps that Chaney had played his gruesome hunchback and herded in the age of the blockbuster. We had hours yet to burn before dinner, and Mutter seemed tired, crashing finally from his massive influx of white sugar, and so we sat on the cathedral steps and stared out onto the amputated streets linked by light cables that snaked blackly in the dirt, waiting for that night's shoot. There was something brutal in all this excess, something that demanded reckoning from its size and breadth alone. It was America, I suppose. Before I even knew what that meant.

When the miraculous becomes common, the common becomes untenable.

We watched the sunset through the false fronts of Dodge City and ambled back to the main lot. At the commissary, we flashed our cards and were shown to a private dining room sectioned off with a heavy swath of medieval tapestry complete with heavy oak wainscoting and crossed broadswords over a false fireplace. There was the blue smell of ice and spilled booze in the air, far laughter and disembodied moans, the desert-fire scent of marijuana, roast meat, and gratin cheese, anonymous bodies. We were brought two miniature tureens of turtle soup. Mutter was served a tankard of dark beer. Chaney showed up for the meat course, a slab of bloody beef loin and two crisp squabs, their startled heads still attached. Chaney spoke as he cut and chewed the steak.

"That was one helluva picture you got there, kid. You're a more than fair actress."

"Thank you," I said stiffly. "It was necessary with our budget."

"You could write your own ticket with this waif act you got going. What is your problem anyway? Weak glands?"

"I do not wish to act, Mr. Chaney."

"My kid, Creighton, says he's got the bug but he simply doesn't have the paste. But you could really be something. Pickford won't live forever, you know."

Yes, but I suspected I would. And I could hardly see mincing around in front of a hand-cranked box, forcing my way through numerical emotions, as a fitting tribute to eternity.

"I do not wish to act," I said again.

"That's right. So you told me," he said, staring at me, chewing distractedly. "Very effective picture. I wasn't quite sure how you achieved that effect of such claustrophobic dread." He continued to stare at me. "Quite a trick." Was he testing my authorship?

"That was achieved with single-frame intercuts, roughly twenty to the foot, I believe." Volker had insisted I shoot a whole B-roll of extreme close-ups. Rats, wide staring eyes, mouths stretched in silent screams. The idea was to slip something past the audience's attention, without their consent. To give them the feeling of being "voluptuously invaded," as he called it.

"Those images fly by so fast you can't actually—"

"*See* them. Yes, Mr. Chaney," I said. "I know they are there only because *I* put them there. Are you now satisfied? Or would you like to know what stock I shot on and at what speed?"

He said nothing for a moment. Just grinned his warm and decaying grin.

"Where did you learn to do that?" he said, still smiling. He seemed to enjoy being impressed.

"My father," I said with a touch of fear and even less longing.

"He still in the business?"

"We've lost touch."

"You say you *cut* your picture?"

"I never said it. But it could be reasonably implied. Yes. Took goddamned days to assemble ten seconds of film."

"How do you feel about working up?"

"You mean like Lubitsch? Like Lang?" I said sarcastically.

"Those boys got directing credit, kid."

I was silent. My soup had cooled to a green muck.

"I know Lois needs an assistant," he said finally. "That is if you could stomach this mug for the next couple of months."

"And what would I be doing? Soaking rushes and binning footage? I've made two films, Mr. Chaney. *Two*."

"Let me make this easy on you. Germany doesn't count, kid. America's the only market that counts. You don't see Clarence Brown or Billy Wellman bucking for work in Berlin. But you're in good company. The promise of this country is that you can always start over. Every day, if you have to. In fact, this country loves nothing more than a comeback. The underdog, the shill, some poor dope bleeding on the ropes—Americans eat that stuff up. You go one round and win, headline. But you have your ass handed to you ten times before finally wearing the belt, they'll love you till the trumpet sounds."

"And if I don't wish to be loved?"

"If you don't wish to be loved you're in the wrong business, sister. That or your name is Joe von Sternberg."

CHAPTER 24

I met Lois well past her apogee, past her tenure as Universal's highest-paid director, past her second marriage and her mental collapse, past her moment of ultimate martyrdom when she appeared flayed as a flapper Christ before Uncle Carl begging for any substantial scrap. I met her there on the bench, over the rolls and rolls of someone else's shots, someone else's visions, hoisting the blade, making the slice in time, stopping the moment, freeing the next, cleaning up messes. She was bloated from antidepressants, her fingers yellow from nicotine. Her hair, infused with an unruly gray, resisted the ministrations of pins or nets or spit. In the dark, as we cut, she bit the bodies of her Pep O Mint Life Savers so hard they threw sparks from her open lips. It was clear to me from the first day that she resented my presence. In the near dark, I didn't bother pretending to breathe. And this, with my natural furniture stillness, let her tolerate me, let her believe she was still alone.

Lois worked with the editor's door wide-open. She hated the

smell of developer, the gamy stink of the rabbit-skin glue. She associated these smells with labor. And she missed having power. She knew what power smelled like: fresh leather upholstery, a hand-rolled Upmann, fresh ink. So she made me do the wet work, and she never once wondered why my bare fingers never blackened in the nitrate baths.

"This is Sisyphisian," she would slur some days. "Sisyphisic. Sissy-shit." She pulled openly from a gin bottle during lunch breaks, swallowing hard in response to my offer of my useless sandwich. "You know why this horror crap will never catch on?" she might say. "It's the waiting. You have to wait too damn long for something to happen. The whole engine of the thing is designed to produce a thrill. But if you stack the thrills too closely you desensitize the viewer. So you're left with your thumb up your ass for a reel and a half until something pops out at you. You don't understand a thing I'm saying. You're too young. But this horror crap is just math. Just humorless algorithms."

I resented her slurred dismissals. There were no equations that could sum up dread, no quotient that consistently equaled fear. The heart of horror is loss, the languid asphyxiation of hope. Not bug-eyed men in bald caps. And Lois knew loss like the smell of her stale sheets. But she was active when her pictures still said something, still had social relevancy. Women in the workplace. Female ambition. Abortion. These were her themes. She just couldn't shrink herself to fit on the trolley through the dark ride.

"Look at her. Looks like she just got goosed on a bad date," she would ramble on. "I mean, Jesus. How hard up was poor Mary to agree to this shit? Now you got falling chandeliers and ol' Lonny boy looking like my last husband's hard-on in a string tie. You have that binned by the way? See what you can do with this shit. I'm goin' to Little Persia."

Little Persia was the back room where a few old rugs had been stacked. She created a kind of burrow back there and each day, usually an hour after our day had started, she would retreat there. Sometimes I would hear her laughing quietly beneath a tannic stink or hear the slosh of a bottle. What was she doing? Smoking opium? Drinking wood polish? I hadn't the faintest idea. But when her absence began to coalesce into half a day, I took her at her word and began to monkey with the footage.

Volker.

Anticipation, the flesh on sharp and frozen hooks. Then a chill. This would be the time he would make his entrance, when he would assume the strings and fill me with such capable dread. But nothing came. No voluptuous panic, no violating whisper as my joints engaged his will. Nothing. I was merely one. The distance over water had stilled him. Completely. And I mourned him. I mourned his fullness and the dank coil of his confidence. I missed the first tremors of despair as the rot of his mouth filled the cavity of mine, as his stiffness filed backward and darkly through the bones of my lap. I missed these sensations because of the promise that had always followed. The insight. The *talent.* And so I thought perhaps the promise might flower if the sensations could be replicated. This is why I reached for the pencil, rejected it as too gentle for the task. The knife. The dull one we used to scrape the glue residue. It had heft and girth, but most important, it harbored the cold. And the cold was necessary. I slipped it under my skirt and stabbed. The pale girth of my thigh gave with a dull rasp. I struck my belly, my hip, the cold sealed lips of my sex. Nothing. The ceremony sent no signals across the sea, revealed nothing more than cadence. Cadence. Stab. Progression. Stab. The crude accumulated code of invasion.

How did it go?

It was trust. As when eyes might meet and something kindred might become stone and fall and ripple there. Then tingle. As the ripples enter beneath the flesh with no less resonance, no less delight. Then fear. As the ripples, now inside, loose promise, loose consent, but not their terrible motion. A fugue of violation. Congealed pieces of me fell in dry gobbets to the floor. Trust. Then tingle. Then fear. *Violation.*

Trust. You see the Phantom in his mask, his horror hidden from view. He takes a genuine if violently strident interest in Christine's talent. He promises death if his demands are not met. The opera brass scoffs. Death comes.

Tingle. The Phantom comes for Christine, takes her to his lair, his bed, his organ (which organ?). He plays for her. She is enchanted, enthralled, aroused.

Fear. Her fear that he might not be a lover, a husband, a human under that mask. She gauges; she gathers; she slinks; she reaches. She must know his true face, the face of her angel and she . . . yes, *she* rapes *him.* She *violates*; she bares; she flays; she humiliates by removing his mask. Christ, where is that close-up? Cut to the goddamn close-up of Chaney's face behind that organ—that poor, stripped, humiliated face.

Surprise? Sure, *horror* even, but the Phantom is not the aggressor, not this time. She is, and we feel for *him.* The freak. The fiend. We pity him. We fear and covet him in one gesture, one shameful selfish gesture. Her gesture. His defeat.

The rest is the denouement of coitus interruptus. Soul mates shunted by rural audience expectations and bad teeth. The picture will have only one real scare, but Pasadena housewives will wonder at the moisture at the crux of their girdles when the house lights come up.

"What the hell is going on in here?" Lois stood there, the tips of her bob frayed and wet from the drool of her narcotic dreams. She must have been summoned by the dry sounds of my hacking knife. I see real wonder skitter across the blurred surfaces of her eyes as she watches the divots in my inner thighs fill like the throats of croaking toads. She sees the dull knife still with its dusting of pink, still in my hand. She smiles.

"I knew this place was a kind of purgatory," she slurred, "but I'll tell you this, girl. I've never seen *that* particular brand of penance before. You get the cut? No pun intended, sister."

"Yes, Ms. Weber," I said, still pinned by the shock of my exposure.

"Good. Give the footage a cure. And be sure to rinse that knife."

CHAPTER 25

But even before I met Lois, I had left Mutter our very first day, with the simple assignment of finding a place to live. The task was far less daunting than it sounds. Uncle Carl's plan for a studio was to create a kind of jovial labor camp where employees could live, eat, play, and work all within the confines of the studio's several sprawling acres. There were barracks with washrooms, a bunkhouse attached to a working ranch that, when not used for exteriors, produced a fair share of beef, milk, and eggs. Hammocks for the gaffers were strung treetop-high in the fly system of the stages. Portable trailers came furnished with four-poster beds. Pup tents and campsites proliferated, not to mention several other options. Mutter had only to flash his man-of-a-thousand-faces passport to attain access to any of these. So I straightened his cap and reminded him where the commissary was and didn't bother to watch which direction lured his attention.

He was without his cap, a thin line of red ochre drawn at the intersection where metal meets flesh, his row of bolts equally embellished. He took my small hand, happy in his role as guide. And aren't we grand, the two of us, leaving "work," strolling on the evening "streets," walking "home." What had he chosen for a nest? Cots behind the castle battlements? A hayloft in the boom-town barn?

"You seem rather pleased with yourself," I couldn't help saying, noticing Mutter's crooked grin.

"Yes," he said.

"What's all that on your head?"

"Paint."

"Yes, paint. But what for?"

"Tonight."

"What happens tonight?"

"We come home."

He led me through those self-consciously tortured streets to near the shins of the Santa Monica Mountains, at the most out-ward stretch of the backlot. I smelled this "home" before I saw it. Thin tendrils of blue smoke broke the low rise of a hill and there was the village. An Indian village. Black-haired children with seal-pup eyes, bodies as brown as lacquered furniture, ran naked behind spinning hoops, then stopped when Mutter appeared, ig-noring their toys and running to him, little legs churning under their fat little bellies. The women dropped their cooking. The men stilled their horses and all moved toward us in a fragrant, heavy wave of welcome. It was a salad of nations. Navajo sheep-herders, Comanche horse ranchers, Sioux and Cheyenne who had spent years barely breathing in tar paper shacks on agency land remembering nothing but where they'd stashed the bottle. They had all come here Anglicized, hair shorn over the ears like white men, shod in hard-soled shoes, choking down Jesus with dairy products and soap. But here they had to assume historical precedent, had to morph into the public's romantic image of them, so they grew their hair long. Worked shirtless until they were as dark as the anthropological record. Learned the language and crafts that had been beaten out of their parents at reservation schools. They became "Indian."

Mutter held a child in his arms while two other children, older, naked from the waist up, hung on him in a human cape. His smile never left as he moved into the crowd that slowly began to resume work with glittering eyes still on his return. How had this happened? How could they so welcome a stranger? How had these people compressed a lifetime of the familiar into a few hours? The crowd parted slightly, and at the apex of the thronging bodies an old woman stood with a squat young woman. The old woman was no taller than me, and two cigarettes were stuck in her shriveled face, each burning at different lengths, insurance against her hoop of smoke never being broken. She nodded and the young one, blushing when she peered at Mutter, handed us tin bowls of a rich, gamy broth. I saw pieces of spicy bark and aromatic leaves floating in the steam, and in the bottom of my bowl, proudly submerged, was a paw, the skinned knuckles glistening bluish in the greasy liquid. Dog soup. The traditional celebratory meal, as common to them as birthday cake. Mutter raised his bowl to his lips with one hand, drained it in a single swallow, and handed the baby back to the younger woman, who placed a caramel pudding–colored breast in its mouth and took Mutter's hand. I watched them merge into the teeming activity, watched his massive form become integrated, quelled by the daily life of the studio Indians whose job it was to threaten with rubber tomahawks and fall from slugless bullets. How had it happened?

That night, they lit a bonfire in the body of a rusted-out Model A and beat drums stolen from the studio's prop house.

Men leaped around the curling flames, shaking the tips of their J-toed cowboy boots in the dust, some in dungarees, others still in the hair pipe and buckskin of the day's wardrobe. Mutter, shirtless, his slabs of muscle rippling like water under a strong wind, howled phonetically the chant the other men knew by heart. The young woman stood with several others, the black pits of her baby's eyes kicking hard yellow in the firelight. She grinned and whispered to her friends, her lips and eyes curling in union each time they took in a cycle of Mutter's passing.

"He will make some girl very happy," the old woman whispered to me as she sat down. She offered me a cigarette, which I took but did not light. I watched as she crumbled a cigarette in her rooty fingers, sprinkling the loose tobacco upon the ground before she stuffed two more in her mouth.

I watched her shuffle through the flap of a teepee and then turned back to the dancers. I was passed a bottle of solvent-smelling fluid. I passed it on to another watcher who drank deeply from it. There was heat from the fire if I cared to feel it, heat from the bodies around me if I cared to join them, but I felt neither heat nor cold. They were objects that reflected light, moist tubes that made sounds, faces that pulled and dipped and wrinkled into the semblances of feeling. They were like all the others, the stuff of stories, marionettes of meat and tears whose lives only mattered to me if captured on film. This made me a purist and all purists are alone.

But Mutter was different. My feelings for him were different. It cut to watch him happy without me. Yet this made no sense. With what was I feeling? He was a habit, a condition occasioned by his proximity that brought an illusion of continuity, of comfort. But I loved him. Against reason, against the tangled retrograde of my state, I loved him. I was not jealous of his new friend.

That was something I could provide no one and thus could not begrudge him. He was nature to me, my last piece of home, and I realized I could not remain but neither could I simply leave.

"Maddy," he said behind me. He sat down sweaty, his great chest heaving. Had he heard my thoughts? "Maddy," he said again. "Friend." And he thrust forward a puppy, mottled brown and white, still smelling of bitch's milk.

"I hope you don't expect me to eat that," I said.

He grinned. "Friend. For you."

I took the creature, feeling it quiver coldly in my arms.

"What about you?" I asked, looking up at him.

"Always friend," he said. He did not sense my conflict. The puppy was a party favor, not a proxy.

"I cannot stay, Mutter."

"But this is where we stay. This is home now."

"Not for me."

"But why?" His voice cracked and a thick finger brushed his nose.

"No pillows," I said, smiling, and he read my real reasoning there, I think. I handed him back the puppy.

CHAPTER 26

Weeks passed, and each time I met Mutter for coffee or lunch, he was tanner, healthier, somehow more handsome, even though he had fallen out of the habit of wearing his cap. His speech improved. He was filled with stories of camp life, of rivalries and reunions, of births and injuries sustained in the dangerous stunts that comprised most of the Indians' work. He mentioned names as if I were acquainted with their owners, as if I knew John Little Foot, who had crushed the head of his humerus leaping from his horse onto a runaway stagecoach. Or Mary Iron Feather, who had just given birth to triplets.

The father of Mutter's girlfriend's baby returned to camp after being on extended loan to First National Pictures. His name was Benjamin Pope but he was known as Big Ben due to his extreme size. He was one of the few Indians who had broken the traditional mold of generic savage and was routinely cast as an Italian gangster. He had worked as a two-bit fighter at local fairs throughout the West and had a single cauliflower ear and busted nose to prove it. His rage at being replaced in camp, not to mention in the bed of the mother of his child, cleared a circle around the two rivals within minutes of his arrival. They would vie for Jane's favor, for Jane was the only name Mutter ever called her, and the winner would take all.

There was a carnival atmosphere to the competition, whose only event was the bending of metal wheel rims pried loosed from the spokes of an old wagon. Ben, with biceps writhing like pythons, twisted his into a cold pretzel. But Mutter, taking his cue from the romantic theme of the prize, cajoled his into the shape of a heart and thereby won the day. The two had since become as close as brothers, Ben teaching Mutter to ride and Mutter showing Ben how to shoot. Ben even said he would put a good word in for Mutter to Uncle Carl, as the studio was always in need of big fellows who didn't mind wearing a little rouge when taking a hard hit to the jaw for a dollar a day.

And where did I spend my nights and early mornings when not cutting with Lois? I realized after the camp dance with Mutter that my chosen refuge needed to be near the business, inside the business. The only night skies I cared to sleep under were studded with twelve-watt bulbs. My sunsets glowed from forty-foot cycloramas flamed to life by carbon arcs. There needed to be no locks on my interior doors, no secrets behind them. Candy glass could never cut me when it shattered in my windows. There were many stages to choose from, but most had muslin skins for ceilings to allow for shooting in natural light. Only a handful were "blackout" boxes, and the one I chose, the one known, before they tore it down in 2014, as Stage 28, I chose for personal reasons. Lon had told me at our first dinner that on this stage was built the opera house set for *Phantom*. It had once accommodated the grand staircase but after shooting only the stage and theater boxes remained, soon to be repurposed as opera houses from all over the world. It smelled like a swamp in there, for half the stage had been flooded during shooting to create the Phantom's subterranean sewer. It had never been thoroughly drained and had doubled as a toilet for a weary crew not allowed to leave the set. The uric reek and ashy stink of drowned cigarettes still lingered. At first, the smell had whispered lovingly of ancient burials in peat bogs, of sleeping mummies, necks broken or neatly slit, tanned tea-colored beneath their boggy quilts, and perhaps my Celtic roots tempted me to forever brine myself in what remained of the foul slosh. But that horsehair-and-plaster facade of the theater boxes provided a safe, reliable pocket that might keep me just out of nature's reach. It was the opera house set that kept me close to Lon, or at least his belief in me.

Even with no key lights to make it sparkle, I was enamored of its gold leaf, its incredible attention to detail, its breathless, graceful enormity. It had been made by Italian master craftsmen who had constructed a working replica of Venice for the 1915 World's Fair in San Francisco, slow artisans who spoke no English and moved in the refined cadence of craft only they could hear. Uncle Carl had paid them each a dollar twenty-five a day plus board and promptly fired them once the set was completed. As testament to his managerial methods, one could still see on the camera-shy surfaces loud protests of profanity, all in Italian, labeling "Uncle" Carl Laemmle as a fucker of pigs, of crippled cows, of cross-eyed whores, of his own cursed and booted mother.

I spent my evenings in one of the theater boxes. Box five. The Phantom's box. I would lie on my back in a nest of rat droppings and racing forms, gazing lovingly at the dark rippled irises of the hung lights as if they formed the figure of Orion. It was quiet in there, cool and hollow and huge, but it gave me the feeling of being tucked in a papier-mâché womb. It was abandoned most of the time. But once in a while a producer or scout might wander in and knock on my delicately molded boxes or stroll my collapsed stage wondering aloud, "You think this joint could double for the Albert Hall?" I was proprietary of the building. It was my home after all. And on those occasions, when I heard a foreign footfall, tentative upon the damp silence, voices lowered as upon entering some ghostly church, I could not resist a moan. I'd wait until they were beneath me, then will my dry lungs to fill. With slow pressure, trying not a grin, I'd let out through my parched throat a long and sinuous death rattle. It filled the enormous space with an almost ecclesiastical dread.

"Jesus, you hear that?"

"Cheese it, brother!"

My ridiculous wail was not diminished by my hollow laugh as I heard those shoes recede at speed. I guess that's how the legends started. It got to the point where all I'd have to do was tap on the walls or let a yellowed Santa Anita racing form flutter to the ground like a grim autumn leaf in the spectral half-light. One night it rained. And a couple came in. Young dress extras from some eighteenth-century melodrama. She righted her pow-dered wig from their run. He pulled his brocaded pantaloons from his crotch. They were wet but not soaked. He pulled her to him. She playfully slapped his face. I don't know why they in-terested me. Maybe because there was no coin in their affection, no real barter in her flirtatious slap. But that wasn't it. It was them. Their youth, cold and wet and still burning. The math was simple. Without even having to count I knew they were my age, if I had been allowed to age. All those years offering up myself in payment to Volker's insight had not put me off wanting to be touched. To be looked at like that. I longed to be one of them. I hated them. And I peered over the edge of my box and watched them wrestling there on the damp concrete. The cheap satin of their costumes rasped loudly where they made contact, filling the stage with the loud and ironic sound of silencing ghosts. I filled my lungs and let out a slow rattle, my moan staying just inside the sonic signature of their grappling bodies.

"Did you hear something?"

"Come on, help me with this damn thing."

"Henry, Jesus! *Stop* it! Did you *hear* that?"

The silence rang, stoked only slightly by the sound of their increased breathing.

"Nothing." His hands dipped beneath the heavy drape of her skirt.

"*Henry!* Stop it!" she said sharply, and I could not resist.

"*Yeeessss, Henry,*" I wailed dryly. And I jumped up on the rim of my box and screamed, screamed with all my frustration and fury. "*Keep your goddamned mitts to yourself, buddy!*" The sound I made would all but rival a neglected gate hinge, and with balls of rat turd clinging to my face like some medieval pestilence and my hair plastered to the extreme bias of what passed for my sleep I must have looked like some narcoleptic brat suddenly awoken from a nap in her breakfast cereal. They stiffened instantly. He ran before she did. But there was no comedy. Only a residue of longing. There had to be more to my existence than the tedious hopscotch of studio politics and balled ambition. For many nights after that I would lie in my box and try to picture a face, a young man's eyes, stolen from some slouching grip, a pair of hands from a junior gaffer. And I'd fumble in the rubbery and confused darkness beneath my skirt but nothing stirred. Without

reference to the actual sensation there was no icy fire. The closest
I got was remembering the tang of a lemon ice with the artist's
wife a lifetime ago in Vienna. But a child's confection was not
what I wanted.

AFTER THREE MONTHS OF MUTTER LIVING LIKE A GENUINE RED INDIAN AT
his camp and me terrifying the occasional trespasser from my
box, the cut of *Phantom* was finally locked and we had our first
screening with the changes I had made. I didn't even bother in-
forming Lois of my final cuts. I simply drowned out yet another
of her meandering sermons on the necessity of the non-narrative
montage in conveying the spiritual aspects of cinema while I
waited for the seams to dry.

Chaney by that time was at war and smart enough to know
it. He knew Uncle Carl was bound to reject any cut merely to
prolong the star's tenure at the studio, thereby preventing his
return to Metro in the hopes that he'd default back to Universal.
So Chaney needed a hit, a big, fat-titted hit that would unequivocally close his Universal chapter. To do this he needed consensus; he needed an audience. So he took a risk, an enormous risk
in hindsight.

"You knock this out of the park, you'll never look for work
again," he said to me in the lobby of Grauman's Egyptian, where
he had rented the entire theater for the preview.

"Mr. Chaney, I had no idea an audience would be seeing this
now." If I'd had a heartbeat, it would have been thundering like
a hummingbird's.

"Of course not. If you knew that, you would have tried to
only *please*. You wouldn't have done your best work."

"But I can't guarantee—"

"Who can, kid? We'll know in the first reel, right? This town wouldn't be any fun if *all* the dice were loaded."

We took seats in the back row. We could see just the tip of Uncle Carl's thinning pate several rows ahead of us as we waited for the lights to dim. Classical Bach on a roller rink Wurltizer, the picture seemed to be playing well. Not much shifting. A few coughs, but the heads were quiet in silhouette, attention rapt. Then it came. Christine couldn't take any more guessing. She sneaked up behind the Phantom, the anticipation palpable. The theater seats creaked like wooden ships in roughening water. Then she did it. She ripped the mask away.

Chaos.

Laemmle's wife screamed. Another fainted. Two grown men leaped on the seats of their chairs. The rest of the movie played like the Sea Serpent at Pacific Ocean Park. It didn't let up until the final scene, where there was a collective sigh of released tension. Lights up, then silence. No one said a word. Slowly, people rose from their seats. Laemmle's wife, head down, was the first to leave the theater, followed by patrons wiping their brows, wringing their dresses, murmuring. And beneath it all, Chaney grinned like a working-class cat with a golden canary. He finally turned to me.

"Kid, you just bought yourself an official straitjacket in the looney bin," he said, and I beamed. At the time, exchanging my white coat for such a restrictive garment seemed a definite upgrade.

The theater emptied of all but Uncle Carl. He stopped by Chaney. I'd slunk into the confines of my chair, invisible.

"Quite a picture, Lon," Uncle Carl said in his comic German accent.

"I'll say," Chaney replied, lighting his fiftieth cigarette of the day.

"However, there are a few things—"

"Bullshit, Carl."

Uncle Carl bristled. Few had this license.

"You heard 'em," Chaney continued. "I suppose that scream your wife let out was German for 'What a stinker'?"

"Now, Lon, I wouldn't say that. It's a perfectly *fine* effort . . ."

"It's a solid gold fly over the fence, and you know it. Now you're going to do what you do best. You're going to release this picture *as is*. Not a single change. Not one edit. And after you get the feeling back in your arms from raking in your killing, you're going to put this kid under contract."

Uncle Carl looked to me with a rubbery shock on his face.

"Don't worry, Uncle," Lon smirked. "You'll thank me."

We never discussed the picture again, never pondered its finer points, the cutting on the axis, the building of tension with increasingly closer coverage, the way I'd made the Phantom appear a complex, tragic, even *romantic* figure. It was all understood. Hollywood never discusses. It simply rewards.

CHAPTER 27

There is comfort in the places of rot, silence in decay, a soothing lull as wood returns to its softness in soil, metal dims its shine, and bodies disassemble back to the belly of the world. And it was here, in one such place, beneath the pilings of the Santa Monica Pier, well after midnight, where the mildew and brine purred like myrrh from the sodden piles, that I thought of love again. There was a contour in the damp sand, a cold shallow pit of compression where two bodies had lain, the imprint of an ample ass that feathered backward up the beach, dipping into two gentle divots where the balls of shoulders had been. I spread my small fingers over this hollow, sensing the lost sounds that might have synced with the action, a silk rustle of hemline cresting to midthigh, a creak of cartilage from the joints that had held him poised, breath in tandem then peppered with laughter or what was taken as laughter before the intentions changed and the words no longer mattered.

On her back, what had she felt? Thought? Prayed? Had she known his name? Had they been promised or just met? Was his breath of liquor or cotton candy or had she even noticed? And as the bodies moved now in my mind, I slithered into that shallow grave dug by at least some variety of affection and slipped my fingers between my cold thighs and waited for a flush that would give flesh to the image. I heard my name. I saw the familiar lace-up boots. Chaney stood there with a flashlight in one hand, shining the light in my unblinking eyes.

"There you are, kid," he said. "We've been looking all over for you. Whatcha doin' under there anyway?"

"Aw, for Chrissakes, Lon, leave the kid alone. We all need our dark places."

The last voice was new to me, a lazy Kentucky drawl barely discernible under a gloss of standard Hollywood affectation that made one think of some small English-speaking country that was not the United Kingdom and definitely not the sticks. The voice's owner crouched to his knees and I saw the director for the first time. He wore an ivory tennis sweater two sizes too small for him, a collar and tie, and above this a broad head with an aggressively receding hairline and a violent bristle of mustache that looked remarkably like a nail brush pressed to his upper lip. I sensed no eyes, no shape to his nose or jaw; he was merely follicles shouting hair. I was not impressed. He was beside me in the damp sand before I could respond to his mumbled introduction. He crossed his arms over his chest and chuckled the way the living do when they are brave or drunk enough to mock death. And then he turned to me.

"You know," he began in a whisper, his breath sharp with whiskey, "this reminds me of when I was a kid. I used to play the living corpse in a traveling spook show down south. They used to stick a straw in my mouth and bury me for up to eight hours a go in a cardboard box. You believe that? They'd dig me up and pull me out, dust me off, and folks would ooh and aah and that was entertainment back then. But I kinda liked it. Being deep in the dark. Made me feel safe and kinda whole. You know what I mean?"

And his eyes lit with a flicker of recognition. He knew that I did.

"Listen, let's get outta here," he said, taking my hand and pulling me into the sky and stars and light of the boardwalk. "We don't want to miss them jockeys."

On the boardwalk, the nighttime pier teemed with day-lit life. On one side, pragmatic barns with vaguely Moorish battlements housed the amusements. Cars were parked along the white railing, the windshields swiveled to let in the damp breezes. Music throbbed from the heated yellow glow of portable Bakelite radios. Sloppy couples drank from scoured ketchup bottles, from one another, as men stripped to their undershirts fondled the breasts of their dates. Seabees up from Point Mugu strutted in their dress whites, tattoos bluing under battleship tans, while hatcheck girls argued with pomaded rent boys, vying for the eyes of passing trade. The director took it in, his eyes nearly watering from delight at the low ebb of life all around him. Some he paused to speak to, offering squares of gum or cigarettes, desperate for a few words from those authentic lips. But Chaney remained aloof, a bishop of the average, his face so common and still so known as to be almost invisible.

We passed the briny stink of the bait shops, a dance school that promised proficiency in something called the Charleston, boat rentals, pretzel stalls. We came to the end of the pier and there, life was most potent. And music, a lazy jelly roll trot flowed inward on tin drums and muted brass, swaying, shirking, shivering on a limping vortex of golden light, sweat, and tobacco smoke. We had arrived at the La Monica Ballroom.

The jockeys the director had referred to were people, couples really, who shuffled about the filthy dance floor of the ballroom like after-hour brooms. All were in various states of exhaustion, leaning into the dregs of formal embraces just to stay upright. It was commerce, a dance marathon, popular then when the prize was a thousand bucks just to spend a week on one's feet. Nine hundred and twenty hours of dancing had already lapsed. Twenty couples remained and each told their story in the fallen debris around their combined ankles. Chicken bones and soda bottles, cigarette packages, empty tubes of lipstick, cracker crumbs. Some still wore the bibs of stained napkins tucked into their shirt or dress fronts, evidence of meals consumed hours ago while exhausted on the hoof. They slept in shifts, sometimes violently rousing the other when the allotted time for rest had passed. If they both collapsed, they were roused and led from the floor. If rousing was ineffective, stretchers were employed.

On the upper galleries, the spectators, fresher than the competitors, jeered and hollered at favorite couples, some holding up patterned bedsheets with *ATTA BOY ROSCOE* or *SHOW 'EM YOUR STUFF, PEARL* painted on them. It was up there, where the smoke and peanut shells collected, that the director led us, his red feminine mouth pursed with excitement.

"I got twelve grand on number fifteen. Can you believe that? It was touch and go during the fox trot, but that bitch he got with him there got legs like a howitzer. Ain't *no way* them kids is goin' down."

I noticed his sordid glee brought out his native drawl, and sweat glistened on his broad brow as he nipped from the neck of a small flask.

"May I say, Mr. Browning, I'm quite a fan of your work," I began. I had been instructed by Chaney to say this. I was of course lying. I had seen none of his pictures. But Browning did not want to talk shop. Number 15 had just hit a patch of rough weather. Try as she might, the amazon with the thick legs could barely hold him up.

"Come on, you gorilla-assed bitch! Hold that cocksucker to rights!" Browning shouted. "Keep it movin'! Keep it movin', ya iron-plated half a whore!"

But the deadweight of her partner beckoned with the entropy of the ever-after, and she went down, proud and hard as the *Bismarck*. Browning imploded and two stretcher men scrambled to the wreckage. She could not be roused, and there was an awful panic as members of the orchestra were enlisted to try to hoist her bulk to safety. In the end she was rolled off the killing floor, her dress and sweat-soaked arms gathering dust and cigarette butts like some demonic Christmas loaf.

"Well, there goes the goddamned night!" Browning shouted. "Twelve grand, you bum! Twelve *goddamned* grand!"

It was a cursory meeting, a test run to see if perhaps I could work with the director on a property he and Chaney had been developing, a property that had already enjoyed one infamous German incarnation as a motion picture and countless retellings in other mediums. But Chaney knew he could put a very special stamp on *Dracula*. It could be the part he was remembered for.

Browning was publicly reticent, but privately he needed to prove to a studio he was worth the risk again. I didn't tell them none of this was news to me. Just like I didn't tell them of the afternoon meetings I'd been having with Junior.

In the years that followed, pictures found their voice and the bottom fell out of the banks.

CHAPTER 28

The consensus in those years was that talking pictures were a clever but somewhat vulgar fad that would hopefully wear out and leave us all blissfully back in the strong silent dark. No one realized synchronized sound would completely change not only the experience of the cinema but also the types of players who would then be drawn to them. Much has been made of regional dialects and foreign accents completely destroying budding careers. The truth was, speaking gutted the magic for many. Few can remember *hearing* their dreams. Sound made the medium more totalitarian, more common, more like daily life. And few players had gotten into the game to approximate a quotidian experience. Silence was international. Sound was regional. Once actors were exotic messengers from a muted world, agents of a kind of divine but temporary madness whose voices echoed like angels behind our flickering optic nerves. Sound sobered everything, made us dull. Made us sane.

The Laemmles embraced the new technology, as did all the

captain pimps of Hollywood. Soon the boulevards were filled
with promises of talk. *Dracula* would be the first talking picture
of its kind. Uncle Carl hated the idea of some greasy supernatural
ghoul draining pert little blondes by their jugulars, while his son,
Junior, hoped it would be pure rube currency, sex and death as
palatable as bacon and eggs. They made a compromise. If Junior
could get the rights, he would front-burner his father's World
War I message picture and Pop would clear the way for things
that go bump in the night. That was where I came in.

"But I have no influence with Mr. Chaney," I said.

"He likes you and listens to you. That's platinum in this
town," Junior said.

"Mr. Laemmle. Lon's and my relationship is based on professional respect and I hardly think it fitting to appropriate it for
some front office intrigue."

"Front office intrigue? Jesus Christ, where do you think you
are, kid? Do you know who the lowest creature on this lot is? It
ain't the copy girls or even the poor schmucks who mop up in
the men's room. It's the clever bastards in the editing department
who play with pictures all day. You want something better? Okay.
But first you gotta get outta the dark. You gotta get me Chaney."

"I thought Metro or Paramount Lasky had the rights."

"Where'd you hear that? No one's got the rights. Not yet.
But it's a cinch. Schulberg's too much of a snob to allow stage
blood on his profit sheet and Mayer's terrified of the production
code."

"But Metro has Chaney," I said.

"But Metro doesn't have *you*."

"I don't understand. If your plan is to procure the rights
to *Dracula* yourself, wouldn't that be all the incentive Chaney
would need?"

"Why do I feel I'm always talking to my rabbi with you? Listen, say Universal doesn't have as deep of pockets as some of the other studios and the rights don't come so easy. Chaney's my insurance."

"If you're not happy with my work here Mr.—"

"Son of a *bitch*! You're a tough little nut. You look outside the window lately, sister? Those people ain't standing in line to get a good table at the Derby. Those are *breadlines*." He reached for a cigar. Talk of the economy always forced his hand to a three-dollar cigar. "Half the town would crawl on its belly for a walk-on and you're making me spell it out. I mean, you gotta eat, don'tcha?"

Silence.

"Well don'tcha?"

"You know what I want from this studio and it's not the blue-plate special."

Junior grinned. "Again with the directing," he said, shaking his head. "Why are you such a glutton for punishment, kid?"

"I very much enjoy my work here on the lot, Mr. Laemmle. But I respect that it is your prerogative as head of production to relieve me of my contract anytime you may see fit." I didn't tell him my real fear, that the real earth and real trees off the lot were filled with the siren song of the everlasting, that to leave this plywood empire would leave me as vulnerable as a dead branch in a breeze. I didn't tell him that in my stalled heart, lungs, and brain was imbedded the very grail of spiritual practice, that I was the flat-chested apotheosis of prana. That I needed the falsity of Hollywood like a drunk needed a drink.

"All right, all right. So *you* don't need to eat. But I bet that hulking friend of your does." He smiled when he saw this new tack hit its mark. "He's happy here, right?" he continued, leaning back in his chair. "But if this town teaches us anything, it's that we could always be *happier*. You put a bug in Chaney's ear about this, your pal will have a job here for *life*."

"What about directing?"

"Jesus! Get me Chaney and I'll think about it."

Mutter was soon after employed in front of the camera for the first time, following his Indian brothers into mock battles only he had actually lived through. He was hired as an action extra in *All Quiet on the Western Front* because production needed tall bodies to stand in the foreground to force the perspective of the outdoor scenes. At least that's what they told him.

He didn't know about my tacit agreement with Junior to enroll Chaney, so I just smiled and nodded when he told me the news. It is a testament to the innate hokum of Hollywood that Mutter never mistook these battle sequences as the real thing. I had heard of shell shock, traumatic repression, latent what-do-you-call-it, but these proved merely academic terms. Mutter was as happy as a puppy in the surf diving into muddy hand-dug shell craters. It was as if the explosions, the flying earth and bodies, held no memory for him, no monsters under his bed. It was simply play—noisy, wet, filthy, exhilarating play.

I was collecting checks, trying my best to maintain contact with Chaney, feeling my own pressure to win him over, but my duties had very little to do with actual production. I was binning dailies for bread-and-butter comedies, delivering script changes at all hours of the night. I even cast a few extras for the six-day horse operas we shot in the wilds of what is now Encino. There was a rumor in the commissary that Mutter's girl was pregnant, and I imagined him, briefly, poised above her small dark body actually fulfilling what he had been dared to do to my mother all those years ago. There was a surprising distance in the thought, but still I was doubly content with my bargain with Junior. I could never confirm his impending parentage as he never took his meals in the commissary. He ate in the open, out of steaming pots and smoking grills, animal grease on his fingers, smiling, I imagined, at the camping trip that had become his life. At least he had found someone. I had no idea I was about to do the same.

The system was simple. I'd get a call at about five thirty in the morning requesting basic Western types: twenty cowhands, a few baddies for the posse scenes, a bartender, nonspeaking, with attendant barflies, and I'd load myself into my modified Packard flatbed and head over to Gower Gulch. That Packard was a marvel. With its blocked clutch and brakes, my shorter legs could reach the pedals. It had a hand throttle that allowed me to modulate speed with my fingertips. A straight four, it was bored out for hard duty, and with its two-ton struts could carry or climb nearly anything. I got it cheap from one of the studio's transportation managers. Spent a weekend in the wilds of Sherman Oaks teaching myself how to drive it. Best automobile I ever owned.

At that hour of the morning, the Cahuenga Pass was full of birdsong. I'd buzz the empty road in the still-cool sunshine over to Sunset, where George Washington Smith was building the first of his West Coast palazzos, and continue east to Gower Gulch. There's a mini mall there now, trussed up with fake Western fronts and a paved parking lot, but then it was just a big dirt parcel surrounded by a split rail fence. This was Paramount's backyard but also the only place in town to pick up a few Western day players. They'd come still in their gear, batwing chaps and roughed-out boots, hooks buckled to their belts, on horseback or foot. Texas shitkickers and Montana bulldoggers, New Mexican Apaches with frowning jaws and eyes as pretty as their ponies.

Boys and men, ropers, punchers, cooks, and fence menders, all as lean as piston rods and twice as functional. They'd muster as soon as they heard the first trucks pull up and then we'd walk the line.

I knew all the scouts from the other studios, but we never said as much as hello. We respected one another's type and left it at that. Metro wanted cowboys who could sing. Paramount wanted only those who looked like John Gilbert. But Universal wasn't so picky. We just needed hands who could take a twenty-mile-an-hour fall from horseback for two bits an hour and not gripe. That usually left the majority for me, and the 'pokes knew it. So as soon as I pulled up it was hats off and shy white smiles and "Morning, Miss Maddy" this and "Howdy, Missy Maddy" that. I was the queen of this rodeo. And I loved it. You must understand I was at the foothills of my sexual peak, at least chronologically, and these lean and lanky specimens were fodder for the rare nights in my box when my dreams did not fail.

CHAPTER 29

He was young, about my age in years. As tall and straight as a young sequoia with shoulders so lustful they whispered sinfully under the yoke of his snap-front shirt. He had sky-blue eyes and a shock of brown hair with a pure-white streak just left of his widow's peak. He'd survived a strike of lightning as a boy and was thus marked. His name was Lucy Kinnon, but he'd been known as Lucky ever since his flirtatious brush with atmospheric discharge. A spray of pale copper freckles dappled the bridge of his nose and these, along his with tangled teeth, never fully allowed him to be the man who lived in the roughness of his hands and hard, lean muscles.

I lusted for him on the spot. He carried a battered guitar with him wrapped in a worn sheet of Christmas paper. The Metro scout was the first to notice him and asked if he could actually play that thing, to which Lucky mumbled he reckoned he could.

"Anytime, son," the Metro scout snapped, and off came the wrapping paper, as gently as a newborn's diaper, and he slung it with a length of twine over his broad shoulder and out came norteño, as sweet and ancient as anything I might have heard from a roving orange picker. And when he finished, the scout sniffed and asked if he knew any white men's songs, to which Lucky addressed the dust once more, saying, "I suppose I do but don't rightly feel like playin' 'em."

This was too much for the Metro scout but just enough for me. I packed him shotgun and left the rest of that morning's haul in the back, gripping the slats of the flatbed, and listened to him strum all the way down Hollywood Boulevard to Highland.

That first day, I put in a good word with that day's director (John Ford, perhaps?) and got him a few lines. He was happy with the bump, and we had lunch together, where I pretended to eat a piece of cherry pie while he wolfed down three burgers. He told me of his father's place in Perris, not France, he said. A small cattle spread where he'd worked since he could stand. The day laborers hired for castrating and branding season were the ones who taught him how to play and gee, if I wasn't the spittin' image of his baby sister. Something sunk in me at that, but I rallied and gave him my plate of shredded pie and asked him if he wanted to see the studio.

I led him through Little Europe, past the colonnades of the casino at Monte Carlo to the steps of Notre Dame. And his face, his shiny, open face, was like a new penny. Well, tie me to a tree or dip me in spit. Rural references took on the luster of Keats as he quipped over everything he saw. *How the heck they figure that? I'll be dog* danged *if that don't look like* real *stone.* The sun was going down. The arcs were being set for the night's shooting and I felt the day begin to lose its luster. I knew the hard physics of this world, knew he had no contract in his sights, knew these moments would be our last together. But I simply

wanted to drink him in, see the way his limp thumb flicked the
cowlick from his eyes, the way his lips shuddered shy of those
crooked teeth before he smiled. And in my mind, I could give
him warmth, a heartbeat, a future. I could age the playfulness in
his eyes to full passion and lift his callused hand to my stunted
breast and he would feel something that could torture him there.

"You've been real white, Miss Maddy," he said, his eyes relaxing at the waning sun. I hadn't even begun. (Though I must
admit I had no idea what the reference to my complexion meant.)
"I need to thank you for this swell day." I came prepared. He
watched me as I sipped from a small covered cup I had brought
with me. He might have assumed it contained something in-
nocuous, water or lemonade. I didn't let him know it was filled
with a solution of borax and harsh peppermint oil. I was tired of
too many nights of stalled fantasy. This evening I would pass the
threshold. And for the passing I needed all the kissable freshness
I could muster.

"Have you known many girls, Lucky?" I asked. He looked
mildly shocked. This coming from a creature who could still wear
pigtails, who could blame him? He looked away, his simple cogs
beginning to turn. Then he looked at me with his crooked smile.

"A few. I guess."

"Well?"

"Well, what?

"Did you know them well, Lucky? These girls?" I took another swig from my cup and noticed small strips of my throat
rolled down to my silenced guts with the caustic mouthwash.

"How do you mean?" he asked as innocent as New Year's
Day. I moved closer to him. Could he feel my radiant chill? Was
there some kind of promise on my face that could breech my
ridiculous pug nose and full baby's lips?

"I mean, did you know them well enough to do this?" And I removed my hand from the pocket of my skirt, where it had been nearly broiled by the heat of a chemical hand warmer. I placed it on his.

"Holdin' hands ain't nothin'." He grinned. "I done that back in the school yard."

"Did you, now?" I asked, stealing ever closer. Was he interested at last? I could feel a nervous heat spark from the top of his hand. His breathing jerked. He righted. Then he blinked and looked at me.

"How old are you, Miss Maddy? If I can ask."

"Oh, so much older than I look." I lifted my cooling hand up the length of his arm until it rested softly beneath his ear. I let my fingers play there on his neck, as I had imagined, as I had so many times dreamed. His eyes closed with a crush of pleasure.

"I reckon I was wrong about you remindin' me of my baby sister," he whispered through his loosening jaw.

"I don't want to remind you of anyone, Lucky." I brought my head to his shoulder, my face nuzzled there among the warm salt of his neck. Did I dare it? My tongue was let loose from behind my teeth and I noticed it made a contact of sorts. A kind of gentle stab that sent a shiver through him that sprung the muscles of his arms and crushed me instantly to his chest. His lips brushed the stiff surface of my cheek and I could feel them flutter there, tentative but burning.

"Not like that, Lucky," I whispered.

"Well, I don't mean no harm but your tongue's a little cold."

"So warm it."

And I was on him. Our lips crushed together flatly. My tongue leaped like a buccaneer past his teeth and I could feel it roil dryly in the claimed warmth of his mouth. I forced his hand hard upon my chest. There was a galvanized flash of passion, one small but harsh leap of procreative memory in the pit of my stomach. Then nothing. The creature was still cold. The experiment had failed. I could sense him sour, feel his arms begin to falter, to slip from my shallow waist. His eyes opened in panic and then he reengaged and now there was a pressure on my ribs, a frantic push as he tried to rid himself of the rictus of my embrace. I did not feel the blow that tore my lips from his. I saw his eyes begin to wild and he coughed, rasped deeply for breath and then he puke-choked into his open hand. His eyes filled with a naked disgust I will never forget.

A cricket.

In his palm was the quivering hull of a cricket.

It must have crawled, unnoticed, up into the ledge of my hard palate. How long, I'll never know. Lucky dry-heaved, then smeared what was left of it on the thigh of his jeans. He backed away. He said nothing. His jaw worked, his lungs even seemed willing, but nothing came out of his stunned mouth. No scream. No shriek. Just his eyes, wide, shattered, reduced to a terror so raw and enveloping I could hardly stand to look at him. But I did. I watched him as he finally swallowed. Watched as his eyes finally began to hood in revulsion and perhaps hate. Watched as his shoulders and hips relaxed in the hope that I would not follow. Watched as he turned. I even watched as he ran. The dead are playgrounds, Volker had said. We are never alone.

That night, curled in the damp filth of my box, I did not need to sense Volker to know what he would whisper down the canyons of my bones. How he would snicker at my failed lust.

You stupid girl. No wonder you chose a theater for your perch. That's the closest you'll ever get to a normal life. You should have accepted the invitations of the soil. Only one thing will keep your head above the stone. And that is desire. Cultivate it wrongly and you see the result. Rightly, and the worms might be cheated one more meal. I would cultivate rightly. I would never act on such an impulse again. I went back to writing Chaney, hoping work might finally seal up where my heart had been.

Then one day a package was sent to the studio with my name on it. It was the American version of Stoker's *Dracula*, complete with both Deane's and Balderston's plays with a note: *Read these and get ready. Lon.*

CHAPTER 30

Chaney collected me in a modified late-model Zagelmeyer Kamper-kar, in his line-dried plaid and lace-up boots, his head sweet-smelling and still wet. A father, a suitor, a peer? He was unannounced, unplanned for, a sudden lark that demanded immediate accord. I had no trouble getting the time off from my duties at the studio. Junior thought this was all part of my plan.

"I can't work in the city," Chaney said on an intake of his cigarette. "We'll rough it for a night at my cabin in Big Bear and then maybe a week in this heap. Have you been to the mountains around here? Just breathtaking."

I didn't answer. I felt the stares of the secretaries as I hoisted myself into the passenger seat. For a man who'd made his living on appearances, he had no sensitivity for how things looked. The whispers rose around his cheeks like gnats and he simply ignored them.

"You think this is all right?" I asked, regretting it the second it came out of my mouth.

"Hey," he said, splitting his face into a smile. "We're just pals, ain't we?"

The drive was beautiful, cradled with dense evergreens and flowering brush, and I felt the lull, the tug of the dirt that sped past my window. But he was somehow a talisman against all that. Or was it my desire to succeed well cultivated at last? He had packed a small lunch, some cold cuts and fist-size apples, but offered me nothing. He knew I would refuse. And there was an almost unbearable intimacy in his knowing this.

"What's your take on the book?" he asked, watching the road, not me. "You said in your letters you might have some ideas about the material."

I looked at him blankly.

"That's why I sent you the book and stuff, kid. You okay, Maddy?"

I wasn't sure how I was supposed to make myself indispensable to him, how I was to fulfill my unwritten contract with Junior. I thought maybe I would take the same tack I had with *The Toymaker*, come up with shots and bits of business that might actually make it work. I wasn't sure if he would take me seriously, if he knew what every director knew: that words were just a blueprint for a picture and every director must be second kin to the pencil and the hammer. My ideas for *Dracula* hadn't come easy. Not like the sharp and sinuous vomit I had experienced with Volker. There were many nights in my perch above the killing floor of Stage 28 where the pages had refused my concentrated forays, had remained stiff and prim and immutable as I tried to seduce them into cinematic repose. It had been a seduction *of* the dark *in* the dark with little to recommend the silent romance but the confused congress of words and whispers. I liked the book but had my issues with it. However, I wasn't sure how he felt about it, so I was gentle, almost casual when I said, "The epistolary format will be a challenge." He raised his eyebrows and laughed.

"The *what*?"

"The letters," I corrected. "The fact that the book is composed of letters, *correspondence*, is difficult to adapt." I scrambled to sound like I knew what I was talking about. "I assume you'll be sparing with the dramatic versions you sent me."

"You see me duded up like some half-baked headwaiter?"

I smiled.

"I want the *essence* of the book," he said. "The action. Take it out of the drawing room, off the damn stage."

"Who'll be doing the adaptation?"

"You think I brought you up here for your conversation, kid?"

"Me?"

"Who else? I've seen your pictures." (Plural? Had he seen *Zipper*?) "You understand how to get those scares under the skin."

It was that simple. His faith in me had become founded with little more than his instinct.

"The first thing I'd change is Renfield," I said with as much confidence as I could muster.

"You think a dame should play him?"

"I don't think *anybody* should play him. I think he should get the air."

"The air? Listen to you. Real American, huh? Why axe old Renfield?"

"He dilutes the basic tension, I think."

"Which is?"

"Incestuous sex, yes?"

"Hey, hold on. *Incestuous?*" He looked to me. "I thought this was just a two-reel dark ride with a little fluid exchange."

"You are serious?" All my reticence seemed to evaporate. I was back in Germany, back in Zann's hot little office fighting for my reason to exist. "He is a tragic creature of appetite, an aristocrat of the Other."

"Why tragic?"

"He can *desire* mortal women but he can only *love* those he sires. In effect he gives birth to his own sex partners. You understand? He can only love his *own* daughters. Hence, incest."

"Censors are gonna love this."

"He is a creature constantly running, consistently hiding, shunned, hated, misunderstood and yet deeply desired. He is confounded by an earthly existence to such a degree that night becomes his day. He has confused sustenance with intimacy or perhaps he is the first to truly define the nature of intimacy. He is part god, part ghoul, living only half a life—a life that will never cease and thus never culminate into the only thing he truly desires."

"And what's that?"

"Release."

"Well, sweet Jesus, if you haven't done your homework."

"Too much?"

"There's more?" He chuckled. I felt his eyes on me then, and I willed some color to my face. "I'll need a treatment by the time we leave," he said. "Wait'll you see the makeup I have planned for the son of a bitch." And we continued to drive.

His cabin in the woods was an idyllic thing. Made of stone and shingle, it had a set of comfortably sagging wood steps that led up to a wraparound porch. It seemed the product of age, of weather and long talks. But upon careful inspection I saw the seams. The steps had been cut at ingenious compound angles to simulate wear. The porch, equally guilty of the set-shop touch, had even been aged with careful dry brushes of blue and gray. The inside seemed modest enough, a single room of raw wood paneling with a river-stone fireplace. An enormous tin bathtub supported a pine plank top that doubled as the only vertical surface apart from an iron bed. Four mismatched chairs were easy to dismiss as dimly practical until one assessed the masterful carving at the headrests. A zinc-lined water heater hid behind a sliding panel, a luxury even in fine homes at the time, and a telephone hid coyly behind the wicker of a carefully aged creel. It was a set. An environment designed to evoke rustic calm as quickly as a shot of nicotine. But cigarettes were far too urban a protuberance for him when he came here and were replaced with a cherrywood pipe that he stuffed, tamped, and lit even as I was coming through the heavy front door.

"Drop your gear anywhere," he said as he shoved the pine tabletop to the floor and opened a steaming tap that filled the tub in mere minutes. "You don't mind if I wash up."

Not a question. Not even a request. He had his clothes peeled and in crumples around him before I could answer.

He stood there in two flavors, naked, tanned to the throat and elbows and pale everywhere else, one of those two-toned orange Creamsicles in the shape of a man. His lack of modesty could have been an affront, should have been. Was I so sexless as to not even merit a blush?

"Hand me that mug and brush, would ya?"

He lathered his jaws and lip, sinking into the steaming water, exhaling liquored smoke, gaily carrying out the duties of his toilet without so much as a glance in my direction.

"I've been thinking about what you said on the way up here,

about the count seeking release." A drag on his pipe, then the rasp of his straight razor down the slope of one horsey jaw, "and that's there in spades. But we can't play down the sex angle, the gothic romance, the effect he has on the two girls. His kiss, the bite he puts on them, must be almost a benediction, a sacred rite."

"Blood of my blood. Flesh of my flesh," I said, quoting the book (and the Bible) to the best of my recollection.

"Exactly. A sexual Eucharist. Hand me that towel. The last rites and the transubstantiation all in one go."

"Hays will get the church groups circling the wagons."

"Hays won't know what hit him. He'll be squinting so hard to see our ingenue's nipples he won't even notice the blasphemy. Let me get this fire going."

He was in a plaid flannel robe now, the color up in his cheeks from the hot water, his feet leaving winking puddles on the broad planks of the floor. The fire caught with a single match. More Hollywood magic? And he reached for his portfolio, the stem of his pipe rattling cold in his teeth.

"I want to show you this makeup I've been working out, see what you think."

Imagine a well-lubricated machine, so perfectly calibrated to its function of reproducing the grotesque, the tiny cunning details of the discarded and the damned that even nature might balk at its veracity. And this glorious engine wants your opinion. It was too much to hope for. Then I thought of Laemmle. My ridiculous mission.

"So Metro has the r-rights?" I stuttered. "Because last I heard . . ."

He paused to light his bowl.

"What have you heard?"

"Nothing. I just thought the rights were still up for grabs. Uncle Carl . . ."

"Uncle Carl is in for a mighty rude awakening, honey. I signed the contract last week. *Dracula* is officially a Metro super jewel."

So I had failed. I had convinced him of nothing. In fact, in agreeing to write the treatment for him, *I* was the one who would be defecting. But I couldn't languish in another failure. I was too happy. Have you ever sat in a room with the genuinely imbued? Have you felt the sea change as his vision atomizes, rises, and begins to shift the cogs of his heating brain? Where is loyalty when history, real artistry, stares back in shaded black crayon?

He was a meticulous draughtsman, as a few remaining sketches of his can attest to. And there before me was the face of the count, exactly as Stoker had described him: an older man, made a night creature well past his boyhood, seemingly against his will, feral, tentative, the nervous glint of the predator, the reluctant glance of the executioner. Long graying hair, wild and matted as raw hemp. A heavy mustache. The tips of two sharp teeth making gentle divots in the meat of his lower lip.

"The teeth are problematic, I'll admit," he mumbled. "They have to be plausible but can't override the sexuality. Murnau got it right with Schreck's ratty look but a mug like that won't make the Pacoima housewives swoon. Go with the canines, it's too wide a splay. The jugular would open up like a fireplug. Go with the lateral incisors, you have practicality on your side but the look is a little front heavy."

He thought everything through like this.

"Maybe he carries a small knife," I suggested.

"Stoker is clear about his sharp teeth."

"Stoker didn't make pictures."

He smiled at this and I reminded myself to blink. "So you think no teeth?"

"I think," and I must admit I paused for dramatic effect, "I think teeth. But only just *before* we see him bite. In normal conversation, he has teeth like anyone else. But before he bites . . ."

"They grow. Like little dental erections."

"Sorry?"

"Jesus. What am I saying? You're too young for that. But your *idea* is terrific. A face like a Swiss Army knife."

"Perhaps he gets younger after he feeds," I offered.

"And he *ages* when hungry. His appearance will clue the action. That's a girl. Let me show you the harness I rigged up for the wall-climbing scene."

And it went on like that all night, a steady precipitation of details misting up the windows of that close little cabin. The count would not wear evening clothes. He would be arraigned in all black, his version of tiger stripes in his hunting grounds of ever-night. He would have an accent but only a slight one, a taint, not readily placed. His sexuality would be tethered to the animal, not the manners of the drawing room. His hands must be clean, no fur like in the novel, but the nails could be long, well manicured, slightly effeminate, but dangerous. He would wear a heavy cloak, not a cape. He must struggle with the social graces, with the expectations of his moneyed prey. He would look only the women directly in the eye. But the most startling discovery I made that night was his plan for the wolf transformation. Chaney wanted to show it, show the count transmogrify before the slack jaws of the audience into the black wolf of the novel. Half a decade before Henry Hull would awkwardly launch the virgin effort of this effect in *Werewolf of London*, Chaney had planned a seamless twenty-six-stage progression that would rival his already impressive accomplishments. He had even discovered yak hair as the medium of choice. It was the same stop-motion build we had used when the creature grows flesh in *The Toymaker*. But I said nothing. I was so excited, so enamored of working again I didn't care if he believed the idea had all been his.

UNDER A NEUTRAL-COLORED SKY, WE STOOD IN THE STREAM. THE AIR, the coolness, alluded to but not felt, not by me, sucked all shadow. The light was even, dull but present, democratic, and Chaney whistled with the lit pipe in his teeth, his sweet smoke testament to his breathing. And I read back what I had written.

My bare feet were in the stream with him, to the ankles. I could feel the tiny mouths of the trout nibble at the dead flesh of my heels and I nudged them forward, away, toward the actor's drowned worm. But it was me they preferred.

"The bastards aren't biting," Chaney complained.

"Why don't you try over where I'm standing?" It was what I imagined a good marriage would be, the comfort, the ease, the mutual respect, and that extra treasure of being able to create together. When I imagined sex, and I admit I did, there was always a bleed of Lucky's face through his features. Lon's confidence, his shoulders, and his athletic thighs perhaps. But Lucky's eyes. And smile.

We spent a week like this, eating outdoors (me surreptitiously disposing of my tiny chewed-up wads), walking in the evaporating pine mist of late morning, always talking, always challenging, me with my hard pad and pen and his slow mantra of "read it over again." At night, by the snapping fire, he spoke of the system, of an artist's place in it. How nothing was owed. That all must be earned, and this was the reason he'd refused to help his son follow in his footsteps.

His natural mode of expression was gestural, the words floating like raw stuffs around him, waiting to be shaped by the clean and precise movements of his hands. Deaf parents, he would offer when my eyes were drawn to their rhythmic flailing. Was I the only one fortunate enough to know this?

"To portray a role, you have to embody it. Pain is fleeting; film is forever."

THE MORNING OF OUR LAST DAY, CHANEY LIT HIS FIRST PIPE OF THE morning and tumbled into a coughing jag so violent he burst the blood vessels in both his eyes. Only after he spewed up two coffee cups of red did he let me call the ambulance. The truth was, Chaney had been in precarious health for many months. Metro had even suspended his contract with the caveat that if he showed significant improvement over the summer he could have his pick of projects.

August. Hospital day.

The actor had been vomiting up ever-deepening hues of sunset, the thin red of dawn, the heart blood of twilight. Chaney's only son sat in a corner, a boy too tall to be a boy yet too awkward and untried to be anything else. He waited for his father's end as hopelessly as he waited for his father's love. I'd been summoned and I went. But I paused when I saw that broken boy. Chaney motioned again that I should come to him. And it was the only time I felt a pang of conflict for the great Mr. Chaney.

"Kid," he rasped in my ear. "Lend me some."

I bowed my head closer, not sure to what he eluded, ignited with shame by his son's bleary gaze on my back. I smelled bleach, formaldehyde, the sour tobacco stink of his plastic breathing tube.

"Lend me some," he croaked. "Some of what you got."

His eyes were wide, peeled to youth, to behind youth. An infant left to the lions.

"I need it. I need it now. Whatever made you the way you are, I need a little piece of your ever-ever after."

HIS COFFIN WAS DRAPED WITH AN AMERICAN FLAG, UNHEARD OF FOR A mere actor. Hollywood stopped in its paces, the whole town, for two minutes of silence. And I stood well outside the cortege of relatives and business associates and thought of his last words to me. Had he known what I was? Had he sought me out on mere pretense, hoping in our conversations about the minute habits of the undead that he might uncover some rare and practical gem of mine? Had he hoped I'd somehow *save* him? Hadn't he known that even if I could, I loved him too much to ever do that?

Hollywood never mourns for long.

Phones ring again.

And when mine rang it was a call from the wilds of the Malibu colony. A call from Browning himself.

CHAPTER 31

He sent a limo, of course. This was the standard first foray in any serious negotiation, but I was still unclear what he wanted of me. His call had been little more than a terse reintroduction and the time I could expect his car.

The interior was a portable Schwab's Pharmacy. Chrome racks held every confection then in commercial production: dimpled bags of Boston Baked Beans, Milk Maid Royals, nonpareils dusted with every color of sugared granule, licorice sticks stacked neatly as cords of timber, and that new confection, the one named after the inventor's horse, Snickers. In a silver bucket ingeniously fitted to the inside of the door, several Moxie sodas, in all flavors, frosted in their bath of ice. But what caught my attention was the Oswald the Lucky Rabbit chocolate bar. Hadn't such a confection provided Mutter with his freshman bout of American sweetness? I thought of him then, the back of his thick neck turned from me, alive and vital and living his own life. I sat back and wondered if the rumors about his girl being pregnant were true.

Mr. Browning was never alone. He had a very real phobia of himself, I imagine. But people were of no real interest to him. Only their artifacts. Carnival banners were everywhere, hung from the hand-painted ceiling and the lip of the dark oak wainscoting, old sideshow canvases rolled and creased so many times the paint was mere ghostly traces. *Delwood the Dog-Faced Boy. Cleo the Fish Girl. Rondo the Ineffable "It." Is It Male or Female? You Decide.*

And canvas was not all. He had carnival punks from penny-ante shooting galleries, rigged coffins from tenth-rate magicians, a false-fronted Chinese treasure chest, a chess-playing mechanical harlequin with a dead man's grin, two-headed babies yellowing in magnifying brine, prosthetic limbs, detachable noses, a plaster iron maiden lined with cracking rubber spikes. The man himself sat with his back to me, facing a sputtering fire. I could hear the crackle of crumpled paper and see the fire brighten as dry balls were tossed into it.

I approached quietly, improving my view of him with each step until I could see a script in his lap, each page torn and tossed with focused efficiency. The script was *Dracula*; *Property of Universal Pictures* heading each page. He was barefoot, in striped pajama bottoms, a week's worth of growth crowding his perennial mustache.

"Mr. Browning," I said.

"Present," he nearly yelled.

"I've arrived, sir."

"Deducible. But is it a fact?"

He turned to me. His eyes were nearly swollen shut. He sneezed and reached for a tumbler of amber liquid.

"He would have been magnificent," he said, taking a swallow of his drink. "Better than anything I ever did with him."

"Who?"

"*Lonny*. Keep up, goose."

I moved to crouch by the fire, facing him, but he waved me away.

"I prefer you in my periphery, sister," he said. He poured himself another drink. "Have you read this shit they want me to ringmaster?"

I crouched by the arm of his chair and peered over the torn pages in his lap. I recognized the text from my own research.

"The Balderston. Yes."

"Broadway. Now they want respectable spooks."

He broke off here and I saw the child in the man, alone in the dark, the bogeyman express, terrified and alone. But I could not stomach it to reach out and touch him.

"So what do you plan to do?"

"Do? I told that kraut dwarf to shove it."

"So you've *passed* on the project?"

"I don't know. Maybe I should do it. I kinda feel I owe it to Lonny."

"So you will?"

"Christ. I'd rather swallow red-hot thumbtacks. I'd rather drink toilet water. I'd rather clip that little thing of skin under my tongue and gargle with saltpeter . . . but they *got* me."

"Contract?"

"No. *Me*. They got *me*. The same way they got you. The way they got all of us. Glamour. Cheap, chintzy ten-for-a-penny glamour. All hooey. All goose shit. But we'd walk on bloody stumps just to be next to it."

He was right, of course, but still I was confused as to my function.

"Mr. Browning, I'm not clear why you called for me."

"Not clear? It's clear as mud, kid."

He got up then and strolled over to a gothic revivalist table piled with empty bottles and books. He tossed objects to the floor whose concussions were broken by the thick rug under his feet and found what he was looking for. A film can.

"I watched this six times. *Six*. And every time it got better."

He tossed it to me and I scrambled to catch it. It was a print of *Zipper*, still with German titles.

"*That*, sister, is a fucking masterpiece. I would have castrated myself with a rusty razor if I could have made a picture *half* as good. You hear me?"

I felt a flutter as of real excitement, but nothing came to the surface. I was too out of practice with compliments. I managed a smile.

"Thank you, sir."

"No. *Never*. Genius never says thank you."

I felt a distinct chill in the air as that last comment hung there, cloaked as it was in envy, shame, and anger. I wanted to change the subject. Ground the conversation.

"Who do they want in the lead?" I finally managed.

"Well, if old Uncle Carl had his way, I'm sure he'd put a necromancer on payroll, raise his great-grandfather from the grave, and stick the old fucker in the cape and spats. Just to keep things in the family." He slumped back into his chair and stared once again into the fire. "I don't know. Paul Muni maybe? Who knows. I'm pushing for an unknown. But so did Sisyphus."

"Have you seen the Los Angeles production?"

"What, with that Carpathian lingerie salesman, what's his name?"

"Bela Lugosi. And I hear he's devastating in the role."

"No. Strictly nuts to that."

"So who?" I asked.

"Oh, it'll go to Lugosi. No choice. No marquee lead will touch this stinker with a pool cue."

"Why?"

"It's a goddamned fairy story, that's why. Strictly kid's stuff."

"Are you quite sure of that Mr. Browning?" I felt more than vague propriety and was offended.

"*Nuts!* It's the goddamned twentieth century, kid. You think Joe and Jane Schmuck will part with real Yankee green to see a *spook* story?"

"But the supernatural aspect is what gives it—"

"*Diapers!* Strictly nursery time!"

"Oh, Mr. Browning, if you only . . ." I stopped myself. But my anger was building.

"Look, it's a simple rewrite. Two Hungarian madmen escape from some Budapest nuthouse and are convinced they're vampires. One won't go in for the bloodsucking and so sticks to rats and vermin. The other guy, well, he likes his delusions straight. It's the story of two con men, two shysters out for a little rub-a-dub and some high-class tail. It's *London After Midnight* in gypsy-ville."

"No!" I almost yelled. "You will *destroy* it if you shyster it up, if you make this picture talk out the sides of its mouth!"

"What?"

"If you bothered to exhume yourself and spend some time out there on the streets, you'd see the *last* thing people want is what they know. They've got a bellyful of what they already know, Mr. Browning. Foreclosures, scams, huckster promises. It is *you* who must keep up. And it is *not* fantasy. Not fantastic at all. People *want* to believe there are such things. And they are wise to do so."

"Christ. You're talkin' like a tent show swami. You make this thing with the supernatural angle you'll hear crickets." His world was the con, the freak, the desperate. The downtrodden but very *explainable* world of the petty criminal.

"Crickets? I'll hear crickets, you say?" And before I knew what I was doing, I fumbled with the buttons of my blouse and thrust his filthy head to my smooth chest. "What do you hear in there, Mr. Browning? Crickets? *Anything?*"

"Jesus! What the hell are you doing?"

He struggled to pull away, but I held him fast.

"Educating, Mr. Browning. You think you know all there is in nature's basement? You haven't scratched the surface. Listen!" He put his head slowly back to my chest, grinning stupidly, then looked up at me.

"So no heartbeat. Big deal. Classic two-penny gaff. I knew a guy who could lift a *truck* with hooks through his eyelids."

"Lon *wanted* it this way," I sputtered. "He understood the uncanny like you *never* could."

"Lon is *dead*, sister!" he spat. "Kaput! Blooey! Yesterday's pot roast!" I was burning to make my point, desperate to shut his drunken, foul, unbelieving mouth. But what could I do? And if I did it, how would I go on, him knowing what I really was? What would happen to me? To Mutter?

"What if I was to tell you you *must* make this picture as Lon imagined it," I said as calmly as I could. "Not for his sake. Not for mine. But for *yours*. For one simple and unassailable reason. Because it's *true*. It's *true*, Mr. Browning! Such creatures *do* exist!"

He smacked his lips and made a rude and very long-winded

farting sound. "*That's* what I'd say." He giggled. "And shame on poor, miserable Mr. Chaney for wasting his last precious days being taken under by a low-down shit-heel like you!" That was it. Something snapped. And I thrust him away and reached for the closest sharp object I could find. It was a dagger-shaped letter opener and I plunged it deep into my chest.

"*Hey!*"

Browning screamed, leaping away from me, as I dragged the dull knife down the length of my torso, the skin tearing with the sound of old leather. Dull pink dust trickled from the wound as I reached my hands into the gash and pulled at the brittle bear trap of my split ribs.

"Look, Mr. Browning. *Fairy* stories? *Nursery* rhymes?" The shriveled fist of my heart hung like late-harvest fruit on the withered stem of my arteries. "No, sir," I said, taking his hand in mine and closing his stiff fingers over the desiccated organ. "*Such things do exist!*"

An hour later, after the wound sealed and he had me open it again for a second, third, and fourth time, giggling each time with fiendish relish as the flesh reknit with a faint crackle, he finally got to the point of our meeting.

"Lon said you'd make me change my mind," he said. "He wasn't kidding."

CHAPTER 32

Uncle Carl looked as if he'd swallowed a live guppy. It was the only time I saw tears in Junior's eyes. Of the small group of us who suffered through that first assembly, only one of us was grinning. That was Browning. And I think that had more to do with his luck at track than the nitrate offal cooling in the take-up reel of the projection booth. Apart from a few on-set visits, my influence was stridently banned from the picture. Still, I couldn't help feeling more than partly responsible for the overheated wake we were all being forced to endure once the lights came up.

"Put it on the road, Junior," Uncle Carl finally said.

"But, Pop."

"Put it on the one-nighter circuit, son. Let's try to get back what we can out of it."

"But with a few edits . . ."

"Gold leaf on sheep shit is still sheep shit, my son." It was the only time I'd heard Uncle Carl curse.

It went to midnight whoopee shows, where it played to houses packed with self-soiled bums and junkie whores too jittery to ply the streets. The highlight of its East Coast run was in New Haven, where a few rambunctious students released a flock of live bats in the theater. The local press, unaware the bats were a student prank, praised the studio for its creative publicity. To cover all bases, a silent version was even struck. But even that played to mostly empty houses.

Then, somewhere in the Midwest, in some rinky second-run house, in a town with a greater population of cows than people, a strange thing happened. People began to line up.

It started, as with all innovative American entertainment, with a religious backlash. The son or daughter of some Cotton Belt Methodist must have come home bug-eyed and salivating, mumbling about the blood being the life. And when it was finally gleaned that the traumatized child was *not* reciting the Eucharist, an all-out crusade began. Reels of celluloid exploded in bonfires, effigies with straw widow's peaks and flour-sack capes were torched at sporting events. Local pastors flooded the weak radio signals of rural communities, denouncing the "unwholesome and deviously satanic" allure of this new abomination from Tinseltown. It was Lugosi as a caped and coifed John the Baptist heralding, in spirit, what would be the first coming of rock and roll. The approbation of children makes things cool. Their parents' dollars make them commodities. Shows that sold out at midnight would sell out for the first few showings of the next day. Lines wrapped around city squares, through cow pastures, over the low hills of Civil War battlefields.

Then the conflagration came to the cities.

And how did father and son thank those fat cherubs of solvency as they came triumphantly through the stucco gates of that San Fernando elysium? They dropped Browning's contract.

"But she was a hit," I said, watching Browning sip his breakfast from a silver flask in a corner of the commissary.

"She took too long to turn a buck," he said, blinking. "And timing is the name of this fucking game, kiddo."

"Where will you go?"

"Back to Metro. I don't think Sam will ever be done with me. Not until he can convince himself he actually understands one of my pictures." But that wasn't why he had agreed to meet me. He had other news. And he took his time getting to it. "At least you got something to look forward to," he said, smirking. "I hear Junior's putting a man-made-creature picture on deck. You heard about this? A man-made-monster picture. Sound familiar?"

Was it too much to hope for?

"You're sure about the theme?"

"Sure. Some crazy professor makes a man out of spare parts. Ain't that your picture?"

"They have a script?"

"Do they *ever* have a script?"

"So what do I do next?"

"I'll tell you what you *don't* do. You don't go breaking through doors demanding your shot. That leads to one of two things. First, they'll see you're desperate and pay you a pittance to compromise yourself into the gutter. The second thing they'll do is reject you out of hand as too stupid and green to not know when you should keep your cards to your chest. Your best option is to write a vital treatment, if only to let them know what they'd be missing. Then you wait. Just remember, everyone loses who *really* plays in this game, kid."

Maybe that was true for Browning. Slightly less so for Chaney. But not for me. I had the insight. I had the pedigree. I had the inside track even if Junior was unaware that I was in the race. This was what I had been waiting for. This was my desire patiently cultivated now bearing luscious bloodred fruit. But such a tree has thorns.

I decided I needed to "Americanize" my concept. Write an updated treatment with the themes of *The Toymaker* and forget that the film, in one form, already existed. Realizing the necessity of such a document was far different than actually producing it. At least for me, whose payment for her best creative insights always involved the rhythmic ministration of some long and blunt instrument. It was one thing to field ideas with Chaney, but I had never gotten to write that treatment. This was new. I was alone. The prospect of writing it, what I would have to endure to achieve it, was terrifying.

I found my perch in box five and curled into my nest of yellowed racing sheets and the damp charnel-house reek the rats left behind. I burrowed deep in the pungent filth, erasing all question of light, prying open the thick black void that was what passed for my mind. I did not have to wait long to imagine I heard him. His amused tenor would have been indistinct from my own had I the ears to hear it. But this was not possession. This was an anchor of habit that brought me down to these cold and instructive depths. He was as memory would have painted him, his face a blur that flickered in the fickleness of recalled horrors. A single eye with teeth that sprouted indelicate fingers.

Your creature needs to have once been human, he began. *Not those quaint clockworks from your original. He is repurposed, without his approval. A victim of an existential rape. Perhaps you know a little something about that. Americanize it? Why, there's a brute and simple sodomy. Make it bigger, faster, louder, with an impassioned hate for anything that has come before it and you have made it American. Put your monster in a man's modern suit, age it, ill-fit it and you will have what these cheeseburger eaters call modernity. But we need something more than that, don't we? You can't sense it. You have brined too long beyond pain, beyond death. Beyond fear. You've grown soft in your rictus, yes? What we need is the blade between the skin and muscle, to excite the nerves while the patient still kicks. But not here. We must go back. Back to when death was still undiscovered. When loss still crouched, distant, in its hard black egg.*

I was suddenly on a dim treeless street. The air itself seemed to rain dread. I could smell the stink of charring bodies as dark motes of diseased flesh swirled in a dry gray snow. The plague fires burned greenly. Vienna. The street was familiar now. I stood before the abandoned house of my artist. The windows were boarded. The front door gaped.

Inside.

The walls were ravaged. But there was no passion here. Only the thin whispers of panic, the artifacts of terror that still dripped and swung and fluttered. The stairs broke the silence in small tortured concussions as I mounted them. And there was the room where we had worked, where I had lived, the floorboards curled from rain. And there was the low bed where the artist had taken his wife one last time before she died. Before he died.

And there they lie.

The bones of his back so sharp in life, honed further by the skin that had tightened in rot. And she beneath him, stiff in a final bliss that was clear even without the amplifiers of her eyes. She was a dry creek beneath his skeletal truss. And where they joined, only the maggots danced. Do you wonder how the dead feel pain?

They dream it.

For what was that now on the floor? So small and shivering and frail? It was me. But from an angle I had not witnessed. Why were its fingers bound, its toes tied tightly in dull webbing? Fear doesn't throb for the dead the way it does for the living. It does not stab or alert. It echoes. Slowly. An ache pierced through the belly by hooks, shambling, through the dust, lost. There was a shadow above me with limbs as gnarled as dead branches, a needle in its leafless fingers.

Where does the needle go, Maddy? it whispered.

Where does the needle go?

My lips had already been stitched shut, so my scream was muted as it imploded in muffled terror in the confines of my throat.

In the eyes.

The needle went into my eyes.

Above me was Lucky. But not as I remembered him. Neglect had shorn the lips from his face, the charm of his crooked teeth now ghastly without their fleshy veil. Murmurs of movement where his eyes had been. And the needle. Plunging over and over into the ripe and swollen freshness of my eyes.

I don't want to remind you of anyone, Maddy.

And the reek of the grave blistered forth from his lagging jaw as he moved his skull upon my lips. I pulled away with a shudder of revulsion.

Not like that, Maddy, he mocked as his fingers burrowed blindly into my scalp, forcing what was once his face to mine. His tongue was a tangle of worms that gnawed greedily through the stitches. They fell, cold, in a thousand disparate tangles of appetite, chewing my living gums and cheeks. Wet bodies frothing the rising blood. Writhing and filling. Filling and writhing. Hot tears. God, I could still shed them.

The terror would not ebb.

Then shoes. His immaculate shoes that could belong to no other.

Do you remember now, child? Is your attention duly primed? Shall we begin?

WHEN THE TREATMENT WAS FINISHED I SENT IT TO THE FRONT OFFICE and waited. When word came, I went to the studio laundry and stole several clean sheets and a cake of harsh laundry soap. In the dead of night, the night before my meeting, I opened one of the wall spigots behind the stage and doused my naked body with icy water. I lathered the soap hard, in my hair, my open eyes, inside my mouth. I washed the grave off me. All memory and thought of anything decayed and neglected and reeking. I swept my box of its filth, then flooded it with chill water and scrubbed the graying boards with the claws of my hands, breaking like tubes of chalk the tips of my fingers. When it was clean, I lined my box with the sheets, folding the corners precisely to the peripheries. Never would I exist in rot again. Never would I dream like that again.

CHAPTER 33

My walk to the front of the lot was purposeful. The first time it had been so. My treatment was good. A little florid perhaps, but solid in its conviction. I was aware of the irony of my trajectory, how I was headed to where I had begun. But a beginning was what I needed to make. To *finally* make. My creator was a woman. And she had made her monster from a man. Not a spare body. Not a nameless corpse from an unmarked grave. A man she had known. A man she had loved. A man she had murdered. Because he had hurt her. Had tried to break her. And in such an attempt had broken himself. Now he was fixed. Remade to love her, to fill her loneliness with cold caresses, her hollows with the rictus of rot. To never stray, to never leave her. To love her the way he had first loved her when he had brought *her* back from the dead. True, it never would have played the Rialto in Van Nuys. But that wasn't the point. I had proven I could do it. On my own. Such passion, such vision, such *resolve* could not be denied.

Junior's secretary showed me into his office immediately upon my arrival. The studio may have faltered, but Junior's surroundings had definitely flourished. Gone was the practical tiger oak, replaced by well-fed deco curves in pearl-colored Bakelite and milky plaster, a desk supported by stylized palm leaves that spoke more of female thighs than tree-lawn fauna. Sconces like overturned breasts seemed like organic ripples in the plasterwork. In a chair that at once seemed forbidding and ridiculous, a frond-backed thing that resembled an albino peacock's tail, sat Junior.

"Miss Ulm," he greeted me as if I were a shareholder, a lit cigar between his teeth. He was not alone.

The man in the chair opposite Junior's did not stand to greet me. He blew the smoke he held in his mouth through a distracted downturn of his lips and smiled ingratiatingly, looking to Junior as if acknowledging me was not in his contract.

"Charmed," the man said with a clipped high London accent. He was blond, pale, immaculate in a demeanor that was only tarnished by the mocking grin that never seemed to leave his lips. A man so reposed in his own intelligence, arrogance, and cream-colored linen that conversation with others seemed more a concession than a pleasure.

"Jimmy here's just come off a big hit for us, *Waterloo Bridge*," Junior said, motioning to the man, "and has been given his choice of properties—"

"I'm going to stop you there, Junior."

Jimmy turned his lithe body toward me.

"You see, Miss Ulm, this studio has such an appalling *lack* of amusing ideas that *choice* seems hardly to have entered into it. I need something different. Something other than the *war*, you see. And you seem to have done rather well, financially at least, with that vampire dross."

"The rumor is Browning never would have attempted *Dracula* if it wasn't for our little Maddy here," Junior quipped hopefully.

"So it's *you* the cinematic pantheon has to thank for that hysterical mess. I didn't know whether to laugh or weep," he said to me with a vague smile. What the hell was this? Here I had come to plead my case to Junior, to field his praise and assuage his doubts in private. And suddenly I was on display; Junior with that cloying used-car-salesman grin and this supercilious bastard all but kicking my tires.

"What Jimmy here is trying to say . . .," Junior began.

"What Jimmy is trying to say is perfectly relatable by Jimmy *himself*," he breezed. "I chose *Frankenstein* as my next project, Miss Ulm, because I thought it might prove a bit of fun. However, it seems the management is slow to believe that I will treat the subject with the proper gravitas."

"What's a fright picture without the fright?" Junior interjected. *Frankenstein*? It was the first I had heard of it.

"It was felt that you, who is rumored to have an insight into the genre, might be able to assist me in attaining this lamentable bathos. I told Junior I do not collaborate. That my success, as well as my failures, are only of interest if they are my own. He insisted we meet, however. Which quite obviously we have." Jimmy stubbed out his cigar and, standing, pulled smartly on the tails of his waistcoat.

"Jimmy, wait," Junior said, pulling the soggy wreck of his cigar from his mouth. "Maddy here has a real track record with this kind of thing. She was great with Chaney, and I think she might be good for you too. Give her a chance. That's all I'm asking."

"A chance to what, Junior? I've seen these pictures to which you refer, and frankly, I have no interest in emulating *any* of them. Your success in this genre can quite simply be relegated to the shock of the new. You only procured the rights to *Dracula* because Metro lost interest after Mr. Chaney's demise, yes? From here on out you will have to do something truly spectacular or watch your precious horror franchise be usurped by studios with better budgets and, frankly, better taste."

Jimmy turned to me with a smile.

"Now I'm sure you are a perfectly charming child, but simply put, you *are* a child. I mean no offense other than what stating the obvious could inflict."

"You're making a mistake, Jimmy, this kid—"

I raised my hand for silence.

"He's quite right, Mr. Laemmle," I said. "I know what I appear to be, Mr. . . . ?"

"Whale."

"Just as I am sure you know what *you* appear to be. How stagnant would our careers be if our mere *appearances* proved the truth? All rumor aside, unless you have seen the two pictures I directed for UFA, you know nothing of my work. To judge me on what has been religiously *denied* me could only be construed as the height of idiocy."

I turned to Junior. "Mr. Laemmle, *Junior*, I want to direct. I've wanted to direct since I arrived here. And you said *produce*. So I produced something. My treatment."

"What treatment?"

"The one I presumed about which you called me here."

"The lady-doctor thing?"

"Did you read it?"

"I looked at the coverage."

"And?"

"What? This isn't Krautville, kid. You can't *do* that stuff. The creature *schtupping* the dame and the dead flesh and the pins in the eyes. C'mon." Junior grinned at Jimmy, but Whale stared at me shrewdly. Had he read my treatment too? "But in the broad strokes it's very similar to *Frankenstein,* you gotta admit. That's why . . ."

I had no idea then just how similar they would make it.

"What is this *Frankenstein* you keep referring to?" I insisted.

"Jimmy's next picture. The man-made-monster thing." So that was it. A decision had already been made, my role in the endeavor already cast.

"I see." I was sick inside. Shattered. But I refused to let it show. "So my being summoned is just an attempt to get me to hold the hand of yet *another* self-important neophyte who doesn't have the first *clue* about the genre."

"I wouldn't put it that way."

"Why not *me*?" I blurted. Why is it always so horrible asking for what you want?

"Why not you *what*?"

"Why not let *me* direct this *Frankenstein*. You said yourself I'm the best qualified." Whale could barely contain the amused smirk that tap-danced across his face.

"I never said *that*," Junior said, raising his hands defensively. "Come on, kid. You know how this is going to play out. I'm not sayin' you don't have something."

"So why not give *me* the chance?" My voice broke in its passion. "I've done *everything* this studio has asked of me. And more. Can you honestly imagine this picture without the *spark* I could give it?" I was suddenly aware of my child's stature, my narrow shoulders, the glut of knee that held my fragile weight. I could have just as easily been negotiating to stay up past my bedtime.

"I'll answer that one, Junior," Whale said. "Because, my dreary little doll, he *owns* you either way."

And there it was, the truth of my indentureship served up with a sweet-smelling smirk from a snarky fruit in ecru-colored linen. Junior looked to the immaculate nap of his carpet.

"Then I have my answer, Mr. Laemmle, and you have my notice. Good luck with your picture, Mr. Whale. I'm sure you'll tiptoe around our *hysterical messes* and find a *spectacular* solution to your script. By the way, modern dress is the key. But I imagine you read that in my treatment. Good day."

And for that moment, as I passed from their sight, through the office door, I was unemployed, falling faster than a stone, nauseous, terrified, yet somehow somber in my resolve. I had just principled myself into a breadline (metaphorically speaking). I would give Mutter my regards and . . . but even *I* couldn't buy my own bullshit. Should I slink back? Beg for any position? Make coffee? Run scripts? What the hell had I done? Did it matter? Yes, goddamn it, it mattered. I was worth what I wanted and it was clear I would never achieve that at this studio. I would always be a dark talisman, a gothic good-luck charm, worthy of affiliation but not the helm. How far was it to Paramount? Could I dodge the love songs of the weeds and gravel long enough to make it over the hill to Metro?

I did not have long to ponder this. Just outside the studio gate, a white limo idled. The door opened at my approach.

"Get in," Whale whispered from its cool, flower-scented interior.

Partnership? Not really. More like a lifeline, I suppose. I leaped at it.

"I've always loved a strong exit," Whale said, nodding to his chauffeur to drive. "And yours would have made Barrymore shit his knickers *green*. We'll probably end up hating each other. But I have a suspicion what we do together might outlive us both."

He was only half right, of course.

CHAPTER 34

These would be the parents of the creature: a sallow, ageless, chronically underappreciated German-born adolescent and an arrogant, self-important but still frustratingly brilliant queen. Whale didn't bother to tell me why he changed his mind. I supposed he found me amusing. And amusement held a premium for Mr. Whale.

"It's a frightfully poor story, really," he exhaled in the interior of his limo as we drove to the heights of Hollywood. "The only amusing element is the brash doctor's presumption at getting that poor lump off the slab. That and the fun one could have with the creature itself. That was the title of the original stage production you know, *Presumption*. It was the age of Kean, so you can imagine the floodlights doused with passionate spittle from the wildly pontificating actors, the creature spouting in rhymed couplet."

"He should be mute," I said, watching the residences out my window flash like schizophrenics from Moorish to Mediterranean to Tudor.

"Pardon?" he asked, turning to me.

"The creature. He should say nothing."

"An infant of pure ethos?" he said, lighting a cigar and smiling.

"Pathos. We should feel sorry for him."

"That lumpy, sutured mess?"

Who said anything about sutures? The bastard must have seen my German original.

"Children should love him," I said. "Only those who *betray* him should fear him."

"Certainly break with convention. And who would be my antagonist if the creature now fondles our heartstrings?"

"The *idea* is the villain," I said calmly.

"That tone does seem to lurk beneath the prose of the book."

Why was he keeping up this ruse of the book? All my instincts screamed he had no intention of doing anything remotely recognizable as someone else's work.

"I never read the book," I said.

"Well, you have unnerving insight for such an illiterate. Bite of lunch?"

We had stopped at his apartment. A simple walk-up, small but elegant with one large window facing the Broadway Holiday Building. Tasteful trappings. Framed originals. Small bronzes. And on the wall was a watercolor portrait of a young girl curled under scrutiny, nude, in garish oranges and greens, a whitewash over her stomach. I recognized it immediately. It was me. Painted by my artist a lifetime ago. The last view of myself alive.

"Herr Schiele," I said under my breath.

Whale gave a small start.

"Do you know Egon Schiele's work?"

"Quite well," I said.

"Few do. But I must say there is an uncanny resemblance between you and the subject."

"There should be," I said evenly. "I *sat* for it."

The director paused. And then a smile filled his face as he assessed my obviously impossible claim.

"You know, child," he said. "You are far more interesting than you initially appeared. David?" He called into the kitchen and there appeared a man, shirtless, with an apron around his waist. He kissed the director fully on the mouth.

"Lunch won't be much, last night's tagine and a green salad," David said.

"Set another place," Whale whispered, looking to me.

"Oh my," David moaned. "I hope it doesn't drink milk. I used the last in our coffees this morning."

"I won't be eating," I said, stepping forward. "But I do appreciate the gesture." I bowed. I had learned never to shake hands.

"Formal, isn't it," David said, curtsying. "What's it called?"

"Maddy something. But really, David, you should try to be more civil. She is frightfully clever and we will be working together."

"Madeline or Magdalene?" David asked, lighting a cigarette.

"*Mädchen*, actually," I answered. "My mother was nothing if not literal."

"Oh, my favorite kind of mother. You can stay." And he flitted off into the kitchen and moved bowls and opened drawers while Whale moved me to the sofa.

"My guess is we'll get stuck with an adaptation of the Webling for a text, but I'll want more comic relief. I like the idea of a mute. Limits our casting choices, but it makes sense. I've already worked out the look of the thing."

He fumbled through a portfolio before removing a sketch that he handed me. Mutter's face gazed back at me.

"Where is the original?" I asked.

"Pardon?" Whale exhaled a stream of smoke.

"Lon made the original drawing of this makeup years ago. Where is it? Or is plagiary another of your hidden talents?"

"My, you have done your homework."

He stood and reached behind a chair and there it was, faded a bit but still Mutter. Serious, slightly afraid, trying to concentrate, trying to earn his box of chocolate. Heartbreaking.

"I know the man who sat for this."

"You are full of jests, aren't you?"

"We came from Germany together. He fought in the war."

"You're serious?"

"Deathly. Would you like to meet him?"

"I do so hope your precociousness will eventually strike me as charming."

CHAPTER 35

Whale did not like the outdoors, nor the rough or wild places. His idea of roughing it was a poolside sherry at the Beverly Hills Hotel. In those days, the backlot, the Indian village, would qualify as wild. He did like the shirtless half-breeds and stuntmen parading around in tight dungarees and sweaty deltoids, however. And a smile never left his face as I took him deeper into the circle of teepees and hollowed-out car bodies that now doubled as domiciles.

Mutter stopped when he saw me. It had been several months. From his hand fell the fist of his son, who was walking now, his head as round and furred and normal as any human child's. Mutter stared at me and I could see his mind working, remembering, checking for sweetness, for fondness, before he smiled and approached me. I leaped into his arms and he held me tightly, embracing me off the ground.

Seeing Mutter was not a revelation for Whale. I believe he saw the real-time resemblance of his creation as a usurpation of his creativity, an affront to what he needed to protect and project as *his* originality. I wish I knew then how far he would go to defend it. I remember him standing in the cow shit and crumpled hay, his outline darkening in the fading sun, the raw real life all around him, the sloppy families and happy, naked children with sooted noses, the supper fires just beginning to smoke, and he, in his elegant high boots, his face inflamed with a slight disgust, looking as out of place as a Limoges figurine on a bomb range. It was the only time I would see Jimmy Whale at a loss for words.

Whale was an artistic aristocrat, a man burdened with an almost regal responsibility to distinguish himself. He was aware of Hollywood's unspoken code of candor and insisted each worker in his sphere refer to him as Jimmy, but this seemed more an invitation to complicity than a genuine gesture of warmth. People were treated civilly only as long as they did his bidding. I, alone, was solicited for my opinions, an act he found so circumspect it took place only in private.

"The ending's no good," Whale said one day over a lunch of shrimp salad and a glass of Montrachet. "This business with the ice floes will appear . . . What is the American slang?"

"Hokey?"

"Precisely. Primarily because their breath won't fog and believability is most essential with the fantastic. It needs a touch of Revelation, an almost biblical undoing."

"Locusts? Frogs?"

"Too much sugar on your Wheaties, dear?"

"Fire?"

"Perhaps, but something literate."

"Hanging? *A Tale of Two Cities*?" I offered. (To work with Whale without at least a cursory knowledge of world literature was to risk a tedious tongue-lashing that always ended with an elbow crook stuffed with some dingy leather tome.)

"I see where you're going, the flesh rounding full circle." Some of the corpse had been taken from a hanged man in Shelley's story. Or was it my original he was pilfering? "I like the symmetry, but it's too prosaic. It has to be a metaphor for quelled audacity, a failed dream."

"A windmill?" My last reading assignment had been the heft of Cervantes.

"Quixote's giants. I think you have something. Trapped in one's ambition, one's affront to the natural order, immolated in the dream, destroyed in desire. Marvelous. Can't you see those massive sails streaking sun-bright in the night?"

He would always remember the inspiration as his own. Just as he would my suggestion of modern dress. He would later tell the press the idea had been his unrealized desire to do Shake-speare's *Timon of Athens* in the guise of American bootleggers.

One idea that was his own was the casting of the titular doctor. For the part of Henry, Whale gave very little thought to casting a friend and colleague of his, an actor he had directed in his hit *Journey's End*. The studio at this point had reduced the budget by a hundred thousand and had very little leverage in convincing Whale to hire a name.

Colin Clive's alcoholism was legend, as were his nervous ex-cesses, his shell-shocked magnetism, his early demise while still beautiful. What was not so well reported was that he was a kind, chivalrous, preternaturally sensitive man who spoke three lan-guages and insisted on calling me *ma petite tant pis* (my little too bad) because he was convinced my pallor and thin frame were the result of some wasting disease. He was constantly slipping me cold shingles of toast dripping with great yeasty smears of Marmite, convinced of the yeast derivative's restorative powers.

Whale had still not cast the role of the creature. He believed that the right actor would simply materialize, like some hideous Venus from a mechanical clamshell. He would go on to claim authorship for every aspect of the picture, including Freund's chiseled shadows and Pierce's iconic makeup. So I knew he would never accept an actor who had not blossomed under his strict curatorship. Seeing Mutter and not considering him for the role confirmed as much. We had not discussed the essential of a sympathetic creature, not past our initial meetings. And I think Whale thought a monster picture required a fairly requisite monster. I felt differently. I knew the monster was the paternal maker, the creature the child victim. How, in my present state, with my strained maternal relationship, could I have felt differently? So I was actively looking. In the basements at the janitors taking their sullen cigarette breaks. Among the burly carpenters in the set shop. Unusual office boys and the chauffeurs of certain stars. I was looking for eyes. Sympathetic eyes, loving, yearning, ill-begotten but caring eyes. With the part irrefutably mute, these would be the actor's only arsenal.

I found the eyes I was looking for one day on the lot, under a fringe of pomaded bangs, beneath a craggy brow, headed expeditiously to the men's room. I followed them in. A tinned knight and a clown were just dipping back into the flies of their costumes. And what could I be other than a midget in drag to their distracted eyes? I stood my ground behind the set of eyes and waited. He was of average height, of average build, perhaps on the thin side. From the back, his shoulders were not very broad. And I thought of the challenge to wardrobe. Then he turned around. He had a wedge-shaped head, dark complexion with sunken cheeks.

"Are you lost, my dear?" his gentle voice cooed, softened further by a sibilant lisp. His eyes were perfect, warm and dark as two mugs of chocolate.

"No," I finally answered.

"Are you looking for the ladies loo?"

"You're English?" Somehow I thought this might endear him to Whale.

"Enfield, yes. Are you sure I can't help you?"

"I'm here to help *you*."

He tucked and zipped.

How that smile of his could ever be considered sinister I'll never know.

"Then this must be my lucky day," he said, moving to the sink to wash his hands.

I told him about the new production, how I felt he would be perfect for it, and how he simply needed to meet Mr. Whale. He nodded ingratiatingly, indulging the obviously deluded child who rambled beneath him. Whale was deep in preproduction by then and forced to take whatever sustenance he required from the lot. I told him to be in the commissary tomorrow, precisely at lunchtime.

"But I never take lunch in the commissary." He smiled. "Too much cutter. I bag it most days or go without."

"Well, then here," I said, giving him a quarter. "Have a roll and coffee tomorrow. But be sure to be there."

He fingered the coin, a faint yearning in his eyes, then held it out for me to take back.

"I'm serious. This could be big," I said.

"And by what name goes my generous benefactress?"

"Maddy," I said. "Maddy Ulm."

"Boris," he said. "But I think you should call me Billy. Billy Pratt." His given name was William.

"Be there, Billy," I said. And those warm eyes blinked warmly but noncommittally and I watched him join a chorus of other under-fives dressed in pinstripes and spectators.

Whale refused lunch the next day. And the next. Every day at noon for a week, I would spy Mr. Pratt sitting alone, nursing his tea and roll in his best suit. And every day I would offer my apologies and slip him another quarter for the next day's ruse.

It was a Friday when Whale, exhausted and merely wanting a cup of tea, finally stopped in the commissary. I forced him to sit under the pretense of my own hunger. Having never seen me eat, he seemed oddly fascinated by the prospect of actually watching me consume a meal. I searched the tables to no avail. Mr. Pratt was nowhere in sight, probably bored by our little game. But still I piled on heaps of steaming roast beef and potatoes. Panicked, I feigned delight at the culinary delights that awaited me. Sitting down, I had just stuffed my dry throat with a particularly undercooked bit of potato when Whale announced that he had to return to work. The noxious bites of beef simply flew into my mouth. I felt them back up in gelatinous layers in the proximal end of my esophagus. My gusto distracted Whale from his departure and I kept packing in the tasteless food.

"Easy, child. Save room for your pudding."

I felt sure my throat and chest would explode from the pressure when Whale's eyes narrowed past me.

"Hello," he said distractedly. "Won't be a tick," and he shot up and raced to a table behind me. I, of course, was splitting. Literally. Thankfully, the damage was behind the buttons of my blouse, and as I recused myself to the ladies' room to purge the dead flesh from my deader hollows, I spied Whale gleefully lighting a cigar as he invited Mr. Pratt, who must have slipped in during my performance, to join him.

When I returned, Whale waved me over with an avuncular dip of his hand, the gesture of that odd ever-clean uncle who liked to linger in the clinging steam while the boys took their bath, and said, "I've found him." Mr. Pratt looked distressed. It was clear he thought I deserved the credit for his "discovery." But I knew differently. I shot a warning glance to Billy. His face reassembled in innocence.

"Well, Miss Ulm." Whale exhaled with a tint of boredom. "Meet the creature."

"That's marvelous, Mr. Whale," I demurred. "He's *perfect*."

CHAPTER 36

I was sitting with Mr. Pierce, the picture's makeup artist, mid-summer, in the cold white of his home studio amid the rolls of mortician's wax stacked like toy cigars and smoked bottles of solvent-smelling collodion, watching him eat a spongy cake of feta cheese as he held forth on the morphology of midfacial prognathism and the unique yet purely speculative contention that middle-Pleistocene Neanderthals had no concept of a future tense. They were children in that frozen wilderness, he explained, dim to the need for complex tools. And yet death, which with their cognitive deficiencies must have seemed a rough repeating surprise, still yielded elaborate, even compassionate, burials. They loved. And might have died out because they so loved. Frankenstein's creature would have their large-boned bodies, their rough gait and brooding suborbital torus, but not because he was a club-wielding brute straight from the Sunday funnies. Rather because the creature was a childlike son of Adam. Simple, hurt, hungry for love, and ultimately hateful when that love was withheld. At least I didn't have to convince Pierce of the necessity of the creature's nature.

"Yes, yes, Jack," Whale would whisper dismissively after he'd heard Pierce's reasoning, "but I can't have an overgrown infant parading around wet-eyed for eighty minutes. He must be terrifying. Unequivocally ghastly. You do understand, old man, don't you?"

"I understand this makeup must tell the truth of the character."

"When has a tin of lip rouge ever been party to the truth?"

"Precisely," Pierce said in his accented English. "Beauty makeup *is* a lie. But this cannot be."

"Just stick to my sketches; there's a good man."

These summer sessions at Pierce's home studio were the only luxury Whale afforded us. Billy sat patiently in the chair, the great peak of foul-smelling meringue above his eyes outgassing stridently while Pierce left to make coffee. He had suffered through weeks of several failed makeups, each time winning nothing more than Whale's polite disdain. He never complained. So that afternoon I assumed it was the Elgar on the wireless that was making his doe-like eyes water.

"Dear me," he said, trying a reluctant smile. "I do look a fright. I seem to have fallen asleep at the Brighton shore and a whole flock of seabirds has had its nasty way with me." Unpainted, his cotton and collodion brow did look a bit like a carefully molded turd.

"You'll look better once you're painted."

"Ah, yes, and such a flattering morgue green. I can just see the offers jostling for supremacy once we wrap."

"You'll be wonderful."

"Listen to me. Crying in my tea for cream. I suppose I should be grateful for the chance to eat."

"What's wrong, Billy?"

"Isn't it obvious? I'm forty-four years old and for the first time in my oh-so-humble career I have a role I have *absolutely* no idea how to play. An odd-mannered corpse."

"Oh, he's much more than that."

"Is he? Whale doesn't seem to think so. The pinnacle of his direction to date has been to tell me to cut back on the fags."

"Forget what Whale said. Or hasn't said."

"My dear girl, I couldn't possibly." I looked in the mirror at Billy's reflection. There was a gentleman sitting there beneath all that reeking white muck. I would need to soften my approach.

"I should think having once been dead would give the creature a rather exclusive view on living," I said quietly.

He looked at me in the mirror, his eyes wide with a soft curiosity. "And what would such a view be?" Did he know he had solicited my confession? Why did I feel such a sudden sense of pending relief?

"Off the top of my head," I said, trying to sound casual, to sound speculative, "I'd imagine there'd be a pervasive sense of not belonging. Not awkwardness, mind you. Or even being some endearing misfit. But having to look at the world as through a piece of shop glass. Everything you see—the sky, the sun, the faces of animals and people, nothing belongs to you. Nothing is yours. You can move through the world, even touch it. But you can never *belong* to it. And yet that knowledge does nothing to dispel your very real desire for it. It would be to know the world only secondhand. To have to face every false day, every counterfeit night knowing what others only glimpse at their very end: that the world was never really yours to begin with, that everything you held dear, had fought for and loved for had only ever been *borrowed*." Billy was silent for a long time. Had he heard? I might have given him the only real direction he would receive during the entire shoot, but I had no idea if he had understood me.

"I never noticed that before," he said finally.

"What?"

"Your fingers. The tips of your fingers are black." I could not hide them before he picked one up in his warmth and winced at the coolness. What could I say? An effect of the blood pooled there from my stilled heart?

"The nitrate stains," was all I offered. "From when I worked in editing." He was unconvinced, but it was clear he did not care to believe anything else.

"It's an excellent effect," he said. "We should tell Jack."

"I will."

"You are very dear, Maddy," he said to my reflection. "I would be quite happy if you could find your way to be near me during the shoot. I feel you'd be a great comfort to me."

I was well past the false front of my years. And the way he looked at me then, the warmth of the room and his eyes stirred feelings I hadn't felt since Lucky. But that is the real fruit of Volker's legacy.

To be near.

And nothing more.

CHAPTER 37

Billy, signing his name Karloff, was bound by a standard minimum contract for artists guaranteeing him no less than one week of employment. There was a rider attached ensuring the studio additional provisions regarding retakes, added scenes, and trailers, but nothing that spoke of infinite fame. Not that first sweltering August day of shooting. Especially not to Billy in his gasoline-smelling face and six-inch asphalt-layer boots. Whale dragged him through sixteen hours of grueling takes, with no breaks, no respites. No wonder Mr. Karloff would later be instrumental in the formulation of the Screen Actors Guild.

It wasn't all forced humility. One pleasant but difficult surprise was seeing the picture's shooter on the first day. It was none other than Karl, the fried-potato-loving cameraman who had tutored my wrist all those years ago at UFA. He was loading his bulk onto the location bus when he stopped. He pushed violently past several dress extras on his way to hug me.

"My God! Maddy, dear!" he said in German, lifting me off the ground. "What in heaven are you doing here?"

"Karl! Jesus, *Karl*!" What the hell is he going to say about my changeless state, I mused as he put me down.

"I thought you'd be up to here by now!" he said placing a pudgy hand to his shoulder.

"Yes, well. Still not eating enough, I suppose. I miss those omelets." He looked at me. Endeared. Confused. A meeting completely out of time and context.

"You should be directing this pap."

"Don't remind me." I hoped my smile seemed genuine and wasn't poisoned with the panic I was feeling under his searching gaze. Whale arrived, thankfully, calling out to me, and the company roused into ranks. "My master's voice," I said, rising up on tiptoes to kiss Karl's loose cheek. His smile was still stiff, his mind churning with questions I didn't dare answer. It was sad that I was forced to avoid him. He might have been a real friend.

I cooled in the shadows as much as I could after that chance meeting. Could I have imparted more of my sensibility to the picture had I not been forced to haunt it? I'll never know. My biggest regret was not running more interference with the actors. Whale was relentless. When Colin showed up an hour late his third day, unsteady, either from nerves or spirits, Whale made an enormous show of stopping work to welcome him.

"Well, well, look who decided to drop by. Restful evening, Clivey?"

I remember Colin near tears.

"What's that? Oranges and lemons?"

"Say the bells of Saint Clements," Clive answered, willing himself to smile.

"Get a bucket," Whale said calmly. When no one moved, he pointed directly at me and hollered, "Get a *fucking* bucket!"

After I brought it, setting it quietly before Clive in the neat silence of the stage, Whale grabbed Colin's hand and, choosing a digit, shoved the actor's finger down his own throat until he vomited. The poor actor heaved and whimpered through several waves of nausea. When he had finished, Whale said, "All better? Care to join us in the business at hand?"

Clive wiped his mouth and nodded.

"And if you ever appear on my stage in such a condition again I will have you castrated, old boy. Yes? Positions!"

That was how he ruled. I had to choose my battles carefully. But I did what I could. Billy got the worst of it, I'm afraid. Whale was always pretending not to remember his name, and when he did it was always some humiliating bastardization—Morris Stroganoff and the like, truly childish—geared I suppose to keep Billy always on the fringe of satisfaction, never having pleased his master, which, as Whale well knew, was precisely the core of the creature.

We had one company move, our first day, to Lake Malibu. A fleet of limousines lined up in front of the studio at five in the morning to take us there. It was rumored that I was originally cast to play Maria, the little girl who gets chucked in the lake. Of course this was never true. Whale mentioned the possibility once, to which I immediately turned colder than usual. He saved some kind of face by mumbling, "Of course you're right, the part requires innocence, appeal. Not some sour little know-it-all with a German accent." Had he forgotten the undisclosed country of our tale was supposed to be Switzerland? The part went to little Marilyn Harris, who was better known around the lot by the scrotum-shrinking demeanor of her overbearing mother. I had few words with Harris. When she saw that I rode with the director she asked sweetly, "Gee, how do you get on *that* side of the camera?" To which I answered, "By refusing to be on *your* side, I suppose." The drive was tolerable, peppered with Whale's preening stories about his days in Blackpool's vaudeville. When we arrived, Billy was agitated.

"Have you eaten?" I asked.

He was leaning on his slant board, smoking a cigarette, his eyes more blistered than the character called for.

"I had some tea."

"You need something more."

"It's not that, Maddy," he said. "If I ate anything, I'm sure I'd spew." He lit another cigarette.

"What then?"

"The *scene*. This blasted scene with the little girl."

"What of it?"

"Whale wants me to throw the poor thing in after the daisies, and I think that's rather out of character."

"You terrorize Elizabeth. You kill Waldman."

"This is different. It's a *child*. The monster would never hurt a child. It would be like hurting himself."

"Have you told Whale?"

"Incessantly." He spat and threw his still-smoking butt to the dirt.

"I see. Tell him to shove it. Tell him if anyone knows this creature from soup to nuts it's you, and if he knows what's good for the picture he'll leave you alone."

"Maddy!"

"You don't have to say it like that. You can cross the pond and give it some good British starch."

"I can't risk a row. I'm dead on my feet as it is. I just feel all the effort we've put into lending this poor oaf some humanity will all be undone." He said it. He used that wonderful, warm, all-inclusive pronoun. *We.* He *had* understood me. "All for the sake of a man who enjoys pulling the wings off flies."

"True. But only the *lesser* flies."

Near the lake, little Marilyn Harris was polishing off the last of her lemon meringue pie. It was six thirty in the morning. Her mother always indulged her like this on the days she worked. The first assistant director called for places, and Billy pushed himself to his feet. I took his hand.

"Just remember," I said, "it's your ass up there."

"I don't like it when you speak so coarsely."

"Your *bum* then up there. Your glorious stumbling *bum* they'll remember."

We shot the scene in parts. All the segments leading up to the toss of the little girl were easily Billy's best work in the picture. But when it came time to shoot the actual throwing, Billy froze. At first he complained about his back. Then he stumbled, nearly dropping the girl. Finally it came to a point where he wouldn't reach for the girl at all. He would stand there, his head hanging, little Marilyn licking stray tufts of meringue from her fingers, then looking to Billy, and saying, "It's okay, Boris. I'll float."

Whale called, "Cut."

Striding up to Billy, smiling, he said, "What's this, dear boy? Are we at a linguistic impasse? Having trouble with the word *toss* perhaps? I could say *throw, chuck, heave,* maybe *jettison. Jaculate?*"

"I simply can't do it, Mr. Whale. Every instinct in my body is in riot against it."

"Every instinct in your body is under *contract.* I thought that was clear from that officious little piece of paper you signed."

"I understand, Mr. Whale, but it's . . . *wrong.* For the creature." In his boots and false cranium, Billy was nearly seven feet tall. And Whale, in his spotless cream vest and cravat, was just under six feet. It was a parable in reverse. A slim Goliath emasculating a hulking David.

"I see. Well. What say we try this? You *don't* chuck the brat into the drink. And I send you back to under-five gangsters and day-playing red Indians. And I'll jolly well sod back to England. And we can forget this whole ridiculous mess. Yes?"

"I wouldn't care for that."

"Wouldn't you? What's the alternative, then?"

"You could do it on the cut," I spat out.

"I beg your pardon."

"Maddy, *please*," Billy whispered.

"He could hold the girl, feint toward the lake, and then you could cut back to, I don't know, the daisies or something. Floating."

"Floating *daisies*? And all this time I was toiling under the misapprehension we were shooting a *thriller*."

"It will work, Mr. Whale," I said. Billy looked like a snail fresh from the roof of its shell.

"I've no doubt it would, Miss Ulm. But that is not what *I* want. Or has my director's prerogative fallen chummily into the breach of consensus?" Director's prerogative. Christ. I had forgotten what it was like to even *feel* like a director. My ambition had taken on a distinctly maternal cast. And one look at Billy's face told me I was failing even at that. "What do you think, Mr. Karloff? Shall we try it my way? Just for a *lark*?"

"I could give it a go." Billy said to the ground.

"Really? I'd hate to impugn those Kean-like instincts of yours."

"No. You're quite correct, Mr. Whale."

"Oh, I'm *so* pleased," Whale quipped, heading back to his seat. "When you're ready, *Boris*."

For several decades the fates accommodated Billy, as the child-drowning scene was the first to get the ax by the censors. Of course, when it premiered in Los Angeles, the scene was in. But all over the country, when it was rereleased in theaters, and later shown on television, the scene always cut just as Billy reached for the kid. Now it's been "restored," returned to Whale's original vision, but I can't watch it. Not without feeling Billy die a little each time and seeing in my mind Whale's supercilious blond head chucked into the frigid waters and held under until the end credits.

FRANKENSTEIN **WAS A CHRISTMASTIME RELEASE, AND IN THE THEATER** where I saw it, there was a wreath framing Billy's face and plastic garland and holly swagged about the box office. I was not allowed into the editing room. In fact, Whale fired me on the last day of shooting.

It was the burning of the windmill and the throwing of Henry's body onto the flaming sails. A dummy was employed whose loose joints kept bending unnaturally with every take. The company was frustrated, but I, having taken and observed all the abuse I could swallow, was working on being amused.

"Find this funny, do you, Miss Ulm?" Whale said indignantly.

It was three in the morning. He was tucked into his director's chair, bound in a greatcoat and muffler against the mild morning chill. I was in my flimsy blouse.

"I find it a damn riot."

"Do you? And I suppose you could do better?"

"I think throwing a *pot roast* stuck with *broom* handle arms would look better than this shit." Whale was silent. Then he looked to the first assistant director.

"Get Clive padded up," he said, lighting a cigar. Clive had gone home, nursing a hangover after he he'd been told he would no longer be needed for the night. "Oh, yes. I'd quite forgotten that," Whale said spritely. "Then let *Boris* have a go. He was a *truck* driver in a previous incarnation, I believe. This should be child's play." That was the last straw. Billy was a wreck. Weeks of a grueling schedule, not to mention a slipped disk in his lumbar after hauling Clive up the windmill steps take after take, had left him noticeably impaired. Film might be forever but so would the damage to Billy's spine that would already never properly heal. I watched in cold fury as the costumers peeled Billy of his two thick layers of wool pants and strapped him in football pads. I wanted to go comfort him but slinked away when I felt Karl's eyes on me. Billy looked so disoriented and alone, absolutely ill as they fitted him with Clive's hairpiece and cutaway. Whale twittered with the script girl as I watched Billy mount the windmill steps as if they were the gallows. I didn't know what to do. The first cried, "Flames," and the gas jets blared, forcing Billy to flinch as he wobbled near the railing. Whale screamed, "Action." I leaped to my feet before I knew what I was doing. Whale simply grinned as he tossed his hand up near Karl, forcing him to keep rolling. I scrambled up the side of the windmill and landed softly near Billy. I couldn't feel the heat of the gas flames, or even the hot wind of the sails as they twisted slowly beneath me. I could see the faces looking up at me and I saw myself back home before that first frightful fall that had begun it all. It seemed I was forever taking dives off high buildings to make my point.

"Maddy," Billy said to me, sweating so hard his wax eyelids had slipped to the tops of his cheeks, "what on *earth* are you doing?"

In that moment he was Mutter. I was back in Germany. I was just beginning.

"Don't worry," I said, climbing into his arms. "I'll be fine. Just throw me like you did the dummy."

"This is *monstrous*. No!"

"Please. You *have* to trust me."

"But I'm not in proper wardrobe. *Please*, before you get hurt."

"You've quite made your point, Miss Ulm." Whale's voiced boomed through his megaphone, a contraption I noticed he used primarily as a pedestal for his ashtray. "Please do come down so I can fire you properly."

"Oh, Maddy," Billy said. "He can't be serious."

"No?" I said climbing up on the railing. "*Fuck* him." I gave Billy a swift, cool kiss, peeling his panicked fingers from my arm. And dropped into the ether. I felt nothing when I landed, of course. A jostling. A jab. What terrified me was Billy's cry. His scream. There were more screams as I hit the ground. I felt Whale's hand on my shoulder as he turned me over.

"Maddy! Maddy!" Whale cried, trying to rouse me with the tips of his fingers. "For the love of Christ, what have you done?"

"How was that, you blond bastard?" I said sitting up. "*Real* enough for you?"

I didn't wait for his reaction. I was on my feet in an instant. I will always regret not turning to see his face. But some things cannot be topped. Some exits must be clean. My contract was suspended the next day and I was told to leave the lot until further notice. I had no personal effects, nothing to box and carry, so I headed over to the Indian village to make my good-bye.

Billy was there, I remember. I guess Pierce must have told him about Mutter. He had Mutter's boy in his arms and was telling him that he was part Indian too, but a different kind of

Indian. East Indian. He didn't ask me how I had survived the fall, but there was a caution in his eyes, a cooling between us.

"I'll have your contract reinstated, Maddy," he said soberly. "He can't let you go like that. You're just a child. You have to eat."

"Do I?" I asked, smiling.

He let the comment pass.

"I've seen your friend," he said, glancing over to Mutter. "If this picture's a hit, Whale will never let him stay on the lot."

"Mutter will be fine. I barely recognize him in the pictures he plays."

"There's already been talk. Why do you think Laemmle insisted I wear a cloth over my head to the set? To spare the stenographer's nerves?"

It was true. Carl Senior had insisted Billy not show his face from the makeup room to the stage. *Modern Screen* had even run a shot with Pierce escorting a pillow-headed Billy by the hand.

"If Whale can barely share credit for the look of the monster with the man who created it, how do you think he'll fare against the real thing?"

"Nothing's going to happen to Mutter. It's me they're angry with. I needed a break anyway."

A bell rang then, some kind of clarion that signaled the beginning of a meal, and Mutter collected his son and smiled at me, casually, as if he saw me every day. I watched him turn, blending with the other Indians heading to dinner, and realized no good-bye would ever be necessary. But it would be a very long time until we saw each other again.

CHAPTER 38

I had money. Lots of it. Having worked and lived on the lot for so many years, my weekly checks had simply accrued. Hollywood bought cars, but I couldn't part with my flatbed. Polo ponies? A share of Chasen's? Perhaps my own eatery where customers don't eat at all, just sit in boxes full of moist earth and have edifying conversations with the worms and rot?

Maybe a home. Hollywood bought homes. Big homes. Sprawling homes. Estates. Mansions. Compounds. Now that might interest me. I needed a place to hide.

There was a burgeoning development in the hills at the end of Beachwood Canyon, a bucolic emission in milky Moorish stucco from the breathless drafting table of S. H. Woodruff. Busby Berkeley had a home near the stone gates. The development had begun in the twenties, then fallen out of favor with the Depression. I had heard a huge push to revitalize the district was under way. It was the reason for that great white sign on Mount Lee.

Hollywoodland. I could live in Hollywoodland. Water my

palms and bougainvilleas and patrol the wide hot streets. Take in the view of the reservoir. The gray haze that was beginning to gather over Santa Monica.

Five minutes from Hollywood Boulevard—the Sylvan Beauties of the Hills of Hollywood lend subtle charm to the Homes of Hollywoodland and *Husky limbs and lusty lungs for the Kiddies of the Hills.*

"You'll need your parents to cosign if you're serious."

"Why? I don't need a loan."

This gave the agent pause. He was roundish and short, well fed, in a tight-fitting blue suit. Brown shoes. His hair was dark, thinning, and gave off a slightly funereal smell, stale lilac and meals alone. He wore one of those pencil-thin mustaches, more paint than virility, that were so popular among the aging juvenile leads in town.

"You payin' cash? What are you, the next Pickford?"

"I'm the brain that decides the trajectories of each new starlet's eyebrows."

A freshly paved road was all the invitation necessary to take a drive in Los Angeles, even if the journey were a mere three hundred yards up the lazy south-facing slope of Beachwood Drive. We passed Moorish fortresses, Spanish haciendas, Norman castles with curtain walls and ivy-covered keeps (built to repel the garden snails and finger-size lizards I surmised) with great peaked bartizans that overlooked the scrub sage and silence.

"Feel that?" the agent said, giving his steering wheel a graceful turn. "Nice wide roads, generous sidewalks. You can walk here, which is nice. And do you notice what's missing? Huh? You see it?"

I don't think he understood the impossibility implied in his query.

"No phone poles! No wires ruining the view. Everything underground. *Class!*"

We passed a reflecting pool studded with flesh-pink lilies worthy of *The Rubáiyát*. A balding man in black socks and shorts was filling it with a garden hose.

"Your parents going to be joining you soon?"

"Pardon?"

"Your parents? They coming to live with you?"

"Of course."

"I sold Baby Peggy a nice, fat Spanish job a few years back. Ten rooms. What's a family of hillbillies do with ten rooms in the Hollywood Hills? Bootleg? Who knows. Hollywood money, boy! Where they coming from?"

"Who, please?"

"Your folks, sister. Where they comin' from?"

"Germany."

"Ah! Right! Old Deutschland. I was trying to place your accent. *Mutter und Pop*, eh? I got no beef with your man Hitler, the way he's wanting to run things. That egg is okay. A little stiff with the Hebs, but it's about time someone was. You ain't a Jew, are ya?"

He did not wait for my answer.

"Let me tell ya, I'm as white as the next guy and I ain't got no vinegar for my own color but, sheesh, them Jews are tough nuts. I had a kike couple the other day, I was givin' a house away for nothin', a two-bedroom, one-and-a-half-bath, view, and still they wanted me to landscape the joint before escrow. You believe that? Look, folks, I say, planting flowers and trees is half the fun up here, plan your own personal Eden. But that old ball and chain he had with him wouldn't budge. Grass and palms, they wanted. And not seed, mind you. Hell no! *Sod!* Listen, I say, you're takin' the strained peas right outta my kid's mouth. But no washee, sister! I tell ya, them folks can sure shave a dollar. Here we are."

He pulled his car into a clean drive shaded by drowsy willows. The house was a charming old-English-style wattle and daub with plaster "nogging" studded with imitation straw lathered between the exposed timbers. Two quatrefoils, over herringbone bracing, formed two surprised eyes that faced the street from the top floor. Rosebushes lined the stone walk. The mailbox was shaped like a witch's head. I fell in love with it instantly.

"No bunk, kiddo. Now you can wash down your Wheaties in your very own Hansel and Gretel."

I moved in on a blistering day in September. That is to say I took the front door key in my small hand, thanked the agent, shut the door, and sat Indian fashion on the swept oak, facing the empty white walls. I had no furniture for the rooms. No clothes for the closets. No carpets for the floors. No cans or toothbrushes for the cupboards. No preference where the footboard faced. No bed for that matter. To me, the house was little more than a human garage. Apart from a few picture books and the pink-and-cream dress the artist's wife had given me in which I passed a single Sunday afternoon, I had never owned, let alone purchased, something merely for my own amusement.

I felt safe. For although the house was made of natural materials, it was not raw nature herself. And the intoxicating call was not within my new walls. I owned sinks and pipes and switches and wire, walls and planks and counters and crevices, paint and nails, fixtures, plants, a driveway. I was indeed like that old or ugly groom who takes a pretty wife, not for the dusky evenings during which he can exert himself upon her but merely for the reflection her figure provides, the possibility that he *could*. I would have friends, dinner parties, high teas, a servant. I could create a salon of cool elegance where the finest artists would congregate and we would talk about the rareness of real beauty and emerging criteria for cinematic art. I could bind them with stories about my past, about the bitter mornings and hard superstitions of my village. But from my lofty present, from my chintz-covered couches and sterling service trays, my past would seem quaint, all that ugliness reduced to sips and nibbles and sympathetic looks. And when it was time to leave, to say our good-byes, I would not retire alone. I would take a companion to the back rooms with me. I would pan for him. Scrounge and mine and quarry for him. If that failed, I'd hire someone to attend all the rough places of the West, the rodeos and honky tonks. And Lucky would be dug up for me. For that's who he would be. Lucky. With Billy's eyes and Lon's marvelous mind. My own little slab creature of comfort. And his duties would be only in his eyes. How he beheld me. And in his arms. In how he held me.

But I did nothing. After years of constant action, I stopped. Time played its old tricks. That first day and for many more after, I saw the sunshine come in sheets through the clean, mullioned glass. My eyes traced its long tracks upon the floor until it was cold in decline. It was night then, a whole bucketful of night. And the next day I watched the light drag itself across my floor again. And again. For many weeks my thoughts went as blind as a garden worm.

Then there came a knocking. The room was markedly cooler, if I cared to feel it. I could hear voices between the knocking, whispers and twitters of "But I don't know who lives here," and "Who cares, just knock again." The sound of laughter softened through noses. I wasn't curious. I was lonely. I wanted to see another's face. On the lot there was constant warmth and movement. But in these "better" neighborhoods, to know one's neighbors was to not know them at all.

I got to my feet. My body was stiff from disuse. I cracked and creaked and plunked my way to the front door.

"Trick or treat!"

Loudly, in tight unison from three disguised faces. Three boys, I surmised, roughly my age in appearance, although it was hard to tell under their makeup. They smelled of laundry soap and whole milk. The first, the one standing to the front of their small phalanx, had his face smeared a chalky white, his mother's concealer perhaps exploited as a base. On his head, to give it a smooth appearance, he wore a black velvet yarmulke with *Congregation B'nai B'rith* embroidered on its edge, a black triangle of construction paper pinned beneath the words to simulate a widow's peak. The richness of his cape and the satin of his lapels meant he came from money. Only the wire-frame glasses he squinted through diminished his getup.

Next to him, under a brow painted green, pounded from the butt of an empty Eight O'Clock Coffee can, was a plump little Frankenstein's monster whose entire cranium shuddered each time he coughed into a clean handkerchief. He must have cribbed the image from the promotional posters that papered Sunset Boulevard for the picture had yet to be released. The last boy wore a miniature satin smoking jacket, his face trussed up in bandages of toilet tissue, a pair of dark glasses covering his eyes.

"I don't recognize you," I managed to say.

"You will, girly, once the picture's finished," the toilet-paper-faced boy said. "We're still in preproduction."

He was meant to be the Claude Rains character from *The Invisible Man* and I would have to wait another two years to make the connection. Still, it was clear they were children of Hollywood and had the motive instincts of the young Turks they were.

"So what's the story?" the diminutive Jewish Dracula said, pushing his glasses to the bridge of his nose. "You gonna treat or we gotta trick?"

"I'm afraid I don't understand."

"She doesn't understand, fellas," he snorted. "This from a girl lookin' like one of *my* brides. Come off it and quit stallin'."

"Yeah, make with the sweet stuff. And none of that old-lady dish candy," Toilet-paper Face said. "We ain't no grandmas."

"You really don't know what day it is?" fat little Frankie rasped, embodying Billy's sweetness far more than he would ever know. "It's Halloween, kid."

This was a tradition that was just beginning to establish itself in American cities. But I had known the night all my life.

All Hallows' Eve. That was the night in my village when the women would spit in a circle and bar the door from the wandering dead. When all fires and candles were put out to bury us in the safety of darkness and we would tremble under our covers until first light. Leave it to the frivolous Americans, I thought, to remake our most terrifying night in white sugar and molded plastic.

"So what's it gonna be, sister?" Dracula threatened. "We ain't got all night."

"Leave off, Bud." Frankie sighed. "She doesn't have anything."

"Then she pays the price."

"Leave off."

"I said she pays the price. *Egg!*"

The toilet-paper-faced boy pulled a stinking yellow egg out of the pocket of his smoking jacket and dropped it into the palm of the bully vampire.

"Don't say we didn't warn ya." And the egg arched slightly before slamming into the bridge of my nose. I felt my head snap and the skin there give, felt the sulfur-slime slip into my mouth.

"Run!"

"Why'd you do *that*?" Frankie whimpered as his friends pulled him into the street.

"Shut up and vamoose already!"

I shut the door and put a hand to my face. My nose felt weird, less perpendicular than usual. I walked to my bathroom, the first time in several weeks I had entered that room, and turned on the light. I turned the taps. The plumbing groaned. Then the water ran rust colored, then clear. I splashed the cold on my face, washing off the rotten slime. I've never liked mirrors. Their lies are invariably uncharitable. Their truths even more so. But I looked into the one hanging above my bathroom sink for a mere assessment, a survey of the egg's damage. The bridge of my nose near the tip was somehow dented, a slight disagreement between the cartilage and the bone. A small pressure from my fingers popped it back into place. Then, still staring at myself, I took a fair assessment of what I saw. Black hair with a conservative part in the middle, lusterless and longer than I remembered. A face of papery white, large eyes a congested blue with long black lashes, Volker's lashes. A small but full mouth, pretty, I thought. But serious. Far too serious. I smiled. My cheeks wrinkled in compliance but my eyes stayed dilated, the pupils as big as bullet wounds. I opened my mouth. My teeth were dull. My gums ashy. My tongue gray. The veins had all receded beneath my skin, leaving it smooth but hard-looking. My fingertips were indeed black. I would have to wait forty years for the proto-punks and Goth girls to bring this look into vogue. What was I going to do until then?

I heard voices, more children, from across the street. They would soon be at my door and I didn't want another egging. But what could I give them? The only thing I had multiples of in the whole house were the kitchen cabinet knobs. These I removed with my bare fingers, a fingernail slipped into the screw-slot splintering in the process. I soon had a drawer full of them, and placing them on the foyer floor, I waited for the next knock. It never came. Word must have spread about me, about the strange little girl in the empty house who didn't know shit from Shinola about this special night. And so I was shunned. Ten, eleven o'clock. At midnight I began replacing the kitchen knobs and then stepped out onto my porch. The street was quiet, smelling faintly of burnt pumpkin and the coming dawn.

"Happy Halloween, you ratfuckers!" I shouted. A few porch lights snapped on and I ducked behind my door and bolted it for the night.

CHAPTER 39

The morning came. Then the night. Then another and another until the days blended into a numb kind of pablum. I heard voices raised, recognized the smell of dawn, cut grass, cooking turkeys, burning leaves. Time meant nothing. My phone rang three weeks before Christmas. I learned it was Billy as soon as I answered it. I coughed hard to clear my throat of dust and the particulate of dead spiders. Then I greeted him.

"Dearest girl," he said in his tender lisp, "where have you gone to?"

"I bought a house. I'm sitting in that house."

"Lovely. I'm thinking of doing the same but I need a garden. Something more than these barren patches that pass as verge out here."

"How did you get this number?" was all I could think to say.

"Why, the directory."

"The what?"

"The phone directory. Apparently you do have a phone."

"Yes. I'm speaking into it."

"Are you quite all right, my dear?" I was anything but all right. I felt like a piece of dismally animated Spam with eyes. I tried to laugh to reassure him and out came a dusky screech.

"The reason I called," Billy continued politely, "is a screening of the picture is this evening and you simply must be there."

"What about Whale?"

"Don't bother about Whale."

"He *fired* me, Billy. The last thing he'll want to see is a surly ex-employee."

"You were never surly, dear. You were amusingly firm. You taught me how."

"I wish that were true."

"*Now* you're being surly." I couldn't help a chuckle.

"Oh, Billy. I miss you."

"Then by all means come."

"I can't." Karl would be there. Enough time had passed for him to formulate an actual case against me. And too many people had seen me take that fall. And get up and walk away. The rumor mill had to be operating at maximum capacity by now.

"I want you there, Maddy. There might not have *been* a creature if not for you."

"And that means a lot." Jesus, did it mean a lot. Billy, after two decades in the business, was roughly eight hours away from instant stardom. By midmorning tomorrow he could have his pick of directors. And I had to pluck my dank hat from that ring, had to scuttle into the shadows and lurk in this cavernous new-build for reasons obvious only to me.

"Billy, I'm glad you called."

"I worry about you."

"Don't. I'll be here. I'll *always* be here."

CHAPTER 40

I waited in line for two hours at the Golden Gate Theater in Whittier to see the thing. I had to duck a flotilla of nurses with Christmas holly pinned to their uniforms who were hired to check blood pressure before allowing customers into the theater. It was pure Junior gimmickry. Those with peaky diastolic numbers had to sign waivers before they could purchase their popcorn.

It cut together nicely, I thought, a bit choppy in parts, with Whale's trademark disdain of social convention purpling a bit for my taste. The sound was dreadful. But Billy, with his breech-birth entrance and those jump-cut close-ups on his face, was beautiful. People got up, left, took a breath, headed back to their seats. I saw a mother with two toddlers, one on each knee, cover her eyes with her program while both her children grinned like hungry mice in the flickering light. There was a riot of uneasy movement through most of the picture and a palpable sense of relief when it ended. People were quiet as they filed out, speaking in hushed and guilty tones.

"You don't think some quack could really *do* that, do you?"

"I hear Hitler's already got plans to resurrect Frederick the Great."

"Mae Clarke looked lovely."

"Really? I though she looked puffy."

"Who's this Karloff fellow?"

"Who cares, so long as I never meet him in a dark alley."

Going to the pictures was a mistake. It fueled my yearning in a way I didn't think possible. I came back to my cold, dark house and sat on the living room floor, not bothering to turn on any lights. What was I off the lot? How could I find the will to function in the tedious comings and goings of the audience, just another body outside the studio gate? I was a creature thrummed into existence by agencies outside natural laws—or perhaps an expression of her deepest secrets. I was a thing best suited to haunt bedtime closets and the dust beneath single beds. I was only plausible in black and white, lit by artificial lighting. And yet wasn't I moved by emotions as if my heart still pumped? Where did they come from, my loves and hates and passions and boredom? Were they water from the rock? Was I evidence of the absence of God or a testament to the heat of his vacated throne? Did I even desire to be understood? Reasoned? If nature selected for survival and man for appearance, what had I been selected for? The flickers? Was I *Homo cinematicus*? Or some flotsam from the dead end of descent?

The cells of my body knew they were cooked and longed for a return, but still I persisted. Why? Perhaps my mother never forgave me for the pains of childbirth. All I knew was that it had been a mistake to leave the lot. My pride was nothing in the face of this tedium. But I couldn't force my way into the dance. I had to be invited.

So in the twilight of a daydream, in what would seem no more than a few moments of blissful despondence, I passed out of consciousness.

I awoke, if one could call it waking, to the sound of a knock on my front door. It was a sound I remembered hearing, many times, a shout through closed lips. But something in this knock was different. More plaintive? More seductive? I can't say. My time away was over.

I was covered by an inch of dust, as if I had sprouted downy feathers, and the hollows of my mouth and ears writhed with the wet-white bodies of baby termites and ants. I shook them loose like change from a deep pocket and tried to stand. My joints snapped, bones dumb to their function, and I fell once. Then a second time. How long had I been in my trance? Finally I pulled myself by the elbows to the front door. I pressed myself to my feet, unsteady, feeling strangely hollow. My neck and spine sang like splintering wood as I opened the front door.

"Telegram." A young man in a Western Union suit lifted his eyes to my face in tandem with his pen. His eyes caught, as if snagged from behind their sockets and I heard a faint intake of breath. I must have looked a fright. "Sign here," he finally managed to say, his wide eyes never leaving my face. I scribbled my name, took the thin yellow envelope offered me. His hand shot reflexively to the brim of his hat, but his action was aborted there. It was still stalled at the brim of his hat when he mounted his motorcycle and puttered away.

I tore the telegram open. It was from Billy:

Dearest girl, stop. Where have you been? stop. Phone on the fritz? stop. Call me at once. stop. Billy.

There was only the dense compression of my breath on the mesh of the receiver when I lifted it to check. My kitchen taps groaned but no water flowed. My light switches were impotent. I found my car keys, lifting them from a cocoon of dust, leaving a clean shadow of their shape on the floor. Outside my front lawn looked like a forgotten graveyard, weeds as high as me. My truck turned over only after several tries, the cabin cold, reeking of stale gas. As I drove to the small market at the foot of my block I noticed the changes. Ivy I remembered as tawdry sprigs now covered my entire garage door. And when did that sycamore grow so shady? There were cracks in the pristine sidewalk. A new Ford in the driveway of a home that I remembered being for sale.

I dropped the coins in the pay phone. Billy answered at once "Billy?"

"Maddy, dear girl. There you are. Where have you been? On holiday?"

"Hadn't we just spoken?" Through the glass of the phone booth I saw a woman in shabby calico leave the market with a box of milk and a newspaper. I couldn't see the date but recognized Roosevelt's dark circles on the front page.

"Just spoken? Dear heart. It's been *three years*."

I tried to get my bearings, to find my sea legs. Time was like a listing ship.

"Three years? Of course."

"I thought perhaps you went back to Germany to see your family what with all the dreadful changes going on over there."

"No."

"Have I caught you at a bad time?"

"No. Billy? Is that really you?"

"Yes, darling. Maddy, listen, I really would love to see you, catch up and all that. I have loads to tell you and I'm afraid I'm going to solicit your help."

"My help? In what?"

"I think it would be easier if we met. Tea?"

His address was in Laurel Canyon on a parcel of land that overlooked Sunset. It was surrounded by gardens. Hollyhocks and foxgloves. Heraldic rosebushes that came from clippings descended from the time of Henry IV. It was a Tudor home of blond and russet brick with doors and shutters carved with patterns of folded linen. He had obviously prospered in the time we had spent apart. A butler greeted me in hunter-green livery and said Mr. Karloff was in the back garden and was expecting me to join him out there. I followed the servant through wide but tasteful rooms until two French doors opened on a shirtless man in shorts and a top hat.

"Maddy! Dear child," Billy said, taking a dressing gown from his butler and slipping it on. "Look at you. I was expecting a young lady. You haven't aged a day."

Before I could answer, I was ambushed by a piebald sow that immediately began to nibble my cold fingers.

"Violet!" Billy snapped. "Stop that at once!"

Pigs are carrion eaters and her bites were not affectionate.

"Stop it this instant, you dreadful creature!" Billy shouted, and he pulled at the pig's hindquarters while I dipped my free hand into her mouth to extract the middle digit she had managed to detach. In a movement that I hoped looked like slipping on a ring, I reattached the finger.

"I hope she didn't hurt you, dear. I've never seen her act like that before. Jeffery, see Violet back to her room and no dried corn this supper. She's been beastly. Tea?"

And we sat in front of a silver service on chintz-covered wrought iron overlooking a garden right out of a summer in Surrey.

"Shall I pour out?" Billy asked rhetorically.

"Nice to see you've done so well," I said.

"Yes. Our little friend, the creature, has been quite good to me. I owe him everything."

This was just like Billy, to share the credit of his success with a two-dimensional fictional construct that only captured the public's love due to his humanizing effort.

"I'm surprised Whale let you take any credit at all."

"Jimmy's mellowed quite a bit. Success has had the opposite effect on him. Instead of making him insufferable, it's made him rather paranoid, I'm afraid. He's constantly trying to outdo himself. Of course nothing has matched *Frankenstein*. That's why we're making a sequel."

"A sequel? But you died in the mill fire."

"Apparently not. Box office has amazing regenerative powers and it seems I slipped into a subterranean well and lived. Horribly scarred, of course, but alive nonetheless. And I speak. I suppose the shock of a near death, or rather *re*-death experience, scared the verbiage into me."

"You can't speak. The whole soul of the creature is his animal-like vulnerability."

"My argument, precisely. But Jimmy was very persuasive."

"I can't believe he has changed that much."

"Then perhaps it's me who has mellowed. Biscuit?"

"You're going to do it? You're going to play the creature again?"

"That hideous galoot has been rather good to me."

"What do you want me for, then?"

Perhaps I was too blunt. Billy was delicate, and I saw his eyebrows raise and then narrow in a kind of benevolent indulgence.

"You were good luck for me that first time."

"What does that mean?"

"Simply that I'd like to have you on set."

"As what? A kind of mascot?"

"I wouldn't put it that coarsely. A friend. A *muse*."

"A muse. So no real function."

"Being a muse has a tremendous function."

I had forgotten the tedium that led to my slipping away for three years. I should have been leaping at the chance to just breathe the sound stage air again.

"I mean, I'd have no other purpose than to be there for you," I said, trying to gain my composure.

"Yes. I'm afraid you're right in that. Think about it. Mull it over. We don't shoot until next month."

"I don't need to think about it. Of course I'll do it. I'd do whatever you ask of me, Billy."

"I'm so pleased."

"What about Whale? Won't he object?"

"I think he'll be amenable."

Then it was clear. Billy had already spoken to Whale about me. He was fulfilling his promise to me in the only way he could. Whale had agreed to my presence but only under one condition, that I be there in a purely observational capacity. But I didn't care. I'd be back in the warmth of the arc-light-heated air, back on the killing floor. All of this went unspoken, just like the questions he had about me, about my not aging, not changing, went unspoken. What did he think? That I had some glandular condition? A midget with an excellent skin care regime? I left him his illusions, and he left me mine.

CHAPTER 41

The feeling on the set of *The Bride of Frankenstein* could not have been more different than its predecessor. No longer were we the upstart innovators grinding by on a shoestring. (And I tax *we* with the word's broadest inclusionary meaning imaginable.) Now we were the precedent, the pinnacle. What no one knew was that we were coming to the end. Never again in the Universal horror cycle would a film match our humor, our horror, our quality, our humanity, or our originality. We were the last of an often-to-be-imitated breed. For me to leave no real thumbprint on such an undertaking was disheartening in the extreme but still exciting. It smelled like history. It felt like history. The press had a constant presence on the set. Pierce was always ready with an eyebrow pencil to pose for the cameras, and Billy posed with teacups and pinkies for more publications than Roosevelt.

Whale had free reign and he hired his friends, people who

could keep up with him in conversation, who shared his tastes and prejudices. I suppose when he hired me on the first picture he had hoped I'd be one of these. The only exception was Billy, whom he still treated like a truck driver. But Billy didn't seem to mind. He said once, "If ever I require authentic warmth, that's what real family is for." I kept to the sound stage as much as I could, even "slept" there when sweeping up was done for the night. I was afraid of seeing old faces. Too many questions if they saw me. I couldn't count on everyone being as proper as Billy. But Mutter was on my mind quite a bit. I wondered how he was getting on, how much his boy had grown, if he was happy.

And so one evening I scurried up a piece of laboratory apparatus and crept out of the transom to the street. The studio was not doing well. The streets were shabby, the backlot in dire need of paint. It was as if a hard destructive wind had blown through the lot. The castle keeps showed their ribs of two-by-fours. The casino at Monte Carlo had been scavenged for parts. Notre Dame looked like an abandoned car wash. The old European street seemed to be the only set still living. It was lit that night, flagged arcs throwing slanted shadows on the forced age of the buildings. An eerie shorthand of illumination I had helped write. Foggers sighed their sinuous breath to the knees of vague dress extras in funereal black. You want to know what real horror is? It was being tethered to the shadows that night, lashed to the decayed peripheries along with the withered sage-brush and cigarette butts. It took everything I had to not barrel down there like a half-pint banshee and scream, "Curb that spill on cobbles there! Let that smoke settle! You got that backlight as hot as it will go? Now let's *really* push their faces in the shit, this time. Let's make them *feel* it!" I shouldn't have wandered.

I receded back into the shadows. Perhaps seeing Mutter again would buffer my spirits.

The Indian camp was gone.

I retraced my steps in my mind, checked my trajectory, but I had made no error. The teepees, the fire pits, the lean-to shacks, all were gone. Only the car bodies, rusted old jalopies, tireless, windowless, fit sadly as dens for the coyotes, were left.

This wasn't natural history. One could not kneel and sift through the silt and find an arrowhead, a beer top, a child's tin whistle. There was nothing, no trace of Mutter and his friends ever having existed there at all. It was an hour before dawn, in the lonely cool that had once held so much promise for me, had once shadowed me through nights when I roamed the lot as if I owned the place. Now I needed to talk to someone. I needed to know what had happened, and I willed the sun to hurry.

The sheen off the women who peopled Junior's waiting room had tarnished since my first years at the studio. These were hard creatures with no illusions about quick stardom and industry charity. They knew they were going to start on their knees and seemed ready for the work. Buttons had been bitten from blouses. Few wore stockings. Eyebrows were painted on as thin as cheap noodles. They were all eyes, lips, and tits, pure bundles of joyless accommodation and the hate between them was palpable. They barely seemed to notice me. They must have thought I was a sec-retary's daughter, a script girl's niece, a nothing. Only when my name was called and they realized I sought the same audience as they, did they suck their teeth and mumble.

Junior looked awful, bloated, hair thinning, ravaged by cred-itors and unsavory appetites.

"You the same Maddy Ulm who used to work here?" he asked, not looking up at me.

"The same."

"You ain't her sister?"

"I have no siblings."

He looked up at me and his eyes seemed to glaze.

"What's wrong with you? You look exactly the same."

"Thank you."

"I don't mean it like a compliment. It's not right. Gives me the jimmies."

"I want to know what happened to Mutter."

"Who?"

"My brother."

"I thought you just said you didn't have any siblings."

"You *know* who I mean, Mr. Laemmle. What happened to him, please?"

"You expect me to know what happens to every mug who can take a flop off a horse?"

"You promised me he'd have employment here for *life*. Or are your promises as thin as your hair these days?" He reached for a cigar. His box was empty. "Then why did you agree to see me?" I asked.

"Professional courtesy."

"But that courtesy doesn't extend to actually answering my question?"

"I got a studio to run. Leave your address. I'll see if we can't get you back on the lot."

"I'm already *on* your precious lot, Mr. Laemmle," I said, rising, not waiting for an answer. "How long do you think *you* will be?" In the waiting room I was stopped by a female voice.

"Wait, please," she said.

I recognized her from my first day in Junior's waiting room. She hadn't aged well, had chosen the shabby jowls of three squares a day instead of a place where a smile could softly land. She led me outside.

"Look, it's been tough around here lately. Layoffs like you can't believe. Junior doesn't act it but he's scared. The studio's one bad picture away from receivership and all he knows is the family business."

"You're breaking my heart."

"Same old yarn, I know. But he didn't want to do it. But he had to. It killed him, really broke his heart."

"What broke the bastard's heart?"

"Closing that camp with all those Indians. He had to break up families, people his father had hired when they were just kids."

"Do you know what happened to them?"

"Some went back to the reservation, I guess. Or got as far as a bottle and a flop on Franklin Avenue."

"*Mutter*?"

"He feels bad. That's why he doesn't like to talk about it."

"Do you know where *Mutter* is?"

"He had nothing to offer, not really. But he *did* promise."

"Where is he, please?"

"He's here. On the lot. Lives in a shack behind Stage Twenty-eight that used to be a recording booth. Night janitor. Works for two meals a day and a cot. Not a bad deal if you think about it."

"Thank you."

My plan was to leave the lot and never come back. Simply get in my truck and drive to the top of Mulholland and find a nice dung heap and call it home. My studio days were over. I was little more than an actor's lapdog. A ghost too stupid or stubborn to shut up and actually haunt. But with this final humiliation, I needed to face a hard reality. Junior had promised employment for life. He never stipulated what kind of life. But my feet wouldn't pass the gates. Before I knew it, I was creeping around the Phantom stage to that dilapidated shack behind it.

The door was little more than a few nailed boards fastened with a hook and eye. Being locked from the outside, I felt it safe to assume Mutter was not at home. I lifted the latch and stepped inside. The walls were papered with Oswald the Lucky Rabbit chocolate bar wrappers, his three fingers and vacant grin in frightful duplicate from ceiling to floor. Mutter had a small cot, made with a patched Beacon blanket in an Indian pattern. A single photo tacked to the wall: Mutter and his wife, a tree with its arms around its resident squirrel, and a bright-faced boy with dark hair and his father's eyes. Under the bed, a tin plate and a fork were stacked near a chipped commissary mug. And over the bed was a huge stolen one sheet, a lithograph of Billy in full monster makeup, menacing and underlit, the words *Warning! The Monster Is Loose!* blazoned beneath. And that's when the idea came to me. Maybe it was seeing that European street all lit up for business that fueled me, the hot shame of the shadows, like my seat in the opera house, a taste, a tease, my mocking, useless vantage point. I had an eternity to reconcile with my ambition, but Mutter wasn't so cursed. He deserved more than a flop and a cold lunch exile, sealed up like a dirty studio secret in some shabby closet. And I would make sure he got it.

I waited for hours, more than hours. Half a day perhaps until I finally heard the rasp of the hinges as the door creaked open. Mutter filled the doorway, but I could tell, even from his silhouette, that he was thinner, bleaker, less. It was getting dark and he carried a lamp with him, which he lit and placed on the floor near the bed. Then he saw me.

"Maddy? Home?" he said.

His voice cracked. But that could have been a trick of the duration of his day.

"Hello, dear heart," I said in German.

"English?"

"Not anymore," I said.

CHAPTER 42

My plan was simple. The clothes would not be hard to come by, an old castoff suit, a pair of heavy boots. Mutter's height and bulk, even in his diminished state, would not require him to go to the studio's extremes. Unknown to the staff on the lot, the studio was already in receivership by then, just months away from a total takeover from the Standard Capital Corporation. The theater chains had been sold. A bum Western had cost Junior his credibility with his usual investors. His grandstanding during our last meeting had been his last indignant salute to a passing parade.

He needed a clean exit, a way to keep the scuppers from filling, and *Bride* was his last ace. So he flogged the horses, making enemies of all who worked on the picture. We didn't have long to wait for the opening. Post-preview word on the street was the sequel was better than the original. Theater chains prebooked the picture for a year. The premiere would be a strictly spat-and-spangled affair. Standing room only. Whale had already worked

out a sweetheart deal to leave the genre and remake *Show Boat*.
Each person seemed to be getting what he deserved. Everyone
but Mutter. All that was missing was an invite, and for that, I'm
sorry to say, I enrolled Billy. I had not been much of a muse,
had been skulky and silent most of the time. But Billy was still
obliging when I asked to be invited to the premiere. He even had
a tiny black satin shift made for me for the occasion. There was
guilt. And then there was justice. And none ever took the higher
ground in me.

I parked around the corner from the theater the night of the
premiere. I didn't want the cameras to spot my shambling truck.
I told Mutter to wait by the fire exit while I dodged the press and
snuck into the theater, stealing down the empty aisles to backstage, where I opened the fire door and told Mutter to wait for
my signal. It was tart perfume and cigarettes, gowns and gamy
furs that reeked of mothballs as bodies hauled themselves over
a red carpet. The flashbulbs in those days were like small explosions, and a feeling of siege, of pending war, was very ripe in the
theater.

The crowd outside, the average public, was dressed in rags,
smelling of dirty soup and long days, but still found energy to
work up a passable frenzy for more make-believe. Junior made a
speech no one would remember. Whale stood up and waved like
the queen from her carriage. The houselights dimmed like they
had thousands of times before.

When it ended, the applause broke heavy and I freed myself
from my seat. That was my cue. I scurried up the aisle. Unnoticed. That is until I spoke.

"Ladies and gentlemen," I began as throats cleared. "What
we have enjoyed here is a treat rare in motion pictures. But where
do these nightmares come from? From what corners of the day-

shunned consciousness do these specters rise? From front offices and memos? From typewriters and red pencils? From makeup chairs so like the labs of the mad doctors they portray? Or from the mind, one fixed, fertile blond-tressed brain whose vision rivals that of Shelley herself?" There was a smattering of applause here. Whale even began to stand. "*No*, ladies and gentlemen," I said forbiddingly. "All those guesses would be right. But, upon closer inspection, adamantly *wrong*. Great images require great inspiration. And so the real question is *not* who is responsible for these enticing artifices but who or what *inspired* them. That inspiration is not a figment. He is real. He exists. And in the parlance of the good doctor himself, he is *alive!*"

And Mutter wobbled onto the stage. I could find only a moth-eaten suit jacket in the end, the backlot night watchman's Sunday best I lifted from a hook in his sour little shack. Mutter wore this over his patched and stained overalls, so the image I had hoped for, the hard, obvious, protean impression of the *real* creature fell woefully short of its mark. I had shown Muter how to shamble, how to stiffen his knees in imitation of Billy's definitive gait. He lumbered to center stage and stood there painfully exposed, his eyes shifting to the wings, looking exactly like what he was: a poor hulking schmuck, pitifully down on his luck, who had gotten lost on his way to the men's room. With no spotlight, even the flatness of his head was lost.

Laughter. They all laughed.

"What the hell is this?"

"Some kind of gag!"

"Show's over, kid."

It was more confusion than outrage. More irritation than a clear case for credit. Mutter scuttled off the stage, shirking from that awful hail of derision. It was Hollywood, and everyone

assumed Mutter was just another costumed imitation. My shouts
of, "*There* is your Frankenstein monster! He's real! Stop! Touch
him! He's *real*!" only made things more perverse, desperate, and
worst of all, poorly produced. What stopped me were the tears
in Billy's eyes. He had predicted this outcome ages ago. Even the
crust of all my actual years could not protect me from yet another
of my fervent childish impulses.

From the stage I saw Junior's eyes go cold, his jaw tense.
Whale smirked and took David's arm, but I could see he was
rattled. The success of the monster franchise had landed him
squarely at the top of the A-list. Nothing could be allowed to
contest his right to history. My attempt to better Mutter's lot
might have fallen flat but lesser rumors had eventually gained
footing. It would not be enough to merely chuck him in a janitor's
shed this time.

I should have gone to the press. I should have sat with one
journalist, one photographer, and spelled it out in plain English.
But my taste for an audience was too strong. I had inherited all of
my father's brash showmanship but none of his cunning.

Junior had Mutter served with his extradition papers the
next morning. An undocumented immigrant. He must have
awakened some poor INS official the night before to get the
order, some groggy bureaucrat with a yen for horror who went
along with it, no questions asked. Mutter had twenty-four hours
to leave the country. Sitting in the slatted light of Mutter's shack
I did my best to explain the situation to him. But the giant's ears
refused to fill. I finally defaulted to bedtime German to soften
my explanation, murmuring simple words like *must* and *leave*
and *home*. *Home* caught. *Home* sparked recognition. So why had
his huge face fallen? Why were his tired eyes filling? I did not

understand until he reached toward the wall and gently tore the photograph of his family from its nail.

I had forgotten. Stupidly. Selfishly. Real living leaves roots. Leaves branches.

"Come?" he whispered. "*They* come home too?"

There was no word in any language that could dampen the blow of my response.

I drove with Mutter to my bank and liquidated what was left of my account in crisp hundred-dollar bills. I waited in my truck while Mutter shambled to the stoop of a cold-water flat near Olvera Street, his hand filled with the only thing I had left to give. How long would my money last them? Five years? Ten? What did it matter when I had cost them everything?

I had no welcoming shadows to retreat to, no filthy theater box in which to burrow until the nightmare passed. I was exposed to the unflinching indelibility of my hideous mistake like a worm in the Los Angeles sun. There was only one decision left to make. And I had made that the moment I saw Mutter kiss his wife and child good-bye.

I had come to America in a trunk. I could go home the same way.

CHAPTER 43

We had been scheduled to dock at Hamburg, but congestion on the Elbe had us redirected to Bremen, a smaller port still under local authority. We shuffled down the gangway amid lives that spanned several trunks and those that rattled inside biscuit tins. Stale wool and cold sausage, mostly German nationals, but a few Americans were among us, businessmen defined by their two-toned shoes and shaved chins and neatly folded top coats that draped over the crooks of their free arms like steakhouse maître d's. Europeans are born knowing how to form lines. Americans are taught how to avoid them. As we funneled into the tables set by the immigration officials, it was the Americans who flashed their blue passports and were waved through with a curt nod while the rest of us slowed to a bovine stop. The officials were young men, some just sprouting the mustaches that would delineate them as civil servants. Brushed wool caps and bright brass buttons, they smiled and clicked as papers and photographs scattered over the tabletops. When it finally came to our turn, we were asked for our tickets.

"We have only the one I'm afraid," I said, handing over Mutter's. "I lost mine." Lying was less complex than pretending to breathe. "I was sick, you see, and it fell out of my pocket while I was indisposed."

"You are feeling better now, I trust, fräulein?" said one with real concern. This young man had sisters. "Might I trouble you for your papers?" We had no papers, no documentation of any kind, I from my obstinacy of remaining essentially nameless, Mutter as a casualty of his life.

"Lost as well, I'm afraid."

"During your malady or previous?"

He had blond fuzz on his upper lip that reminded me of stubborn milk and did much to trivialize his officiousness.

"Previous."

"Ah. And where was your port of departure?"

"Los Angeles, America."

"I see. Your papers were lost in Los Angeles?"

"Just so."

"How is it you were allowed to board without proper documentation?"

"An oversight, I suppose."

"Why did you not report this?"

"They seemed anxious for our departure."

"I'm afraid you will have to register with the local constabulary. Wait over here, please."

Comfortable chairs, open air. We could have been on holiday. Mutter closed his eyes in the sun. Had he forgotten his family already? Or was that another selfish figment of mine?

Too cowardly to open his buried wounds, my attention drifted to the longer line of those leaving the country. The officials at the departure tables were not young. They did not wear the quaint brass and bonnets of the locals. Their uniforms were gray and they wore the faces of stern fathers. I recognized their armbands from my memory of Weimar street corners. They opened suitcases, removed candlesticks and silver soup tureens, spoke harshly to the well-dressed women before them who only lowered their heads. Men, husbands, brothers reached into breast pockets and sometimes hands were slapped away, other times the offered money was accepted. Many were detained. None left with all their belongings. This was not the Germany I remembered, where police and postmen were always officiously polite.

We were finally collected by a fat little official who licked his fingers before opening the door to his car. He wiggled into the driver's seat like a roosting hen, nodding into his rearview mirror before accelerating slowly. The police station was quiet. A drunk slept on the sergeant's desk. It felt like a setup for a Buster Keaton. We were shown into the captain's office, and he rose as we entered. He was a nervous man with a receding hairline who wiped his hand on a starched handkerchief before bowing to us.

"Please sit, you must be famished," he said.

We sat and took the shortbread that was offered. The captain had only cleared his throat when Mutter devoured the entire plate. Behind him was a framed picture of a humorless man who bore a marked resemblance to Chaplin, had Chaplin had a dour brother who wasn't so skilled at jokes.

"So begin," said the captain, rattling some papers on his desk, freeing one and smoothing it with the damp flat of his hand. "I understand your papers are lost?"

"My ticket was lost," I began. "Our papers were stolen."

"Stolen? And you have come to report this?"

"Our papers were stolen in America, sir," I lied.

"And what were you doing in America?"

"Working for the Hollywood motion picture industry, sir."

"In what capacity?"

"I wrote and edited and consulted on several pictures while my brother (it somehow felt safer to maintain a blood relation) was employed as a stunt man and janitor."

"Are all American film industry stunt men janitors as well?"

"No, sir. His was a special case."

"And your work papers?"

"Stolen, sadly."

"I see. Is it safe to assume that your papers were stolen by your Jewish bosses?"

I like to imagine that he asked this last question with some distaste.

"No, sir. Respectfully, I do not think it would be safe to assume that. I do not know if the man who stole them was Jewish," I embellished, offended. "I only know he was hungry." If I was going to make up our story I thought I might as well feel righteous about it.

"I'm curious," the captain said, his demeanor relaxing as he allowed himself a yellow smile. "Is it the practice of the Hollywood film industry to hire its personnel without proper identification?"

"From my experience, sir, there *is* no consistent practice in Hollywood."

"Just so. I'll have to inform the consulate. Well, names, places of birth, that kind of thing to start. We'll begin with you," he said, pointing to Mutter with the nib of his pen.

Mutter looked stricken.

"Is there a problem?"

"Can't I speak for him?"

"Can't he speak for himself?"

"That depends."

"Upon what?"

"The nature of the questions." The captain's eyes had not left Mutter since he became the subject of conversation. He scribbled something, blinked, and set his eyes upon us again.

"Name?"

"Wilhelm Ulm," I said. Was I thinking of Billy?

"Would you characterize your brother as mentally deficient?"

"No, sir. I would characterize him as wounded in the service of the fatherland."

"I see. Will you have him remove his cap please?"

I looked to the captain, mute.

"Please?" he asked again.

I reached my hand to the lip of Mutter's cap; he started at the gesture and then relaxed when he met my eyes.

The captain's eyes narrowed as he surveyed the damage. "Where did you get that, my boy?"

"Verdun, I believe," I answered.

"He must have received the Iron Cross for that."

"Quite possibly," I whispered.

"But, sadly, without papers I cannot be sure he *is* German. Let alone a veteran."

And I had given a false name for Mutter. Now there would be no record of his service.

"I'm afraid," the captain continued, "your case is too delicate for these clumsy fingers. I have no choice but to refer you to a more sensitive review."

There was nothing sinister in his tone, nothing that could be construed as silky compliance with some dark directive. I would have cast him as a petty bureaucrat overwhelmed by political contingencies far outside his control, a dress extra in *Casablanca*, perhaps. But not a villain. Not a devil. They came later.

We were removed after several hours and loaded into a large gray van. Our driver was very handsome. A boy from a northern farm, I guessed, from his broad shoulders and full lips. His clear, pale skin was beautifully enhanced by the black of his uniform. He wore no pips on his collar tabs, designating him as a basic trooper, but there was ambition in him, clear in the ways he kept our papers crisp on the seat beside him. His grip on the wheel was at precisely ten and two. Our seats in the back had been equipped with restraining devices, leather belts unsubtle in their purpose. Small rings for the wrists, longer, loose belts at the height of the chest, small rings again where ankles would naturally rest. He made no request that we should employ these devices and so we sat stiffly. It was clear just from our short walk that we had crossed some political frontier. What nervousness that quivered in me was assuaged by the fact of us. We were German. Even the most cursory investigation would reveal that. He started the van and I watched him as his attention drifted to our paperwork on the passenger seat. He picked up the top sheet, studying it, then gave a look, almost helpless, to the closed door of the police office, swallowed, turned off the van, and then turned toward Mutter.

"Stand, please," he said, and I realized from his accent that I was right about his northern heritage. Mutter seemed fascinated by the holes in the restraints.

"Mutter," I said. I waited for the young man to repeat his request.

"Stand please and lower your trousers."

My silence was enough for him to clear his throat and explain.

"The police have neglected to answer the ethnic question. I must perform the Jewish test. Lower your pants, please, and your undergarment."

The young man lowered himself stiffly to his knees. Mutter stood and undid his belt. He lowered his pants to the ankles and his billowy shorts to the thigh-curve of his ass. The young man removed a pen from his inside pocket. This he would use as a probe. Mutter's attention seemed drawn out the van's windows, but the sudden temperature change had an awakening effect on his bladder and a thick yellow arc glistened near the young man's face. He veered in disgust, rocking back to his feet.

"He will desist immediately."

Mutter smiled. Relief? Retort?

"He will *desist*," the young man said, but his only response was the hard liquid report that seemed to last an eternity.

"You will clean this up," he shouted.

"With what?" I asked.

"You will clean this up!"

I used the flat of my shoe to break the surface tension of the puddle and watched it flow into the hard rubber grooves of the van floor. The young man bent again to his task but as soon as he made contact with his pen, the independent organ, now voided and carefree, rose into the air like a snake to the charmer.

"He will desist!"

"I'm afraid he has no control over that, either," I said.

"He is homosexual?"

"I would think from the evidence it would be safer to assume he had an unnatural affection for writing implements."

"I cannot tell if his foreskin is intact."

"Then I suppose you'll just have to wait."

"You will divert him."

"Please?"

"You will slap him, hard. On the buttocks."

"That could have the opposite effect," I said.

"You would rather *I* do it?" His eyes flashed.

"No."

"You will count to three and slap. Hard, mind you."

I counted and my hand cracked on the firm flesh. The organ bucked but did not deflate. The tip bobbed slightly like a snout testing an unusual scent and, finding it to its liking, swelled all the harder.

"You have not hit hard enough. I will try."

"No. Let me."

But he threw his hand across Mutter's cheek with the sound of a shot. Mutter's face snapped to the side, red spittle hitting the windows from his loosened jaw. His hand found his chin and his eyes traveled from surprise to confusion to anger in a slow jog. Mutter raised his hand to strike as the trooper placed a hand on the holster of his Belgian HP. I leaped up to his balled fist.

"No, my dear heart. Not that."

The diversion had its intended effect and the young man's attention fell back to Mutter's groin.

"You will pull up your pants and refasten your belt," he said, standing. He seated himself and restarted the van. "He is *not* a Jew. Or if he is a Jew, not a very good one."

We had not been on the Berlin streets, had not seen all the pulpy bonfires in the civic squares, all the banners and rallies and sloppy beer-hall reprises of the "Horst Wessel Lied." We had not heard the terms *undesirables*, *useless eaters*, or the lyrical *living not worthy of living*. We did not know that real Germans existed now only on party passports. Did Mutter know that simply by the dint of being Mutter he had broken several of the still-fresh Nuremburg Laws? I had never heard one of Hitler's speeches. And even if I had, I never would have imagined any of it applying to us. Mutter was not deficient; he was wounded. An iron man of the fatherland made *literal* from his wounds. Not less so. Why were we being treated this way?

CHAPTER 44

We were taken to the ironically named Süssigkeitburg Schloss, or Candy Mountain Castle, rumored to be, in a mere twenty-odd years, the Bavarian model for Walt Disney's centerpiece of his first amusement park. We were greeted by nurses in starched pinafores and white collars who smelled of liniment and soup, whose clean red knuckles held us carefully as they guided us up the steep front stairs. Our paperwork was handed to a female orderly who sat behind a modern desk in a magnificent frescoed foyer, cherubs fat on mischief and good wishes lounging on baroque clouds and smooth shafts of rendered sunlight. She looked at our pages quickly and stamped them separately and we were moved down a wainscoted hall, under crystal chandeliers that had once lit courtly manners. We were shown chairs. Told to sit and wait for the doctor. Wait for selection. I was nervous at the prospect of an examination. But I no longer cared what happened to me. Mutter, on the other hand, could offer nothing but fascination, a testament to brilliant

German field surgery. We heard shouts that bent in the open spaces and so could have been songs. And Mutter, head cocked to the sound, said, "Song?" And I thought I could hear the swallowed words of "Lili Marlene." The door near us opened and a nurse showed us in.

It was a bright room with lancet windows that faced the garden. The walls had been reduced to white, but still a bit of their original splendor showed through in a pattern of raised flowers and shadowed vines. There was a file cabinet, a desk, a chair. In the center of the room was a large zinc-covered examination table with a slight curb around its periphery. The whole table slanted imperceptibly to a small drain. A woman with a smile full of long teeth stood as we entered. She was large, wide-hipped with hearty calves beneath her white stockings. Her hair, blond as flax, was braided and secured into two tight loops at either side of her head. She was conspicuously missing her left arm, the white cuff of her lab coat pinned in a neat crease, cuff to shoulder.

"I am Dr. Hedwig Flosse," she said in a deep but melodious voice. "You may call me Heddy," she said, bowing her head slightly to me. "But you," she said, turning to Mutter, "will call me Dr. Flosse, as I reserve the usage of my first name solely for the children."

She smiled and her cold fingers brushed my colder cheek.

"You will undress," she said in the general direction of Mutter as she gazed at his papers. "You may leave your shorts on."

I ruffled my fingers in a motion of undressing and Mutter unbuttoned his shirt.

"You have been with him long?" Dr. Flosse asked, taking Mutter's shirt and folding it carefully.

"We—" I began.

"I must tell you," she said, raising a finger toward me, "I cannot indulge the ruse of your sibling relationship. It is clear to me you share no morphological traits of heredity."

"Yes," I said. "We have been together a long time."

"And has he gotten worse?"

"Worse?"

"His cognitive faculties. Have they diminished?"

Mutter was on the table by now, his massive feet dangling over the clean checkered floor.

"Hard to say," I answered. "Is fear the same as diminishment?"

She felt the glands under his neck, raised his arms, struck two fingers on the drum of his chest.

"Have you noticed decayed linguistics?"

"Please?"

"Speaking in sentences shorter than usual?"

"Perhaps. But he has never been consistent."

"Do you want to know why?"

I nodded.

"There is lead in that plate on his head. It has been leaching into his brain for several years, I suspect. Slowly destroying brain tissue. Open." The doctor opened her mouth, and Mutter mirrored her action. "It destroyed the Romans, you know. Lead pipes."

"I thought it was from eating hummingbirds and buggering boys."

She moved to a small cabinet with several glass jars of various liquids and powders. I saw one clearly marked *cocaine*. Another marked *methylene blue*. She opened a drawer, rummaged around, and removed a pair of chromed pliers and a small silver hammer.

"I want you to watch his feet while I do this. Tell me if he curls his toes." And she set the jaws of the pliers on one of the bolts at his forehead.

"What are you doing?"

"Removing his plate. It needs to be replaced with a non-reactive alloy."

"Shouldn't he be asleep?"

"He's a big, brave boy," she said, patting the wide belly of his shoulder. "Watch his feet, please."

It took over an hour to remove that plate. I stood helpless while her one bulbous forearm swelled under the pressure of her grip. When the bolts stuck, she tapped them with her hammer to loosen the calcified bone. Mutter grimaced but never cried out, and the bolts made the only sound as they hit a metal dish. When the bolts were all removed, a series of dark holes glared back. A crown of black night. The doctor rummaged in her cupboard, coming back with a silver chisel. I noticed the nurse who had shown us in furiously scribbling notes.

"They are going to fix you, Mutter," I cooed. "Fit you with a shiny new plate. Isn't that nice?"

Mutter's smile stalled beneath his wide eyes.

"I want to hold his hand," I said.

"It won't affect the procedure."

Mutter's palms were wet. I could feel his racing pulse in the thick tips of his fingers. His chest was a stoking bellows, pulverizing the air, working up a white heat. His hand closed over mine, and deep in his throat a scream was forming, soft as a train whistle, gaining force, losing distance. Then my own eyes clenched tightly as my head was racked with his screams. His grip loosened finally and he fell to the table in an oak-heavy faint.

"That's enough!" I shouted. Dr. Flosse nodded to her nurse. The nurse grabbed me with one hand and viciously backhanded me with the other. I fell to the floor, then scuttled to the corner of the room.

"I am sorry for that, my dear," Dr. Flosse said calmly. "But nothing must interfere with the procedure. It is very delicate, you understand. Would you like a sweet?" I shook my head. The doctor smiled and turned away, whispering words with too many syllables to her nurse. They prodded with fingers, the nurse's pencil, at the gelatinous red cabbage so vulnerable now in the eggcup of Mutter's face.

"You have killed him," I said.

"He has fainted. There are no nerve endings in the brain. I'll revive him in a moment. Please sit."

I did as I was told. There was nothing else to do. Mutter's eyelids fluttered. His chest rose and fell. The nurse tied a sterile cloth over his open skull. The doctor examined the plate she had just removed. When her interest waned, she went to her cupboard and removed a glass ampule, which she broke under Mutter's nose. He started, roused, sat up, and then immediately slumped forward.

"You will help me with him," she said.

"Where are you taking him?"

"To get cleaned up. I have the measurements for his new plate. It won't take long to fabricate."

I helped her lift him to his feet. His tongue seemed to be working at odds with the confines of his mouth, saliva leaving silvery traces down the sides of his chin.

"He will need time to recover. But his verbal skills will return," the doctor said. "In fact, I believe he will improve."

She led him down the hall, his feet shuffling beneath him. His head lulled to my side and his eyes opened wide, but there was no recognition in them. Just pure, mute animal. He seemed to be able

to stand on his own, and the doctor loosened her grip on him, but
I refused to loosen mine. When we reached the end of the hall, I
noticed more patients accumulated there, a few with single nurses
or in small groups led by a nurse. They smelled of crumbs and
sleep, their hunched or twisted bodies barely covered under the
white cloth of their thin robes. They had faces too small for their
melon-like heads or the faces of old people on bodies as young as
mine. One man, with only half a mustache, had fins instead of
arms. A very tall and slender woman sang to the back of her hand,
her lips dry and crusted from never being still.

"You will have clean uniforms and hot meals after you are
clean," Dr. Flosse began. "We have all been through this before.
Please make liberal use of the soap. Especially those sensitive
places we've talked about."

There was general laughter at this. A few made scrubbing
motions with their hands.

"That's right, my darlings. You remember. Scrub good and
hard. You must all be clean if you wish to be healthy. You can
come with me," she said, taking my hand.

I pulled it away.

"I want to stay with him."

"I assure you that is not necessary, my dear," she said kindly.
"It's just a very light cleansing mist. "

"Mutter?" I said. The giant rolled his eyes to me and smacked
his lips.

"Maddy," he said dully.

"You see? He will be fine. Stand by the door if you wish. But
no peeking." And the doctor winked at me. I loosened my grip.

"What about his head?"

"The showers are not very high. Please." She gently pushed
me aside.

"Slowly, slowly, my pets," she said as the throng shuffled in. "There's plenty of hot water for everyone."

The patients squirmed and rocked out of their robes as Mutter fumbled with the buttons of his shirt and trousers. He was nearly a foot taller than everyone else and there seemed to be a kind of game as to who should enter the showers first. Shortest to tallest seemed to be the rule. And every time Mutter tried to cut into line, he was lightly slapped or hissed at until he was buffeted to the very back of the line.

"Careful, dears," the doctor chimed soothingly.

Then I noticed it. A heavy rubber seal around the door of the showers. Its handle was of the industrial-freezer variety, a heavy clasp with a locking pin.

"Mutter," I said. "Mutter, wait." But his turn had come. A nurse handed him a white bar of soap. He nodded to her, then shuffled into the room, the door closing with a soft compression behind him. I rushed to the door before a nurse could drop the pin in the handle.

"Wait! I want to go with him!"

"Child, get away from there!" the doctor screamed. Then I heard the distant sound of a van's ignition shudder through the walls. A nurse gripped me hard around the waist, but I threw a elbow with my full force at her stomach. She collapsed long enough for me to pull the handle and open the door. The patients turned toward me with a start as I rushed inside.

"Mutter, *don't*!" I screamed. The door hissed closed behind me. I heard the tick of the pin as it locked into place. The huge sunflowers of the shower heads began to sigh as I pushed my small frame among the milling bodies, trying to get to Mutter. Several closed their eyes and smiled in a memory of warm water but quickly opened them as the room filled with a clear shimmering vapor. I could see Mutter's confused face laced among the moaning heads. I pushed on the door, but it would not budge. I beat on the shower door until I felt the small bones in my hands shudder.

"Mutter!" I screamed. "The door! *Smash the door!*"

The coughing began. As the chamber filled with the exhaust, the patients formed the last herd, moving instinctively away from the center, like a cloud of birds eluding a hawk. But the confines of the room, the hard angles, were nothing like the sky. We were stirred, flightless. Poor backs hid heads. Knees began to fail. A few ventured toward the center, still making weak scrubbing motions. They were the first to fall. When their lungs reached past the capacity to expel the exhaust, the real panic began. Upward went the herd, screaming, crying, scrambling over the mounting heap of the fallen. I clawed my way to Mutter and held fast to his hand. His raving child-eyes were wide in horror. *Use me; hold me. I'm here. You are not alone.* My mind was a smear of panic. The words. What were my mother's words?

"*Tooth!*"

"*Nail!*"

"*Hair!*" I shouted over the deafening hiss.

There wasn't time. There wasn't nearly enough time. I rode the tremors of his hand with only the pressure of my own. His grip finally relaxed. His bulk began to falter. He fell to the floor, his eyes still open, still confused. In some final desperate gambit, I placed my mouth over his, to offer perhaps a last few cubic centimeters of uninfected air, but no exchange filtered through his slack lips. He was still. They all were still. But my eyes stayed clear and steady. My ears still echoing with the cries that had faded.

I heard the door unlatch, smelled the freshness of the hallway. Male orderlies lifted the bodies out in pairs. I burrowed beneath Mutter's body away from the light that grew stronger as the lifeless obstacles were systematically removed. I felt Mutter lifted off me with a grunt of "Jesus Christ" from the struggling orderly. I stood up with a hiss, my hands like claws. The orderly went white. Then he screamed.

"She's still alive! One of them is still *alive!*"

I scrambled for the exit. I felt myself pushed back into the room. The door slammed. Panicked, muffled voices began a tumble of orders. Calmer voices joined and then I heard the van's ignition again. The exhaust filled the room. The engines were revved, the engine exhaust descending loud as woodland rain, but I sat cross-legged on the floor and wept. It was a tearless cry, more of a sustained convulsive spasm than recognizable grief. I vowed to tear out the throat of the first human through that door. I counted the minutes, and when several had passed, the hissing from the shower heads stopped and the door was cautiously opened. I crouched. When I saw a body materialize, I leaped screaming, tearing. I was slammed to the floor with an effortless blow and felt myself lifted by my throat. Dr. Flosse held me firmly in her one good hand.

"*You're a liar!*" I screamed through the forced narrowness of my larynx.

"No more than you, child," she said, dropping me to the ground. "Pretending to be just a common brat. When all along you were this glorious *gift!*"

CHAPTER 45

I was coveted. Like a child covets a novel breed of titmouse and keeps it smothered in the confines of a candy box until it eventually becomes numb from too many kisses. Initially convinced that the key to my condition lay in the logic of my cells, Dr. Flosse began a series of exhaustive tests and intrusions. I was measured and probed, weighed and topically examined. And when my morphology fell into the predictable median, when she was forced to report me as nothing more than infuriatingly average, she went past the skin, to the birthplace of puzzles. I was baked, poached, frozen, and sautéed. Placed in silver stainless-steel vats of corrosive enzymes and caustic alkaloids. Agitated and analyzed. My skin was smeared with photoreactive nitrate, photographed by photostatic radium cathodes. My bowels were bloated with barium enemas, photographed again, exposed to gasses of chlorine sulfate, injected with enough potassium chloride to stop a buffalo. My eyes were doused with lice killer, my tongue drenched in lye. I was kneaded, compressed, stretched, and tangled, left out in the rain like a neglected tricycle. And all the while I silently relished her subterranean frustration as each new horror met with unerringly similar results. Then one morning, with a particularly icy resolve, she strapped me to her table. Holding her scalpel as lightly as a realist his blending brush, she opened me up with two deft pulls of her one good wrist. With the care of a midwife, she removed each organ. Placed each in clear jars filled with a hydrating solution of potassium sulfate. Then she placed the specimens around me. Heart, lungs, liver, spleen. Cut flowers tempting a rifled garden plot. She stood back, her one arm crossed over her chest, admiring, yet still flummoxed by her work.

"You are confounding," she began slowly, "because to observe you is to lose faith in observation altogether. You are a miraculous pebble in the shoe of science, my dear. Somewhere inside that flat little chest of yours is the key to an inoculation against death."

She delivered this speech while putting me back together, packing my organs into my hollow abdominal cavity as gently as company china after a holiday meal. She was unused to soliciting compliance from a subject, uncomfortable at treating her patients as people, so she overdid it, giving my liver what she must have conceived to be an affectionate pat while tenderly fitting it with my gall bladder, referring to my colon as *shotzi* and the shriveled drape of my omentum as *dass liebes Ding*.

"Tell me, please," she asked, looking down at me. "Is it witchcraft? Some special incantation that has made you what you are? I heard you shout while your friend expired. What did you say? Tooth. Nail. Hair. Is that correct?"

Even if I chose to relate the story of my transformation it would be of no use to her. I was completely ignorant of the particulars. And as for being impervious to external forces, the tedious exercise of her experiments, not to mention the general flatness of her company, was doing much to wear me down.

"I understand will, Maddy," she said, casting a cold eye on my torso as it quietly knit together. "Do you know how I lost this arm?"

"Probably got it caught in the ravenous teeth of your girdle's zipper," I said, sitting up.

"I cut it off myself." She let that linger as she dropped my blouse to my lap. Then she seated herself on her low examination stool. "I was one of the first white persons ever allowed in Tibet. It's true. I'd come as a representative of the *Schutzstaffel*. My specialty was Asian religions. I'd planned on being a professor before the Reich. I was there looking for the *Bardo Thodol* or the Tibetan Book of the Dead. Our Führer has always had a weakness for esoteric texts. I found nothing, of course, except a blizzard. And an avalanche. We were buried under ten thousand kilos of snow for two days. We managed to avoid hypothermia by excavating a small den in the loosely packed debris. I recommended vigorous chest massages, sleeping in pairs. When we finally tunneled out, I realized I was the only Caucasian to survive the ordeal. The rest had perished from exposure or perhaps fear of intimacy. I was there with two tiny Tibetans, a lingual gulf between us, and no food. We walked for miles until our bodies finally gave out. I had little to negotiate with. I did not know the terrain like my indigenous guides. I needed them. Protein, preferably animal protein, has arguably the highest concentration of calories, so the choice was clear. The sacrifice would be mine. They are stronger than they look, those little brown Tibetans. But after fifteen minutes of merely pulverizing my upper arm with some igneous shale, I realized they had made dismal progress in shattering the bone. I completed the job myself, fabricating a kind of remedial serration in the blade of the shale. I was through the bone in no time. When it was off, we split it into three parts: the distal portion of the wrist including the carpals and metacarpals, the median section just above the condyles of the humerus, and the humerus itself with its portion of both bellies of the biceps. We ate it cold, like a particularly resistant steak tartar."

Her efforts to win my compliance did not end with her horror stories. She also tried more traditional methods. I was given the consort's room in the castle, a room whose original function had been one of inspiring compliance as well, albeit of a different kind. It was done up like the precious dress the artist's wife had given me, in pink-and-cream watered silk with the French love of the curved line. It was so adamant in its insistence of luxury, so persistent in its desire to saturate the senses, that it was difficult not to be won over by it. The doctor would come at night, at bedtime, with a silver service set with a pot of hot chocolate and freshly baked cookies. She had decided to take a materialist view. I think she thought if I were reminded of what it was to be a simple child, I would eventually develop a child's sense of insecurity and low esteem. And that first night it seemed to work. Though I could taste nothing, the textures were soothing, the warmth of the liquid in my mouth not much different from the heat that gathered on my satin sheets where the doctor sat. It was the attention I loved, her cotton candy blitzkrieg. She dropped her officious enamel and came as a kind of child herself, full of a child's questions.

"What is it like, Maddy, to know you will never age and decay?" (Disappointing.)

"How does it feel to know you will outlast the shape of the shoreline?" (Lonely.)

"Do you feel like a god or a stone?" (Neither, actually. But if I had to choose I guess I feel like a bit of meteorite that orbits regular lives. A concrete housefly?)

"Are you sure you will not tell me the purpose of those three words you screamed in the showers?" (Quite sure.)

I supplied none of these answers, merely thought them. I was not expected to answer. This was a seduction, a test of membrane integrity, a way to see by sly observation just what it would take to break me down. Her attentions had their effect. In the days that followed, she would wake me gently, with the same silver tray as in the evening, and so complete a circle, creating a ritual, an expectation. She would "do her rounds," which I fooled myself did *not* amount to shower head dispatches and tortures. If I was not beginning to like her, at least I could tolerate her. I would dress and we would walk the grounds or play croquet in the garden, and when I looked up and saw the frightened faces of the patients looking down on me, I did not imagine their fates but smiled at them and looked away. It was the only way I knew I could continue.

She eventually drew the conversation away from my physiology. She asked me about my past and when I told her of my time in Hollywood, she pretended to be impressed. She found a hand-cranked motion picture camera, an old Bell & Howell, and several tins of color film, somewhat novel at that time. She allowed me full access to the grounds for my "gelatins" as she called them.

I couldn't think of a narrative and was more interested in experimenting with color balance, so I shot a series of unrelated vignettes. The clouds with a polarization filter. The children, mostly twins, at exercise in the main courtyard. The mason who had come to build the large iron-faced oven in the basement. He could clown like Harold Lloyd and even wore the same glasses. (It was this footage, later shown at the trials, which helped achieve the conviction and execution of Dr. Flosse along with several other doctors from Sonnenstein, Grafeneck, and Hadamar.)

I had a darkroom at the top of one of the towers, a cylindrical space like an empty oatmeal container, where I kept my basins of chemicals and drying racks. I'd spend hours in the solid dark, experimenting with developers and bath durations. When I had something interesting, I was allowed to show the other patients my footage. We'd set up benches in front of a hung sheet that covered the elaborate hearth of one of the sitting rooms. We'd dim the lights and wait for the infectious shushing and yelps that accompanied any sudden change in ambience to die down, and then I'd start the show. I used a soundless eight-millimeter projector. I provided the narration with such pronouncements as "Angels in the briars" over an image of several pairs of twins taking the air in the rose garden, regaining their constitutions after the morning's experiments, or "Wake up, sleepyheads" over panning shots of patients under disturbed dreams, pulling on their restraints.

The joy these images brought to the patients who could recognize themselves was enormous. "That's me! That's me!" would crackle like candy cellophane in the flickering dark, and the mantra, once picked up by the bulk of the viewers, would sometimes never diminish. I wondered if there was a cruel aspect to these evenings, if there was a perversity in providing a few hours of normalcy. But I reminded myself that I was a prisoner as well, and what I provided could never be mistaken as hope. I kept them calm and diverted, and I suppose there was some complicity in that. But I never saw it that way. It was merely a way to pass the time before the inevitable. I had, after all, crossed back over the water.

CHAPTER 46

I became aware of him slowly. It began as a faint dawn of panic, the sensation of having forgotten something important and the sinking realization that you are too late. But it soon gained focus, focus in my lower belly and groin. And I could feel a kind of desultory tingle there, a halfhearted assault that teased the edges of desire as it steadily grew in intensity. The first cold fingers of February. Icy tongues of scorched metal. He was approaching rapidly from a great distance. I hung my reel of dripping film in the complete darkness and looked down to my hands. My small child's bones had begun to throb with a faint greenish glow. They flickered and guttered as the sickly verdant light flowed frigidly up my arms and shoulders, beating the flesh behind the darkness, raising my chilled structure to blinding skeletal relief. I was a beacon. A light to guide his way. Finally. But this light was not content to evanesce. This light had teeth. And abruptly I was shot through with an icy shock so strong I was thrown from my small stool. I heard his thin, cruel laugh echo in the close room.

"Volker?"

Certain veins are never deaf to the promises of the needle.

His reply was the rasping of the walls as they grated against the floor. I stood as the room began to shrink. And when the confines of the space finally cupped me in its coffin-size palm, when I could struggle no more, the walls began to writhe. At first I thought it was spiders. He was fond of spiders. In the weak light from my anatomy, I thought it was webs downing softly against the hard angles. But it wasn't. It was hair. Human hair, neglected under the lid. Hanks of seething tendrils spewed from the ceiling, floor, and walls. A dead dowager's braid. A young suicide's tresses. Worming blind in the dark. A glut of the keepsake of the dead snaking dryly around my ankles and up my thighs, cresting with the stink of rot and failed lilac over my shoulders and finally down my throat. Tickling, clogging, stifling. And there, finally, the longed-for staleness of him on my tongue, his sweet caustic breath filling my airless lungs. The thunder of his approach filled me with a sickly excitement I could not contain. I leaned against the tight walls and fumbled with the folds of my skirt. My knees opened without complaint. My entire body was slack with desire, with an ever-cold and neglected longing that reflexively shunted fear like a chest unhasped by a single terrible whisper.

"Poppa." I moaned in dusky expectation. Even with my unaided ambition slumbering six feet inside me, the *need* of him still rankled, a ghostly itch from some ancient amputation. But nothing fluttered my deserted flesh. I could sense him, could smell his vicious spice in the air, but he refused to surge.

"Maddy," I heard him whisper harshly, free from the intimate tissues of my skull. "What are you doing, my girl?" I sat up.

He was congealed there, his outline solid as a reflection in a dark and undisturbed pond. "Not like this, child. *Never* like this."

"What do you mean?" I said as a slight shame shivered through my nerves.

"Look at you, sprawled there, *spread* like a common whore. After all these years, this is how you've soured?"

"*Soured*? Isn't that what you wanted? Isn't that what you've made me *only* fit for?"

"Pull up those knickers," he hissed.

"But I don't understand." I didn't know what I was supposed to feel. What weakness of mine was required to signal his supremacy? The ceaseless mechanical horrors of my last few years had taught me the only benefit of my condition: *the dead have no fear.*

"You've grown old, Maddy," he said with a touch of sadness, retreating. "My little girl is gone."

"But I am so much *more* now." How many nights had I tossed in my consort's bed while the woman raged inside this useless girl?

"Alas," he whispered, "without fear the rose has *no* sweetness."

I righted my clothes roughly as I stood, feeling sickened by the extreme of my so often deferred passion. Humiliated by a reflex I could never have engendered without addiction. I crossed to my worktable and dunked a fresh reel in its bath, looking at him. He was his same impeccable self, his lips still full and sensual, the tines of his mustache still crisp as a vivisectionist's hook. Fury seized me and I threw the shallow tub to the wall with a metallic crash.

"Why have you *come*, Volker?" I shouted. Dry sobs bent my back. I turned from him shuddering in the smallness of the wide room.

"Why have I come?" he said soothingly. "Isn't it obvious? To continue our work."

"Our *work*? I haven't needed you for my work in *years*!"

"Is *that* what this is?" he asked, his fingers fondling the stuttering images of twins still dripping with developer. "These home movies of the damned? I was so hoping I might find you a success."

"I *was* a success!" I screamed, trying hard to believe it.

"*Never*," he whispered with a grin. "You were a lapdog to your Hollywood pimps and now you are more so to these goose-stepping comedians. I taught you nothing. You contented yourself with scraps. Like a mongrel so beaten by its master any slight recognition seemed a feast. You whispered your passion. *Never* shouted it," he spat. "You insinuated your vision. *Never* owned it. Oh, you need me, girl," he said as his dark eyes flashed. "You need me *badly*. You can choke down the lie of your accomplishments all you like. But that is a biscuit of cold shit I'll never swallow." He had been many things to me. A cruel puppet master, an intractable advocate, a tyrannical drug that shored up my ever-crumbling confidence as it drained my capacity to dread. But never this. Never a disapproving father. I didn't know what I feared most. "There *is* still work to do," he continued, his voice broadening theatrically. "Still nightmares left to be hollowed. Magnificent terrors still to be harnessed. But not if you don't have the heart to claim them." His eyes were wide. But not with terror. Something much worse sat in his pupils, an angry child fingering a ridiculous rubber knife.

"What would you have me do?" I laughed, picking up my upset tub and footage. "*Horror* grew up, *Poppa*. Just like your little girl. It put on uniforms and spit-shined its boots. These people have washed horror in soap and starch and made it stand in line."

"Then *smash* their lines. *Poison* their soap and starch."

"My God," I said with a faint curl of disgust. "Look at you. You still believe the boogeyman is waiting under the bed. What half-shadowed thing could we throw up on a screen that could compete with this? Even if I *wanted* to, how could I? Look around you. The conviction of these walls is quite adamant, I assure you."

In answer he simply smiled. "Do you remember the time you fell?" he said, beginning his soft retreat, the almost imperceptible blurring of his clean and vivid dimensions. "You fell so far and hard a *choice* sprang up. Do you remember? And what did you do? Did you retreat? Fail? Pretend you were less than what the desire in your soul knew you to be? Do you really think the walls of this place are any more covetous than *oblivion*?" I felt the quickening of some tiny rebirth, the haunting at the corners of my eyes where tears might go. "All you need to do is what you did then. *Will* it, my girl," he said, his image growing fainter. "All you have to do is *want* it."

And I stepped toward him as a frightened child might approach her father, and he paused. And then he grinned, his eyes flashing a terrible solid black, his teeth bared clean by a menacing peel of his lips, and rushed into me, screaming, tearing, lacerating the very core of me.

And was gone.

I kept making my little presentations, although the audience changed each week. Every night I pondered of escape. I got used to the screams in the early mornings, the stink of burning bodies at night. I know now we were in dress rehearsals for the Holocaust, that every major player made his grim debut in castles like ours all over Germany. I watched as the first drafts on the etiquette of extermination were written. Each night before "bed," Dr. Flosse would alert me to refinements in the system. She had discovered that "selecting" family members, that is separating them before the gassings, actually achieved results in the long run. Without a familiar face to embolden them, she found they were less likely to resist her, especially when they were told they would meet with their loved ones shortly. The confusion and vulnerability of the initial separation engendered the beginnings of a calm compliance that only the element of hope could complete. She considered the "specter of hope" so necessary in the "fluid processing" of certain victims that she made a special note to her bosses in Berlin "that under no circumstances should children ever be separated from their toys. They are comforting symbols that can bear no fruit of rebellion and so should be indulged." She even thanked me for an insight I had helped her discover. Before my arrival with Mutter she had been flirting with the idea of "processing upon arrival." She was curious to see if subjects with no previous experience with the facilities, i.e., those who had not taken actual showers on the premises, would resist processing. That was why Mutter had been mixed so soon with others who had established a familiar routine. And thanks to Mutter's example, with my help, she could safely report that subjects would process just as compliantly with merely a bar of soap and a useless towel. I, however, was the exception and could not be considered relevant to statistical evidence. But her words stirred nothing in me, no pity, no outrage. I simply eyed the walls of my prison, wishing, like the living wish, that something might come and release me.

CHAPTER 47

One day word came that the doctor's efforts would be rewarded with a visit from Reichsführer Himmler himself. The castle was in a dither, as if the newly engaged were entertaining their soon-to-be in-laws for the first time. A menu was planned, silver polished, the main dining room cleared of its vivisection tables. French food was considered publicly decadent but privately desired and I remember slabs of foie gras and brioche toast, duck simmering in champagne and oranges and a huge Alsatian tart in a replica of our castle. Several of the more cognitive patients were given reprieves and fitted with white serving jackets and told from what side to place a dish and from what side to pull it. One, a microcephalic named Gertzi, who also loved to watch me thread the projector, was given white gloves and the job of sommelier. He practiced for an entire week, filling a wine bottle with dyed water and emptying it out into a line of stemware until he could achieve a perfect pour without leaving a single drop on the linen.

A day before the visit, we were informed Himmler had a cold and would not be attending but would send his attaché in his stead. How could one be disappointed that history's most notorious war criminal, the meticulous architect of all their untimely deaths, was unable to make it to supper? But we were. The patients actually cried when they heard the news. They pulled their hair. They mewed like kittens. I had to find Gertzi's cork from his practice bottle and sneak it into the kitchen to scorch it. I used the blackened end to draw a quick mustache and I hunkered and swiveled and pratfalled until their smiles returned. I was reprimanded by the lead cook for making sport of the führer. How could I tell her I was doing my best Chaplin?

The evening of the dinner, our guest was late. The soup, turtle with pearl onions, grew a skin. It was raining outside, a very businesslike German sort of rain that desired only to fall, not detain. But the patients, dressed in the clean starch of their borrowed linen, were trembling. It began with Gertzi, a low sort of keening from a distant point in his throat, lulled louder by an involuntary rocking, a swaying, as certain piers are swayed by the gathered force of passing waves. Soon a shout broke from him, a spray of panic over the sour gunwale of his lips that drenched the others. And the voices spiraled upward, shot from the cannons of their poor throats, foghorns of the lost. I could have quelled their nerves with a little frosting in my face, a few slip-falls to the flat of my back, but the doctor had confiscated my cork and banned me from the soiree under the pretext of punishing me for defaming the Reich. But I had made a science of stealth. I had sneaked out from my room and could see them through the porthole of the kitchen door.

"Stop this at once!" the doctor shouted. Threats worked as well as compassion. The doctor smoothed the apron front of her dress, a cruel-looking thing of black muslin that clapped like stage thunder when she walked. Her face was still flushed with her instructive anger when the officer entered, unannounced. The doctor snapped her fingers once and the patients fell to muster.

"Rain," he offered with a formal bow of his head, taking off his leather greatcoat and shaking it with a graceful veer of his torso. The raindrops crackled to the floor, not daring to moisten him. He was the most staggeringly beautiful man I had ever seen. High cheekbones. Full lips. Impossible eyes. We all seemed struck by him, and it was the doctor herself who finally broke his charismatic spell and took his coat and led him to the dining room.

"You will please forgive us if we go directly into dinner," she said.

"Of course," he said, removing his peaked cap. He wore the uniform of the SS-Totenkopfverbände, as velvety and black as deep space. But where most members of his unit were still sporting brown shirts in deference to their roots in the SA, his collar was white. This was a look that would not meet with sartorial favor until after the invasion of Poland. He was a trendsetter, this one.

I could see them as they entered the dining room. The officer sat with his back to me. "I will have wine, please," he said. "Something cold and yellow and not too sweet. We will dismiss the soup. What is the main course?"

"D-duck," the doctor stuttered, still standing.

Gertzi poured beautifully, poured with the silence and grace of a spring brook, and stopped when the officer raised two fingers to his glass.

"A half portion of the duck, I think," he said. He had a beautiful voice, deep with a slight stickiness of laryngic bass

(American cigarettes?). What Lubitsch would call "conversational charming."

The dinner proceeded. The patients acquitted themselves reasonably well. Nothing spilled, sloshed, or dropped. But, apart from Gertzi, they were not graceful. In effect, they were like hand-carved versions of devices better suited to fabrication in metal. But the officer, who never gave his name, was politely indulgent and even whispered "Thank you" when his plate of neatly piled bird bones was shakily lifted from its place.

"You seem a remarkably resourceful woman," he said, addressing the doctor, the only other diner at his table. "A realist, Frau . . .?"

"Fräulein . . . Flosse," she corrected.

"Fräulein—pardon the assumption—Flosse. That is why it seems remarkable to me that you would assume the veil of your silence enough to hide something of this magnitude from the Reich."

The doctor drained of color. Wasn't he going to compliment the meal? The rustic yet passable service?

He went straight to business. The Party had this effect on men, even sons who had been raised with the manner of small talk. Though confused, the doctor knew she had transgressed and was nervous now to appear more ignorant than guilty.

"Sorry?" she said, waving her cup away when Gertzi took a chance on refilling it.

"We know of the female child," the officer said, lighting a cigarette.

The doctor opened her mouth, but the officer, seated rather near her, used the pad of his upturned index finger to close her flummoxed jaw.

"Please," he said, smiling. "I have not come here as the agent of any personal retaliation. Your motives, though your own, I'm sure were in keeping with Party precepts. We simply want the child."

How I longed to embarrass the bejesus out of the doctor, to burst through the kitchen door and fall on my knees, hands held out for the cuffs, saying, "You got me, bruddah! Take me to the chief," doing my best Chico Marx. But I was quiet. It seemed the officer was doing a remarkable job himself.

"I'm not finished with her, sir," the doctor managed to say.

"I see," he said, leaning back, exhaling Ronald Colman–like. "Then perhaps you would be willing to draft the communication denying the führer his personal request?" He waited for his sentence to have its effect. Then, "Oh yes, my orders are to take the child back to Berlin. I assure you, Fräulein Flosse, there is no regret in failure. Only in refusing to comply."

"When were you thinking of taking her?"

There was genuine sadness in the doctor's voice.

The officer was unmoved.

"Immediately. Tonight."

"But that is quite impossible! She's not packed! She's not prepared!"

"Be sure to make that your main justification when you draft that letter to the führer."

"Might I request some time alone with her? To say goodbye?"

The doctor's eyes were wet now. She lifted the metal-like fabric of her apron to her eye, folding it somehow into a cone with which she daubed her tears. I was amazed she did not blind herself.

"Of course," the officer said breezily. "I am just curious, however. How much time does an officer of the Thousand-Year

Reich need to say good-bye to a degenerative medical anomaly remanded from her fruitless analysis?"

Shame vied with contempt in the doctor's eyes.

"I shall have her ready at once," she said.

I raced through the kitchen and up the back stairs and deposited myself under my satin sheets. I was grateful I had no beating heart to give away my exertions. As I lay in my consort's bed, looking up to the silken vortex of the canopy above me, I thought of the patients, of Gertzi, all stunned into silence by the conversation they'd only partially understood. That evening their coats would be collected and exposed, in a special airtight closet, to an open box of Zyklon B. The gas would perform the task for which it was invented: to rid clothing of lice and more tenacious vermin. In the morning, the patients would recount their triumphant exploits of the previous evening as they filed out of their cells. They would pantomime plates landed and lifted softly as songbirds. Gertzi would pour and pour again from empty hands his ineffable bottle of cold yellow wine and they would follow one another, smiling sheep, into showers where they would never be tutored in the correct use of soap.

Dr. Flosse finally made it to my room. She had changed her dress, which was a relief to me, as I was free from having to compliment it. Her face was fresh from a few handfuls of cold water. She wore her officious skirt, her white lab coat, a touch of perfume. It was the impression she wanted to make, the way she wanted me to remember her. The doctor had difficult news and I listened, quietly, curious how she would deliver her lines.

"Berlin has sent for you. The officer is waiting downstairs."

She had grown fascinated with a loose flesh-colored thread from my comforter. I tried not to disturb this fascination as I uncurled from my sheets and removed my nightgown.

"You'll like Berlin," she said briskly. "Lovely city. Sidewalks and trees and little schnitzel vendors."

She removed an ironed handkerchief from the pocket of her coat and blew.

"I know Berlin," I said, pulling my blouse over my head. I gave her no indication that I was fully prepared to go.

"Of course. You're to meet the führer, a rare honor. He has a delightful dog that he has taught to be a vegetarian. Perhaps he'll let you feed it some raw carrots or something."

I had never mentioned an affinity for animals, but it was not me of whom she was speaking. It was her construct, her charming little unbreakable doll that was now being forced from her grasp, leaving her alone in her play pit of ash.

"He has a charming car, the young officer who is to drive you. Perhaps he'll let you sit in the front seat." And her tears came like some grotesque eruption, brimming past the ability of her hanky. The bed quaked with each explosive sob.

"Ach, you must forgive me," she said with one furious mop of her face, but I was not even listening as I worried the buckle on my left shoe.

"You say he's downstairs?" I asked, fully dressed from the doorway.

"Who?"

"This officer. With the car."

"Maddy . . ."

"Yes?"

"Now that you're leaving, won't you please . . . could you just *tell* me the significance of those three little words? The ones you shouted that day in the shower?" I had denied the knowledge to Chaney. Had grasped at it only in the frenzied terror of losing Mutter. Under sober reflection, my condition was something I would not thrust upon my worst enemy. So it was with complete candor that I looked into the doctor's bleary eyes and said, "Trust me. If I understood them, you would be the *first* I would tell."

I saw her shoulders feint, an involuntary twitch that, if expressed, would turn into an offer of embrace. But she checked it, aborted it in the sinew. Something in her knew this was too great a request. We were past saying anything else. Good-bye would be absurd.

I was down the stairs in a blur of small pumping knees. The large front door of the castle was open and through it I smelled the wet cobbles of the driveway and the lingering smoke of the officer's cigarette. He waited behind the wheel as I approached the car, a large Mercedes four-door, beading the light rain under fresh wax. He exited the car and crossed to the passenger-side door, grinning, his cigarette in his lips like an American movie star. I must have looked frightened, for his smile broadened as he opened the door for me.

"What's the matter, honey?" he said, tossing his dying butt to the gravel. "Don't you recognize your own long-lost mother?"

CHAPTER 48

I was silent for a long time as she drove. Feelings surfaced, firing wildly inside my skull. But it wasn't like my first rediscovery of her at the nightclub. My feelings had cooled, coiled in me like things apart, parasites of the heart. Had I been normal, I would have looked from eyes at a different height, the promontory of a matured body. I would have known that I had outgrown her. But I still felt as I appeared, small and adrift. She kept looking at me, her cap now off, the dark auburn roots of her short bleached hair guiding me back to something familiar. But her eyes betrayed nothing. No fondness or disgust. Only assessment. Even though the dead do not age, they do change, like cliffs and riverbeds change. We are carved and pitted from the inside and so can be new to one another.

"Where are you taking me?" I finally asked, feeling an ease in so general a question.

"Out of Germany. The party is ending here. Everyone who's even remotely entertaining is being rounded up. "

"And how did you find me?"

"Your father told me."

Father. The word was a cold breath that inflamed my embers. I choked my ambition down and turned hard upon my mother.

"Why do you wear that uniform? Are you one of them now?"

"This? It's a *costume*," she said, trying to smile. "We've always been fond of dressing up in this country. I used to fake my lust under Weimar. Now I fake my compliance under the Reich."

"Well, they're not faking theirs."

"I had no idea you had such an interest in *politics*."

And she meant it in the etymological sense, in its most basic meaning, as in the business of people, the affairs of the living. The situation in Germany had nothing to do with us. We were bystanders. Ghosts.

"I thought I raised you to be more interesting than that."

"*Raised* me? Jesus Christ. *Mollusks* show more interest in their offspring."

I was surprised when she slowed the car to the shoulder. She breathed deeply, staring through the mottled surface of the windshield. She turned to me. Her eyes were full of tears. Real tears. It seemed impossible that I could wound her.

"Give me your hand," she said.

I gave it to her and she gently placed it inside her tunic.

"You feel that?"

Her heart beat, a solid rhythmic thrum beneath my cold palm.

"And this."

She drew my finger over her cheek and caught the moisture there. Her tears were warm.

"I'm no different than you, Maddy. I worked the same charm on myself that I did on you."

"I don't understand."

"I wanted you to be strong. To fend for yourself and grow strong the way I grew strong."

"Abandonment is not strength."

"Neither is self-pity. Your grandmother did not want to teach me this charm. She called it *die Art Fluch*. The kind curse. She warned that the dead awakened were not less themselves but more so. But I thought I saw myself in you. The same hard green reed of a girl that I was."

"But a *girl*," I said, looking at her. "Always a *girl*. Never like you, never ripe. Never a woman."

"What was I to do? Tell me. Could *you* watch your own child *die*?" I looked away. Mutter's thick fingers ebbing heat on the shower room floor. His lips that had refused a last desperate breath. "Look at me," she said. I raised my head. "You understand, Maddy. I can see it in your eyes."

We were both silent then. It wasn't some maudlin spring awakening, an end of act swelling of waxing strings. It was more an assessment of our situation. Germany was lost to her as Hollywood would have to be reinvented for me. My only hope of a new discovery, a new venture, was in her.

"Then teach me," I said to the upholstery. "*Teach* me how."

And she drove.

CHAPTER 49

I told her my sensory ability had been spotty at best, based on recall more than direct stimulus. Smells seemed somewhat easier to achieve, tethered as they are to memory. But taste was nearly impossible. Her basic premise was simple enough: reality is defined by one's attention. I should have known this, she said, purporting to work in an industry that survived on the manufacture of perception. Wasn't I a creature of Hollywood? I told her that I felt like such a creature because I had obviously associated with Hollywood's limitations. She told me to stop that. I was only limited in my ability to experience my surroundings because I *believed* I was limited. It was much harder to do this while alive, she conceded. Our biology was always challenging our innate gods. When I asked her—in a fairly whining tone, I'm ashamed to admit—why she hadn't told all this to me before, she scoffed. No one, in her experience, could ever *teach* anything worth knowing. She said life is a strictly bespoke business. Experience the only worthy tailor. But she never said she was sorry. Then she quoted Buddhist scripture, a two-thousand-year-old koan:

> *While living, be a dead man.*
> *Thoroughly dead.*
> *Then whatever you do, just as you will,*
> *Will be right.*

We could make our flesh warm, our hearts beat, if we chose. This she said was especially convenient while fucking. She said it just like that. Fucking. And I said I doubted I would ever be attracted enough to anyone who would find me accessible in that way. She told me to keep an open mind. Experiencing new sensations was all a question of "listening" to the experience, becoming "one ear" she called it. Free of the tyranny of "what is," we could augment our experience of anything the same way one increases the volume of a radio. It was all fiddling with knobs, according to her. Tuning into what we wanted. Tuning out what we didn't. The world was just one massive sending tower, broadcasting limitless stations, all for our listening pleasure.

We headed back to Bremen, to a small hotel by the sea where some friends of hers were waiting to sail to America. They were Jewish artists mostly, composers and set designers, someday directors who had managed to be sponsored by the payroll pledge fund. The American government didn't seem particularly alarmed by Nazi invective but was heartily annoyed by the influx of refugees and had severely limited emigration visas. The only reliable way to get into the country was by sponsorship. Several well-known European actors and directors, working in the States, had set up a fund whereby a percentage of their studio wages went toward passage, food, even instruments and scoring paper. We were being funded by the accumulation of three marathon benefits held by Marlene Dietrich at the Cocoanut Grove. Every shake of her ass and flash of her kneecaps was another life saved.

Volker came to the dock, mingling with the marine mist. He lifted his head and nodded as our ship pulled out. His eyes were bright and I could see the outline of the terminal through them, could see people milling onto waiting boats, lifting luggage, children, the last tangible memories of their homeland. He smiled. He knew his work was done. I had no words for the feelings rising in me. I had never mourned a father before.

CHAPTER 50

We arrived back in Los Angeles on a day when the clouds were low and cold, the sidewalks chilled from a sudden rain. My mother was silent but I could see her eyes searching the gray streets for the glamour, as everyone's eyes first search, not knowing that the only glamour this desert holds is what one brings. She had said good-bye to her friends at the dock at San Pedro. They had contracts to fulfill. We only had each other. Her eyes brightened as we drove through the stone gates at the top of Beachwood, but fell again as I pointed out Busby Berkeley's house.

"It's so small, Maddy. Are you sure he lives there?"

"I've seen him with his dog."

"He walks his *own* dog?"

My humble truck was disenchanting enough (I was thrilled it still started after a jump from a pier-front busboy), but my house was the real coal at Christmas.

"It looks like something out of our village," my mother said, not even bothering to cover her disappointment.

Inside, the taps were dry, the light switches worthless. The only furniture was the trunk my mother had brought with her and from it she removed a candle stub, lit it, and then proceeded to explore the rest of the house.

"Maddy," she said, chiding me softly, "why do you live like this?"

Moving smoothly from room to room, her candle held high like the hero in a vampire picture, she said, "You might as well be buried, my girl."

"Why do you use the candle?" I asked. "We don't need the light."

She exhaled impatiently as a teacher might with a child who has failed yet again to grasp the simplicity of arriving at a certain sum.

"Why do you fuss about only what we *need*? There are joys in this world, my girl. And candlelight is one of them."

That night we broke some dried branches from a dying sycamore and lit a small fire in the grate. We lay down before it, our bodies flat to the hardwood, stretched out like the corpses we were. My mother was clarifying the conditions of our existence, segueing from theory to actual practice in a light and meandering tone better suited to a sorority sleepover than the cold necromantic catechism of what would be ours forever. We were no longer mere factories of reaction. We were inside cause now. Beyond death and therefore life's limitations. For instance, she asked if I was comfortable there on the floor. When I said I wasn't, she laughed and said that the hardness of the floor had nothing to do with how I felt about it. The floor was only half the conversation.

My back was the other half, and if I chose to "hear" comfort, warmth, luxury, or any combination of the three, I had the ability to do so. Eventually I wouldn't even need to feel the floor to be comfortable upon it. I would carry comfort inside me.

"But what happened to the duck?" I asked.

I said it without explanation, free of context, testing the growing intimacy that only her direct reply would confirm. She smiled and turned to me, beautiful in the firelight, and said, "Where all duck that's unfortunate enough to end up in orange and champagne sauce goes."

I had watched her consume the entire dinner without ever having to void her mouth in a napkin and I was curious, even jealous.

"We shit out this black liquid stuff," she said, laughing like a girl who had "shit" too loud in company. "I don't know how it works."

I seized upon this at once and theorized that our bodies, now no longer dependent upon nutrients, no longer needed to bother with the functions of digestion and absorption and performed, probably by some kind of diastolic friction, a simple reductive shorthand.

"Perhaps," she said to my lengthy explanation.

"Is it always liquid?"

"Why do you want to know about *shit*? We get to enjoy food. That's all that matters."

"I don't understand."

"We'll work on it tomorrow. Let's get some sleep."

"Why would we sleep?"

"To dream of *love*, silly. Why else?"

There was an automat on Hollywood Boulevard not far from Grauman's Egyptian called the Hornblower. Nautically themed,

it had ratlines for room dividers and voluptuous figureheads sup-
porting each booth. For a handful of hot nickels, you could feast
like a privateer and never bother sitting. My mother thought it
a perfect spot for my first gastric dry run, so we headed over the
hill, trying to beat the lunch rush.

"Maybe we start with a dish of Jell-O," my mother said,
heading toward a window where a quivering stack of toxic-green
cubes peeked through.

"I don't like Jell-O."

"You've never had Jell-O."

"I don't like the look of it."

"Then the chocolate pudding."

"Shouldn't we have something substantial first?"

"What for?"

Her logic was unassailable. She deposited the nickels. To
the minute flourish of a three-note boatswain's whistle, the tiny
window lifted automatically. Wiping a thin metal spoon on her
blouse, she handed me the dish.

Now, don't do anything. Just look at it. Anticipate it. Wait for it.

I looked up into her shining eyes. Her lips had not moved.

*Smell it. Still cold on Christmas morning. Hot from a sweet-
heart's hand. Toasted. Sweet. Earthy. Primal. Cup your palm around
the memory of it and place it on your tongue. The scent with clever
feet. Taste. The scent with deepening roots. Feel it spreading on the
palate, cousin to the smell. But louder. High up in sinus, carpeted on
the tongue. Creeping like fog. Like delicious milk chocolate fog, turning
to rain, now standing water, richer, into cream. Into a dense toasted
sweet, roasted gale.*

A tiny storm of love.

"Easy there, sweet chips," my mother said out loud. "Small

bites. You don't want to be sitting there with Eleanor Powell and have brown shit shootin' out your nose."

And she dipped the head of her spoon into the muddy goop and demurely placed the bite between her cunning little teeth.

"That crap's not bad. Get another," she said, taking my dish with relish.

The plates began to stack. There were the remains of an Irish stew, a shepherd's pie, a macaroni salad, two chicken pot pies, a liverwurst open-faced, a side of bread-and-butter pickles, a plate of borsht that stained the corners of our mouths like circus clowns, mashed potatoes with chitlin' gravy, a matzo ball soup, calf's tongue in mushroom sauce (forty nickels!), and a lime chiffon pie. I felt filled but not stuffed. Rather like a tube of toothpaste that had just been given an initial squeeze.

"What are we going to do with the rest of the day?" I asked. It felt strange to put forth such a question, but I liked being under her tutelage. It was a relief after so many years of fending for myself. I wanted the lessons to continue.

"I don't know about you, but I'm looking for work," she said, her voice crisp after a sip of coffee.

"You should try the studios. It's a cinch they'd put you under contract."

"Why the hell would I do that?"

"Don't you want to be a star?"

"Are you kidding? Too much work. Hell, I can rope a rich joe, give him the tumble of his life, and be eating the same fancy chow and wearing the same fancy frock as the poor dumb dame who sweated under hot lights for fourteen hours." She already sounded American.

"Don't you want to earn your own money?"

"What for? The money don't know the difference."

"But you'd be reliant on a man."

"That's what *he'd* think."

Again, her logic was unassailable. If you looked like her. But I couldn't be content with her particular brand of consumerism. I would never be happy in the crowd, feeding from the shadows. I was my father's daughter, odd as that sounds, and I wanted one final tilt at that tinsel-covered windmill.

"I thought you'd given that up," she said when I told her my plans.

"There's more than one studio in this town," I said.

"They want them young, honey. But not *that* young."

"Well, Jesus," I said sullenly. "Don't spare my feelings. Just have a nice hot shit right on my dreams why don't you."

At the mention of feces, even as a euphemism, I felt my bowels suddenly liquefy. My mother saw the change on my face and immediately burst into laughter.

"Too much, too soon, sweetie," she said, trying to hold me up.

I slapped her hand away.

"Christ, I don't know if I can make it to the bathroom."

"Ball it up, darlin'."

I hadn't had to control a sphincter of any kind in two decades.

"What do I do?"

"You could stick your thumb up your ass but that might be a tad conspicuous."

I must have moaned or something, for her smile faded and she took my face in her hands.

"No feeling can manifest without your permission, Maddy. Do you hear me? Wish it away."

I felt like the hull of the *Titanic* just moments after the kiss of that first iceberg.

"Look at me. There is no pressure in your belly, no pain in your guts. You feel nothing until you are *ready* to feel it. Okay? Nothing until you are ready."

I was a first-time skater letting go of the rail. I took a cautious step and stood up. A loud, high-pitched whine escaped through the fabric of my skirt. I felt a pressure and a tremulous belch rang out of my throat along with an acid surge that made my eyes water.

"I think I threw up a little."

"Choke it down. That's a girl. Better'n soda pop. Now tighten up and walk to the ladies' room. There you go."

What came out of me was a christening of sorts. It was not foul. There was a watery sweetness to it, if anything. And from the confines of that stall I heard the women come and go, talking of the days of Valentino, missed periods, the cost of the local Red Car. How hot dates needed to be treated like just-baked pies, set on the sill and left to cool lest one would be burned. Or at least that was what her mother had told her. I could pass as one of them, but something was lost, a new vulnerability revealed. My mother drew strength from the lies. I felt somehow beholden to them. She had enjoyed our reckless feast, had ignored the faces pressed to the glass that watched us suck down the food our bodies didn't need. I had felt there was something obscene in the indulgence. But I wanted her to stay.

Could we be like mother and daughter? Not likely. But we could be friends, close girlfriends who shared at least portions of their lives. And given enough time, enough talks, perhaps one day we would be like strangers who had grown to *feel* like family.

CHAPTER 51

My mother wanted to be found and so she conspired to get lost. *Zipper*, as Zann had predicted, had indeed made her a star in Berlin. But beyond her first rush of ascendancy, she found her celestial position offered little prolonged advantage. Unlike me, she realized the necessity of her self-generated shadows. She wisely became a sister to the moon. The only light she craved was what she could borrow. What she wanted was access, a kitchen full of cookie jars low enough to disguise her reach. She dismissed the stage shows at both Grauman's Chinese and Egyptian. The story of Myrna Loy being discovered in the pre-picture chorus was a cautionary tale for her. She needed to be at ground level, in the cramped heat of the nightclub where eye contact and the scent off her heated skin would be as effective as mace. She tried the chorus lines at the Cocoanut Grove, the Roosevelt ballroom, the Embassy Club, but she lacked the generous fleshiness of the women of the day. She was lean and kinetic, almost cruel in her litheness, and the modernity of her form was lost on the men hiring.

As a last resort, she applied as a cigarette girl at Lickter's in the Chinese Theatre store next to Grauman's. She was given the job, provided she "fatten up," and was told to come back in the costume of a tobacco-producing country. Cuba, the Dominican Republic, all the island plantations had been taken by sullen Chicano girls from Echo Park. She decided on the Russian steppes, where a particularly harsh varietal grew that, once cured in vodka and kiln-dried over yak chips, was a necessary component in a pipe blend favored by Spencer Tracy.

Finding a costume was easy. The elite Nazis of her association had been avid role-players. Their bedrooms had been more like black box theaters than places of repose, and they had spared no expense costuming their illusions. My mother's trunk held unparalleled treasures, and among them was an assortment of titillating getups, all of which had seen action among the most solvent *Oberführer*. She had Dresden peasant dirndls complete with wooden shoes and tear-away bodices, a pair of crotchless lederhosen, Slavic shawls embroidered with geometric depictions of gypsy girls in compromising congress with all assortment of woodland creatures, ghetto fishmonger skirts of distressed silk with a gold lamé star of David. But her favorite was a black sable *kubanka* with a matching thigh-length greatcoat given to her by a *Brigadeführer* whose fondest memory of the front had been the almost melodic rape of a doe-eyed soprano from Minsk. This outfit was perfect for her tenure at the smoke shop and it would be a simple trick of the mind to keep the sweat from beading on her forehead as she coyly lifted and bent under the heavy wool and fur.

My mother never spent the night with one of her conquests. Once finished, she was dressed and into the raw night like a shot. She nurtured obsession in them but always with a carefully reverse-engineered longevity. Overfondness she knew would breed overexposure. I could count on seeing her for at least a few hours before the sun came up. She had started small, an associate producer at Metro, an agent at William Morris, both of whom yielded little more than change for the powder room. Then one night Gary Cooper came to her cigarette counter, desperate for a pack of Craven A's. She laughed later, that still-dark morning, when she told me how shy he had been. He spent the first hour after their clothes were off performing rope tricks from his Montana boyhood. But she assured me the rumors about his endowment were true. He had far more in common with horses than her other boyfriends. The night after her tryst with Cooper, twelve dozen roses and a silver-appointed saddle arrived on our doorstep. She sold the saddle for fifteen hundred dollars to the parade master of Pasadena's Tournament of Roses. Other stars followed, and with them came more lucrative loot. Gold cigarette cases, emerald-encrusted telephone dialers, a pair of champion-blooded Borzois she sold to a breeder in Glendale. She kept nothing. Every gift, no matter how extravagant, met with the same frigid assessment. Everything was hocked.

In two months we had a house full of furniture. Chinese deco rugs absorbed the sound of our two-in-the-morning laughter. We sang in German with Greta Keller from a phonograph given to my mother by Irving Thalberg, the only gift she kept. When she intimated to a Danish count that her mode of transportation was of necessity the Red Car, a cherry-red Bugatti was gathering condensation in our driveway the next morning. Having never bothered to learn to drive herself, she made me pilot the thing to a dealership on Sunset Boulevard wearing false whiskers and dark glasses. Our comfortable domesticity was a new frontier for her. And I was the perfect cover. What could cool a waxing passion that had reached the ebb of its usefulness faster than telling her lover she had a needy little girl home?

CHAPTER 52

It was winter of a new decade and I was campaigning hard for a Christmas tree, hoping that pretending to be a family might quell the real fire in my gut. I had seen plastic wreaths wired to the grills of limousines, seen the mechanical elves in the windows of Robertson's. It didn't have to be an elaborate decoration. Just a little tree with a few lights and tinsel whose modest glow would keep me company while I waited for the night hours to pass and my mother to come home.

For the last few years she had bristled at the idea. Christmas Eve was a big night for her, what with all the parties and the general feeling of expansiveness that she could so easily engorge into personal gain. And she'd gripe that it was an unnecessary expense, that there was plenty of cheap glitz on the streets if I were feeling sentimental. But I always thought she was uncomfortable with the druidic implications of a tree. Like most self-made people, she did not like to be reminded of where she came from.

"Just a small one. No bigger than me."

"No, Maddy."

"But I'm the one who's here alone most of the time."

"That's your choice."

"But it's Christmas."

"Only because some thieving converted Roman said so."

"Jesus Christ, I don't want to get into some dreary historical dialectic. I just want a pretty little tree to stick in the fucking corner for three lousy weeks or so. Is that really so much to ask?"

"How bad do you want it?"

Her gray eyes flashed at the prospect of winning something from me. I should have known all along this was her real intention. I paused and looked at her. She could not contain the gleeful smile devouring her face.

"What do you want?" I asked cautiously.

"To have you come with me to that party."

Decent lager and bratwurst had become treasonous as America flirted with a second war with Germany. I agreed, perhaps sullenly, with her rabidly liberal refugee friends who saw a declaration was long overdue. Weimar was home to us. Not this third try at some starchy and humorless reich. They were having a huge blowout at the home of one of the composers. It would be an opportunity for her to see many of them, but also an opportunity to take the pulse of the town. A new breed of power was surfacing in Hollywood, and its chief priests were sure to be at this party. The problem was it was to be a family affair, wives and children, and she was uncomfortable showing up in an obvious shade of scarlet. She needed me to sell the benign domestic angle while she worked her dark snares belowdecks. The fact was I was desperate to go to this party, to be among the anointed few who still breathed the stale studio air. But I couldn't let my mother know that. Not if I wanted my tree. "I'll want at least a ten-foot tree, then."

"If we can stay until midnight," she said.

"Eight-foot, and nine thirty."

"Six and ten."

"Done."

IT WAS ONE OF THOSE PLACES IN THE CANYON BUILT FOR A VIEW. IT WAS meant to resemble a Norman castle with battlements above the modern top-story windows and a plywood portcullis over the driveway. Attached to the simulated stone was an enormous sign, Vegas-worthy, which read: *Freedom H. Q., Operation: Steel Boot = Hitler's Ass* with a rather convincing forced perspective pictograph of a bent and soon to be bowel-addled Führer gaping at the viewer in sheepish surprise.

The gravel of the driveway was littered with cars, plain, early-model Fords, and I could see my mother begin to frost at the prospect of a wasted night. Many of the cars were occupied, rocking gently like dinosaur eggs or steaming from the inside, all five windows milky as cataracts. As we passed one, a couple, wet and rumpled, burst out of its cabin in a warm sea-scented fog. Both the man and woman wore little black plastic chip-like mustaches that clung to their upper lips by a tiny claw pinched to their septums. At the entrance was a bin of these little mustaches with a sign admonishing each guest to *Nehmen jetzt eine!* (Take one, now!) Parody is the last station on our trip toward dismantling fear, and it seemed imperative that everyone be in on the joke.

"Stick this on," my mother said, shoving the hard plastic

square up my nose. "Part of the deal is you can't be a fucking wallflower all goddamned night, get it?"

"You just added at least a foot to the tree," I said, adjusting the plastic square.

We moved into the throng of bodies expelling opinions, laughter, smoke. Children raced through the larger legs and torsos, expert, as always, at such work. They had fists full of cake or flailing slices of cold meat, hit-and-run scavengers. One had even found a half-drunk bottle of rye. One boy, a plump little thing dressed as a pint-size de Gaulle, sized me up and promptly threw a slice of bologna in my face.

"Oh, Maddy's got a crush!" my mother jeered as she disappeared into the fray.

I removed the thin slice of composite meat. Not having a handkerchief, I began to scrape the residue from my face with my fingers.

"Who knew young love could be so tenacious?"

I was offered a worn but laundered handkerchief from a young man who did not look it. His head was large but well shaped, the bald dome crowing like a pregnant belly. He wore glasses and spoke with his lips covering his teeth, an affectation of many European immigrants who had yet to amass enough spare capital to indulge in straight, white American teeth.

"Curt," the young man said, offering me his warm hand.

"Maddy," I said, taking it.

"Pleasure," he said, bowing slightly, and that was all I needed to know to assume his origins.

"What part of Germany are you from?" I asked.

He blushed. "Is it so apparent?"

"Only to one from your homeland."

"But you barely have a trace of accent."

"I've been here many years," I said.

"Surely not so many. Are you here with your parents?"

"My mother. She'll blow soon. And like the white whale announce her location as a challenge. One need only be patient."

"She sounds enchanting."

"If you like whales."

We had moved to the drinks table by this point and I stood quietly while he poured himself a Scotch and me a glass of watery purple liquid. We found seats on a beleaguered love seat. He reached over to me and gently removed my mustache.

"Unless you're planning on invading Poland this evening," he said.

"I forgot I had it on."

We circled the niceties, as well-bred Germans are wont to do. But when my last name was finally revealed, his formality shattered.

"Oh, sweet merciful Jesus, no!" he shouted. "Not *the* Maddy Ulm? Not the infamous Vampire Girl of Universal City? Not the Phantom of Stage Twenty-eight? My God, child. You are a legend on the lot. You should hear the accomplishments ascribed to you."

I was shocked but curious.

"Tell me," I said, trying to smile indulgently. At that moment, a flurry of green cocktail olives rebounded off my forehead. The plump little de Gaulle snickered from his blind behind an ottoman and ran for cover, hoping, I assumed, that I would follow.

"More of Cupid's tender darts?" Curt said, laughing.

"Please continue."

"Are you sure you wouldn't rather have a bit of fun with him? He seems lively."

"I'd much rather hear about my legend."

"Well, the stories are ludicrous but vastly creative. Apparently you were an intimate of the infamous Lon Chaney, Man of a Thousand Suitcases . . ."

"*Faces*," I corrected.

"Ah. That makes more sense. Anyway, seeing you now it's clear that's an obvious fiction. But some say you actually were instrumental in the cutting of his *Phantom*."

"Interesting."

"Others say you were the real genius behind *Dracula*. But I have seen that picture and understand genius as applied to that endeavor only in the broadest context."

"Prudent."

"There are others. I think the most interesting is that you were the model for the famous *Frankenstein* makeup. Can you believe that? I'm sure Mr. Pierce would find that rumor of particular interest."

"Incredible. I look nothing like him," I said, laughing as convincingly as I could. I was amazed at the veracity of everything he told me but, of course, I remained silent. "Where did you hear these . . . *pearls*?" I asked, taking a nauseating sip from my cup of purple.

"The bit about Chaney came from his son, Lon Jr. I'm working with him on his next picture. I must say he wasn't my first choice."

So Creighton had grown up, changed his name, and entered the game after all. His father would be furious.

"What's the picture?"

"Get ready and don't laugh," he said, settling his glasses firmly on the bridge of his nose. "You know what? I should preface this by saying I *am* a real writer. My original draft was really

far more Kafkaesque than the middling tripe they've forced it
into."

"Don't tell me. Your story is about the corruption of man.
How an average joe can be hideously transformed by pervasive
and intolerant forces beyond his control. The good German who
wakes up one morning to find himself a monster."

"That's uncanny. How could you know that?"

"Simple. You're a good German boy fleeing the Nazis. What
else would you write about?"

"You don't suppose him turning into a *wolf* is too obvious a
metaphor?"

"Too obvious to whom? The typical American hausfrau and
ten-year-old boys? Which, if you're under contract to Universal,
will be your prime demographics."

"So you know the *hell* I've been going through." He grinned
wearily.

"Only that they probably *loved* your original concept but felt
the ideas to which you so tastefully *alluded* to in your original
draft could be better served if *seen* in a more obvious and, hopefully, *profitable* stop-frame metamorphosis."

"Oh, it's so humiliating."

"Your bosses have never been big on subtly, trust me. I sense
a lot of fur in your future, *mein Freund*." For a moment I reflected
wistfully if coldly on Chaney's plans for his wolf transformation.
"Just remember *yak* hair is the key."

"Christ." He moaned with a smile.

"Don't despair. You've most likely compromised yourself into
a very lucrative franchise."

"What the hell have I gotten myself into? The whole thing
is devolving daily into this great steaming pile of superstitious
hog shit."

"I don't know if I'd call it *superstitious*, exactly."

"Don't tell me a cynical girl like you believes in *werewolves*."

"People had a sensitivity to such things in my village."

"You must have been very small."

"I remember they would draw the pentagram in white chalk on their front doors as protection against such creatures."

"A star?"

"Yes. Symbol of the faithful."

"Faithful to what?"

"The old gods. The gods of the skalds."

"Vikings?"

"Visigoths, actually. Werewolves, as they are commonly called, were really berserkers, members of the fighting elite. It was told that as a last line of defense they could turn themselves into wolves. A small pack of them was said to be able to destroy an entire Roman legion. The white star was to remind them of their roots, that the people who had drawn such a star were of the same faith as they, had the same allegiance to the old gods. And so might be spared."

"This is fascinating. Especially that stuff about the star. People in Europe right now are dying, marked with a star. How do you know all this?"

"My grandfather. And his, and then his, and on back. Everyone knew these stories in my village. We had a wolf's skin the size of a man over our mantel that was said to be one of their pelts."

"I thought the berserkers were just militant fanatics who could swallow their tongues and go into furious trances. Probably an allusion to some psychotropic substance taken in the heat of battle to increase ferocity."

"The wolf is the last vestige of our indigenous self."

"How old are you?"

"Ageless," I said, grinning behind my drink. I hadn't had a creative adult conversation like this since I'd worked with Chaney.

"You're giving me the heebie-jeebies. Is that correct?"

"Heebie-*jeebies*," I said, smiling.

"Those too. Jesus, kid. You need to lay off the grape juice."

"There was a saying in my village, a kind of poem, really. You see, the ignorant set all cautionary thought to rhyme. It's so they don't forget how miserable they are. How did it go? *Even the man who loves his gods / And burns the willow bark / Must avoid the night when the moon is full / Lest the werewolf steal his heart.*"

"The full moon? I never heard that before."

Suddenly, my face exploded with a burst of clammy white cake and green frosting.

"Eros is back at his trebuchet," Curt said.

"Excuse me, but this must end." I shot up from my seat and was on top of the badly winded boy in seconds. "Where's the fire, shit pins?" I demanded, bending a pudgy arm behind his back.

"Oww! Lay off!"

"Only if *you* lay off air-dropping the appetizers."

"What? Get off me!"

I reluctantly let him up. His lip quivered as he rubbed his shoulder.

"That's not how you get a girl's attention."

"Who says I want your attention?" I had forgotten how tediously defensive children could be.

"Listen, if I agree to have *one* drink with you will you promise to leave me alone for the rest of the evening?"

"A drink?" he asked, blinking. "You mean like a juice or a pop?"

"Anything. A beverage. A little *conversation*, then *no* contact either personal or in the form of projectiles. That is my offer."

"You won't play Seven Minutes in Heaven?"

"I don't know what Seven Minutes in Heaven is, but I suspect it has little to do with one's final reward."

"You talk stupid."

"Forget it," I said, getting up.

"No. It's okay," he said, grabbing my arm. "We can have a drink. I think your talk is funny."

Luckily I was spared his company.

There was an incredible rise in voices. I jostled through the bodies, toward where the voices were the loudest. I saw the flushed skin of my mother tower above the jeering heads of the crowd as she stood, topless, on a grand piano. Two shirtless men, in bow ties only, bent their pale backs over half the keyboard each and began playing a very bluesy rendition of "Bei Mir Bist Du Schon." My mother stepped out of her skirt to high cries and swung the flimsy garment over her head before launching it into the crowd. As she sang, I couldn't keep a nugget of pride from lodging in my throat. She was wonderful.

CHAPTER 53

I got my tree, all seven feet of it. I spent six hours weaving multicolored lights through its fragrant branches, lights I had purchased along with a few ornaments and a box of tinsel at the Woolworth's on Hollywood Boulevard. I had seen it begin to work its slow and delicate magic on my mother, who would drift into the living room, completely nude, for various assessments, most of which were vague grunts that could not be completely confused with disgust. But now that it was nearing completion, she became more vocal.

"You're not using real candles? What kind of German are you?" she said, crossing her arms over her ample breasts.

"Why don't I just douse the whole thing in gasoline and throw lit matches at it? What's the matter with you?"

"I remember trees like that when I was a girl."

"I thought your family feared the winter solstice as the death of the sun or something and spent the winter months cloistered in the dark, spitting into corners."

"You make fun, but I remember a winter, many years before you were born, when my father took me to Ulm. There was a huge silver-point fir in the middle of the dry-goods shop. A magnificent thing, as high as a roof beam. With real candles clipped to every branch. I watched for an hour while the shop owner's wife lit every one. And when she finished, she gave me a gold paper crown and a tiny piece of rock sugar. I'll never forget it. When I mentioned I might like a tree like that in our house, my father beat me with his shoe and locked me in the cupboard. Trees were not to be enslaved in the worship of the one God. He had very particular beliefs about such things."

"Is that why you hate Christmas?"

"It's why I never allowed myself a fondness for it."

She came closer to me and I could see tears in her eyes.

"You've done a beautiful job, Maddy. Perhaps a little less tinsel next year, but beautiful."

It was strange to think of her as some hipless child, flat and scrawny with no sexual hammer, capable of anything as useless as wonder. She had this way of having one believe she had always been the way she now appeared. Seeing her softened was almost too much to bear. So I resisted an embrace and smiled back at her moist face. The moment was mercifully broken by the ringing of the phone. She answered, looking at me while she spoke. Then she held the receiver out to me and I took it. It was Curt, the owl-eyed writer of werewolf tales, inviting me to the lot for lunch. It seemed the fates of celluloid horror were not finished with me quite yet.

CHAPTER 54

I must admit the proposition of returning to the lot held none of the vindicated glory I had hoped for. I surmised my conversation with Curt had sunk yet another of my untenured hooks into him. He saw in me what all the others had seen, a way into the crypt of the uncanny that would not leave him looking foppish. Most likely he had already incorporated a few of my carefully dropped crumbs. The star and the poem (which was a pure fabrication on my part), perhaps. I figured we'd talk shop for a few hours and maybe he might convince his keepers to toss me at least my old day rate.

The guard at the gate knew my name. Not in the glow of some fond personal recollection or by my reputation. He had merely looked down to his list, found the words there, like hundreds of others, and given me directions to the Welsh moors. My favorite sets have always been exteriors. Landscapes of inner space, they are always more dreamlike for being by necessity purely artificial. This one, where the werewolf would do most of his leering and strutting, was beautiful. Sparse trees and low rocks, a slight rake up to the cyclorama where a leaden sky was painted. They were using the high condensing foggers, and a bit of residual mist spilled languidly through the carefully hidden nozzles. A perfect killing floor. Curt was sitting in a chair behind the director, next to an enormous bearlike man wearing paw-shaped socks and gloves with sharp nails.

"Maddy," Curt said as I passed. "There you are. Sorry I couldn't be here earlier. Have you shown yourself around?"

"Just a bit."

"I was able to incorporate some of the things we talked about." Here we go, I thought to myself. Another round with Universal's little go-to ghoul.

"Marvelous," I said dryly.

"I wanted you to meet Lon. He's been asking all kinds of crazy questions about you and so I told him I would bring you to the set."

So that was it. That was why I had been summoned. Cynicism always hides hope. And once that's gone, nothing is left but the void. It's the one vacuum nature cannot be bothered to fill.

Lon stood up and shook my hand. He was an enormous man. In his face of what I assumed to be yak hair and a black rubber nose, he looked truly feral. He fumbled to remove his lower plate of canines before speaking.

"It's a real pleasure, Miss Ulm," he said with earnest. "I really appreciate you coming all the way down here."

"My pleasure, Mr. Chaney." In his eyes was the same boy I remembered from that horrible hospital room. The fractured lump on too small a stool. The boy of all back and no front.

"Pop just told me so much about you . . . Well, I was wondering if we could meet sometime. Not here, away from all this craziness. Somewhere we could talk. Would you be all right with that?"

"I'm sure I'd love to." What in the hell did we have to talk about?

"Great, I'll have it arranged."

And that was that. Interview concluded. I supposed I could have stayed, watched the scene quicken to life. But I had made my contribution and wanted desperately to leave.

On the drive home, I became aware that my contributions were becoming increasingly brief. Perhaps I had come a dreary full circle, where ambition in one as young as I looked was as ridiculous as that same ambition in a woman of my actual years. But I wasn't quite prepared to accept that insight.

CHANEY'S SECRETARY CALLED ME ONE SATURDAY MORNING AND TOLD me in spritely tones that Mr. Chaney expected me to meet him that afternoon at one thirty. It was an order barely disguised as a request. A real Hollywood pro, this girl. So I agreed, confused yet strangely convinced of the subject of our conversation. I had lived the life he should have lived with his father. Even a warmed-over piece of that might be some comfort.

The venue for our meeting was the Van de Kamp's at Ivar and Yucca. A diner in the shape of a windmill, it seemed the perfect setting for a seemingly innocent creature's demise. He sat at a back table, unrecognized, wearing round dark glasses and a gray fedora, a cup of coffee growing cold before him. He stood when I arrived and removed his hat and glasses, taking my hand. His face was puffy, too much booze or emotion or both. When we sat, he put the dark glasses back on.

"Will you have anything?" he asked as the waitress replenished his cup.

"Nothing, thank you."

"It's not a last meal, Miss Ulm," he said, smiling.

"I'm not hungry, thank you."

"I'll have a Denver omelet and french fried potatoes, please," he said, and then turned to me. "I've thought of this meeting for most of my life. Can you believe that? Even as a boy away at boarding school, I used to set a pillow at the end of my bed and pretend it was you. My father always said you were special, said it with uncomfortable regularity, if you want to know the truth. He told me of your glandular condition, how it kept you looking like an innocent. But I must admit, seeing you again, in the light, you really do look like a child. Which makes this all the more difficult."

"Mr. Chaney, perhaps this isn't—"

"Please, Miss Ulm. It's been fifteen years with a splinter in my brain. If I don't do it now, say the things I need to say, I never will."

"Of course," I said quietly.

He looked down at his cup and tears began to seep from beneath the rims of his lenses.

"Jesus," he said under his breath. "Just a little kid."

I did not know if he referred to himself or me. Then he laughed and shook his head as if to clear his mind of sentiment.

"All my life I have hated you," he said evenly. His eyes glanced up to mine to gauge my reaction. "Does that surprise you?"

"Not at all. I never liked your father's attitude about you. I always thought it harsh. I remember the last time I saw you was in a small chair."

"And you were at his bedside."

"I was mortified that he made you watch while he whispered to me."

The large man shook with a sob worthy of his size. He snatched the paper napkin from under his flatware and vented his nose.

"Do you remember what he said to you?"

Of course I did. But what could I say? The large man was wide open. He needed something, some cork of closure to staunch the last ten years.

I looked him in his great sagging eyes and said, "He asked me for a cigarette."

The great face went pale and then a shudder began from deep in his belly. Then a laugh broke that shook the whole table.

"I'll be damned," he said with breathless relief. "That's just like him. All these years I thought . . . Hell, I don't know. A *cigarette*. Son of a bitch."

His food arrived at that moment and he lathered it with ketchup and several shakes of salt before he began devouring it.

"I know Pop didn't want me taggin' along in his footsteps. I'm sure he'd be good and sore that I changed my name. But the studio made me. That's the truth. The name. They thought it would be a draw. I know they only want me for these pictures because I'm big. Monsters are supposed to be big. But I really like it, you know. The dialogue, the scenes. Working out little bits of business with the other actors. I had a scene the other day with Claude Rains and he's, you know, a real pro and it felt just like folks. Just like two professional joes doing their jobs."

I watched the food enter his lips, the broadness of his brow that would wrinkle to accommodate a bite. I could see him at his mother's kitchen table, an overgrown boy, so grateful for a plate of buttery love.

"The only reason your father would *not* be proud of you, Mr. Chaney," I said, "is that you have proved him wrong. And your father hated being wrong. Having to bear his name might be unfortunate. But you do not have to bear *him*."

"You really feel all that?" His swollen eyes crested with an almost sickening hope.

"Absolutely."

He dropped his fork and reached out for me, a sad but bursting smile on his face. I felt his hands on the thin tubes of my arms, the fingers tensing as he lifted me over the end of the table. He hugged me hard, until I thought my sternum might fracture.

"Gee, you're a swell . . .," he said, halting suddenly. He didn't know what to call me. His heart, which I guess he never learned to trust, was telling him I was something far older and more urbane that what he saw. But he was in the habit of trusting his eyes. He could remain simple and safe if he trusted his eyes. "You like ice cream? Let me buy you an ice cream."

On the drive home I was rattled. What had I gained from this confrontation? An unsolicited bowl of mint chocolate chip made nearly inedible under the scrutiny of his oafish gaze. A stifling hug I did not want. A two-hundred-pound man prone to alcoholism and flights of mood had said he hated me. Even with my pronounced physical resilience, I couldn't mollify my fear. And this was why I'd made the effort? To referee his childish bouts with inadequacy? Feed him lies about his supposed talent? Build him up so I could make my escape unscathed?

I had pity for the child. Much less for the man.

CHAPTER 55

At the beginning of the postwar boom years my mother had the idea of selling the house. It was a bad time to be German, especially in a predominately Jewish enclave like ours. I wasn't working, and the house was simply bursting with over a decade's worth of equity. Her plan was to buy a ten-unit courtyard building on Hollywood Way in Burbank, close to the studios. This last bit was a concession to my own delusions, but she was always skilled at nurturing fantasy. The rented units could pay for themselves and would take the pressure off her hustling so hard. It was easy to forget how old she really was. Looking at her one could easily assume she would find a fascination with a new cologne, a new car, a new cock. I pretended I didn't care, that I would do whatever was easier for her. But deep down I was crushed. My house on Beachwood Drive was the culmination of all my efforts on the lot. But I signed the papers when the time came, watched the moving van loaded, handed over the front door key.

It was a pretty little apartment complex. Several of the units were rumored to have been actual backlot fronts from some studio's old European street. I was surprised my mother didn't want something more modern, but who could argue with the price? The only problem with it was the view.

A vista of heartbreak.

For all I had to do was stand in the winter-yellowed stubble that passed for the grass of our front lawn and turn my head to the right and there, like a potbellied chalice in some knight's tale, was the cylindrical taunt of my last ambition, the Warner Brothers–First National water tower. It didn't matter that Warner made its bones with cookie-cutter gangster pictures and cheap musicals, that the closest they got to horror were the rows of morning makeup chairs stuffed to capacity by bottle blondes still belching the dregs of the previous evening's boilermakers. It was a studio. It had stages. And it had people working in those stages. People laughing, screaming, tirading, and dreaming. People *living* the only way I knew how. In service to the tinsel. Genuflecting before the glitz. I suppose I could have bullshitted my way onto the payroll as a script runner or fourth assistant director. God knows I knew my way around the ballyhoo. I could even imagine the face of the sharp first assistant after I laid down my spiel, the keenness of his gaze as he looked down from the lofty height of all nineteen of his years and lied unknowingly to me when he winked and said I had a future in this business. What could I do? I had nothing to offer this new fascination with singing sailors and high-diving leading ladies. Volker's sapling had grown into a tree, an outdated bit of spook-show set dressing made up of chicken wire and plaster repelled by the grating Broadway playback and garish tints used to feed this new insipid genie called Technicolor. Surely there were eyes now raw from beholding Esther Williams's perennially chlorinated pelvis. Ears that might bleed if they had to suffer another bombardment from Garland's barbiturate-addled vibrato. So where were they? So what if times were good, if Hitler had gone from *Time*'s Man of the Year to unglamorous stiffening on a bunker floor? So what if musicals boosted annual receipts in the midbillions, if preparing peas no longer chipped a two-dollar manicure but sprang, creature-like, from frozen sleeps in nifty bags? What had become of all those richly textured and complicated shadows? Had they really only become fodder for braying ex-vaudevillians like Abbot and fucking Costello? My mother became worried about me. I stopped pretending to eat. I didn't bother to sleep. All I wanted to do was ceaselessly pore over the trades and rave about the industry's inexorable slide into abject mediocrity. It never dawned on me that the majority of future film historians would ignore my best efforts for similar reasons. The world was becoming tawdry, blissfully superficial, and ignorantly optimistic. And worst of all it was doing it in nauseating *color*.

"Maddy, let's get out of the house," my mother might say. "I know the barman at the Beverly Hills Hotel. We could have daiquiris. Sit in the sun by the pool for the afternoon."

"What on earth would possibly make you think I'd waste an unnecessary second in the *sun*?"

"You need to get out."

"And do you really think I'd want to spend an entire afternoon seeing your tight-trunked ex-conquests parade by like peccant sheep making goo-goo eyes at their lost Bo Peep?"

"Did you mean to do that?"

"Do what?"

"Make it rhyme like that. That was wonderful. You really should start writing more. You have such a marvelous ear."

"What the hell are you talking about? I'm trying to *dissuade* you, not fish for cheap compliments."

"Then go across the fucking street and ask for a break. There's not a job on that lot you couldn't do."

"Oh Jesus! We've been over this. What the hell am I going to do with a lot of tap-dancing morons? I couldn't stomach it."

"They're making more than musicals, Maddy."

"See, you did it too. You put four *m*'s together. Should you start writing *your* memoirs?" She ignored my comment.

"I heard they employed that author you like last year," she said steadily. "What's his name? The alcoholic with the drawl."

"That describes more than half of this town's staff writers."

"The *famous* one. With the books. Howard says he was hired to write replacement dialogue for his Bogart picture."

"*Faulkner*? Jesus. You want me to be as miserable as fucking *Faulkner*?"

"Then call your friend Billy. I know he's still working."

"He wouldn't take my call."

"How do you know?"

"I *don't* know, but I *don't* want to find out."

She looked at me with a severe but still bemused expression on her face.

"One of these days, Miss Maddy *Ulm*, you're going to have to do something just slightly out of that narrow comfort zone of yours. Either that or I'll start saving up for a nice new pine bedroom set for you. In Forest Lawn." I was miserable. But not quite ready for that.

"You'd have to start screwing studio heads again, if you're serious. Plots like that are expensive."

"Only the best for my baby."

There was something pleasant in our domestic bickering,

an almost perfect simulacrum of family. I liked that we argued under the guise of the ages we appeared, not our actual ones. Looking back, that would have put us uncomfortably in "Baby Jane" territory. We were an odd pair. But I hoped not quite ripe for such parody.

SOMEHOW THE YEARS PASSED. MY MOTHER SEEMED TO ENJOY THEM. WE made up birthdays for ourselves and celebrated the random dates with box-made cakes and stupid trinkets. We sat snickering in the dark with the doors locked on Halloween night. We decorated our yearly tree with magazine clippings of her old conquests and strips of her gaudier costume jewelry. But deep down my embers were still glowing. I still combed the trades. Still kept more than a symbolic eye on the distant studio gates.

I remember something called rock and roll was on the radio. How the loopy three-chord guitar breaks made me lonesome for Ellington and the real soul-quenching riffs of Bubber Miley. I had taught myself to cook. Nothing fancy, stripped-down versions of sauerbraten, bratwurst with spaetzle and canned cream spinach. I'd wanted the meal to be special, so I'd sprung for a forty-cent can of fancy brined mushrooms to garnish my packet of pork gravy. My mother had taken a new beau, a young man in a gray suit who worked as a junior VP of programming in this new field called television. He was a fairly lucrative mark but chapel bells were ringing in the distance, so I knew his tenure would be short. That's why I had to act fast. And this guy just happened to work for the alphabet network. And if the *Variety* blurb I couldn't stop thinking about was true, this bright young Turk was the only one in town who might make my life interesting again.

The table was set. Her highball was ready. I watched as she sipped, then tucked into her pork cutlet and sauce.

"It's not overdone, is it?" I asked as casually as I could.

"The pig or this whole evening?" she asked, still chewing. She had seen right through me, but I played innocent.

"What do you mean?"

"Maddy, there's a reason you were never comfortable in front of the camera. Just *ask* me."

"You mean I didn't have to go to all this trouble?"

"That depends. Is this about Bob and that *Variety* article?" The article had not been specific. It had merely stated the network had acquired the rights to several classic Universal horror pictures they were looking to repackage with a host.

"Just tell me if they found a host yet."

"Jesus Christ."

"See. I *did* have to go to all the trouble."

She pushed her plate away and curled her fingers around her drink. "Maddy. Why do you want to do that to yourself?"

"Do what? For years you've been telling me to look outside of my comfort zone."

"Yes, but this *Shock Theater* thing or whatever they're calling it. You don't know his angle."

"What angle? What has he said?"

"We don't do a lot of talking. I just know his *type*."

"They need a host, and no one knows these pictures like I do."

"I just think your instincts about yourself have been pretty accurate."

"Meaning what?"

"You're not an actress."

"I can always count on you for support."

"That's exactly what I *am* doing."

"Pissing yet again on my one chance? We go from total neglect to *pissing*?"

"That's not fair. We've had a lot of good years."

"*You've* had a lot of good years. I've made do. I've *idled*."

"That's *your* fault, honey. And this isn't your *one* chance. If you knew anything about it you'd know it's not much of a chance at all."

"Why can't we let your friend decide?"

"Oh, he'll jump at you. He's heard the stories. He knows what he'd get."

"And you still won't call him?"

"When have I ever pissed on your chance?"

"When? When *haven't* you?"

"Are you really so stupid you haven't realized you've led one of the more *interesting* lives this world has ever offered? Make being bleak your *style*, Maddy. But don't make it your *life*. Do something with it."

"I'm trying to."

"No. You're desperate. And you're selling yourself short."

"Oh, please. Don't tell me to start writing again."

"Why not? What else are you going to do? You really want to cap it all off by being a *television* hostess? That's your grand exit?"

"Who said anything about an exit?"

"It's television. That's all this *can* be."

"Obviously you have no respect or understanding of my life's passion."

"Jesus. This has *nothing* to do with your fucking movies."

"Are you going to call him? Or should I?" I said flatly. I could be just as stubborn as she when I knew what I wanted. "It might be weird if I did it."

I HAD TO LEAN ON THE SINK BEFORE I DID THE DISHES. I COULD HEAR HER running her bath, could hear her snatch up the phone receiver in her bedroom, the rotary grinding angrily as she dialed. I didn't realize by virtue of her calling him that night, not waiting at least until morning, that she had more than a small if conflicted concern for my wishes. I was too deep in the muck of my last chance. Maybe I'd never get another opportunity to *make*, maybe my tiny white coat really was tucked away for eternity. But at least I could *curate*. I could guide, I could enlighten those poor blue-glowing faces chewing on their reheated chicken and gray peas before the box. I could *matter*.

THEY SENT A CAR.

Not the movable drugstore of Browning's overture but a limo nonetheless.

I was ushered into the waiting room like a to-go order of Chasen's steak tartar, told I wouldn't have long to wait, and given a glass of water and a copy of *Time*. The only other occupant of that featureless room was a darkly beautiful girl with high cheekbones and pale eyes, wearing what looked like a sadomasochist's version of a nightgown. She said nothing when our eyes met, just bent her red lips down to her hand and continued to gnaw on the long plastic tips glued to her fingers. Within mere minutes the doors to corporate Vallhalla opened and I was gently summoned inside.

"Miss Ulm," the young man behind the desk said, rising to shake my hand. "You don't know what an incredible pleasure it is to finally meet you. You feel a little cold. Can I get you a hot cup of something? Tea? Chocolate?" I tried to imagine his hands on my mother, his mouth lingering upon places I'd rather not fixate. His charm, such as it was, was carefully corralled inside his eagerness, a well-bred boyishness so different from Whale's flippant genius or Chaney's working-class glamour. It was curious to me none of her conquests were handsome. Not like Volker had been. Perhaps that was deliberate on her part, a conscious selection that would not foul the exchange and leave her vulnerable again. "I just . . . *gosh*!" He continued grinning. "I've heard so much about you and to finally *meet* you. The *stories*? My, goodness. Please. Have a seat."

I refused his offer of refreshment and sat.

"You know, my father worked on the original *Frankenstein*. Assistant gaffer. He swore that picture would have fallen apart without you."

"It seemed to manage," I said trying to gauge his acumen. Was he just another, sleeker version of Junior? Or something entirely new?

"I just want you to know how thrilled we are to have you with us, Miss Ulm. It's really going to make . . . I'm sorry—" He stopped himself, his eyes glinting puckishly, like a boy with a toad in his pocket. "I hope you don't mind, but I just *have* to ask. I mean, now that I've got you in the hot seat. Is it true you knew the guy Jack Pierce based the creature's makeup on?" I hadn't trod on Mutter's memory for years. He rose in my mind then, a silent crash of images: his hands upon me still damp from the Danube, his eyes sparked by love and shifting firelight, chocolate on his teeth, his howl, his eyes again like startled birds, the curve of his throat on the shower room floor.

"Yes," I croaked. "I suppose there was a *guy* as you call him. More of an inspiration, really. Pierce is a very great artist, you understand . . ." The images began to slow. It was only then I realized a thick and somewhat greasy tear running down my cheek.

"Gee, I'm sorry," he said, snapping his pocket handkerchief to life and offering it to me. "I didn't mean to . . ." I waved his square of clean white linen away and flicked the tear from my face with a finger.

"It's nothing. Many, many years ago, that's all." I cleared my throat of its dust, trying to ignore the questions burning in his eyes. "I understand you had the good sense to purchase a few of the pictures with which I was associated." He grinned, mining my comment for what he must have hoped was even a hint of irony, relieved the conversation had found its corners again.

"We did, yes."

"And which ones are these?" The question seemed to throw him. As if he couldn't quite reconcile my tone with the fact that my head didn't crown the top of the chair.

"Well, the whole trifecta, actually. *Frankenstein, Drac*—"

"*Trifecta?*"

"Sorry. That's a horse-racing term. I mean—"

"I am aware of the word's lineage. I just don't quite see how such a term applies to the topic of our discussion." He looked at me and suddenly sat up noticeably straighter.

"Sorry. Bad word choice. Universal was willing to sell us the rights to several of your . . . *pictures*. We thought we'd start out with the first three. *Frankenstein, Dracula*, and *The Phantom*."

"I assume you are referring to Chaney's original. Not that candy-colored flotsam with Claude Rains."

"Actually, the silent element was problematic. So unfortunately we—"

"Problematic? "

"Well, television is a *sound* medium after all," he said trying to be delicate. "We just thought . . ."

"I suppose that can't be helped. But it's not the *aural* issues that concern me. It's the progression. The accrual of sophisticated cinematic techniques that ultimately defined the genre."

"We're not really concerned with showing the movies in chronological order."

"May I ask why not? You should at least begin with Browning's *Dracula*, if only to—"

"See, that's what I thought. But *that* one's my favorite."

"Is it really?"

"You know, when you're *young* with *girls* and everything . . . *Hey*, what was Browning really like?"

I admit to being a little thrown by the question. A public summation of Browning's character would not be easy.

"Mr. Browning? How shall I put this delicately? Browning was . . . an *asshole*."

He couldn't help a sudden whoop of laughter. "No!"

I smiled at his slip of decorum.

"I'm sorry, but that's the inescapable truth," I said, unable to stop a chuckle myself. "A sort of besotted carnival barker, at least in my association. Loved these horrible tight tennis sweaters for some godless reason."

Bob had a very sincere laugh, loud and easy and not self-conscious. He was becoming quite charming.

"You see, *Dracula*, despite its faults, was really the first of its kind in many ways. The first *supernatural* horror film, and this concept was quite outside of Mr. Browning's wheelhouse, shall we say."

"Wow," he said almost dreamily. "I always wondered what it would have been like to have been on the set. Lugosi creeping down that stone stairway, with those X-ray eyes of his . . ."

"Actually it was quite like being on a chicken farm during a blackout."

"What?"

"The soundproofing in those days was primarily chicken feathers and they have a rather distinctive musk."

"I'll be damned," he said, coming from behind his desk and sitting on its lip, facing me. "So why the armadillos?"

"Pardon?"

"In Dracula's crypt you have this shot of these crazy *armadillos* rooting around. I never got that."

"Oh, the Hays Office, I suspect. They had a *hell* of a time with the censors. And showing vermin, *rats*, was one of their many prohibitions. So Browning got around that by depicting the frolicking habits of a bit of Texan wildlife. I've never understood it myself."

"Great stuff." He chuckled. "You sure I can't get you something to drink? A Nehi? Water?" A beverage offer in the middle of a meeting is never a good sign. But this was different. This was going well.

"Perhaps you better tell me what you had in mind," I said, leaning back in my chair, stopping short of calling him "young man."

"We're basically a network *affiliate*, Miss Ulm. The best we've got is local access, Sacramento on a windy day, if you know what I mean."

"Universal must have given you the rights for a song."

He looked around the room. Anywhere but at me. I hadn't made my comment with any tooth, but the implications were clear.

"Pretty much," he almost whispered. "The idea was to breathe some new life into these movies, these *pictures*—"

"I wasn't aware they were in need of life support."

"I personally don't think they are, Miss Ulm. I'm quite fond of them. They bring back some very pleasant afternoons. But we are dealing with advertising dollars here. Unlimited reruns with no overages. We're looking down the barrel of a ten o'clock slot, which isn't choice, but I think this will be so unique we'll get the share."

"I haven't the faintest idea what you're talking about."

"Sorry." He rubbed his face. His hands were small. A woman's hands. "Bottom line, these pictures have a very *unique* demographic. At least today."

"Which is?"

"Boys. *Children*. Like yourself," he corrected quickly. "That's why we thought a young host would be such a cinch. We've come up with a name for you, for the host character. Penny Dreadful and her pet bat, Rollo . . ." His voice began to fade in my skull. It's a strange sensation drowning in your own expectations. When ambition, as familiar as the hard ground beneath your feet begins to thin to a viscosity that could actually clog a lung. "I think we've got Mel Blanc locked to do the voice of the bat . . ." The sea change that darkens by degrees. This horizon was new in the subtleness of its finality, lit as it was by lightning as bright as his teeth and flashing eyes. I saw his jaw continue to labor under the excitement it seemed desperate to generate. "A couple of Jack Benny's best gag men have come on board to help with your banter . . ."

I didn't need to listen to hear what he was saying. He was simply nursing a lucrative trend that had begun with those two damn comedians back in 1948. It's a simple and immutable trajectory in Hollywood. First you are the vanguard, the oft imitated but rarely duplicated paragon of the genre. Then a few breadlines later, another world war, and they gut you and stick you with brass poles and wooden ponies and make you go round and round for the kiddies.

"I see," I said, trying to smile, to pretend to swallow. "So your plan is to heighten the aspects that haven't aged quite so well. To focus on the *kitsch*, as it were. The *camp*." I was unconvincing with the forced casualness of my assessment. I could tell he knew my heart had broken some.

"I wouldn't quite put it that way but, yes," he said gently. "We just want to have *fun* with them." It was almost an apology.

"Nothing wrong with fun."

"No."

Fun. Why does *fun* hold the world's premium? Shadows are much more flattering. Dread resounds so much deeper than giggles. Everyone looks better in black. The glaze upon my eyes, the stiffness in my body had little to do with my condition then. I was suddenly on that same isolated curb as Junior, watching another parade drift past. The only thing left were the good-byes.

"To your credit you've been very kind, Mr. . . . ?

"*Please* call me Bob."

"Well, Bob, I feel that under closer scrutiny of my prior commitments, such an undertaking would prove quite impossible at this time. I hope I haven't inconvenienced you." I stood up, fighting a bit for balance.

"I understand, Miss Ulm," he said, standing to meet me. "You sure you won't reconsider?" I said nothing. What could I say? "The pictures *really* are terrific."

"Oh, I don't worry about the pictures. They'll outlive all of us. At least *most* of us."

I shook his outstretched hand, willing my palm warm in the process.

"On the upside you got a sure-fire second choice out there."

"You mean the cheesecake corpse with the press-ons?" He almost snickered, with an embarrassed nod toward the door.

"You mentioned the show's demographic yourself," I said, creaking toward the exit. "You really think you'll go wrong with a dose of big-titted necrophilia? Give her a chance. Trust me. She's ahead of her time."

CHAPTER 56

There was no creamy white limo waiting for me at the gates this time. No desperate phone call or telegram from a well-mannered friend to rouse my ambition back into action. James Whale drowned himself in his swimming pool in the spring of 1957 and I couldn't help a pang of professional jealousy when I read of his final production. I would allow nature to finally win. I would give in to her call of soil and silence and dark. But only on my terms. Just like Jimmy. I decided to take one of our apartments for myself. I didn't tell my mother the room's real purpose. I let her believe the years had simply shown us to be very different people and I was much more comfortable with less clutter. When carpeting came into vogue, we splurged to have all the units done and then realized the new floors highlighted the wear to the cabinetry. So we had the cabinets and walls painted. That's where my efforts at domestic insurgency ended. My mother never understood the reasons behind my forced austerity. How could I tell her the best tombs never come with foldout sofas and dinettes? My mother coped by keeping abreast of trends, by raising her hemlines, frosting her once-opaque lipstick, cutting her hair. And I was all prepared for my suburban internment when one last bit of business demanded attention.

The event took place in a junior ballroom of an airport hotel. We had been allotted four hours for our celebration, having to make way for the wedding reception of the daughter of a prominent pool supply salesman. There were card tables set up with stacks of glossy black-and-white eight-by-tens, monster masks, and horror-themed glassware sets, a rusty piece of tubing said to be part of a scissor arc used in the original *Frankenstein*. It was a semipopular if respectfully enthusiastic gathering. It seemed the custodians of my life's work had fallen into the hands of three hundred adolescent boys in ties and horn-rimmed glasses, young men who seemed better suited to taking minutes at chess club meetings.

I avoided meeting my host. He would have expected a bent old thing well into her dotage and I never had a taste for prosthetics, so I lingered by the refreshment table, sipping flat Coke and waiting for the king.

He came a half hour before the end, walking briskly into the room to tumultuous applause. A white-haired, white-mustached gentleman waving graciously, holding court as if he were still a mere commoner.

I can't describe the feelings I had when I saw him. The combination of so many conflicting emotions didn't allow for the linear or the lyric. Longing, regret, humor, disappointment, love, these were the base notes. Did he still hate me? Was I *ever* thought of at all? I'd made mistakes in my long and frustrating career, but he was the most lasting regret. I tried to imagine him as a

young man, half-starved, beautifully cadaverous in his padding
and mortician's wax, waiting humbly for his cue behind a face as
recognizable as Christ's. But that young man was gone, thinned
to repeating wisps of shadow and locked boxes of memory. Age
makes strangers of us, and I was content to have just seen him
one last time. He was thronged by his fans and I lost sight of
him. I was planning on making a graceful exit. Then I heard my
name whispered with the sweet sibilance that could only be his.

"Maddy," Billy whispered. "Dear little Maddy Ulm? Is that
you?"

I looked up at him with tears in my eyes and said nothing.
He pushed his glasses more firmly to his face as he continued to
stare at me.

"But you are the living image of her, my dear."

His face was fuller, deeply tanned. He wore horn-rimmed
glasses that gave him a professorial look. The warm brown of his
irises was tinged with the invading blue of cataracts. He would
live only another four years. But the look in his eyes, the love, the
wonderment, made him young again.

"I'm her granddaughter," I said finally.

"Of course," he smiled. "Is she here?"

"She was indisposed," I said. "But she wanted to come. She
so did want to come."

"How is she? Is she well?"

"Oh quite well. Just . . . age."

"Yes. I know." He smiled ruefully and then took my hand.
"You will give her my regards, won't you? Tell her I often think
of her. She was the one friend I had, at the beginning."

"I'll tell her."

"My dear, why are you crying?"

I wiped my eyes with a hard brush of my fingers.

"I just know she had certain . . . *regrets*."

"All that's in the past now. Age has a way of clearing old misunderstandings. Please tell her I have nothing but the utmost fondness for her. And I always shall."

"I'll tell her. Thank you, Billy."

"Billy? I haven't been called that in thirty years."

EPILOGUE

I play the moments back in my mind, threading the events carefully through the sprockets of my memory, priming the bulb, feeding the gate. My first fall, my white coat, the train west, and Mutter's chocolate bars. The creases in Chaney's cheeks, Browning's ridiculous mustache, Whale's indulgent smirk, Billy's smile. They fumble into montage, degrade into jump cuts, and fade with skip-bleaches from too many viewings. But still the images persist. The world reminds me periodically of how I have tampered with history. Seventy-five-year-anniversary DVDs, late shows, revival houses, all reveal how the world remembers. But I prefer my own cut. My own version of the classics.

I had just finished a mental viewing of *The Bride of Frankenstein* when the representatives from Child Protective Services finally gave up their search. I lingered in the dark of my closet until I heard their car doors slam, ignite, and drive away. These jokes of my mother's are getting increasingly tedious. But so little humor passes between us anymore that I'm reluctant to deny her these small connections.

She invites me to lunch. She makes old-people food. Cold chicken salad and iced tea. She's forgotten she doesn't need the nourishment. She's proud of the pace she's kept with the world. We watch her television. She shows me how her computer works. The latest results of her Google search. My name replicates down the virtual page like bad Gertrude Stein:

> *HORROR CONFIDENTIAL: LON CHANEY SR.'s LOVE CHILD!*
>   *Oct. 4, 1973— . . . though Lon (née Creighton) Chaney adamantly denied before his death any such . . . has emerged that another child, Maddy Ulm, discussed in Boris Karloff's final interview, may be his illegitimate . . .*

> *CINÉASTE D'HORREUR—CHEF D'OEUVRE D'HORREUR SILENT DÉCOUVERT!*
>   *Mar. 29, 2013—(translated from the French) . . . attic of Ben "Bongo" Simms, onetime Cincinnati projectionist who discovered the footage while . . . attributed to the early expressionist work of William Dieterle, the Alliance Française calls the footage "the Prussian prelude to Frankenstein" . . . possibly Maddy Ulm (UFA 1920–24) in dual role . . .*

But my personal favorite was this little item from a few years back:

> *HOLLYWOOD'S 100 MOST HAUNTED: A GALLIMAUFRY OF SPECTRAL DELIGHTS FROM THE BALCONY OF GRAUMAN'S MILLION-DOLLAR THEATER TO THE KITCHENS OF THE AMBASSADOR HOTEL.*

Oct. 31, 2010— . . . year-old Saul Ruelberg, then a
dress extra at Universal, reports seeing a "a pretty scrag-
gly little spook," (could this be Maddy Ulm?) who Karloff
called "his creature's real mother lightning" in a . . .

And there I am, old ninety-seven out of one hundred, sand-
wiched between poor Peg Entwistle, whose favorite perfume
supposedly still lingers among the scrub sage after jumping to
her death from the *H* on Mount Lee in the late summer of 1932
and a fifth-generation Trigger who, after choking to death on a
spent condom expediently discarded into his oats, was reported
to have snickered mournfully, albeit spectrally, during a commercial break in Pasadena's 1972 Tournament of Roses Parade.

My arguments against the reliability of these little gusts of
cyber flatulence don't seem to sway my mother at all. She tells me
people know my name. Care about what I've done. I could set the
record straight, claim a few shreds of my legacy, if I'd only start
writing again. But I have my work, the thing I realize I am finally
really fit for. You see, one day the machines will fail, theaters will
close and become obsolete, and all the shiny-mirrored surfaces
of recording disks the planet over will crack and lose their luster.
The world will begin to forget. Forget about our first collective
foray into nightmare. Forget that the sharp and primitive monochrome of black and white once held more mystery, more beauty,
and more nuance than all the gradients of the rainbow. They'll
clamor for the darkness, for what came before. That's when I will
appear. And I will tell the stories.

I'll be the only one left who remembers them.

ACKNOWLEDGMENTS

There are a handful of people who were indispensable in the making of this book. To them I owe a tremendous debt of gratitude and no small portion of my love.

To Mesh, Hungarian wizard and cyber sage, who did a lot of the heavy lifting along the way.

To Mom and Rick and Eric who saw some value in the thing when so few did.

To Noah B. who in many ways saved my life by taking a chance on a cold query one bleak December.

To Eric M. and the editorial mandarins at HarperCollins.

To Sandy Meisner who showed me how to make the doing specific.

And to Stacy and Sophia, my two ladybirds. Love. Love. Love. There would be no point without you.

ABOUT THE AUTHOR

BRADFORD TATUM has worked in Hollywood as an actor and writer in both film and television. He lives in Los Angeles with his wife and daughter.